Other works by the author

Tales From Gaiand Series:

The Legends of Blackhawk (2022)

Copyright © 2023 by Chris Grooms
Cover art and insert map copyright © 2023 by Jamison McGregor

The moral right of the author has been asserted.

All characters and events in this publication, other than those clearly in the public domain, are fictitious and any resemblance to real persons, living or dead, is purely coincidental.

All rights reserved.
No part of this publication may be reproduced, stored in a retrieval system, or transmitted, in any form or by any means, without the prior permission in writing of the author, nor be otherwise circulated in any form of binding or cover other than that in which it is published and without similar condition including this condition imposed on the subsequent purchaser.

ISBN 979-8-9868109-1-1

Library of Congress Control Number: 2023903362

Acknowledgements

To my Lord and Savior Jesus Christ – thank you for my vivid imagination and through you all is possible.
Lisa Anne – what a crazy ride. Thanks for joining me.
Michael – writing strong dialogue is hard—you made it easier.
Samuel – keep challenging me to write better.
Kayla – your continued patience is amazing.
Marisa – welcome to the family.

What you hold in your hands was made possible by dedicated 'beta' readers:
Sandra G.
Karen C.
Rebekka S.

Jamie – as usual, your artwork is perfect.
Sirrah – your words of praise are humbling.
Genie (**Magic Lamp Editing Services**) – your grace and patience leaves me without words.

"Southern Realms"
Border Lands
Western Sea
East Sea
Sea of Marhgot
Gulf of Marietta
Pella Bay
The Firebrands
Balikitan Mountains
Barrington Mountains
The Highlands
North River
North River
Hinderflot Mountains
Blackhawk Territory
Corazon
Sisera
Peril Republic
Westerling
Kenwick
Coastal Commonwealth
Republic of Sanhmar
Ithmar
Peril
South Hampton
Port Charlotte
Free Cell
San Regal
Earhmar
Mar-Haven
Granhmar Island
Maguana
Kellen
Curchan Hills
Calaverde
Port Stanley
Creden Gap
Rockhall
Northbridge
Shallow Cross
Cache Creek
Chain Bridge
Raphine
Jacob's Forge
Beth Amen
Stirling Hill
Tressel
Tejt
Kenly
High Point
Bayside
En Wahl
New Haven
Isle de Kapri
Crawsteri Confederation
Steven's Point
Evergreen
Oakrun
The Greenes
Ringweld
Rampart
Welcome
Chytwynd
Banter Island
Ruby Island
Seven Bluffs
Prosper
Stowan Freeholds
Ragged Point
The Emirates
Al Wadi
Myre Island

Cast (in order of appearance)

Fitzhugh Walsh: A skilled archivist and historian who manages the Arnault (ar-no) Library in Deep Well.

Baroness Sasha Arnault: Founder and former owner of the Arnault Library in Deep Well.

Mora Gallantry: She serves as the narrator and lives in Deep Well. Daughter of Felix Gallantry. Married to Prince Francis III and mother of Kheel.

Prince Francis III: Formally known as Hanser Strigidae until his admission into Auroryies (a-roar-ees). Brother to Princes Cornell II and Tralderonn. Married to Mora Gallantry and father of Kheel. Currently lives in Deep Well with Mora.

Deemos: Serves Belhaaz.

Jaisia (ja-sia): A drow maiden serving Deemos.

Belhaaz: A demon bent on exacting revenge on the inhabitants of Gaiand (guy-and) for his banishment.

Aeros Askin: A kobold Wyvern Charmer and bounty hunter. Leads fellow kobolds Ruune, Scutter, and Qorrey.

Captain Wulf Blackhawk: Hails from Shallow Cross, Blackhawk Territory within the Crawsteri Confederation. Married to Maria Blackhawk. Son of Theodore and Helen Blackhawk, brother to Seth.

Matthew Jakkes: A cleric in the Beth Amen army and serving the Maiden of the Dawn.

Lieutenant Litvak: A Horse Tribe maiden leading a patrol of Volunteers outside Stirling Hill.

Brother Thomas: A Canon of the Dawn guarding the Silvern Cathedral.

Azmaveth Jakkes: Commander of the Canons of the Dawn and Matthew's father.

Talia/The Matron Mother: High priestess of the Maiden of the Dawn and the Silvern Cathedral.

Targinn Mirth: Self-appointed mayor of Welcome and high priest of the Crypt of Belhaaz.

Asp: A black dragon ridden and controlled by Aeros.

Princess Margarete 'Maggie' of the Blackhawk Realm: Wulf's loyal mare.

Paddy Staggs: A halfling bounty hunter employed by Lady Jirocha.

Ashir: A halfling leading Paddy, Tonk, and Redd to steal a valuable artifact.

Prince Wake: A young Prince of Auroryies.

Izzy: A bounty hunter leading Wes, Blouser, and Trit.

Prince Tralderonn Strigidae (stry-gi-day): A Prince of Auroryies. Brother to Princes Cornell II and Francis III. Son of Gallego and Kysellah Strigidae.

Salvador 'Sal' Spencer: Former Citadelle Sentry. Owns Sal's Tavern in Highpoint.

Carjlin (car-line) Feeallah (fee-a-la): A half-elf working at the Motsslyn Inn in Tejt. Eventually restored as a priestess serving the Maiden of the Dawn.

Kysellah Strigidae: Married to Gallego Strigidae and stepmother to Hobby and Hanser. She is Tralderonn's biological mother.

Gallego Strigidae: Hails from Prosper within the Stowan Freeholds. Husband to Kysellah. Father to Hanser, Hobby, and Tralderonn.

Keerrin Feeallah/The Matron Sister: High Priestess of L'Aube Cathedral in Tejt and Carjlin's mother.

Merle and Nellie: A married couple who own and run the Blue Mule Inn in Tetj.

Daniel 'Danny' Caldwell: Half-elf thief/assassin on the run from the Jirocha crime family. He hails from South Hampton, Coastal Commonwealth.

Cleon: Local thug and gang leader in Tejt. JoJo and Hugo work for him.

Seth Blackhawk: Hails from Shallow Cross, Blackhawk Territory within the Crawsteri Confederation. Child of Theodore and Helen Blackhawk, brother to Wulf.

Western 'Old West' Union: Seth Blackhawk's horse.

Jonathon Stockton: A military commander holding the rank of colonel within the Beth Amen army. Son of Asa and Louise and Maria's brother.

Cade Badeaux (ba-do): Patrol leader out of Turkey Foot, Blackhawk Territory. His companions include Trinity DeKyser, Silas Kerwin, and Pyam Tice.

Asa Stockton: Chain Bridge's village Chieftain. Fought in the Goblin Wars. Married to Louise and father to Jonathon, Maria, and the late Gareb.

Ilai (il-eye) Blackhawk: A captain in the Blackhawk Brigade living in Turkey Foot, Blackhawk Territory.

King Jeribai (jer-i-bi) Stockton: King of Beth Amen. Asa Stockton's older brother. Fought in the Goblin Wars.

Sergeant Quinn: A wagon master in the Beth Amen Army.

Captain Yosi Vandermoff: Captain of the Home Cavalry charged with protecting King Stockton.

Dao Chauinard (shaw-nard): Half-orc commander leading the orc army against Beth Amen.

Lieutenant Synane (Cy-nan): A Volunteer leading patrols around Raphine.

Asger Bynjar (by-nar): Chief of the Waraxe Tribe.

Bjarke (bar-ke) Halvard: Chief of the Hilltopper Tribe.

Joseph Locklynne: Appointed steward of Beth Amen in King Stockton's absence.

Essa Jaragua: A drow ranger working as a mercenary.

Scribe Everclay: A drow wizard who is a part of Essa's crew.

Rhent Dubois: A drow fighter who is a part of Essa's crew.

Knot and Packus: Duegar brothers who are a part of Essa's crew.

Naszea Jaryne: A dark gnome assassin who is a part of Essa's crew.

Chara El-Asante: First mate on the *Scamp*.

Lieutenant Rebekka Cathay: Leads a patrol of Jacob's Forge Volunteers. Eventually assumes command of the Queen's Cavalry.

Raniyah (rain-e-ya) Lo'Cain: Hailing from Fairbriar, she is a refugee from the Blackhawk Territory and Seth's love interest.

Lieutenant Luc Tylee: A lieutenant in the Home Cavalry.

Jenga Hodge: Chieftain of Jacob's Forge.

Helen Blackhawk: Originally from Beth Amen, home of the Horse Tribes. Widow of Theodore Blackhawk. Mother to Wulf and Seth.

Louise Stockton: Wife of Asa. Mother to Jonathon, Maria, and the late Gareb.

Maria Blackhawk: Married to Wulf Blackhawk. Daughter of Asa and Louise Stockton and sister to Jonathon and the late Gareb.

Salmista: Helen Blackhawk's horse.

Ezra Blackhawk: Territorial Governor of the Blackhawk Territory. Cousin to the late Theodore and the late Hezekiah Blackhawk.

Colonel Epsen Asbyorn: Commander of Belhaaz's Forces attacking Ripley's Keep.

Major Dag Einar (eye-nar): Colonel Asbyorn's executive officer.

Kheel Strigidae: Mora's and Francis's son.

Skrabb: A half-orc leading the assault against Ripley's Keep.

Prince Sheldon IV: A Prince of Auroryies.

Prince Wrayer Tytonidae (titan-i-day): A member of the Tribe of the Ancients or High Elves. An elven prince serving as an advisor to King Longpine. Son to Prince Isaiah Tytonidae.

Lieutenant Naphtali Lacchi (latch-e): An elf and an officer in the Scarlet Watch.

Captain Roan Ambrose: A skilled elven ranger from the Tribe of Graywild. Served under Colonel Drake in the Frontier Guards. Fought the drow and in the Goblin Wars.

Prince Singjeye (sing-ji) III: A Senior Prince of Auroryies.

Zim Patok: Commander of the Demonstaug (demon-stag) in Udontawny.

Milton Yeager: A mid-level administrator serving Zim Patok in Udontwany.

Prince Gambier VII: A Senior Prince of Auroryies who is supposedly missing.

Chapter One

Present Day 568, Age of the Arch Mage

He rose an hour ahead of the coming dawn. His head hurt, his hands ached, and his eyes remained scratchy and bloodshot. He swung one leg onto the floor, then the other. Fitzhugh Walsh dawdled for a moment, allowing his eyes a second or two to adapt to the gloom. He stood and lit a candle sitting on the bedstand, then shuffled to the window and flung open the curtains. A purple so dark it could have been black blanketed Deep Well. Stars, too many to count, flickered in the early morning sky. He placed his hand against the window and felt the frigid air through the glass. For the last forty-four years, he called this valley his home. He found comfort here, and he performed important work in the archives. He lit several more candles, then plodded to his wardrobe.

His mind drifted as he dressed. He was a young commoner, naïve and inexperienced, when he had first met Baroness Sasha Arnault at the Ateneo Bookshop in Kismill. Fitzhugh froze and stared as she entered. Her allure infatuated him—he had never seen a prettier woman. She wore an elegant sleeveless dress that brushed the floor. An ornately embroidered tunic accented the dress and her beauty. Despite her bourgeoise lineage, the baroness carried herself like a woman of noble birth. Her manner and style appeared impeccable, sophisticated and captivating. He assisted her in selecting a variety of books on a dozen different subjects, from history to the arcana and everything in between. As they roamed up and down among the bookshelves, Fitzhugh discovered the Baroness's thirst for knowledge had matched his own.

He paused his recollections to select the proper scarf to complement his leather jerkin. Fitzhugh lowered himself onto a chair and ran his fingers over the silk scarf. He chuckled. She had given it to him as a gift years past. He leaned back and closed his eyes. He felt her soft touch and smelled the faint scent of her perfume.

She had proposed dinner and he accepted without hesitation. She held his arm as they strolled down Kismill's torchlit streets to the Oyster House near the city's harbor district. Fitzhugh considered himself a king in her presence. Over their meal and two bottles of wine, they discussed and debated the latest philosophies and advancements in science. Her eyes lit up as she talked of her home, an ancient fortress in a secluded valley called Deep Well lying just inside the Border Lands. Sasha shared her vision to build a library and archives to rival the one in the Citadelle of Auroryies. She and her dreams seduced him. He imagined himself as the administrator of such an establishment and spending each day immersed in scholarly pursuits. After dinner, he escorted Sasha to her room in the Keswhick Inn, where they shared another bottle of wine and talked until their words faded.

He awoke in her bed the following morning. She greeted him with a smile, beaming and affectionate. Her auburn hair hung down over her shoulders, her brown eyes inviting and luminous. Her skin was a golden brown and her features soft. Sasha slipped from under the covers and pulled on a robe. She turned and let her gaze rest on him. "My ship departs for Pitch at noon. Join me and we will make our dream a reality."

Fitzhugh Walsh agreed and embraced her dream as his own. A week later, he arrived in Deep Well and learned her wealth knew no limits. The valley, in all its natural beauty, exhibited a splendor he could not describe, but the building housing the Baroness's collection left him speechless. Fitzhugh spent years and her fortune assembling an eclectic compilation of books, maps, paintings, and other works of art from all over Gaiand.

The Arnault Archives and Library, or the Arnault, as she called it, was a three-story structure constructed of marble possessing a salmon hue. An extensive colonnade supported by decorative columns served as the grand entrance. Large windows on all four sides infused the Arnault with natural light. Linen drapes hung from gold curtain rods and shielded the Arnault's priceless contents from the sun's damaging rays. Stone gargoyles, gray and menacing, crouched in the corners and warded the building from evil. The preponderance of the first floor comprised rows and rows of bookshelves preserving hundreds of leather-bound volumes, tomes, and maps. On the second floor, she displayed her expansive collection of paintings, tapestries, and sculptures. Sasha provided the third floor to him as his living space. It was spacious and opulent, more than he needed or ever dreamed of.

He opened his eyes, bringing him back to the present. The first slender garlands of the coming dawn streamed into his bedroom.

Fitzhugh finished dressing, grabbed his satchel, then made his way downstairs to the first floor. In the dimness of the coming day, he donned his fur-lined winter coat, wrapped his scarf around his neck, and pulled on his leather gloves. Fitzhugh opened the door and strode into the receding gray. He inhaled and filled his lungs with the icy air. As he exhaled, the vapor from his mouth reminded him of a dragon's breath. Fitzhugh scanned the silent fortress. Deep Well slept. Only the snow elf guards manning Redoute la Nevicata's ramparts stirred. He stepped off the portico into the snow. It crackled and crunched under each step. He passed beneath the main gate and crossed the bridge spanning Crescent Lake. The torchlight reflecting off the frozen lake's glassy surface created an eerie aura. Eastward he traipsed, engrossed in years of memories.

Fitzhugh gazed across the snowy vale, absorbing the valley's grace and elegance as he plodded on. The Arnaults, Sasha and the Baron, were long gone. Like a puff of smoke, they had dissipated into history. At times he missed her. They were lovers for over a decade, during which he enjoyed her company and body. But that ended when General Bancroft and the demons of Belhaaz arrived. In quick order, the demons eliminated any perceived threat, including Sasha and the Baron. He alone survived their purge. To his good fortune, he and Bancroft shared a passion for books and art. Fitzhugh was ambivalent to what happened around him. His sole care centered on preserving the Arnault and its contents. He considered it strange that under Bancroft's reign, the Arnault's collection grew. He remained convinced Bancroft plundered most of the works. It did not matter how Bancroft or his agents acquired them as long as the works endured throughout the ages.

Fitzhugh stopped when he reached the outskirts of Holly Ridge. The rising sun broke over the mountains, bathing Deep Well in brilliant gold and yellow strands. He cast his gaze over the village. Akin to the fortress, it slumbered. Fitzhugh shuddered against the cold and the recollections. He recalled the day they had arrived, a valiant band of heroes. Bancroft and his minions only whispered their names and forbade others from speaking their names out loud. Despair and apprehension consumed the valley and the fortress. A paralyzing fear gripped Bancroft and his allies. Bancroft knew they came for him, knew they sought him and his demise, and he could not stand against them. Bancroft called them the Bane of Belhaaz, while others within the fortress referred to the heroes as the Defenders of the Southern Realms. Regardless of what they were called, the heroes won. They defeated Bancroft and vanquished his demons and, once again, Fitzhugh Walsh remained the sole survivor. A sly grin broke over his face—he had survived another purge.

On the heels of the Bane of Belhaaz came the snow elves. Centuries of war and persecution had devastated the Snow elves. They needed a sanctuary that would protect them from the demons who desired their extinction. The snow elves arrived seeking a haven where they could rebuild their civilization and renew their fading magic. And Deep Well offered the snow elves the refuge they required to survive.

Striking in appearance, the snow elves owned long features softened by gentle curves with the look of fresh snow tinged by a peculiar artic hue. Their eyes, bright and intense, seemed bluer than a mountain stream. Snow elf hair tended toward a luxurious white that appeared silver when viewed in certain lights. Comparable to their distant cousins from Evergreen, they moved with elegance and grace.

The snow elves brought their treasures, artifacts, and the contents of a vast archive to Deep Well. They placed thousands of years of history and priceless relics from another plane of existence into the Arnault and under his care. Fitzhugh labored for years alongside snow elf professors, sages, and archivists to store and preserve their legacy.

Fitzhugh resumed his journey. He hastened his pace. He didn't want to be late or endure her wrath. Francis stood on the front porch, sipping on a mug of coffee, when he arrived.

"Mister Walsh," Francis beamed, his smile genuine and pleasant. "I hope you are ready to write. She's eager to begin."

Fitzhugh paused at the bottom step. Without warning, fear held him in its icy grasp. Mora Gallantry, the Second Arch Mage of Gaiand, was fascinating and terrifying all at the same time.

It was unexplainable.

Chapter Two

Fall 531, Age of the Arch Mage

A lone drow maiden slipped from the dimness, appearing wraith-like, shaded and menacing.

"He is here," she hissed. Her slender features were veiled beneath her cloak, her face obscured by the folds of her cowl.

Jaisia's sudden presence startled Deemos. He took a second to gather himself, closed his book, and stood. He towered over her, yet she did not flinch. Deemos fixed his calloused eyes on her. "You were not gone long."

"It was easy," she confessed, shrugging her shoulders. "I followed a trail of ale."

"Is he sober?"

"Hard to tell," she admitted, her voice hard and toneless. "He smells."

"No matter," Deemos chuckled, low and wicked. "The kobold will meet with the master now."

◊ ◊ ◊

Deemos suffered Belhaaz's impatience. Rhythmic tapping from the talons grew louder, showing the demon's building frustration. After decades of searching, Belhaaz longed to capture his heir. As the war raged upon the Southern Realms, Belhaaz's enduring infatuation with a child he had never met exasperated Deemos. He failed to grasp the child's importance. Deemos pined for Belhaaz's complete concentration in prosecuting the war, not locating a long-lost offspring. Deemos itched for Belhaaz to join the orc armies in the field. He longed for the master to lead the orcs to victory over the Highlands and Beth Amen. After destroying the Horse Tribes and barbarians, the master's forces would lay waste to the rest of the Southern Realms nations.

Deemos paused near the dais until Belhaaz summoned him on. Belhaaz seemed restless. He shifted his weight under the black robes that concealed his hulking frame. A smug grin deformed his leathered face.

Belhaaz lifted his gaze to meet Deemos. "Aeros?"

"Yes, my master," Deemos confirmed, his bow low.

Deemos heard the master exhale in satisfaction, saw his yellow eyes flicker in gratification. "Bring him in."

"Master, the kobold is—"

"Drunk?"

"Yes," Deemos replied. "I recommend you find—"

"Another?" Belhaaz erupted, his yellow eyes shuttered and furious.

Deemos reeled back a step and held his tongue.

"No! He is the best. Speak of this no more," Belhaaz growled.

Two Odjahary Legionnaires stood at the door. Their crimson skin, gray wings, and ashen armor shimmered in the torchlight. Deemos motioned for them to open the door. Deemos remained apprehensive, standing near the dais, watching the kobold saunter across the bridge. Aeros stumbled but caught hold of the wall and righted himself. He did not falter or slow down. By his gait, by his body language, Aeros was in charge, not the master. Shadows cast by the torches lengthened his diminutive stature. From a distance, it was apparent this kobold had little in common with his weak-minded kin. He was vain and arrogant and brash, qualities Belhaaz admired.

Until he met Aeros Askin several years past, Deemos doubted the kobold's abilities and his reputation as a bounty hunter but at that meeting, Deemos detected a cruelness lurking in his amber eyes, beady and narrow set. Halfling-sized but lean and wiry, his muscles coiled tight as a spring. Fierce and determined despite his size, his sneer revealed rows of serrated teeth set inside a dragon-like snout. Kobolds were the least of the lizard people yet somehow Aeros, through trickery or thievery, acquired the ability to control black dragons, to bend them to his will. Known among sinister factions by the name of Wyvern Charmer, Aeros and his fearsome squad rode black dragons, earning their living as recovery agents, selling their services to anyone who could afford their expensive talents.

Deemos listened to the clawed feet rasp over the stone, heard the bounty hunter's ebony leather armor creak and groan as he neared, and noticed the black dragon scales stitched into the shoulders glimmering in the torchlight. A pendant affixed to a silver chain hung around his neck, a talisman conveying upon him the power to master the dragons. The black dragon charm was sculpted from tourmaline, and its two ruby eyes seemed to follow one's every move. Deemos raised a hand, halting the kobold short of the throne. Facing his master again, Deemos waited for permission to speak.

An ominous grin spread upon Belhaaz's capricious face. Ignoring Deemos, he leaned forward, motioning the kobold closer. Aeros Askin approached, clutching a leather helmet in one hand and a riding crop in the other. He bowed low, waiting for the master to speak.

"Aeros Askin the Wyvern Charmer. Once more I require your services," Belhaaz spoke in a low rumble.

"Proud to serve my master again," Acros proclaimed.

"My heir, Aeros Askin. Bring her to me alive," Belhaaz demanded. "You can locate her in Prosper inside the Stowan Freeholds."

"Of course, my master." The kobold bowed again, spun on his heels and strutted from Belhaaz's throne.

"Aeros," Belhaaz bellowed.

Aeros stopped and faced Belhaaz.

"She is no good to me dead."

The kobold let the moment hang in the humid air. A toothy sneer, condescending and cavalier, deformed his snout into an ugly expression. "Alive, yes, my master."

Aeros pivoted and resumed his exit.

◊ ◊ ◊

Deemos followed Aeros into the courtyard and stood at a distance to observe. The dragon, sleek and raven-hued, curled its lips, exposing razor-sharp teeth. A wisp of steam escaped from flaring nostrils, and a low and dangerous growl, rumbled from somewhere deep inside its bowels, greeted the Wyvern Charmer. Deemos watched the kobold bound aboard his dragon in a graceful leap. A series of leather straps, buckles, and belts secured Aeros to the saddle. He donned his helmet and set his goggles in place. An enthusiastic smack from the riding crop urged the dragon ahead. The massive black lizard unfolded its powerful wings and began beating the air into submission, lifting its massive girth off the ground.

Deemos squinted into the sun as he watched Aeros and his dragon clear the walls, gain altitude, then bank southeast. *Another fool in the master's service.* He picked up a rock and threw it at a cluster of hobgoblin guards gawking at Aeros and his dragon. "Scatter!"

Deemos stormed off, swearing to himself.

Chapter Three

Fall 531, Age of the Arch Mage

Wulf noticed a dust cloud rising against a darkening sky. Riders approached from the west. He grinned. Seth could have told him if they were friendly or not before they appeared. Wulf looked at Matthew. "Riders coming."

Matthew peered west. "Where's Seth when we need him?"

Five minutes passed and now the riders were close enough to count. Wulf tallied thirteen riders, all Horse Tribe maidens. The patrol leader slowed as they neared. "For the horse."

"For the rider," Wulf and Matthew shouted in unison.

"Captain, I am Lieutenant Litvak," she declared, meeting Wulf's gaze. "My squad and I are finishing our sweep around the capital. May we ride in your company?"

"Lieutenant, we would welcome your companionship," Wulf replied.

The lieutenant rode abreast of Matthew and Wulf while the rest of the patrol fell into a column behind them. An awkward lull ensued. Matthew peeked over at the lieutenant. She was young, maybe a year or two older than Wulf. The lieutenant's face, hair, and uniform wore a thin layer of dust. Her grim expression pulled her mouth into a frown. Gaunt cheeks and her hollowed brown eyes gave the lieutenant a haunting appearance. The effects of war did not require a trooper to be on the front lines. Even this far south, the war had terrible ramifications. Had she lost a loved one or a close friend? Matthew started to ask, then decided to leave her alone.

They rode among the troopers until the first outlines of Stirling Hill emerged.

"Gentlemen, this is where we part ways," Lieutenant Litvak announced, her tone hard. "May the Maiden bless your journey."

Litvak saluted and called her troops to order. Then she reined her horse southeast and pushed him into a gallop.

Wulf and Matthew watched the troopers until they disappeared from their sight.

"She looked exhausted," Matthew commented, a sadness filling his tone.

"They all did," Wulf added. He stared into the distance. The nation appeared desperate by pressing their women into service. He could see Maria, his mother, and a dozen other women in Lieutenant Litvak and her troopers.

Dusk loomed to the east. The waning sun, orange and bright, hung in a hazy blue sky as a faint moon emerged from below the horizon. What lingered of the season's leaves clung to the trees. The air, crisp and unmoving, smelled of fall. A musty odor rose to greet them as horse hooves shuffled the leaves. Wulf and Matthew attained the outskirts of Stirling Hill following a three-day ride from Jacob's Forge. Wulf hoped for the allure and prestige of a big city. Disappointment filled his brown eyes when he discovered Stirling Hill was nothing more than a sprawling village, a cow town of rutted roads and low-rise buildings barely larger than Raphine.

Stirling Hill was not Beth Amen's original capital. A century ago, the newly crowned queen relocated the capital from Silver Springs near the En Wahl border to a safer location deeper inside the country. In contrast to the rest of the villages in Beth Amen, Stirling Hill was a planned city and laid out on a grid. Streets and avenues ran parallel to each other, and side roads crossed over them at right angles, with the Palace of Horses dominating the city's center.

Stirling Hill existed in various shades of gray, dull and drab, and sad faces outnumbered the smiling. The capital city suffered under war's exacting toll. It appeared tired and worn down from worry and toil. Absent their spring leaves, the oaks, aspens, and birches were a heather hue, naked and melancholy. Thick smoke and ash poured from the forge furnaces fabricating armor, swords, and other metal products to arm and equip the troopers. The grain mill operated twenty-four hours a day to feed their army. Buildings cried out for repairs and fresh coats of paint. Warehouses and stockyards stood empty and shuttered. There was nothing to store in them. Market shelves were half-full. Coffee, sugar, and flour were becoming scarce. Old troopers pressed back into the service safeguarded the streets. All men of age had been sent north to fight, so now teenaged boys and girls conducted mounted patrols in the countryside surrounding Stirling Hill.

Instead of staying in an inn in the capital, Matthew led them to the Maiden of the Dawn seminary four miles southwest of Stirling Hill. Onto the open plains they rode, where campfires flickered and danced in the distance. Wulf and Matthew were surprised to hear faint, joyful sounds of the lute and tambourine that floated over the darkening expanse. Their labors complete, the herdsmen—the Children of Abel as Asa called them—observed the close of another day and gave the warriors a much-needed sense of hope.

The sun's final radiance was fading beneath the mountains, painting the heavens in a glossy assortment of crimsons, golds, and cobalt as they neared the seminary. From a distance, Wulf and Matthew saw hundreds of torches bathing the sprawling edifice in a soft beckoning glow. The silver domes atop the spires and the cathedral shimmered in the twilight and torchlight. From a half dozen bell towers, the carillons rang out. Their soft tones, deep and low, echoed across the plains, bidding the day goodbye.

Matthew peeked over at Wulf. The wonder he found reflected in Wulf's hardened eyes amused him. It was an expression he had not seen his friend wear. "The Silvern Cathedral."

"What?"

"What you are gawking at is the Silvern Cathedral," Matthew explained. "Clerics in the service of the Maiden gain their initial training and teachings here. Once they complete their primary instruction, the Matron Mother ordains them into the order."

Wulf did not speak as his eyes absorbed the cathedral's splendor.

"There are two vocations we can choose," Matthew resumed, "parish ministry or the ministry of the martial path. The majority select parish ministry. A few opt for the martial path like I did. Martial clerics enter the ranks of the Canons of the Dawn. Forty-one strong, they are called upon to protect the cathedral and, when needed, dispatched to bolster national armies. The Canons stood alongside the Southern Realms nations at the Battle of the Mulford River."

Matthew paused. He could see Wulf only heard half of what he said. "Father John ultimately chose both vocations when he died protecting his cathedral in Shallow Cross from the invading orcs."

Wulf was quiet for a moment.

"Yes, I remember," Wulf said finally. He sighed and then looked up at the cathedral again. "It is beautiful."

The gate was closed when they arrived. Matthew dismounted and struck a gong suspended from an iron pole. He remounted, and they waited. The gate creaked and groaned as it opened. A man, resembling Wulf's above average height and broad shoulders, emerged from the dimness dressed in chain armor. He stepped forward, squinting in the torchlight. "By the Maiden. Could this be Matthew Jakkes?"

"Brother Thomas," Matthew answered.

"Enter," Thomas waved.

Matthew slid from his horse and Wulf did as well. They led their horses a few yards past the gate into an expansive courtyard. Torches lined a gravel road leading to one of many buildings, and hundreds of lit candles hung from the dawn redwoods' ancient limbs. A serene glow washed over the entire grounds. Here they paused as Thomas shut the gate, then set a long iron bar onto metal hooks secured to the stone wall. As they waited, Wulf hugged Maggie's neck. The air, clean and peaceful, seemed infused with a blessed promise of renewing life. He inhaled a sharp breath and let it linger. Hope poured over his body and flooded his soul. He experienced a sensation he had never felt.

Thomas's grin mimicked his girth as he approached. "Hungry?"

"Yes," Matthew admitted.

"Come on," Thomas invited. "You know Brother Hosea cooks more than we can eat."

"Thomas, this is my friend, Wulf Blackhawk," Matthew introduced.

Even in the candle- and torchlight, Thomas noted Wulf's imposing presence, tall and stout. He wore his uniform with pride, his manner confident and noble. Thomas viewed a hardness in Wulf's brown eyes, earned from years of fighting. He noted the scars, ugly and long, on his cheek and arms. Thin locs fell beyond broad shoulders, his facial hair sparse. Thomas cocked his head. Wulf did not hail from Beth Amen. His ebony complexion was atypical for Horse Tribesmen. Thomas thrust out a giant hand and shook Wulf's. "The pleasure is mine, Wulf, and welcome to the Maiden's domain."

"My pleasure as well," Wulf responded, his eyes not quite believing what he saw. He recalled Blackhawk's beauty, and it paled compared to the Silvern Cathedral.

Matthew surveyed the grounds. Nothing had changed since he'd left and he found that comforting. He noticed wagons filled with boxes and barrels parked near the wall. "What's with the wagons?"

"Supplies," Brother Thomas answered. "The L'Aube Cathedral in Tejt sent those as an offering to the people of Beth Amen. We will pull relief supplies from our winter stocks as well. The Matron Mother wants them delivered before winter sets in."

"Thanks. That will go a long way," Wulf stated. "People fleeing the fighting up north have overwhelmed villages like Jacob's Forge."

Brother Thomas placed his arm around Wulf's shoulder and winked. "That's what the church is supposed to do."

As the three men walked down the gravel road, Wulf inhaled the savory aroma from roasted meats and vegetables, watering his mouth.

"Matthew, what brings you back?" Thomas inquired. "Figured you would be closest to the fighting."

"I have been since the first orc invasion," Matthew affirmed. "It's a long and winding tale, Thomas. I will explain over a meal and mug of cold ale."

"Sounds fair to me," Thomas agreed. "The stables are to our left."

After tending to their horses, they resumed their walk to the dining hall. A gracious quiet permeated the grounds, the creatures of the night held their tongues, and even the remaining leaves refrained from moving. The trio walked in silence until they reached a set of double doors.

"You know she will want to see you," Thomas chortled, grasping the door handles.

"I hope so," Matthew asserted. He glanced over at Wulf and winked.

Chapter Four

Fall 531, Age of the Arch Mage

Thomas yanked open the doors, revealing a cavernous hall filled with rows of tables and benches. He stepped in. "Brothers and sisters! Look who has returned!"

A hush fell over the hall as hundreds of eyes snapped to the entryway. At first, a barely audible murmur rolled through the men and women studying the trio. Then it grew to a dull clamor. An instant later, a deafening roar erupted. As one, they rose and made their way to Thomas, Wulf, and Matthew. Wulf saw elves and half-elves mixed in among the humans. The elves' slender features and graceful movements fascinated him. He noted most of them wore robes. The robes' color reminded him of the dawn, a blend of green and cyan, in a clear sky. Chain mail armor, the same dawn blue as the robes, covered the others. Their skin tones formed a kaleidoscope of colors, black, white, and every shade in between. They pressed in on Matthew to shake hands, hug, or slap him on the back. Then, one by one, they drifted back to their seats. One man remained and he stood in front of Matthew. His hazy green eyes studied the young cleric for a moment. Wulf looked over at the man, then to Matthew. Other than a touch of gray in the man's cropped auburn hair, they mirrored each other, each one fair complected and tan. Both appeared taller than the average man. The older man extended his arms and pulled Matthew in. "Welcome back, son."

"Good to see you, Father," Matthew declared as they broke their embrace and stepped back.

"Who is your companion, son?"

"Father, this is Wulf Blackhawk," Matthew announced. "Wulf, my father Azmaveth. He commands the Canons."

"Captain," Azmaveth responded, gripping Wulf's hand. "You're young for a trooper captain."

"Sir," Wulf grinned, a mix of pride and embarrassment. "They don't think so."

"Then neither do I," Azmaveth acknowledged. "Let's get you some food and drink."

Azmaveth waved toward the back of the hall as he led Matthew and Wulf to a wooden table and motioned for them to sit. Their food, a hearty meat stew and biscuits, and ale arrived seconds later. Wulf found the stew filling and the ale stout.

Amidst the revelry, Wulf and Matthew ate and drank. Then, in the space of a breath, the room fell silent as she stood at the entrance to the massive hall. Matthew spun his head.

"Talia!" Matthew exclaimed, his voice almost a whisper.

Wulf lifted his gaze and stared. Her beauty, splendid and elegant, and her mere presence banished a thousand nightmares. She lingered in the doorway alone. There was no need for protectors as she stood among her own. They referred to her as the Matron Mother and only a select few called her by her name. Dawn blue robes hid her slender frame. Silver hair broke over pointed ears and past her shoulders. A simple silver tiara adorned the top of her head. Her eyes gleamed a bright cerulean, enchanting and full of life. She beamed, warm and sincere, as she motioned for Matthew.

Matthew wiped his mouth and hands, then headed for Talia. He knelt and took hold of her hand.

"Oh, dear cleric," the Matron Mother whispered. "How I have yearned to see you in our midst once more."

"Mistress, I am humbled in your presence."

"Come, child," she beckoned. "We have much to discuss."

The brothers and sisters sat unmoving and speechless until the Matron Mother and Matthew slipped from their view.

◊ ◊ ◊

He offered his arm and she accepted. They did not speak, strolling down a corridor bathed in candlelight. For the moment, it was enough to be together. Only the thud of his boots and her flowing robes brushing the stone on each graceful step disturbed the hush. She stopped short of a closed door and waited for Matthew to open it. The moon, full and orange, and a thousand blinking stars splattered on an obsidian portrait, greeted them as they stepped into a courtyard. A thin sheen of dew clung to the grass and trees and the chilled air smelled musky-sweet during their walk. They settled in chairs beneath a dawn redwood, its branches stretching to the heavens.

"Your power has grown," Talia declared, her voice soft and low. "I detected it as you neared."

Matthew met her gaze and held it. "I know."

For a few moments, a simple silence ensued as neither spoke. Talia faced him. "Do you regret your choice?"

"No, do you?"

"No. Your life was never here," Talia confirmed. "I knew when you first entered the seminary."

His eyes met hers. "I hope someday I gain your wisdom and insight."

"You will."

Matthew shot her an odd look.

"Why do you doubt?" she asked, her voice gentle.

"You are the Matron Mother, the wise one."

"In time, you will come to understand." Talia smiled and patted his hand. "So, why do you return?"

"I guess I need to be here, Mistress," Matthew conceded. "Even for a brief time."

She let the moment hang as she considered his words. He looked worn down. She saw the weariness in Matthew's eyes and sensed the apprehension plaguing his thoughts. The fighting and the death were fatiguing his soul. Talia leaned forward and touched his arm. "What do you want, Matthew?"

"For centuries, the monarchs of this land have afforded their protection to our seminary. They embrace our faith and adhere to our teachings," Matthew proclaimed, his tone passionate and steady. "I want our Canons to ride forth and protect this realm. Permit them to stand at King Stockton's side as they did during the Goblin Wars."

"This is not our way anymore," she grimaced, knowing he would not like her answer. Talia wavered as she reined in her emotions. His request stung, stirred up memories she did not want to recall. "Our loyalties belong to all nations, not one."

"The cathedrals in Shallow Cross, Northridge, and Chain Bridge have succumbed to the evil suppressing this land. Father John died defending his. We should be willing to endure similar sacrifices," he argued. An edge appeared in his voice that had not been there a moment ago. He retreated—he would not permit himself to speak to her using a disrespectful tone. "Mistress, this is a battle between dark and light, not nation against nation. We must allow Beth Amen to remain in the light. I beg you to grant this exception."

Talia sighed. "I will give it consideration."

"Thank you," he whispered. It may have been the shadows or his request, but she looked as if she had aged a hundred years in a matter of minutes.

"May I inquire as to this journey you are undertaking?" she asked, thankful for an opportunity to change the subject.

"You have concerns, Mistress?" he wondered.

"Grave misgivings. Your path is unclear. It is hard for me to see. It blurs at the edges and dwells in obscurity," Talia replied. She grasped his hands in hers and peered into his eyes. "A time long ago, I trusted the princes. Even considered many of them my friends. Matthew, those days are gone."

"Mistress, these are the occasions when we rely on hope," Matthew exclaimed.

She gave him a warm look and came to her feet. "Wise beyond your years, young cleric."

Arm in arm, the Matron Mother and Matthew headed inside. He escorted Talia to her chambers. She hugged him and kissed his cheek. "Sleep well."

Matthew nodded then wandered back to the dining hall. He grinned, plodding down the stone corridors immersed in the peace and quiet emanating from the Maiden's cathedral.

It felt good to be home.

Chapter Five

Fall 531, Age of the Arch Mage

Talia rose early from a restless sleep. The day's dawn lingered an hour away in the east. Alone and adrift in her musings, she padded down darkened corridors. She struggled to focus her thoughts and her course felt unclear as she entered the chapel. Talia perceived the Maiden's essence as she felt loving arms wrap around her, compassionate and assuring. She paused and prayed. Saddened by memories from two decades past, a burden weighed on her heart. She saw their broken bodies draped over their saddles. She found her husband's body among them. Talia tried to arrest the escaping tears as she approached the Maiden's statue past rows of empty pews.

A presence kneeling near the altar startled Talia, breaking her concentration. "Azmaveth?"

He rose to greet her. "Mistress."

"By the Maiden, what are you doing here?"

"I think we're here for the same reason," Azmaveth stated, his face drawn in tight lines.

"We are?"

"Let us march north, Mistress," he demanded, his voice low and firm. "Permit the Canons to stand alongside King Stockton as we did during the Goblin Wars."

She let his appeal dangle unanswered. Talia sat down and dabbed at the tears while trying to gather up her emotions. Her composure hung by the thinnest thread.

"Azmaveth, you ask too much of me," she murmured, her gaze fixed upon the Maiden. "Twenty years ago, I buried thirty-nine Canons. I sent them to their deaths, my beloved Zelek among them. I alone am responsible. I can't—"

"Talia," Azmaveth interrupted, his tone respectful. "I fought there and experienced the carnage. I accept the pain and grief you endure. You must release your remorse. You can no longer carry this burden."

She did not respond, her eyes locked on the Maiden. He sat down next to her. "Mistress, we cannot sit by while Beth Amen fights unaided."

Talia did not move, did not shift her gaze from the Maiden. A minute passed. Then another. She took his hand and squeezed it. "You may go."

Azmaveth stood for a moment, motionless. "Do I have your blessing?"

She peered deep into his hazy green eyes and saw his resolve looking back. "Yes, and the Maiden's."

"Thank you."

Talia held her composure as he departed. She heard the door shut. Now that she was alone, the memories washed over her. Thirty-nine bodies, broken and lifeless, flashed before her eyes. It forced her to view each one once more. Talia trembled, her body wracked by grief. She fell to her knees, her body heaved as she sobbed. She lifted her head. A long, sorrowful wail erupted from somewhere deep in her soul.

◊ ◊ ◊

Wulf awoke amid the impending dawn without an ache or pain in his body, his mind and spirit refreshed. He had slept uninterrupted. Not a single nightmare haunted his sleep, as they had for the past seasons. He pulled aside the curtains and looked out. A brilliant morning sun splayed bright streamers of yellow and orange into a sapphire sky. Wulf stared across the cathedral grounds, soaking in the simple but graceful beauty. His soul stirred as part of him did not want to depart this hallowed place. He dressed, strapped Ill Wind to his back, and gathered up his gear, and headed for the stables.

◊ ◊ ◊

-- Talia --

The Maiden's soft voice calling her name woke Talia. She blinked and forced the sleep from her body. Her eyes stung. There were no tears left to cry. She rose to her feet, stiff and sore from lying on the chapel floor. Talia gathered herself. She brushed the hair from her face and smoothed the wrinkles from her robes.

-- You did well, my child, to release the Canons. Now the time has come for you to surrender your torment and regret --

Talia understood, and she wanted to comply. Her faith in herself wavered. She raised her eyes to the statue. "Give me the strength to do so."

-- I will --

◊ ◊ ◊

The grounds bustled with activity as Wulf walked for the horse barns. The Canons formed ranks, three squads of thirteen each. They wore dawn blue tunics beneath chainmail armor and ashen-hued helmets sat upon their heads. Maces hung from leather belts, and they gripped shields in their hands. Their destrier stallions, sleek and muscled, pawed at the ground.

He located Matthew talking to Azmaveth close to the stables as he neared. Matthew flashed a broad grin, facing Wulf. "Hurry, we are riding out behind the Canons."

"Where are they going?" Wulf asked.

"To the Mulford and King Stockton," Matthew yelled as he hastened off. He could not contain his excitement. "I will explain further when I can. Hustle."

Wulf tacked Maggie, loaded his gear, then joined Matthew. The Canons sat astride their chargers and Azmaveth ordered them forward with a wave. The Canons transitioned into a column of twos as they rode past, and the parish clerics fell in behind them. Matthew and Wulf assumed their positions at the rear of the column. Amidst the prayers and hymns of praise raised to the Maiden, the Canons paraded through the grounds to the front of the cathedral. Here Azmaveth halted the procession. As one, the Canons pivoted left and lifted their gaze. Talia, the Matron Mother, stood overlooking them from a balcony, her silver hair and tiara sparkling in the dawn. She raised her hands and a hush fell over the grounds. "May the Maiden protect and bless you. Go forth and stand with King Stockton. Drive this darkness from our lands."

A roar exploded from the Canons and the priests gathered to see them off. Azmaveth stood in his saddle, saluted, and ordered the Canons onward. Out the gate the Canons rode, then turned north. Matthew and Wulf trailed, then headed south.

◊ ◊ ◊

From her balcony, she observed the Canons clear the gate. Azmaveth motioned his mailed hand, turning the Canons north. Talia watched them until they disappeared into the hills. She viewed Matthew and Wulf veer south. Talia lingered, wanting to keep Matthew in her sight for as long as possible. When Matthew faded from view, she closed her eyes, allowing the sun to fold her in its warm embrace.

"He will win?"

-- Yes. Light always defeats the darkness --

"Does he survive?"

The answer the Matron Mother wanted did not come.

Chapter Six

Fall 531, Age of the Arch Mage

Harsh and imposing, Targinn Mirth lorded over Welcome as the town's self-appointed mayor. He was a tyrant, a brutal dictator who wielded his own brand of justice. Prior to his arrival in Welcome, Targinn had served for a brief period as a cleric. Tired of a pauper's life and toiling inside the temple, he disavowed his sacred oath. He discarded his priestly garments and ventured forth, seeking a new career. Over time, he perfected his craft, earning a reputation as efficient and discreet. With time and patience, he attracted a sizeable clientele and amassed a substantial fortune working as an assassin and mercenary. Targinn found the power, wealth, and glory he craved.

Wanted as a fugitive in Chytwynd and the Stowan Freeholds, Targinn Mirth and his congregation of henchmen sought refuge in the Border Lands. They stumbled into Welcome nine years ago and Targinn realized he'd found his sanctuary. Welcome looked abandoned when he arrived, nothing more than a collection of run-down shanties and dilapidated huts. Targinn seized the opportunity to exert his will over the town and further line his own pockets. He drove off and killed most of the villagers and seized their properties. The rest he enslaved. Someone must do those dreadful chores no one else wanted to do. He razed the shanties and huts to clear the land for his own sinister purposes. Consumed by his own arrogance, Targinn appointed himself high priest, then built a temple, gaudy and elaborate, to his latest deity in the village's heart.

Walls, battlements, and towers constructed from gray stone surrounded a grand hall set in the middle of the temple. A single gate, wooden and reinforced by iron, was the sole way in or out. Gargoyle statues, grotesque and fiendish, affixed to the grand hall's entrance, leered at those entering or leaving. Tapestries and ornate furnishings adorned the interior. Gold sconces and chandeliers held torches and candles. Rows of pews flanked a marble walkway leading to a granite dais set at the back of the grand hall. Ribbons of light from thin slits in the walls streaked the grand hall in an eerie pall. When the witching hour reached its darkest point, demons stalked these forsaken grounds. Bleak and foreboding, the Crypt of Belhaaz loomed over Welcome like a black stain upon the earth.

Targinn Mirth used the shrine as a cover for his own illicit operation. He established his own constabulary force, the Myrmidon of Belhaaz, built from the core of his devoted followers. Bald and pallid faced, they tattooed their clean-shaven faces with a narrow maroon stripe running from the eyes to the jawline, declaring their loyalty to Targinn Mirth. The Myrmidon clad themselves in heather gray plate mail armor, and their shields and tabards bore the mark of Belhaaz, five diagonal blood red slashes. These fanatics controlled the chaos and exacted tribute from the business and ship owners.

Word spread fast across the Northern Kingdoms and the Southern Realms and soon those owning questionable pasts and eager for new beginnings flocked to Welcome. Vile and dangerous, Welcome may have seemed a strange name for a thriving town situated miles beyond Chytwynd's northern frontier. However, it was the perfect title for a haven embracing robbers, cutthroats, raiders, and hooligans seeking employment, refuge, or any indulgence gold could purchase. Taverns, inns, gambling halls, and pleasure houses operated all hours of the day and flanked Welcome's wide avenues. Along the Eastern Sea, its location inside the Border Lands kept the civilized from Southern Realms and Northern Kingdoms at a safe distance.

Blessed by a natural deep-water bay and broad sweeps of sandy beaches, Welcome maintained a thriving shipping industry. Nearby pine forests offered a steady supply of lumber for ship construction or refurbishment. Pirates purchased supplies and sold their bounties. With ready access to master shipwrights and cheap labor, brigands repaired and careened their vessels. The careening process consumed an enormous amount of time and energy. They hauled their ships onto beaches and heaved them onto their sides. With the hull exposed, the crew cleaned away barnacles and weeds and fixed any damage below the water line.

Ship captains enlisted new sea dogs and deck hands from a broad assortment of miscreants to replace dead or wounded crew members. Crime families and guilds trading in assassination, piracy, and thieving built expansive compounds in the hillocks surrounding Welcome. These cryptic leagues sold their wares and talents to the highest bidder. In dwellings as large as castles and as secure as fortresses, future miscreants trained in the proper methods to ply their trades.

◊ ◊ ◊

Aeros lingered longer than he should have, especially ahead of his next assignment. But when the ale flowed, there was seldom enough to satisfy his thirst. Aeros loved everything about the smoke-filled taverns—never met one he did not enjoy. With plenty of gold in his pockets, he bought the house round upon round. For at least a couple of hours, Aeros Askin the Wyvern Charmer relished the attention. A golden glow from the morning sun illuminated the eastern horizon when Aeros finally staggered to his room at the Forsaken Inn.

A midday sun, bright and unforgiving, streamed past paper-thin curtains, rousting Aeros from his drunken slumber. He perched on the edge of the bed, holding his head, waiting for the room to stop spinning. He found dressing an arduous task. His fingers fumbled over the buttons and buckles on his leather armor. Once clad, he slung his pack over his shoulder, then ambled down to the busy streets. Aeros paused a moment under the awning covering the inn's front door, allowing his eyes to adjust to the vivid sun suspended in a bright sky. Aeros squinted and headed north.

Slow minutes passed until Aeros reached a trail leading to the top of a bluff. Aeros scrabbled his way to the summit. He found his three companions and the dragons asleep. Asp opened his eyes, craned his long neck in Aeros's direction, and grumbled a low, ominous greeting. As he approached, the Wyvern Charmer saw a dozen empty ale skins discarded near a cold fire pit. His companions, Ruune, Scutter, and Qorrey, rose from their bedrolls bleary-eyed and reeking of ale. They looked like he felt and stank even worse.

Aeros dropped his pack near Asp and leaned into the dragon's massive frame. He felt disdain surveying his companions. "Any ale left?"

Ruune grunted and tossed Aeros an ale skin. Aeros tilted his head back, guzzled the ale, then shuffled over to where his companions packed their gear. "Listen up, rats. We leave in an hour for Prosper."

"Why that nasty river town?" Ruune protested. "Ain't nothing there."

"Yeah, Aeros," Scutter chirped. "No gold. No ale or women."

"We have a job there. Pays big," Aeros snarled. "We fly south following the coastline until reaching Chytwynd. We will overnight on Ruby Island."

"What's the take?" Qorrey inquired, his interest piqued.

"A thousand gold pieces each," Aeros lied.

Ruune, Scutter, and Qorrey shrugged in reluctant agreement, then resumed packing their equipment. *Too stupid to know any better,* Aeros scoffed to himself. Aeros reached into a large leather bag behind his saddle, removing what resembled a fishing net. He knelt, unrolled the netting, then checked it for flaws or tears. He surveyed the net, knowing this was his preferred weapon for capturing his prey alive. Aeros squatted, re-rolled the net, and returned it to the saddlebag.

Asp emitted a low growl and bared his teeth, warning Aeros of impending danger. Aeros spun and watched Targinn Mirth, accompanied by a squad of his Myrmidons, emerge from the trail. Aeros, his palm resting on the hilt of his long knife, stepped to Targinn. Ruune, Scutter, and Qorrey moved to flank Aeros.

Targinn raised an eyebrow and stared down his nose at the diminutive kobold. He wore a crooked smile advancing towards Aeros, his hands extended, palms up. He noticed the talisman hanging around the kobold's neck, the charm providing him dominion over the four dragons. Targinn coveted the talisman, sought it for himself. He yearned for the power, longed for the ability to control the dragons. Targinn knew he could kill Aeros and take the pendant, but the kobold remained untouchable while in Belhaaz's favor. "Aeros Askin, I am disappointed. You did not say goodbye."

"You're a busy man," Aeros taunted, the wave of his clawed hand dismissive.

As the Myrmidons surrounded the kobolds, Targinn stopped short of Aeros. He bent his lanky frame at the waist and narrowed his dark eyes. "Listen here, bounty hunter. Our master's opinion of you would diminish if he witnessed your current condition."

"I'm a recovery agent and my business regarding the master is my own," Aeros countered.

Targinn faltered and stepped back. "Don't—"

"Got no time," Aeros barked, cutting Targinn off. Aeros spun on his heels and pushed his way through the Myrmidons toward Asp.

Targinn halted mid-step as Asp rose to his feet. A wisp of steam seeped from Asp's flaring nostrils, the dragon's glare challenging and intimidating. Aeros climbed aboard, strapped himself to the saddle, and adjusted his goggles. Asp lifted himself skyward with an awkward grace. Ruune, Scutter, and Qorrey followed him into the air seconds later. The Wyvern Charmer and his companions cackled as they swept low over the bluff before banking south, forcing Targinn and his Myrmidons to duck.

Targinn Mirth uttered a string of obscenities and stomped off.

Chapter Seven

Fall 531, Age of the Arch Mage

Morning passed into the afternoon as Wulf and Matthew rode south. They limited their conversation during those hours to a few words, some grunts, and the occasional hand gesture. Wulf glanced at Matthew. The cleric's smile remained etched on his face.

"You know, I slept all night uninterrupted," Wulf announced. "No nightmares."

"I know," Matthew beamed. "I see peace in your eyes."

Matthew fell quiet once more, his thoughts somewhere else. Wulf studied Matthew's shield strapped to his saddle. It was blank, no symbol or device. The Canons carried shields emblazoned with the Maiden's emblem, the rising sun.

"Why don't you have the Canon markings on your shield?" Wulf inquired, trying to get Matthew to talk.

"I am a trooper, not a Canon," Matthew replied, his answer short and his eyes focused ahead. "It would not be proper."

Wulf chuckled. Matthew had stopped talking again. They rode in silence a few more minutes.

"Did you know Rita Dupon doted on you?" Wulf blurted. "Yep, sure did. Talked about you all the time."

"What?" Matthew shouted. "What are you talking about? I don't—"

"So are you going to explain the Canons or not?" Wulf interrupted with an impish grin.

"Uh, sure," Matthew conceded, glaring at Wulf. "I requested the Matron Mother deploy them."

"Why?" Wulf asked.

"King Stockton needs them," Matthew admitted. "And it is time the Matron Mother let them go."

"Was she reluctant?" Wulf inquired.

"Very," Matthew confessed, his gaze shifting back to Wulf. "During the Battle at the Mulford River, the Canons fought where the fighting was fiercest. My father and another war cleric were the sole survivors. The Matron Mother's husband was among the dead. I think she blames herself for their deaths, even after all these years."

"I see," Wulf stated, noting Matthew's far-off stare. Wulf let the conversation ebb. They had plenty of time for discussion in the coming days.

On they rode over the broad flat plains that dominated southern Beth Amen. Daylight waned and gave way to dusk. Wisps of clouds floated overhead as the sky transitioned from blue to gray and then to black. They found shelter in a grove of elms clumped near a creek bank. They removed their tack and allowed the horses to eat the lush grass and drink from the stream. A small campfire provided enough heat to warm iron rations and a mug of coffee. Once they had cleaned their dishes and repacked their gear, Matthew lit his pipe and rested his head on his saddle. "I do not know what to expect when we reach Auroryies. The princes may not even require our services anymore."

Wulf stood near the campfire, scratching Maggie's ears and sipping his coffee. "Me neither."

A peaceful quiet endured for several minutes as Wulf and Matthew listened to the sounds of the night. Wulf sat, his back leaning against a tree, and stretched his legs out. "I already miss my bed from last night."

"And the ale and stew," Matthew added.

"The cathedral was amazing," Wulf exclaimed.

"Yeah, it's a special place," Matthew agreed.

"Why did you leave?" Wulf inquired.

"Restless," Matthew admitted, shutting his eyes. "It was the only home I knew, and I wanted to see more."

"Well, the Border Lands are nice, especially this time of year," Wulf chuckled. "I bet they are nicer than Highpoint."

Matthew laughed, snuffed out his pipe, and drifted off to sleep. Wulf stared into the fire, lost in the embers, fading in and out for another hour, his thoughts drifting to Seth, his mother, and Maria. As the embers waned, he rolled into his cloak. Sleep came quickly and uninterrupted.

◊ ◊ ◊

For the next two days, Wulf and Matthew rode south. On the morning of day three, they traversed the Tressel border and began a gradual descent from the high plains into the Rifting Valley. By noon they attained the broad and flat valley floor. The mid-day sun burned bright, its welcome heat warming the cool air. Distant mountains, rugged and majestic, flanked the vale to the east and west. An early fall snow blanketed the tallest peaks. Fall came later in the Rifting Valley than it did farther north, but the leaves had begun their steady transition from green to scarlet, gold, and russet.

As twilight settled upon the land, they detected smoke coming from the south. A mile farther, the faint outlines of buildings emerged from the dimness. The fall sun was gliding below the mountains when Wulf and Matthew entered a cluster of homes, a stable, and an inn near a stream. Candles burned in the windows of dwellings constructed from logs and mortar. The savory aroma from cooking stoves wafted into the air from the Elmbowl Gap Inn. Tired of eating rations and sleeping outdoors, Wulf and Matthew stopped for the night. Three old men sat in rocking chairs on the front porch, puffing on their pipes as Wulf and Matthew descended from their saddles.

"Evening, gentlemen," Matthew greeted, climbing the steps to the porch.

"And to you as well, Horse Tribesman," one replied.

"We could use a hot meal, cold ale, and a bed under a roof," Matthew requested.

"Don't forget the horses," Wulf reminded Matthew, wearing a meek grin.

"Oh, and a stall for the horses," Matthew added.

"Best biscuits and gravy north of Tejt," the youngest-looking man boasted. "My name is Lamm. Come on in and we will tend to you and your horses."

He moaned and groaned as he stood. "Don't get old, lads. Follow me."

Wulf removed Maggie's bridle and hung it over the saddle horn. He pulled her face close. "Stay nearby."

Maggie whinnied and nibbled at his nose.

Lamm gawked at Wulf and Maggie. He turned to Matthew. "Does she—"

"Yes," Matthew interrupted. "Every word."

Lamm mumbled to himself, then led Matthew and Wulf into the inn. Warm aromas of baking bread greeted them as they entered. Torches and candlelight bathed the dining room in a soft, welcoming glow. A young barmaid delivered food and drink to the seven customers present. Half a dozen tables and chairs cluttered the room. Four Tressel soldiers reclined near the front door and three merchants sat at the adjacent table. A hush enveloped the room as the patrons eyed Wulf and Matthew. Lamm stepped behind a wooden counter and produced two keys. "Three silver pieces will cover your room, stables, and two meals."

Wulf and Matthew set the coins on the counter and retrieved the keys. As they headed for their rooms, they heard a commotion outside. Men shouted and cursed while a horse snorted and neighed.

"Maggie!" Wulf spun and hustled for the door.

"What are you—"

"Maggie's calling me!"

"She can't ..." Matthew yelled. He caught himself mid-sentence. "Yes, she can."

Wulf almost removed the door from its hinges as he burst out onto the porch. He saw three men attempting to steal Maggie. Two had a rope around her neck and were trying to pull her into the wood line. The third writhed in the grass. Maggie squealed. She reared and bucked as she struggled to free herself.

Wulf leapt off the porch and nocked an arrow. He drew the bowstring taut to his cheek and selected his target. "Maggie, stop!"

At the sound of his voice, she froze in place. Wulf released the bowstring. The arrow severed the rope. "Maggie, attack!"

The two men stared at the empty rope in their hands, then at Maggie. Free from her bonds, she lowered her head, fixed her ears back, and exposed her teeth. Thrusting her hooves, she chased the men. Wulf rearmed his bow and fired again. His target staggered and fell face down. The man howled in pain, grasping at the arrow piercing his left shoulder. The occupants from the inn pushed and shoved their way onto the porch to get an unobstructed view of what was happening. One soldier drew his sword. "Trooper, do not—"

Wulf spun and aimed his bow at the soldier. Wulf's eyes reflected the fury boiling in his blood. Matthew jumped from the porch. He held his hands out in front of him, palms up. "Wulf, no!"

The soldier recoiled, his courage evaporated. Wulf turned and sprinted for his horse. "Maggie, come."

Wulf fired again. The final thief stumbled, clutching at the arrow buried in the back of his thigh. Wulf slowed his pace as Maggie neared. He reached for her and pulled her close. Her flanks heaved, her nostrils flared, and her eyes were wide. He removed the rope from her neck and checked her for wounds. "You're safe."

Matthew and the crowd eased to within a few feet of Wulf and Maggie.

Maggie whinnied and threw her head. Wulf marched to the closest wounded thief. The thief cowered as Wulf hauled him to his feet. "No one messes with my horse."

Wulf dragged him to where Maggie stood. "Apologize."

"I am sorry," he stuttered.

"Not to me," Wulf snarled, pointing to Maggie. "To her, and mean it or I will let her eat your face."

Maggie pawed the ground and bared her teeth.

"I am sorry," he murmured.

Maggie nickered, and Wulf tossed the man to the ground. While Wulf cradled Maggie's head in his hands, the crowd gaped and murmured among themselves, not quite believing what they had just witnessed.

An old man tapped Matthew's shoulder. "Come on. She did not understand him."

"With this horse, anything is possible," Matthew admitted, although he was not sure he believed what he saw from Maggie this time.

Matthew moved to Wulf and Maggie. "We good? She's all right?"

Wulf nodded and Maggie whinnied.

"Come on," Matthew suggested. "Let's get some food."

"Bring it to me in the stables," Wulf growled. "I'm not letting Maggie out of my sight."

"Okay," Matthew sighed. Wulf was as stubborn as a Highlander's mule and arguing would prove pointless.

Still mumbling among themselves, the crowd pointed at Maggie and the horse thieves. The people parted, giving Wulf and Maggie plenty of room as they ambled to the stables.

"Trooper," the solider yelled, shuffling for Wulf.

Wulf stopped and faced the soldier and his companions.

"I thought for a second you were going to shoot me," the soldier admitted, his smile meek and his laugh uneasy.

"I was."

◊ ◊ ◊

Morning arrived hushed and without further incident. It was a metal gray, misted fall dawn. Clouds packed the sky—rain was imminent. Wulf and Matthew pulled themselves into the saddle and reined their horses south. They did not talk for the first mile. The sole noise came from the rhythmic plodding of their horses' hooves.

"Sleep well?" Matthew needled. "I did. A warm dry bed. I think I slept in a comforter handmade from down feathers. Can you imagine, Wulf? A down comforter."

Wulf ignored him. He would not allow Matthew to goad him into a meaningless discussion.

Chapter Eight

Fall 531, Age of the Arch Mage

Paddy Staggs shared a few common traits with his good-natured halfling kin. Like his passion for strong ale and good food and lively music. But living a simple country life, working the land, and living in a burrow like a rabbit did not interest him. Paddy put that life behind him upon departing The Greenes decades past. He loved the city, especially South Hampton, and all the amenities and vices it offered. Most often he appeared fun-loving and affable, but Paddy was vain, selfish, and manipulative to the core of his existence. Paddy possessed a swift, violent temper—he did not earn Kyric's or Lady Jiroche's favor by exhibiting kindness. As a skilled tracker, none escaped when he hunted them. Next to Kyric, Paddy Staggs served as the premier enforcer in the family.

Paddy Staggs stumbled home to sleep off his drunken stupor following a night of revelry. He slept through the morning, waking around noon to bright fingers of sunshine that found gaps in the heavy curtains covering his bedroom window. Still intoxicated when he woke, Paddy stared bleary-eyed at the ceiling as the room whirled about him. Paddy shuddered at the sudden thought of Kyric. The drow scared him, although he would never admit it to anyone. He remained grateful Lady Jiroche dispatched Kyric and three other assassins to Peril on a lengthy assignment to assist the marauder Teach Drummond to eliminate a rival pirate fleet. As expected, Kyric fumed, and his last words before departing chilled Paddy to his core. They echoed in Paddy's ears. *I expect results when I return or...* With a wave of his hand, he dismissed the crazed drow from his mind. *A few months left.*

Paddy set his feet onto the wooden floor and tottered to the tub. He bathed in cold water, attempting to sober up. He dried off and wrapped the towel around his body. The halfling reeled from the effects of last night's binge, and he paused several times to steady himself against the wall as he doddered to his closet.

Paddy surveyed his wardrobe, deliberating his attire for the day. *Casual? Business? Maybe formal?* He fancied finer attire. All his clothes fit him to perfection. Skilled tailors handcrafted his garments using luxurious fabrics provided by the finest clothiers in

South Hampton. After thoughtful consideration, Paddy Staggs selected business attire for this day. He looked himself over in the mirror. Pants, matching vest, silk shirt and tie, and a dark suit jacket only worn on one other occasion. *Sharp.* Satisfied at his appearance, he gave himself a wink and a salute.

Paddy carefully removed a metal box from a shelf and set it on the table. He freed the clasps and opened the box. A huff escaped his mouth as he removed a jewel attached to a gold chain. Of all his possessions, this one remained his most prized. The jewel spun and ensnared the sunlight. "So magnificent."

Paddy held it to his face—The Widow of the Desert Seas. Expertly shaped from an enormous black jade gem accented with platinum and gold, his eyes absorbed each detail. Platinum formed the eight legs, and the jeweler had crafted the pincers from gold. With the legs and pincers affixed, the amulet resembled a black widow spider.

The halfling's thoughts wandered back to the night The Widow came into his possession. Posing as spice traders, he and three halfling companions had joined a merchant caravan. They traveled the trade routes south from The Greenes to the northern deserts of The Emirates, enduring soaring temperatures and sandstorms. Qammus sat amidst the sprawling Siba Oasis. Palm trees surrounded the oasis and protected the freshwater springs and crops from the winds and shifting sands. Qammus provided weary travelers and their pack animals a refuge to refit and resupply before resuming their journey.

Agim Fodday, a ruthless and wealthy warlord, governed Qammus with a heavy hand and amassed a fortune by exacting an excessive tax on each traveler passing through. Fodday ruled the oasis from a walled stronghold constructed of clay and mud bricks and a small army exerted his will. Magnificent and opulent, the stronghold Shanaqal rose above the desert and cast an oppressive gloom across Qammus.

For a week, he and his associates cased Shanaqal. Sneaking in at night, they gathered the information needed to steal The Widow. They mapped the grounds, identified entrance and egress points, and learning the guards' patrol routes. Dusk gathered in a cloud-filled western sky when Paddy, Ashir, Tonk, and Redd exited the inn. Using the side streets and alleyways, they reached Shanaqal as the clouds drifted east and hid the heavenly host. Crouched in the wall's shadow, they watched and listened. A minute passed, and then another. They remained undetected. Ashir's tap on the shoulder sent Tonk and Redd over the walls first.

Tonk and Redd had a minute to remove any guards blocking their path to the warlord's chambers on the second floor. Paddy and Ashir scaled the wall then eased down into the gardens. Following a trail of bodies, they found Tonk and Redd shrouded in the hedges near a footpath. Paddy and Ashir climbed to the second-floor balcony and skulked inside the empty room. After a quick search, they located a metal box atop a stand near the bed. Ashir opened the box and confirmed The Widow was within. He closed the lid and gave Paddy the box, then motioned for him to rejoin the others in the garden. As Ashir moved to a bowl of oranges on the table, Paddy escaped by another exit and abandoned his companions to their own fates.

"I wonder…" Paddy considered for a moment as he slipped The Widow over his neck and tucked it into his tunic. He waved at the air. "Ah, they are dead or in prison."

Next Paddy sauntered to an ornate armoire near the window. He released the latches like he was opening a present. Paddy took his time examining the vast array of armaments arranged on a series of hooks and pegs. He gazed over daggers, long knives, a pair of one-handed crossbows, a short sword, and a short bow. Like his clothes, master metalsmiths and boyers custom-made his weapons, each weapon balanced and sized to his stature. *Casual? Business? Maybe formal?* Paddy settled on an ivory-handled long knife and two daggers inlaid with emeralds that matched his business attire.

Paddy grabbed his money belt laden with gold, its heft a source of pride. He snagged a walking stick and donned a satin cloak. The halfling paused before the mirror and checked himself over one more time. He enjoyed his reflection for a long moment then headed out the door. *It is good to be Paddy Staggs on this day.*

A peaceful quiet spread over his South Hampton neighborhood on this early afternoon as Paddy strolled down the tree-lined streets. His stomach growled, and he needed coffee, lots of coffee. His favorite diner sat around the block from his flat. The folks he passed smiled and offered pleasant greetings. Most found his unruly tufts of brown hair, broad flat feet, and cherub-like face adorable. No one suspected this innocent-looking halfling lived a double life. Paddy earned his honest living importing precious gems and exotic spices from every corner of the Southern Realms. It supplemented the income he received from the Jiroche crime family.

Paddy turned the corner and, as usual for this time of morning, the line outside Suzie's Café wound its way down the street. The food was that good. The maître d' spotted Paddy and waved him to the front of the line. Paddy beamed, bypassing folks who had been waiting hours before he arrived.

"Good day, Master Staggs." Bentley opened the door with a slight bow. "Muriel has your table prepared."

"Bentley," Paddy replied. He flipped Bentley a gold piece, then entered the café. *Yes, a fine day to be Paddy Staggs.*

Muriel waited on him, as she always did. She offered Paddy a toothy smile while escorting him to his preferred table near the picture window at the front of the restaurant. Paddy grinned at the waitress who served him every time. She always knew what he wanted. A pot of fresh coffee, six eggs over easy, a stack of pancakes lathered in maple syrup and butter, ham steak, and potatoes. She was his favorite.

He left Muriel a hefty tip after finishing his meal. As the alcohol haze continued to wear off, Paddy strolled to the docks, enjoying the warm sun. It was late afternoon and time to work. His musings, as they often did, settled on money. He wanted to ignore the assignment thrust upon him by Kyric Barjarken. Time and age wore on his body, and tracking became harder with each passing year, yet the money remained so satisfying, too desirable to pass up. Plus, Caldwell was dangerous. For as long as Paddy remembered, Caldwell served as the preeminent thief and assassin in the Jiroche crime family. Brutal and efficient, the half-elf never failed. But the drow guaranteed a sizeable fee to track down the traitorous Daniel Caldwell, and Paddy loved money as much as he loved himself.

As he strolled, Paddy planned his new search strategy. He'd conducted a halfhearted attempt to hunt Caldwell for over a year in South Hampton, knowing full well he would not find him here. He called in a few favors and shelled out some gold pieces to local hoodlums to locate Caldwell. But Paddy understood Caldwell knew the danger of lingering in South Hampton, especially with a fortune on his head. The half-elf was too smart and had gone to great lengths to hide himself. You did not ascend to the top by taking unnecessary chances. When all of Paddy's leads went cold, it confirmed what he already knew. The half-elf had fled the city. He would have done the same thing. *So tracking a half-elf should be easy, right? How many are there?* Paddy renewed his reluctant quest at the passenger terminal on the pier. Two shipping companies operated passenger service out of South Hampton. A visit to Bavard's would serve as his starting point.

The passenger terminal was empty when Paddy sauntered into Bavard's. A tall young man, pimpled and malodorous, manned the counter. Turning on the charm, Paddy chuckled as he neared. Pimple Boy offered a patronizing smile as he spoke. "Well, what have we here? Are you lost, little boy?"

Paddy chortled in amusement, reaching for the ivory-handled long knife tucked inside his suit jacket. "What?"

Pimple Boy grinned. "I said are you lost, little—"

Like a deer leaping a fence, Paddy cleared the counter, driving Pimple Boy to the wooden floor. Paddy knelt on the boy's chest and pressed the long knife to his throat. "What did you say?"

Pimple Boy gulped to fill empty lungs, his trousers soaked in urine.

"Um, how can I assist you, sir?" he murmured.

Paddy smirked and stood. He smoothed his suit, adjusted his cloak, and sheathed the long knife. "Get up."

The young man obeyed the demon-possessed halfling and pulled his lanky frame from the floor. Scared for his life, Pimple Boy pressed his back onto the wall and waited for Paddy's orders.

"Your passenger manifests," Paddy demanded. "I seek a half-elf. Did a half-elf book passage on one of your vessels in the last eighteen months?"

"Uh, in the last eighteen months?" Pimple Boy grumbled.

"Correct," Paddy affirmed. He narrowed his eyes and furrowed his brow. "Is there a problem?"

"No, none," the young man assured him.

"Well?" Paddy insisted.

"It's just a long time ago. Let me see what I can find," Pimple Boy stammered as he flipped the pages of a leather-bound book sitting on the counter. "Would you have a name?"

"Daniel Cald … No, wait. He would not use his real name." Paddy stopped and glared at Pimple Boy. "Try Peter Holmes."

The young man resumed his search. After several minutes, he pointed at the entry. "Yes, right here. Peter Holmes."

Peter Holmes? How often will you use that tired alias? You disappoint me, Caldwell. Paddy rolled his eyes. "Yes, that's him. And?"

"He departed South Hampton aboard the *Bright Star* last year," Pimple Boy revealed. "She sailed for Kenly, a port city in Tressel."

Paddy cocked his head. "When does the next ship leave?"

Chapter Nine

Fall 531, Age of the Arch Mage

He shuddered and hesitated in front of the door. Any conversation with the master unnerved him. The messenger had lit a single candle, then pulled on black robes, clean and pressed. He could feel the frigid air seeping from underneath the door. He reached for the doorknob, then pulled his hand back—his courage failed. The messenger swore, then pushed open the door and stepped inside. He exhaled, his short rapid breaths producing visible puffs. Inside the room, he paused and focused on a marble stand atop a dais along the far wall. A thin square of satin cloth concealed the demon's Scrawlstone.

Beneath the cloth, he saw the Scrawlstone pulsing—the master waited. Imbued with a sinister magic, the Scrawlstone was a gift from the master. The messenger uncovered the stone. A bright light flared and drove the darkness from the room.

He cowered and shielded his eyes. Knocking knees caused his entire body to tremble. The messenger took a long, deep breath in a feeble attempt to regain his composure. "Master, your messenger stands ready."

"Hm, is that so?" Belhaaz questioned, his tone condescending. "I sense apprehension in your voice."

"N-no," the messenger stuttered. "M-more inside the, uh, a-assembly flock to your cause."

"I see," Belhaaz said. "What stands in your way?"

"Prince Tralderonn," he admitted. "He is unyielding. But I have a plan to eliminate him."

"Go on."

"Bounty hunters," the messenger explained. "They are ready to remove the insolent prince."

A long, uncomfortable silence ensued. The messenger squirmed, anticipating Belhaaz's reply.

"Yes," Belhaaz agreed. "Deliver him to Udontawny. He will be a fitting sacrifice."

The light faded and the stone went dark. The messenger replaced the cloth on top of the Scrawlstone and exited the room. He sagged against the door, relieved.

The messenger returned to his quarters and lit another candle. He sat at his desk to pen a set of instructions for the bounty hunters, when he heard a knock on the door. "Enter."

He ignored the proxy entering his quarters. The proxy stopped short of the messenger's desk and waited.

"What?" the messenger demanded, the irritation apparent in his tone.

"The preparations are complete," the proxy reported. "A crew of bounty hunters will wait for Prince Wake to deliver payment and the instructions."

"You are sure Prince Wake understands his mission?"

"Yes," the proxy confirmed.

The messenger folded the parchment and map and slipped them into an envelope. He counted out two hundred gold pieces and placed the coins in a sack. The messenger stowed the envelope and the sack into a satchel and handed it to the proxy. "Leave."

The proxy did not speak as he departed. He wound his way down the torchlit stairwell to the bottom of the tower. The proxy eased the door open and scanned the inner grounds—they were empty. He traversed the inner grounds unnoticed. The proxy crept through an escape door concealed in the Tsoye Wall and out into Highpoint. Clouds masked the moon and stars and shrouded his movements in the Quew Gardens. He slackened his speed when he reached East Street and entered an unlit alley a few yards past Sal's Tavern. He leaned against a wall to catch his breath and wait. After a minute or two, he watched Prince Wake drift a dozen feet into the alley and stop. The proxy straightened and sneered beneath his cowl. He placed the satchel into the young prince's hands. "They wait for your arrival."

Prince Wake nodded in silent understanding. He pulled his cowl up to conceal his head and stepped from the alley. Candles flickered in the windows. Torch lamps cast an eerie glow over the cobblestones. Prince Wake scanned up and down the street. It remained empty and quiet. He hurried for the docks. Prince Wake knew he would find what he sought near the harbor district. He slowed his pace and avoided eye contact as a Sentry patrol moved past him.

Wind blowing off the bay felt chilled and damp as he arrived at the harbor district. He shivered and surveyed his surroundings. In a gentle rhythm, the water lapped against the ships and shore. He detected the raucous laughter and crude singing spilling out of

Skirrit's. He kept to the shadows as he skulked toward the tavern. The prince peeked over his shoulder, ensuring no one followed or watched. He eased into an adjacent alley, disappeared into the gloom, and located the back door. Prince Wake paused and listened. He heard four voices, loud and foul, coming from beyond the door. Prince Wake retrieved a key from the satchel, unlocked the door, and stepped in.

His sudden presence startled the bounty hunters. They pushed back from the table and drew their blades. They advanced, frowning, and Prince Wake halted. A wave of his hand restrained the bounty hunters from further movement. The prince pulled out the envelope and coin sack from his satchel and arranged the items on the table. "Your instructions and half your fee per our agreement."

The four bounty hunters looked at the envelope and sack. When they turned back, the prince was gone, and they were free of the invisible bonds restraining them. A single bounty hunter moved to the door.

"Wes," one said. "Let him go."

Wes glared at the door. "Izzy, I hate them wizards."

"Don't act the fool," Izzy warned as he sat down at the table. He peered into the coin bag and grinned. "Them wizards are paying us a lot of money."

Wes cursed and plodded to his chair. Izzy opened the envelope and read the instructions. He sighed when he finished.

"What's it say?" Wes asked, draining the ale from his mug. "You know Blouser, Trit, and I can't read."

Blouser and Trit laughed in agreement.

"Our target is a Prince Tralderonn," Izzy explained. "We are to take him to a place called Udontawny and turn him over to a man named Milton."

Izzy unfolded the map and spread it over the table. "It's a hike to Udontawny. We will earn our gold this time."

◊ ◊ ◊

Prince Wake hurried from the tavern and headed for another rendezvous with the proxy. Ten minutes passed before he reached the alley and entered. He found the proxy waiting. The young prince stopped and withdrew the cowl from his head. His clean-shaven face reflected the satisfaction he felt from accomplishing the task. "It is done."

The proxy nodded and in a swift motion plunged a dagger into Prince Wake's chest. The prince's eyes went wide with fear and surprise as blood seeped from both sides of his mouth. He staggered, then collapsed to the ground.

"Dangerous times," the proxy declared. Without remorse or regard, he departed the alley.

Chapter Ten

Fall 531, Age of the Arch Mage

Prior to departing, Tralderonn spent the last of the summer purchasing a reliable horse and procuring supplies for his journey. Once all this was complete, he had one more thing on his list. The day before he left, he paid a visit to Sal. The tavern was empty when Tralderonn entered.

"Well, what do we have here?" Sal chuckled, grabbing two glasses. "A renegade prince."

"You're a riot," Tralderonn cracked, pulling up a stool at the bar.

Sal slid the ale glass down to Tralderonn, then walked down the counter. "Where have you been?"

Tralderonn sucked down half his glass, then wiped his mouth on his sleeve. "Preparing."

"For what?" Sal asked.

"Leaving." Tralderonn drained his glass. "I'll take another."

Sal handed Tralderonn his glass. "Oh, where?"

Tralderonn scanned the empty tavern. "Be best if I did not tell you."

"So I am on the extensive list of those you don't trust?"

"Nah, it's not like that," Tralderonn admitted with a shrug. "It is for your protection."

Sal leaned against the wall and crossed his arms over his chest.

"Look, Sal." Tralderonn pulled a long draw from his glass. "The treachery inside Auroryies goes deeper than I thought. I am a threat, and they all know we are drinking buddies. They will come see you, so the less you know—"

"Yeah, yeah," Sal snorted. "The better."

Tralderonn finished his second glass and set it on the counter. "Watch yourself, Sal. The princes are becoming desperate."

"You too, Traldy." Sal watched his friend walk out of the tavern and disappear into the crowded streets. "You, too."

Provisioned and armed, Tralderonn slipped from Highpoint and was gone without notice. Riding north by himself gave Tralderonn the opportunity to reflect. His life as a Prince of Auroryies had concluded in a fiery crash. In the wake of his latest outburst, there was no going back. Tralderonn ignored Prince Xavian's edict to remain in Highpoint and Cornell's pleading and headed north, intent on joining the war effort against the orcs. At least in Beth Amen, he could try to do some good.

He possessed no clue what the future held for him. Tralderonn was homeless—a rebel prince and a rogue sorcerer. The notion caused him to chuckle. What would his mother think? He possessed no formal combat training as a war mage and it did not matter. He commanded the natural magic flowing through his body and it would be enough.

Tralderonn arrived in Tejt during late fall. The leaves were gone, giving the trees a gray, withered appearance, and each morning a thin layer of frost carpeted the land. The sharp air stung his face and suggested winter arrived faster than most wanted. Tressel's capital city sat near the south end of the Rifting Valley, and he embraced the idea of a warm, dry bed, a hot meal, and a cold mug or two. Not interested in the flophouses and hostels on the outskirts, he located a suitable inn near the center of town.

He tied his horse to the hitching post, shouldered his pack, then stepped inside. He paused in a candlelit foyer to give his eyes a chance to adjust to the dimness and gather his bearings. In front of him, a staircase led to the second and third floors. On his right, the dining room and bar. He counted five customers eating and drinking. To his left was the reception desk staffed by a young woman who looked half-elven. Her features were delicate, her eyes a bright blue, and long blonde hair broke over pointed ears. Her eyes sparkled as she brushed locks from her face. The woman's beauty struck him and he found it difficult not to stare at her.

"Welcome to the Motsslyn Inn," she greeted, her smile toothy and cheerful. "My name is Carjlin. How can I assist you?"

Her smile paused him for a second and her eyes ensnared him.

"Mister, you there?" she asked, snapping her fingers.

"Uh, a room with … a bath would be great," he replied. "Oh, and a stall for my horse."

"Is a room on the first floor okay?" she inquired, her brilliant smile never fading. "I will send the stable boy to fetch your mount."

"Sure," he answered. "Thanks."

Carjlin handed him a key. "Fifteen silver pieces, please."

Tralderonn placed the coins on the counter and received the key from her hand. She studied him for a second.

"Are you one of those wizards from Highpoint?" she wondered. Her expression said she knew the answer to her question.

"What?" he responded. "What a curious question. Why do you ask?"

"You paid with Highpoint silver and the staff. Wizards carry staffs."

"Oh, it's my walking stick," he lied. *Curious.* Tralderonn shouldered his pack and plodded toward his room.

Carjlin let him take a few steps. "Well, are you?"

"No."

"I suspect you are," she mumbled to herself.

A bath and a change of clothes improved his mood and now he was ready for dinner and drinks. Tralderonn wanted to stop and talk to the pretty woman behind the counter. Maybe even invite her to join him. Instead, he gave her a clumsy grin and waved, then stepped out into Tejt's torchlit streets. The sweet perfume of fall infused the city, and he sucked in the crisp, clean night air. It was quiet near the Motsslyn, the shops closed and the taverns subdued. The folks and constables he walked by smiled and said 'hello.'

Tralderonn passed an alleyway and stopped. Something nagged at him. He sensed someone trailed him. He peered into the murk for a moment. From the street, his eyes could detect nothing other than what you find in a typical alley: trash cans, refuse, and feral cats. *Curious.*

Tralderonn wandered into the dimly lit Sapphire Pheasant three blocks from the inn. All the light came from the stone hearth set in the east wall and oil lamps burning on the tables. A dozen round tables and chairs occupied the main room. Several patrons, dining and drinking, paid him no attention as he entered. A savory aroma from the kitchen made his mouth water. He sat near the street-front window. When the waitress arrived, he ordered the duck, sweet potatoes, and a carafe of wine. *Hope Sal doesn't see me drinking wine.*

◊ ◊ ◊

"All right, boys, out you go," Sal laughed. Drunk Sentries never ceased to amuse. When the final Sentry exited, Sal started to shut and lock the door. A gloved hand stopped the door.

"Closed. Come back tomorrow," Sal demanded.

"Not quite yet, Salvador," a cowled figure ordered, his voice high-pitched and grating. He pushed through the door, followed by two Lancers. "Or do I call you Sal?"

"My friends call me Sal. You can call me Mister Spencer," Sal stated. "What do you want?"

"No need for rudeness," the figure chastised and started to sit.

"Don't sit. I am closed and it is time for you to leave," Sal insisted. "And take your goons with you."

"Goons? These soldiers are highly trained professionals," the figure replied. "Dedicated to protecting our fine city and its upstanding citizens."

"Yeah." Sal rolled his eyes. "I see how they roust the innocent on the streets and extort from the local shop owners. If that's your definition of highly trained, then your Lancers are true professionals."

The figure removed his cowl and sat. One Lancer positioned himself at the door while the other stood behind the prince, his gaze never leaving Sal. Sheldon motioned for Sal to sit as well. "I am Prince Sheldon, Mister Spencer. And I am going to ask you a few questions."

Sal remained standing, crossed his arms, and glared at Sheldon.

"Tell me what you know about Tralderonn," Sheldon demanded and set his hands on the table.

"He was born in the Stowan Freeholds and became the youngest—"

"Mister Spencer, do you take me for a fool?" Sheldon screeched.

"Yes." Sal saw the prince's pallid cheeks redden.

"Let's try again." Sheldon stood and smoothed out the wrinkles in his robes. "When was the last time you spoke with Prince Tralderonn?"

"Several weeks ago."

"Did he tell you where he was going?"

"No."

A long, awkward silence followed. Sheldon gazed around the empty tavern and then fixed his eyes on Sal. "Okay."

Sheldon pulled his cowl over his head and moved for the door. He stopped and turned back to Sal. "You have a nice place, Mister Spencer. Would hate to see something happen to it."

Sal waited until Sheldon and the Lancers exited to shut and lock the door. He leaned against the door and exhaled. He surveyed his tavern. "It is a nice place."

Chapter Eleven

Fall 531, Age of the Arch Mage

Sunrise lingered in the east as Aeros and his three companions staggered from their bedrolls reeking of ale. After their flight from Welcome, they spent the night on an uninhabited island off the coast of Chytwynd, drinking into the early morning hours. Now with their gear stowed, the kobolds strapped themselves into their saddles. Powerful leather wings thrashed at the air, lifting the dragons and their riders into the sky. The island and the East Sea disappeared as they gained altitude. Aeros checked his compass and the North Star's location, then set a westward heading.

Aeros expected the flight to Prosper would require three hours, and he must conserve the giant lizards' strength for the attack. He ordered them into a V-formation to increase speed and reduce drag on the dragons. Lights from the coastal villages flickered, then passed from view as they flew deeper into Chytwynd's darkened interior.

◊ ◊ ◊

A driving gale blew the rain sideways. She stood alone, her mind numbed and her body frozen with terror. She felt the ground tremble with each step they took. Four advanced towards her, giant lizards, raven-hued and dreadful. She heard their breathing and witnessed their menacing glare. She wanted to scream, but the sounds stuck in her throat. Finally Kysellah's will to live freed her from the stupor holding her in place. The wind and rain lashed at her face, ripped at her clothes as she fled. They came closer and closer. She endured their hot breath on her neck. Kysellah tripped and fell face down into the mud. She struggled to gain her feet. She reacted too late.

Kysellah shot upright in bed, gasping for air. Her eyes snapped to the vase sitting next to her on a stand. A glow, faint and red, pulsed in a steady cadence. The ward, the last of her mother's magic, created for Kysellah four decades ago to protect her. It shielded Kysellah from her father and his agents. She brought her hands to her face and sat unmoving. *Momma.* In the end,

Kysellah's mother had sacrificed everything—her health, her beauty, and her life—to protect her daughter.

She eased from the covers and found her footing on the floor. She fought to control the panic consuming her. Kysellah dashed to the door and yanked it open. Kysellah stepped onto the porch and scanned the eastern sky. Prosper slumbered, and all she could see were a few candles flickering in the early morning dimness. Kysellah fell to her knees, succumbing to an infernal fear, a foreboding dread not felt in years. Despair washed over her like a chilled winter's rain. Kysellah closed her eyes, straining to focus on the danger she sensed.

◊ ◊ ◊

A morning sun, bright and orange, ascended, transforming the sky from dapple to a vivid blue. Aeros peered over his shoulder, then down upon the terrain passing below. Their target neared. His strike required precise timing. Aeros could not afford any mistakes. He reviewed his plan once more in his head. He intended to exploit the rising sun to his advantage. Scutter and Qorrey would attack the undefended village from the east. They would emerge from the rising sun's glare and pounce on Prosper, inflicting damage and pulling attention away from himself and Ruune soaring in from the north. Aeros motioned for his companions to begin their descent. In minutes, the dragons and their riders descended and flew a few feet above the forest canopy.

◊ ◊ ◊

Kysellah's thinking cleared as she gained her feet. She perceived them. She sensed their intent, malicious and foul. Astride dragons, four assailants winged their way to Prosper from the east. Her nightmare was coming true. Kysellah stood unmoving and defiant, squinting into the dawn. She shuddered as a strange sensation swept over her, one she had never experienced or expected. Finally her magic flowed. She felt it, raw and savage, coursing through her veins like a raging storm. Kysellah embraced the arcana. Its sudden arrival did not frighten her. She understood the transformation occurring inside her body. Kysellah's wrath erupted like a dormant volcano. Her fury knocked down a lifetime of barriers and destroyed the barricades that prevented her from employing her own arcane energy. Kysellah felt the magic pulse and snapped her fingers. In an instant, fire ran down her arms and danced over her hands. The flames mirrored the fury in her eyes. She sneered, vengeful and haunting. A wave of her hand dismissed the spell. "I am tired of running."

She hurried into the house. "Gallego! They're here! Get up!"

Gallego wiped the sleep from his eyes and watched as his wife shoved clothes into a pack. He sensed her fear. Kysellah gnawed on her lower lip and sharp lines etched her face. He dressed and moved to her side. Gallego placed his hand on Kysellah's shoulder. The vengeance in her eyes forced him back a step.

"Who, Kysellah?" Gallego asked, his tone hesitant.

"My father's henchmen," she hissed. Kysellah handed Gallego the pack and the vase containing the ward. "Somehow they found me, Gallego. My mother's ward fails, leaving me unprotected."

Gallego looked at the vase with suspicion, then back to Kysellah.

"Run, Gallego," she implored, tugging him to the back door. "The ward has enough magic left to shield you. Flee to Evergreen, then seek safety in Auroryies. Our boys will protect you."

"You're coming too?" he pleaded.

"No. It stops here. No more running," she exclaimed, her voice harsh and low. "You must go."

"Kysellah, I—"

She cut him off and placed her finger to his lips. Kysellah pulled Gallego close and kissed him. Kysellah then pushed away the only man she had ever loved and looked into his confused eyes.

"Go, Gallego. Please," Kysellah whispered.

◊ ◊ ◊

The morning sun hovered just above the tree line when the Wyvern Charmer and his squad of dragon riders attained the Ossabow's east bank. From out of nowhere, they descended on the unprotected and unsuspecting village. Amid panicked screams rising from the docks and village, Aeros and Ruune reined their dragons north. Scutter, Qorrey, and their dragons exploded out of the bright glare, their mighty wings propelling them toward their target with frightening speed. They descended to a foot or two above the water, then attacked the flat boats and fishing vessels first. Powerful razor-sharp talons shredded wooden ships, ripped and tore at the sails. Desperate to avoid the slaughter, deck hands, sailors, and stevedores dove into the water, seeking shelter. The dragons roared in delight at their destruction. Next they raked homes and businesses. The dragons spewed a caustic venom from their mouths, leaving deep gashes in the wooden structures.

◊ ◊ ◊

Kysellah heard the screams from Prosper, listened to the dragons' roars as she watched Gallego bolt into the wood line behind their home. Kysellah hustled to the front of the house, believing the ward would protect Gallego from harm. From the porch, she caught sight of the dragons as they cleared the village. Kysellah snapped her fingers, bringing forth the flames as she stepped into the middle of the yard. She waited, standing her ground as she let the fire build in her hands.

Masked by the rising sun, they winged their way west. Scutter located Kysellah. She did not flee. In defiance, she continued to hold her ground.

Above dragon wings beating the air, Scutter yelled at Qorrey and pointed in the woman's direction. Scutter whooped in delight, bringing his dragon alongside Qorrey. They pushed their mounts faster and raced for Kysellah.

◊ ◊ ◊

Gallego stopped and hid behind a tree. He waited for a second, then peeked back to his home, seeking Kysellah. When she no longer loitered near the back door, Gallego sprinted for his shed. He swore under his breath as his fingers fumbled against the lock. Once it freed itself, he jerked open the door. Inside, he scoured the jugs, vials, and containers lining the shelves. Gallego grabbed three empty jugs and poured a flammable mixture he'd concocted himself into each one. He stuffed strips of cloth into the tops, lit a torch, then sprinted for the woods.

◊ ◊ ◊

Kysellah lingered, menacing and unwavering. She channeled her mother's magic, felt it surge inside her. Kysellah appeared as an angel of death, her hair splayed around her head as if blown by the wind, her eyes glowed red, her face masked in wrath. She waited. She allowed them to come closer. Flames exploded from her fingertips, slamming into the dragons. Sweeping her hands back and forth, Kysellah hammered Scutter and Qorrey with shards of fire.

Desperate to keep his dragon in the air, Qorrey pushed his mount hard right after the first fireball impacted. His dragon bellowed in pain as the flames stripped away scales, seared the flesh underneath, and tore into the wings. The heat blackened Qorrey's skin, melted his leather armor and the reins. The second fireball sent Qorrey and his dragon careening into the woods. As his dragon hurtled through boughs and limbs, Qorrey cut himself free and leapt away. Seconds later, his dragon plowed into the trees and ground below him in a thunderous crash. Tangled in the leaves and limbs, Qorrey clung to a branch ten feet off the ground, trying to remain conscious.

◊ ◊ ◊

Gallego witnessed the dragon hurtle into the trees, heard the agonized screams. He used the trees to mask his movements and maneuvered toward the wounded dragon, carrying the jugs and torch. He slipped behind an ancient oak and peered around the trunk. Gallego noticed slight movements from the dragon. He could see the eyes closed, the chest lifting and falling in an irregular motion. *It's still alive.*

◊ ◊ ◊

Scutter's dragon spewed its venom, two streams of acid splitting the morning air ahead of the first fireball exploding into the massive body. Scutter attempted to avoid the second and third attacks by pulling hard to port on the reins. He reacted too slowly as the fiery splinters pelted his wounded mount, tearing gaping holes in the dragon's wings. The dragon bellowed in pain as wrecked wings flapped, trying to remain airborne. Unable to stay aloft, Scutter and the dragon plummeted. Both died slamming into the ground.

◊ ◊ ◊

Gallego gritted his teeth and crept for the dragon. He froze, felt his courage fail when the dragon's eyes, consumed by suffering and hate, snapped open. The dragon bared its teeth and strained to rise. Gallego pushed his fear aside and hastened his pace. He lit the cloth on the jugs using his torch. He waited a second, ensuring the cloth strips caught fire. In rapid succession, Gallego hurled all three. They exploded on impact against the dragon's flank. The jugs erupted in a deafening roar as the flames engulfed the dying dragon. Gallego stepped back, ensuring he had killed the giant lizard prior to racing for Kysellah. Gallego heard the cracking twigs and spun to face the noise. He missed the kobold emerging from the smoke and flame. Qorrey hit him in the back of the head. Stunned, Gallego fell to one knee as stars danced in front of his eyes. In an instant, he faded into darkness.

Chapter Twelve

Fall 531, Age of the Arch Mage

Kysellah screamed. The acid burned clothing and flesh, driving her to her knees. She brushed aside the pain and forced herself to her feet and pivoted north. Kysellah glimpsed Aeros and Ruune winging for her from above the tree line. Before she could summon a defensive shield, dragon venom marred her again. Aeros and Ruune snatched her up in a net strung between their two mounts as she collapsed. Entangled in the net, Kysellah rolled on her back and discovered the dragon's unprotected underbelly. She struggled to remain cognizant as the pain seared her broken body. Kysellah called forth another incantation and let the lightning erupt from her hands.

Kysellah's lightning shredded the netting and ripped a jagged gash in the dragon's underbelly from its hindquarters to the neck. Ruune and his dead dragon plunged to the earth. The dragon's weight crushed Ruune as they tumbled over the ground. Kysellah clung to the torn netting using one hand as Aeros urged Asp on. Too damaged to hold her weight, the net gave way. From twenty feet high, she fell. Kysellah landed hard on her back, breaking bones and tearing cartilage. As the air left her lungs, she lost consciousness.

Aeros reined Asp north and looked down to his right. He confirmed Ruune, Scutter, and their mounts were dead. He saw the forest aflame, smelled the burning flesh from Qorrey's dragon. Aeros realized he had failed and concluded he was now the fugitive. He knew he could not return to Welcome. By week's end, Belhaaz would place a high price on his head and hunt him for the rest of his days. The Wyvern Charmer turned Asp south and fled.

◊ ◊ ◊

Gallego gagged on the stench of burning dragon flesh as he picked himself off the ground and wiped the blood from the back of his head. He scanned the woods for his assailant, searched for him across the clearing near his home. Gallego detected the kobold limping for Kysellah's unmoving body. Unarmed, he gritted his teeth and grabbed the closest branch. Desperate to save her, Gallego bolted towards his wife.

◊ ◊ ◊

Qorrey cursed, hobbling towards Kysellah. He looked up and watched Aeros and Asp wing their way south. "You disloyal bastard."

Qorrey slowed, nearing Kysellah. He drew his long knife and continued. He saw her chest rise and fall as she took ragged breaths. Her eyes were closed, her limbs twisted about in unnatural positions. Qorrey crouched at Kysellah's side, gripping the long knife. "The battle may be yours—"

Gallego slammed the branch into the back of Qorrey's head, dropping the recovery agent to his knees. Qorrey felt the blow. He sensed it was the old man. Regret swelled inside him—Qorrey knew he should have killed Gallego when the opportunity presented itself. Enraged, Gallego pummeled the kobold's head over and over and over again until the branch broke in half. Gallego tapped into a primal fury he never knew he possessed and beat Qorrey, using his fists until they bled. Depleted, Gallego dropped to his knees and glared at the dead kobold.

Splattered in the kobold's gore, Gallego crawled on his hands and knees to Kysellah. Blood speckled her lips and seeped from her nose. Death held Kysellah in its icy grip and would not let go. Gallego knew he could not save her. Kysellah's damaged body lay in front of him shattered, her garments charred and perforated from the acid and her skin reddened, burnt, and blistered. Gallego cradled her head in his lap and wiped the blood, dirt, and hair from her beaten face.

"You are free, Kysellah," Gallego whispered, leaning in close to her ear. "No more running."

Anguish and sorrow filled her brown eyes when she opened them. Kysellah toiled against the pain pulsating inside her broken body. She mustered a thin smile, staring into Gallego's grief-stricken eyes. She saw his fear, witnessed Gallego's enduring devotion on his bloody face.

"No, my dear," she uttered, her voice, dry and raspy, the words strained. "I have been free since your love rescued ..."

Gallego shut himself away. In a matter of seconds, his future lay in ruins. Deep inside, he hid, suffering in his silent wake. For hours he rocked back and forth, cradling Kysellah's head in his lap. Gallego trembled at the thought of facing the future without her. He pleaded for her to return. When the tears no longer fell, he hoisted her broken body into his arms. He ignored the villagers congregating in his yard, avoided their questions and disregarded their sympathies. Gallego spurned their half-hearted attempts to assist him. He carried Kysellah to the burial site behind their home. He placed Kysellah next to her mother, Elaire. With grim determination, Gallego dug Kysellah's grave and laid her to rest beside Elaire. The tears fell again with each shovelful of dirt he poured onto Kysellah's lifeless body.

◊ ◊ ◊

For several hours, Aeros and Asp followed the Ossabow south from high above, hoping to avoid the villages and farms along the river's banks. Further attention was the last thing he needed. Dread cluttered his mind, panic consumed his thoughts. He pushed all reminders of his failure aside. He would worry about them later. The Wyvern Charmer needed a plan and a place to hide. *Where? Where can you hide a dragon?* he inquired to himself several times. He carried a map in the saddlebag, but he must put some distance between Prosper and himself before landing to review it.

The midday sun loomed overhead when Aeros and Asp landed in a clearing along the river's east bank. Aeros dug into the saddlebag for the map. The chart contained crude drawings cobbled together over the years. He knelt in the grass and unrolled the map. He figured they were two hours northwest of Ragged Point, the Stowan Freeholds' capital. Aeros studied his sketching, searching for a suitable refuge. *There, Myre Island.* With a glimmer of promise, his clawed finger traced Myre Island. He recalled that a swampy wasteland occupied the southeast side of the island. *Yes.*

Aeros and Asp reached Myre Island as the last strands of the day's sun settled below the western horizon. Aeros landed Asp on a sliver of beach on the island's southeast coast. He smelled the nearby swamplands, the stagnant water and rotting vegetation.

Aeros detected subtle movements from the gentle swaying of the mangroves and the bearded trees covered in moss growing along the shoreline. He laughed at his good fortune. He'd found the perfect place to shelter for a while. Aeros removed the tack from the dragon so Asp could search for food. Like a dog on the hunt, Asp barreled into the marsh, seeking his prey.

Too tired to eat, Aeros sipped on an ale skin. The Wyvern Charmer leaned against his saddle, staring east, watching the moon materialize out of the East Sea. Aeros observed thin yellow ribbons and emerging stars glimmering on top of the murky waters while listening to the waves crescendo onto the shoreline. He dwelled on this morning's fiasco.

Her magic, powerful and deadly, had torn through their scaled bodies, driving the dragons and their riders from the sky. She appeared feral, as if raised in the wild. Fury had flashed in her eyes as the arcane energy exploded from her hands. In a violent flash, his three companions and their dragons had died. *How? The job was supposed to be easy.* Aeros exhaled past serrated teeth. They had killed her. He saw her broken body lying in the grass as he fled. He closed his eyes, listening to the master's last order. *She is no good to me dead.*

After his third ale skin, Aeros slipped into an intoxicated slumber.

◊ ◊ ◊

The day continued fading as he knelt in the fresh dirt. Gallego stared at the short wooden stake in his hands as his eyes read the etching. This simple piece of wood would have to suffice. He had nothing else to mark her grave.

"Kysellah," he whispered as he traced her name with his finger several times. Gallego shoved the stake into the ground, then stood. He surveyed his surroundings. Nosy villagers swarmed over the dead dragons and kobolds. Gallego shuffled back into the house for the last time. His home felt empty and cheerless. He managed a meager smile as the memories of his boys and Kysellah flowed over him. Gallego shouldered his pack and placed the ward in his coat pocket. He headed out the back door and disappeared into the woods, not once looking back. Carried on the wind, Gallego heard a faint voice humming a song Kysellah always sang. The tune tugged at his heart, and he felt fresh tears welling in his bloodshot eyes. Despite his sorrow, he joined in.

◊ ◊ ◊

He squinted into the morning sun shining bright off the sand and water. Asp remained asleep a few yards inside the tree line amid the bones and remnants from last evening's meal. Aeros staggered to his feet and gazed over the landscape. He was alone for the time being and maybe long enough to hide himself for good. He hid his saddle and pack beneath a clump of bushes, then drifted into the swamp in search of breakfast.

Chapter Thirteen

Fall 531, Age of the Arch Mage

Izzy, Blouser, Trit, and Wes observed Tralderonn dining in the Sapphire Pheasant from a murky alleyway across the street. For several weeks they had tracked and observed the renegade prince in Highpoint, learning his patterns and tendencies. When Tralderonn departed Highpoint, they trailed him to Tejt, seeking the best opportunity to abduct him. Izzy knew his companions were bored and restless. They did not possess his patience and his love of the hunt. Blouser, Trit, and Wes fought and bickered constantly, and it was becoming a distraction. Keeping them in line and focused became harder with each passing day. He needed to put his plan into action soon. Izzy slapped Wes upside the head. "We take him tonight in his room."

◊ ◊ ◊

He took his time eating his meal, savoring the wine and viewing the folks strolling the streets. He ordered a second carafe. Tralderonn lingered at the table, hoping he might detect the someone or somebodies stalking him. He saw a couple of seedy characters pass, but how could he be sure? *Curious.* Thirty minutes later, Tralderonn drained his last glass, paid his tab, then stepped into the torchlight. He glanced about and saw nothing. Tejt's streets had grown quiet as the night life slowed to a crawl. *Maybe I am paranoid? Curious.*

Tralderonn did not see Carjlin when he entered the lobby. Filled with liquid courage, he thought he could talk to her. *Too bad.* He stepped into his room, then closed and lock the door.

Oddly, sleep came easy and for the first time in as long as he could remember, he did not struggle to drift off. Dreams and nightmares interrupted his slumber. They performed in his mind like seasoned actors in a play. A shrouded figure, dark and foreboding, starred in the opening act. In a menacing growl, it whispered his name. From atop a dais, it beckoned to him with clawed hands. Black dragons and lizard people winging over the

East Sea starred in scene two. A brilliant sun rose over the Ossabow ...

"Momma!" Tralderonn yelled, sitting up. Dread swept over him as wide eyes scanned the darkened room. "She's dead. How—"

The clunk of the lock on the door roused him from a daze. He gaped at the door and detected cloaked bodies skulking into his room. Tralderonn grabbed his staff while springing out of bed. As he gained his feet, a fiery twinge raced through his shoulder, deadening his right arm and causing him to drop his staff. He closed his eyes to clear his mind, to drive the discomfort from his injured body. Tralderonn willed himself to concentrate and shot flaming barbs from his left hand that exploded into the figures. The lead figure screamed as fiery shards seared his skin and ripped his clothes.

Dim candlelight from the hallway poured into the open door, revealing four humans. One laid unmoving and Tralderonn smelled burning flesh and cloth. As he called forth another cantrip, Tralderonn felt the darts strike his chest in rapid succession. *Focus!* he begged his mind as the numbness spread over his body. Consciousness faded in and out. He observed two men hovering over him. *Are they laughing at me?* They kicked him. He felt ribs crack and the breath escape from his lungs. Their fists pummeled his face, the smell of his blood clung to the air. Tralderonn's body and mind began shutting down. He sucked in a breath, the pain raced through his body.

In desperation, he reached inward for a cantrip to corral his assailants together, and he released a brilliant burst of magic from his good hand. The assailants screamed and collapsed to the floor as the white-hot energy consumed them. Tralderonn inched to his hands and knees, each movement excruciating. His hand slipped in a pool of his blood. He yelped, gaining his balance. His left eye had swollen shut, the vision in the other clouded. Tralderonn wiped the blood from his face and discovered the fourth assailant creeping for the exit. Fiery spikes ripped into the assailant, killing him before he reached the door.

He lingered on his knees for a second, trying to breathe. He sensed his broken body and pleaded for it to work. Tralderonn knew he could not stay here any longer. The clamor caused by the fight jerked the inn awake. Doors creaked open and bleary-eyed patrons poured from their rooms to investigate. Tralderonn did not want to answer questions from the authorities or the guests. He dragged himself to his feet using the bed. Tralderonn grimaced, his knees buckled as he dressed and shouldered his pack. He leaned on his staff, staggered for the door, but stopped as he noticed the fourth assailant clutched a leather satchel in his dead hands. Tralderonn yanked the satchel free and slung it over his shoulder. Drawn by the commotion, guests started gathering in the hallway near his room. They gasped as he emerged. He grunted and waved them off when they tried to assist.

Carjlin intercepted him halfway across the lobby, her face contorted, blue eyes a mix of horror and fear. She buttressed him using her shoulder.

"Come," she whispered. "You are still in danger. Tejt is wary of wizards."

She guided him from the lobby and into an unlit alleyway. She shivered against the wind and chilled air whipping between the buildings. With each step, the commotion and confusion at the Motsslyn Inn evaporated as they fled into the night. Half his weight rested on his staff and the other half on Carjlin. She was strong, despite her slender build. Tralderonn groaned on each step, moaned with each ragged breath. He coughed, then spat out a mouthful of blood. More than once Tralderonn stumbled and she kept him upright.

Arm in arm, they lurched through alleys and side streets, keeping to the shadows. Twice the strain forced her to stop and catch her breath. Carjlin's strength waned. He was dead weight pressing against her. They had hobbled from a back street and turned left onto a main road when she heard faint shouts from behind them. Carjlin knew a mob had formed, and they hunted the wizard she lugged. She chomped down on her lower lip and stemmed a flood of fear—Tejt owned an ominous reputation for administering mob justice.

Carjlin found another rush of strength and plowed on. The cathedral was close now and there the clerics of the Maiden would shelter them. At least she hoped so. Carjlin led them into another alley. He tripped, and they sprawled into the garbage cans. The clang and clatter were impossible to mute. She shoved herself to her feet. Her own blood oozed from deep abrasions on her palms, knees, and elbows. His blood covered her arms, face, and clothes. Tralderonn lay in an unmoving heap, drinking in irregular, ragged breaths. His eyes were closed, blood escaped from a dozen lacerations slashing his face. Blood seeped from his nose and mouth. She thought him dead. "Get up."

Tralderonn moaned and gulped to fill empty lungs. He screamed out—the pain felt like sabers piercing his body. She bent down and placed her hands under his shoulders. "Get up."

The shouts grew louder by the second, two blocks away, maybe closer. She could distinguish individual voices and grew increasingly desperate. "They are getting close. Please get up! I can't lift you by myself."

Chapter Fourteen

Fall 531, Age of the Arch Mage

Tralderonn heard her pleas and understood she was risking her life to save his. He wanted to comply, but he could not force himself to move. His body, damaged and maimed, would not respond. Pain like he had never known devoured him. It was too much to bear. He surrendered, he could no longer fight or flee. Here in a darkened alley, Tralderonn Strigidae would die. *Curious.*

A voice from across space and time whispered to him, interrupting his final breaths.

-- What are you doing? -- the voice, feminine and familiar, whispered.

Dying.

-- Why? --

Why not? he shot back. He became indignant at the absurdity of her question. *Can you see my body?*

-- Did I teach you words like quit and surrender? -- she demanded, her tone suddenly harsh and unsympathetic.

Tralderonn hesitated prior to replying. He was ashamed to answer and so he said nothing.

-- It is not your destiny to die in an alley -- she chastised. -- Fight, Tralderonn --

"Momma," he cried out. He waited and then waited some more. Her voice was gone. *Don't leave me.*

"You have to help me here!" Carjlin ordered, her voice a desperate shrill. She no longer concerned herself with stealth. She panicked, knowing a mob would descend on them in less than a minute and both would die at their hands. "Get up!"

Carjlin's appeal shattered the haze clouding his mind. Her voice served as a beacon, reeling him back from death's grip. His eyes snapped open. Carjlin shook, her eyes wide. Lines hewed her forehead and angles crisscrossed her face. Tralderonn labored to his feet, mustering what remained of his strength. She glared at him. "About time."

Carjlin wrapped her arm around him anew, and they lurched forward once more. They shuffled from the alley and froze. Armed with torches and crude weapons, a knot of people emerged out of the dimness. They were frenzied and bent on exacting harsh payment for crimes committed against the fine, upstanding citizens of Tejt. Tralderonn shoved her from his side. "Get into the alley."

She wanted to argue, but his scowl and hardened glare told her otherwise. He propped himself up using his staff and stood erect in the middle of the street. He would not die today. His life would not end in Tejt. Memories of his boyhood in Prosper flooded his mind. He had opposed mobs before. In his youth, the older boys from the village tried to bully him and, on each occasion, he dispersed them using his magic. Most times he used restraint. A simple cantrip or illusion would scatter them. In other circumstances, not so much.

His brow furrowed, his eyes narrowed as he confronted the mob hunting him. Their angry words, accusations, and threats revealed their blood lust. His stance confused them. The rabble slowed their pace, voices, and bravado ebbed away into the night. Muted grumbling, indecision, and angst supplanted courage. They pointed and debated among themselves what to do next, then resumed their progress. They took measured and cautious steps as they advanced. By their actions, Tralderonn concluded talking was no longer an option. Violence was the only choice.

Tralderonn snapped his fingers. A wave of infernal arcana swept over him. Fire ignited in the palm of his hand, then spread up his wrist and forearm. He held the fire, allowing it to build and letting the mob view the flames. Tralderonn had killed four men this night—he could kill more. The instigators in the front recoiled, causing the rest of the mass to stack behind them. They faltered and Tralderonn smirked. They feared him and they should. For a fleeting second, he reveled in their horror. Demon magic roiled through his body unchecked. He wanted to kill them, desired to see them suffer. Without thought or remorse, he could annihilate the entire throng. He could do Gaiand a huge favor and destroy the ignorant and stupid standing in front of him. Tralderonn possessed the power to obliterate the entire city and nobody could stop him.

Again, Carjlin's voice, impatient and fearful, pierced his darkened mind. "Would you hurry? Whatever you are going to do, get it done."

He peered over at her, and his fury subsided. Her expression and her blue eyes begged for him to exercise moderation. *Curious.* He closed his eyes and blocked out the pain and rage. With a wave of his hand, a wall of fire erupted from his fingers. Angry flames spanned the street, impeding the crowd's progress. He heard their collective screams as they withdrew several steps or fled. Tralderonn sagged onto his staff. His strength and body failed. Carjlin rushed to his side and threw her arms around him. "I have you."

Together they lumbered north to a place only she knew. Tralderonn did not ask where they headed or why. He strained to place one foot in front of the other. Somewhere amid casting a wall of flames and the cathedral, Tralderonn's mind quit. Only his will to live compelled him forward. The minutes and the distance they covered passed slowly until they reached the L'Aube Cathedral. She was not sure he was alive as she laid him down on the stone pavement. He did not move. She wanted to cry and scream out in rage at the same time. They had come too far for him to die now.

"Open the gate," Carjlin pleaded. "By the Maiden, I beg you to open the gate."

She pounded on the closed gate, using both fists until they bled. A minute slipped by, then four more. No answer came from within. She placed her back against the gate and slid down next to Tralderonn. She looked over at him. *What were you thinking? You don't even know this man.* Then she remembered the inscription on the Maiden's statue. *Bring unto me your worn, your threadbare. Here, within these sacred grounds, peace abounds.*

Carjlin pulled her knees to her chest and hid her face in her hands. She felt the blood on her palms, a mix of her own and his, smear over her cheeks. She shivered as her sweat and blood cooled in the chilled air. Descending in and out of consciousness, Carjlin heard the mob, re-formed and fueled by a collective rage. They were coming for her and Tralderonn. She sat motionless as they neared. She did not bother to raise her head and count their numbers. It did not matter. Her situation was desperate, and there was nothing she could give to protect them anymore. Her stamina slipped away and her valor ebbed.

As despair vanquished hope, the gate opened. A troop of Canons rushed forth, their shields and armor glimmering a dawn blue in the torchlight, and formed a protective arc. The mob faltered and then went silent. They stood bewildered, looking from each other to the Canons. The crowd leader, red-faced and encouraged by the mob, took a cautious step toward the Cathedral. "We demand the wizard. The girl you can keep."

"You stand upon sacred ground," the commander answered with a dangerous edge in his voice. He tightened the grasp on his mace and shield, then motioned the Canons forward. "Your demands are not valid."

The Canons locked their shields and advanced in unison. The mob leader faltered, watching the Canons march forward. When his mettle failed him, he retreated. Leaderless, the rest of the mob skulked into the night. A dozen clerics of the Maiden poured from the Cathedral. They did not bother assessing Tralderonn or Carjlin's wounds. They lifted Tralderonn onto a stretcher and assisted Carjlin to her feet. As she crossed into the Cathedral, Carjlin felt a change in her heart. *Home.*

Chapter Fifteen

Fall 531, Age of the Arch Mage

A rising sun in the east ushered the duskiness westward. Bright splinters of light sliced narrow strips across the Border Lands, distorting the shadows. The morning sky, streaked with yellows and oranges, was bright and clear, guaranteeing another day of unnatural heat and choking sand. Resembling annoying little imps, the dust devils swirled and twirled over the barren land, springing up in an instant then disappearing as fast.

Deemos stood alone atop the battlements unmoving, his black robes fluttering in a southern breeze. Leery of his displeasure, the hobgoblin guards stayed far away. Sleep eluded him, his manner black and obscene, like the iron walls guarding Scaalia. Early yesterday morning, he felt her death. It forced him to acknowledge her passing. Furious over the kobold's failure, he surveyed the sprawling wasteland in front of him, searching for a sign that would appease his anger. *Did the demon sense his heir's death?* Doubtful, Deemos concluded. Belhaaz did not possess the patience or insight to detect these things. As he worked through his plan, he determined he would not inform Belhaaz today. Impatient for news concerning his heir and her imminent return, the master must wait. At least for now, Prosper was Aeros's last known location. He would begin his search there. Deemos opted to journey alone. His Odjahary guards and the drow maiden were difficult to hide.

Decided on a course of action, Deemos stormed off the ramparts.

◊ ◊ ◊

He entered Prosper near midafternoon unnoticed. It seemed he simply materialized out of the air. In a moment he was there, when before he was not, his appearance altered and no longer recognizable. He could do that. He was not a shape shifter, but he could bend the light and alter people's perception of him. The scowl, hard eyes, and slumped shoulders were no longer detectable. Instead, a handsome man, stout and muscular, is what folk saw. The dazzling eyes showed a friendly nature, and the broad smile, sincere.

Deemos detected the arcana, raw and powerful, spent here yesterday. He perceived a demon magic invoked by a sorceress, a hellfire that could destroy dragons. Like a pungent perfume, it hung in the air as he strolled into the community. The town folks still talked about the black dragons and the carnage they'd inflicted on the village and the riverboats the previous morning. He observed the destruction to buildings and ships, heard the terrified tales of giant flying lizards attacking the hamlet as the sun rose.

Prosper was small, so it would be easy enough to find the home. But as an outsider, the locals may not appreciate him poking his nose into their affairs. Not wanting to attract attention, he would profess he had traveled to the village in search of a relative. He noticed two old men hunched over a gameboard on the porch outside the Riverside Inn and approached.

"Excuse me," Deemos inquired. He smiled, turned on the charm, and waited for the two old men to notice him. "I am seeking my grandmother Elaire and her child, a cousin I have not enjoyed meeting."

The old men playing *alquerque* stopped their game long enough to give him a strange look.

"Mister, Mistress Elaire has been dead for decades," one supplied in a casual drawl.

"Hm, decades. You don't say," Deemos muttered, feigning interest. "The child, then? Can I find her near these parts?"

"I'm sorry, mister," the other provided. He looked at Deemos and hesitated a few seconds before delivering the heartbreaking news. "Them dragons killed poor Kysellah yesterday."

"Dead?" Deemos mumbled. "Are you certain?"

"Yeah, and poor Gallego has disappeared," the first furnished.

Delightful. Her name is Kysellah. Who is Gallego? He allowed the instant to linger a little longer. Deemos wanted to appear saddened by their terrible news. He dabbed away false tears and gazed at the old men. His ruse was working. "Gallego?"

"Her husband," the other added. Pained by Deemos's performance, he resumed. "Took quite a beating defending the missus. But nobody's seen him since."

Why would he flee? The question intrigued Deemos.

"Care if I sit a spell? Would love to hear more about my relatives," he implored. "Drinks on me."

The old men beamed at the prospect of free ale. After a few minutes of small talk regarding the dragons, fishing, and the weather, fresh tankards arrived. Deemos pulled a draw and reclined back in his chair. "So, tell me, did Kysellah have any children? Maybe I can reunite with them."

The old men peeked over at each other and laughed in unison.

"Not around these parts," one declared, wiping his mouth on his shirt.

The other leaned forward in his chair like he owned a secret. "Mister, all three of her boys is princes. Have been as long as I can remember."

"Princes?" Deemos understood what the old man said and the significance.

"Yeah," the second one added. "As in Princes of Auroryies."

Stunned by this revelation, Deemos delayed speaking further. He eyed the wooden floorboards, endeavoring to conceal his surprise and anger. His mind spun and words failed him. He now owned two more unforeseen problems. First, the master may possess three additional heirs. Could they wield the master's arcana? Did the demon know? *Doubtful. I will keep this to myself for now.* Second, they were Princes of Auroryies. Someone inside that cursed Citadelle better have an explanation. Deemos lifted his eyes and used care selecting his next words.

"Wow!" Deemos responded, his broad grin masking his concern. "I did not realize my relatives included princes. Do you recall their names?"

"Uh, let me ponder on that a moment." One removed a ragged felt sugar-loaf hat and scratched his bald head. "Um, yeah, now I remember. Happy, Hollister, and Thaddeus. Right, Rudy?"

"Nah, not even close, Edgar," Rudy scoffed. "Their names were Hobby, Hanser, and Tralderonn."

Deemos stood and set six gold pieces on their gameboard.

"Edgar and Rudy, despite my loss, you have given me a hint of hope," Deemos declared. "If you would be so kind, directions to

Kysellah's former residence would be most helpful. At least I can pay my respects and then be on my way."

Rudy pointed at the rutted road running along the Inn's south side.

"Follow this road," Rudy exclaimed. "Two of them dragons lay in the front yard and one's laying dead in the woods. Can't miss it."

◊ ◊ ◊

He found the house right where Rudy and Edgar said it would be located. The two dead dragons sprawled in the yard made it hard to miss. Pillagers swarmed over the house and the dragons seeking souvenirs and treasure. Armed with carving knives and pry bars, a group of men and boys were stripping off dragon scales. Three women walked from the home carrying armfuls of books and household wares. Deemos possessed no time for distractions, and these looters were removing potential clues. A wave of his hand dispersed the scavengers. He glowered, his comportment menacing and dark. No one dared to challenge him. Some cursed him. Some disappeared back into the village while others stood at a distance.

Deemos paced the ground, attempting to understand how Aeros botched the mission. Death lingered, the smell of burnt flesh and the metallic tang of blood hung in the air. He surveyed the landscape. Long streaks of grass were dead, burned away by the dragons' acidic venom. He found a kobold stripped, his head beaten to a pulp. He discovered two more kobolds crushed beneath their wyvern mounts. *Could Aeros have survived?* Deemos studied both dead dragons. He noted the slashes and gashes lacing their thick scaly hides, observed their leathery wings ripped and shredded.

Deemos followed a trail of blood and located the third dragon lying in a broken heap inside the wood line. His eyes pursued the trail of destruction into the treetops. He detected the fractured limbs and boughs, the shattered trunks caused by the dragon crashing through the trees. As he examined the third dragon, he found injuries similar to those the other two had. However, this one looked burned by something other than magic. Intrigued, Deemos searched around the dead dragon for additional clues. He stopped when he found broken pottery scattered near the dragon. He grasped a shard and placed it near his nose. *Smells like torch oil.* Deemos paused his investigation—there were too many questions. His anger boiled as he gazed across the battle scene. *What happened here? Did she have help? Where did this Gallego go?*

Deemos balled his hands into fists and strode from the woods. He stood in the backyard and searched for any sign that would assist him in stitching this story together. He saw a garden shed and tramped toward it. Deemos opened the door and stepped in. The fragrances from the roots, flowers, and herbs overwhelmed his sense of smell. Inside he discovered vials, jugs, and flasks filled with elixirs and potions organized by name on shelves and a wooden workbench. Among the flasks and jugs, Deemos found a book. He extricated the tome and wiped the dust from the cover. He traced the book's name with his finger, 'Je-Hong's Alchemy Guide.'

He exited the shed with the book and uncovered another hint of magic. It surprised him. He closed his eyes. Deemos perceived a faint trace, old and failing and not of this world. *Elaire? A ward to hide Kysellah from her father? Clever.* Focused on the magic, Deemos followed it until he found footprints leading west. *Gallego? Where do you flee? And why?*

Deemos pivoted back to the house and noticed two grave markers. One was old and faded by age. He brushed away the dirt and grime off the headstone. He stooped down, low enough to just make out a name. *Elaire, the master's former lover.* He knelt next to the second. Deemos scooped a handful of fresh earth into his hands and brought it to his nose. He could smell the lingering magic that infused the soil. *Demon magic.* A simple wood marker said 'Kysellah.'

Deemos stood and wiped his hands on his cloak. He squinted west, then back east. *Aeros could be anywhere by now.*

Deemos gazed north, then south. He sighed. *What next?*

"Welcome," he muttered. Just saying the town's name sickened him. He considered Targinn Mirth a narcissistic half-wit. "As the mayor of Welcome, I hope you have the answers I seek, Targinn Mirth. Your life depends on it."

Chapter Sixteen

Fall 531, Age of the Arch Mage

Paddy Staggs shouldered his pack and strolled down the gangplank, excited to feel solid earth beneath his hairy feet once more. He hoped he had traveled by sea for the last time. The ship's constant movement nauseated him. He recalled his conversations with the sailors concerning Kenly as he swindled them out of a week's pay during a card game. Kenly was not much more than a harbor town, they said. Ship building and repair and a large military presence served as the city's major industries. The city possessed the normal taverns, inns, and gambling parlors one would find in any harbor town, but none of this would appeal to Danny Caldwell for long. Paddy ambled off the docks and entered the city. He looked around and decided he required more information to narrow his search.

A visit to Bavard's Kenly office was the obvious starting point. It turned up nothing. The office records did not show anyone named Peter Holmes booking passage to other ports of call on their vessels. And no one remembered a person fitting Caldwell's description visiting the office.

Paddy trudged the dusty streets choked with horse-drawn wagons moving cargo to and from the harbor, mulling over his options. He caught sight of a tavern a few blocks ahead. The sun-faded sign said 'The Jib Sail.'

The ale house was empty when Paddy ventured in. An attractive mid-thirties woman wiping down the bar counter gave him a wave and a devilish smile. "Welcome."

Paddy removed his pack, hoisted himself onto a bar stool, and enjoyed watching her saunter his way.

"Name's Dolores," she exclaimed, speaking in a distinct twang. "What can I getcha?"

"I'll take two ales," Paddy requested. He scanned over the alehouse, noting each detail. He observed a door in the back of the room and one behind the counter. A quick exit route if needed. The wood floors looked swept and cleaned, but the cutting smell of cheap ale and perfume refused to fade away. The tavern was bright and well-lit from the sunlight streaking in from the large windows. Chandeliers hung from the ceiling and oil lamps sat on each of the fifteen wooden tables occupying the room.

Dolores filled two mugs and set them on the bar. "So what brings a halfling to our lovely city?"

Paddy pulled a draw. "I seek a friend of mine, Dolores. We agreed to meet here in Kenly."

Dolores winked while wiping brunette locks from her luminous green eyes. "Lots of friends are supposed to meet here. Got a description?"

Paddy chuckled, knowing the hustler was getting hustled. He stuck his hand into his pocket and slid a gold piece over the bar. "Lanky white fellow, blond hair, and pointy ears similar to mine."

She pocketed the money into her apron and leaned over the bar and let her gaze meet his. "Elven looking? Killer blue eyes and handsome?"

Paddy rolled his eyes while draining his first mug and nodded. She described Caldwell to perfection.

"Yeah, he came in here for over a year. A regular until four, maybe five days ago. A real heartbreaker he was," she continued, gushing like she swooned over a former lover. Dolores fanned herself using a hand. "Oh, and the smile! He had all the barmaids fussing over him. Already miss him."

Skilled in the game she was playing, Paddy slid her another gold piece. "Any idea where he went?"

Reclining back against the counter behind the bar, Dolores crossed her arms and squinted at the halfling. "Tejt."

"Tejt?" Paddy inquired.

"Yeah, the capital," Dolores crowed. "Long dusty ride to the northeast."

"Did he say why?"

"Nope."

Paddy finished his second ale in three thirsty gulps, then deposited four more gold pieces onto the bar. She grinned and reached for the five gold pieces. He placed his hand over the top of hers and glared. "How do I get to Tetj?"

"Parker's offers coach service to Tejt," Dolores glared back, not intimidated by the halfling in the least.

Paddy shot her an inquisitive look, removed his hand from hers, and slid from the barstool.

"Go right out of here," she instructed, then deposited the gold in her apron. "Their office is at the end of this street."

"Parker's?" Paddy asked as he walked out.

"Yep," she answered. "Enjoy the trip."

Paddy heard her cackling and it reminded him of an old hen as he veered right out of the Jib Sail.

A haze hung over the city and obscured the afternoon sun. The muggy air clung to the halfling's skin as he strolled down the nearly empty street. Paddy passed an apothecary, a general store, a cobbler's shop as he walked. He paused and gazed at his reflection in one of the shop windows. Paddy grinned at what he saw. He snapped his finger and pointed. *Good day to be Paddy Staggs.*

He located Parker's Coach Service at the north end of town. Paddy paused outside Parker's and glanced around. No one he passed had paid any attention to him or seemed to care about his presence. He opened the door and entered.

The foul smell of perspiration and pipe smoke wafted into the humid air as Paddy stepped into the office. Sweat poured from the obese man behind the counter, soaking his clothes and leaving a shiny sheen on his skin. He removed the pipe from between his lips. His grin revealed a mouth full of stained teeth. "Master halfling, how can I assist?"

Paddy returned the smile and turned on the charm. "My good man, I require passage to Tejt."

"Of course, I have a coach leaving in the morning," he replied, wiping his brow with a soiled towel. "And there are seats available."

Paddy frowned. "That won't do, friend. I need to leave today."

"I can arrange, but can you …"

Paddy placed five gold pieces on the counter and grinned. "Will this suffice?"

The man's eyes sparkled as bright as the gold sitting in front of him. "Yes."

Chapter Seventeen

Fall 531, Age of the Arch Mage

Carjlin eased the door open. She did not want to wake him. The healers informed her sleep would benefit him the most. Thin ribbons of waning moonlight slipped past the window curtains, forming odd shadows along the stone floor. She padded to the foot of his bed. Sleep eluded her, and this was her second visit of the morning to check on him. Carjlin knew his name and that he could wield a powerful magic. She knew nothing beyond that. Yet she found herself drawn to him for reasons she could not explain.

He had not moved since she brought him here three days ago. The healers had mended his broken body and used an elixir to remove the bounty hunter's poison from his blood. His breathing was regular now, and his chest rose and fell in a steady rhythm. The bandages were gone, but his face remained bruised, an ugly pattern of purple and blue blotches on his rough brown skin. He appeared relaxed from her vantage point, his mouth fixed in a serene smile. She knew this was not true. Anger and betrayal and loss roiled inside him. A dark arcana, a demon magic, flowed through him. Carjlin sensed the continual battle he waged with himself, a war between good and evil.

"It is so hard for me to be back here," Carjlin whispered. She moved to his side and took his hand in hers. "Did you know my mother is the Matron Sister? Of course you don't. How could you?"

Carjlin stroked his face with the back of her hand. "There is a rift between us that seems impossible to bridge. It started with the sudden passing of my father."

Carjlin felt tears welling in her eyes and she angrily brushed them away.

"He was my world, Tralderonn. He was funny and kind," she continued. "Despite their best efforts, the healers could not save him. Regardless of my prayers and pleading with the Maiden, my father died."

Carjlin released Tralderonn's hand and sat in a chair next to his bed. She did not bother to wipe away the tears streaming down her face.

"Fair or unfair, I blamed my mother. His death shattered my faith in her and the Maiden. So I fled into the city," Carjlin admitted. "For years, I rejected my mother's beliefs and found consolation in Tejt. Does any of this make sense?"

She looked at him for a minute, hoping for an answer she knew would not come. "Anyway, Tejt did not relieve my grief, it was just a way to numb my pain. My mother sought me out on many occasions and begged me to return."

Carjlin hung her head and her tears pooled on the stone floor. "I shunned her, Tralderonn, and finally she stopped trying to bring me home. And now here I am. The one place I swore I would never return to."

Carjlin almost laughed at the irony. She stood and returned to the foot of his bed. "Thanks for listening. I will stop by—"

The door creaking open behind Carjlin interrupted her. Without looking, she knew who entered. *Oh, Mother. Not now.* Carjlin tensed and wiped her face, hoping to hide that she had been crying. She folded her arms across her chest—she was in no mood for a confrontation with the Matron Sister. Carjlin's mother stepped to her side. The Matron Sister placed her arm around Carjlin's waist and pulled her close. She ignored Carjlin's red puffy eyes and the scarlet hue splashed on her face. The Matron Sister leaned in and kissed her daughter on the cheek. Carjlin felt heat rush into her cheeks. She did not expect this warm gesture from her mother and it set her at ease.

"How is he?"

"The same," Carjlin answered.

Several minutes passed in silence and it did not feel awkward. Her mother grasped Carjlin's hand in her own and gave a gentle squeeze.

"I know he cannot stay," Carjlin admitted, trying to head off another confrontation. She peeked over at her mother for a reaction. Typical for elves, it seemed her mother did not age. Her blue eyes still bright, her skin remained flawless and not a trace of gray touched her blonde hair. What Carjlin saw on her mother's face surprised her. No judgment or condemnation, just a sweet, sincere smile.

"Why?" the Matron Sister inquired. Her smile masked her disappointment at Carjlin's words.

"The demon magic inside him," Carjlin stated.

"Yes," her mother agreed. "It is there and strong. However, this man is a refugee in need of our help. I will not turn him away."

"Thank you," Carjlin whispered.

"Of course," her mother answered. "I will leave you alone."

Her mother kissed her again and stepped to the door.

"Mother," Carjlin whispered without looking. She brushed at the tears setting up in her eyes once again. "I want to come home."

"I know," her mother declared, pausing near the door.

"How?"

"The Maiden spoke to me before earlier this morning. She detected a change in your heart."

Carjlin turned and hurried into her mother's open arms. The tears flowed, and she did not care as she sobbed into her mother's shoulder.

◊ ◊ ◊

Keerrin Feeallah, the Matron Sister, paused in the passageway outside Tralderonn's room and leaned against the wall. For a few minutes, she soaked in the silence enveloping the L'Aube Cathedral. Soon the morning sun would usher in the dawn, awakening the Cathedral to greet the Maiden and a new day. She knew in her heart the Maiden had brought this man into the Cathedral. For his own healing? Yes. For restoration of a daughter to her mother? Absolutely. She glanced down the empty corridors and smiled. For the first time since her husband's death, she felt at peace with herself and her faith. Keerrin shut her eyes and offered a prayer of thanks to the Maiden for bringing her daughter home and mending the fracture in their relationship that had lingered far too long between them.

She opened her eyes as the chimes echoing across the Cathedral grounds announced dawn's arrival. The Matron Sister smiled again. "A new day filled with renewed hope."

Chapter Eighteen

Fall 531, Age of the Arch Mage

Wulf and Matthew entered the northern outskirts of Tejt as the sun slipped beneath the mountains that dominated the western horizon. Torch lamps situated atop metal poles provided just enough light to see. Tejt's nightlife thrived in this seedy part of Tressel's capital city. Constables working in pairs patrolled the streets attempting to keep the peace. Laughter and singing spilled out of the taverns and saloons while the high rollers won and lost fortunes in the gambling parlors. Red lanterns marked the entrances to the pleasure houses, beckoning the lonely. Savory aromas released from roasting meats wafted into the air, causing their mouths to water.

They located a suitable stable for their horses, then Wulf and Matthew secured a room at a dodgy establishment on the other side of the street called the Blue Mule Inn. After storing their gear, they headed downstairs to the tavern for a mug and a meal. Tobacco smoke and the perfume of cheap ale inundated the tavern as they entered the main room. An overweight, middle-aged barmaid kept the ale and food flowing to the tables, while a thin elderly man labored behind the bar.

Weary of large cities and wanting to avoid unnecessary attention, Wulf and Matthew sat at an empty table in a dusky corner near the back of the tavern. The barmaid swayed a bit as she neared. She wobbled for a second, then grabbed a chair to steady herself. Her eyes were glassy, she wore her chestnut and peppered grey hair pulled tightly up behind her head, and her wide smile revealed missing front teeth. Several dark stains on her apron suggested she was none too careful in her dinner deliveries.

"Welcome to the Blue Mule, boys. Name's Nellie. My husband, Merle, and I own the joint," she slurred. "What will it be?"

Wulf and Matthew each ordered a mug and a bowl of stew. Nellie winked, then tottered off to fetch their ale and meal.

"Been boozing since noon?" Matthew wondered.

"Yep," Wulf agreed. "I can think of worse things to do."

While they waited, Wulf surveyed his surroundings. Chandeliers holding burning candles and torches affixed to the wall bathed the tavern in a harsh yellow light. Hefty wooden tables and benches near two large picture windows offered a view of the torchlit street. Six patrons sat on high stools at the bar and eight more reclined at the tables, eating and drinking. The customers appeared to be working class folks who paid no attention to the outlanders in their midst.

Wulf and Matthew overheard bits and pieces of the conversation from the table in front of them as they waited for their meal. Two men discussed the fiery destruction of the Motsslyn Inn by a wizard several days past. One demanded they should hold the wizard accountable. The other bemoaned the city's increasing inclination for mob justice.

"Where were the constables?" another man asked. "Never around when ya need 'em, I say."

The first man shrugged and returned his attention to his roast and potatoes.

Wulf and Matthew did not wait long for Nellie to bring their steaming stew and dark ale. As they ate and drank, a commotion outside interrupted everyone's meals.

A man wearing black leather armor burst into the tavern through the front door, quieting the room. His pointed ears and long blond hair showed he possessed elven blood. As the patrons gawked, his bright blue eyes narrowed, and an impish beam washed over his boyish face.

"Ah, don't mind me," he announced, self-conscious from all the attention. "Nothing to see here, folks."

He scanned the room, his eyes flitting back and forth, searching for something or someone. He determined the darkened corner where Wulf and Matthew sat might conceal his body from the men pursuing him. Wulf and Matthew noted his lean athletic build and his array of weapons as he hurried for their table. Wulf grabbed the long knife tucked into his boot and held it in his hand.

"I am not here," the stranger grinned. He pulled his cowl over his head, wrapped his black cloak tight to his body, and scuttled beneath the table.

"You don't think they will find you under there?" Wulf asked.

"Nah," the man answered. "They're drunk and stupid. Plus, I am an expert at hiding in the shadows."

Matthew rolled his eyes. "So much for a peaceful meal."

Seconds behind the man, three hulking men stumbled into the tavern, almost removing the front door from its iron hinges. Disheveled in appearance, each one wore ragged clothes and nasty scars on their pockmarked faces. Stringy and greasy hair hung below their shoulders and their slurred speech was foul and offensive.

"Cleon, I will not tolerate any type of violence in my tavern," Merle cautioned. "Now you and your friends get on out of here or I will hail the constables."

Crimson-faced by anger and liquor, Cleon staggered toward the bar. "Stop talking, old man or I will close your mouth for you. This ain't any concern of yours. That pointy-eared petty crook came in here to hide. Hugo and JoJo, search all the tables."

A nervous energy filled the tavern as some patrons resumed eating and drinking, hoping the hooligans would leave them alone. Other customers, compliant and docile, stood and stepped back from their tables as Hugo and JoJo bullied their way from the front of the tavern to the back, seeking the man. Merle clutched Cleon's arm. "No—"

A big meaty fist slammed into Merle's nose. Merle recoiled into the counter behind him, cradling his face in his hands.

"I told you to shut up," Cleon bellowed, his voice taut and loud.

JoJo and Hugo lumbered to Wulf's and Matthew's table. The two thugs were ugly—boring, plain, and forgettable.

"Tell them to move out of the way, JoJo," Hugo ordered.

"Get up," JoJo croaked.

Wulf and Matthew ignored the men and continued eating their meal. A hush fell over the tavern, every eye focused on the outlanders.

"Hey, Cleon," Hugo yelled. "Got a couple of tough guys over here."

"Yeah? Well, show them who's tougher," Cleon laughed.

JoJo and Hugo positioned themselves on either side of Wulf. Nellie grabbed JoJo's arm. "Leave him be. He is a boy."

JoJo shoved her back, then rejoined Hugo near Wulf.

"Um, this is a bad idea, gentlemen," Matthew warned, shoveling another spoonful of stew into his mouth.

Hugo disregarded Matthew's advice and stooped close to Wulf's left ear, his stench and fetid breath overpowering.

"Your momma's not here to protect you," Hugo slurred. "Get up or I will cut you."

"Don't kill them," Matthew cautioned Wulf.

"Why?" Wulf asked, biting into a biscuit.

"Not worth the trouble," Matthew answered. "And they are not threatening Maggie."

"Enough!" Hugo shouted.

"You're right," Wulf agreed, a roguish smile sweeping across his face. "As usual."

Wulf exploded. A sudden backhand crushed Hugo's nose. The sickening sound of breaking bone and cartilage echoed throughout the silent tavern. Hugo shrieked in pain and reeled backwards into an empty table, clutching at his damaged face. He careened off the table then landed hard onto the wooden floor.

JoJo reacted too slow. Wulf seized him by the back of the head. With his right hand, Wulf planted JoJo's face into the table, shattering his nose, splitting his lower lip, and knocking out teeth. JoJo yelped as the table's wooden planks groaned and creaked under the impact. Matthew grinned, snatched his mug from spilling, and pulled a long draw. Wulf held the thug's head in place as he buried his long knife through JoJo's collar into the table, purposely nicking JoJo's ear in the process.

"Don't move," Wulf snarled.

"Blast, that's got to hurt," Matthew winced, wiping his mouth on his sleeve.

Cleon roared as he drew his sword and rushed to assist his fallen comrades. Wulf wheeled about and drew another long knife from his belt. In a swift fluid motion, he hurled the blade at Cleon hilt first. The hilt bounced off Cleon's forehead, creasing his skin and drawing blood. Stunned, Cleon staggered and grabbed onto the bar to steady himself. He was dumbstruck by the skilled resistance to his bullying and hesitated as he considered his options. He dabbed the blood from his brow as he back-pedaled to the door, then wheeled and sped from the tavern, leaving his hapless companions to fend for themselves.

Wulf yanked the knife pinning JoJo to the table free and sheathed it. Jerking him to his feet by the back of his collar, Wulf issued an order. "Pick up your friend."

Wary of Wulf, JoJo lifted Hugo to his feet. Hugo and JoJo frowned and angled their heads downward. With their faces mangled and blood-streaked, they stared at the floor, avoiding

Wulf's piercing glare. Wulf grabbed each thug by an ear and pulled them to the bar. "What do they owe you for the damage?"

"Five silver pieces will suffice," Merle beamed, holding a towel to his face.

"You heard him," Wulf insisted. "And make it ten. Give him a gold piece."

Hugo and JoJo cursed and coughed up the gold and set it on the bar. They scowled and backed their way out of the tavern. Hugo stopped near the door. "You will see us again."

As the door slammed shut, the patrons cheered and applauded. Merle came out from behind the bar, continuing to press the towel against his face. "Gentlemen, your dinner and your drinks are on me for the rest of the night!"

Matthew drained his mug, then walked to Merle.

"Remove the towel and let me see," Matthew requested. "Ah, not so bad. Hold steady."

Merle cringed when Matthew gently placed his hands on either side of his swollen, misshapen nose. The tavern fell silent once again as the cleric mouthed a prayer. A faint white glow pulsed from Matthew's hands. Merle winced as Matthew's divine energy swept through his body. He felt the swelling subside and the pain dissipate. When Matthew removed his hands, Nellie gasped and stared at her husband in disbelief.

"How did you …" Nellie's words trailed off as she touched Merle's nose. "It's completely healed. It's like it never happened."

"A blessing from the Maiden," Matthew admitted.

"Glad to see you have my back," Wulf barked as he and Matthew returned to their table.

"As a man of the cloth, I abhor violence," Matthew snapped, failing to hide the grin spreading over his face.

Chapter Nineteen

Fall 531, Age of the Arch Mage

The Blue Mule buzzed as the patrons resumed their eating and drinking. Wulf and Matthew stopped short, seeing the cause of all the commotion now seated at their table.

"Daniel Caldwell's the name, but my friends call me Danny," he declared, sticking out his hand. "You were awesome. You saved my skin. Thanks. Those hoodlums intended to kill me. Who taught you to fight?"

"My mother," Wulf growled, sitting down.

Matthew studied Danny for a moment. He noticed the longbow and the twin rapiers strapped across his back and a brace of daggers slung across his chest. "Those for decoration?"

"Naw," Danny replied, his laugh infectious and his eyes mischievous. "I can use them."

"So we are friends now?" Wulf grunted.

Danny maintained his smile. "As far as I am concerned. Who are you?"

"I am Matthew Jakkes and my cantankerous friend here is Wulf Blackhawk," Matthew chuckled. "So, Danny Caldwell, I am not convinced you were innocent in all this fuss."

"Not sure what you mean, Matthew Jakkes?" Danny countered. He sensed immediately something strange about Matthew that he could not figure out. The cleric possessed a calming aura that made Danny feel safe, and the rogue felt an odd peace in his heart. "Waitress, I will have what they are enjoying, please."

Wulf returned to his meal, paying no attention to Danny.

"What did those men want with you?" Matthew inquired again.

Danny bobbed his head. "Ah, they're sore losers. You know, a business deal gone bad."

Matthew chortled. He found Danny's speech and mannerisms amusing. "What kind of business?"

Danny locked his eyes onto Matthew, his smile waned. "You see, I possess certain skills, particular abilities that are not always appreciated by those I do business with."

Wulf peered at Danny over his mug. "You're a common criminal?"

A smug smile reappeared as Danny considered Wulf's assessment. "Actually, I am a master thief. Some call me a rascal or bandit. Maybe even a moonlighter or pickpocket. But one title I do like is rogue. Rogue seems mysterious, you know, makes you think I am a man of intrigue."

Wulf chuckled and drained his mug. "Okay, rogue it is."

Nellie returned carrying Danny's meal and drink and two fresh mugs for Wulf and Matthew.

Over the course of their meal, Danny explained how he deceived the three thugs in a card game. He acted out the scene and played each part as he described his con. He mimicked their voices and aped their mannerisms. Wulf and Matthew laughed at the story until their sides ached.

"What happened next?" Matthew asked, ignoring the tears.

"I followed them into Pinky's. I could tell by their gait they were drunk." Danny started once more. "All it took was a couple of cheap ales to get them interested in playing cards."

Danny leaned back in his chair and sipped on his tankard. "Well, not only were they drunk, but they were also stupid," Danny recounted. "I used a stacked deck and took them for twenty gold pieces each. It was too easy."

For the rest of the evening, Danny regaled Wulf and Matthew with his anecdotes. Most likely they were fables, if not outright lies, detailing his exploits and deeds. Danny revealed to Wulf and Matthew that he grew up on the streets of South Hampton within the Coastal Commonwealth. His mother was elven and his father a hard-working shop owner from South Hampton.

"Despite South Hampton's diverse population, it was tough being half-elf or half-human," Danny expressed. "You know, never quite fitting in among either."

"I can see that," Matthew commented.

"Yeah." Danny went on to convey that common street thugs had murdered his parents during a robbery gone bad, leaving him an orphan just shy of his tenth birthday. "So I turned to thieving as my sole means of survival. What else could I do? There was nowhere for me to go. Hunger and loneliness became my closest friends. It did not take long to realize life on the streets meant you better learn to fight, to fight and win, and to steal to survive."

Wulf and Matthew sat in mesmerized silence as the half-elf described his life story. Danny drained his mug, then resumed. "One day I got caught trying to pickpocket a wealthy-looking woman near sundown. She was attractive, kind of reminded me of my mother. Well, Lady Jirocha took pity. I guess she saw I was hungry and lonely. She took me off the streets instead of turning me over to the constabulary."

Danny paused, ensuring Wulf and Matthew still paid attention. "Lady Jirocha led the local crime family and South Hampton's thieves' guild. She appreciated my brazen yet unrefined attempt at stealing. Under her tutelage, I learned the true art and science of thieving, scamming, conning, and even assassinations."

Nellie interrupted Danny's narrative by delivering another round. Danny gulped down half the mug, then restarted. "Gents, money and fame came fast. By seventeen, I earned more than most do in a lifetime. I was wealthy beyond my wildest dreams and possessed more money than I could ever spend. They appointed me an enforcer in the family by age twenty-five. I enjoyed an abundant life and all the perks."

Danny became quiet, gathering his thoughts. He stared at his ale, watching the bubbles float to the top. Wulf and Matthew glanced at each other, not sure what to say.

Danny sighed. "My conscience caught up with me. Doubts started creeping into my mind and interfering with my job. You know, affecting the quality of my work. I started getting sloppy. I almost got caught during a simple robbery. At the same time, nightmares began interrupting and plaguing my sleep. Every victim flashed in my mind each time I closed my eyes."

Danny hesitated. He peered about the tavern, then took another quick drink from his mug. Like a sinner at confession, Danny picked up where he left off. "Lady Jirocha held the contract to assassinate the leader of the local banking union. She wanted her best for the job, so she chose me. I felt honored owning Lady Jirocha's high esteem. However, I told my conscience this must be the last job, the last murder, the last assassination. It was."

Danny slanted back in his chair, tugging at the tassels on his leather armor as if he had finished the tale. An awkward silence ensued.

"Well?" Wulf asked.

"Well, what?" Danny replied.

"The rest of the story," Matthew demanded.

"Oh, okay," Danny chuckled. He bent into the table for dramatic effect. "There I was, surrounded ..."

Danny dithered, further irritating Wulf and Matthew with his clowning. He laughed at the scowls on their faces.

"Ah, forget it. Another tale for another time," he professed, giving them a dismissive wave. Danny rested his elbows on the table, his thoughts scattered about.

Wulf and Matthew urged him to continue and, after a little back and forth, Danny proceeded with his tale. "It was raining as I perched two stories above the torchlit streets with the intended target in my sights. My victim strolled down a crowded avenue in the company of his wife and a daughter who looked only ten years old. You know, around the same age I was when my parents died. I set the arrow into the bowstring, drawing it tight to my cheek. I sighted in …"

Danny's words tailed off, his expression blank.

"And?" Wulf pressed.

"I waited. And I waited," Danny recounted. He looked down at the table. "I waited some more, and I did not release the arrow. I loosened my draw, allowing the arrow to fall upon the rooftop. As tears streamed down my face, I walked away, leaving the life I knew behind, including thousands sitting in the bank. I realized my life was in danger, so I bolted. I fled east and far away from the family that had brought so much meaning to my life for so many years."

Wulf leaned in his chair, taking another drink. "How long have you been here?"

"I ended up in Tressel months ago. I kicked around Kenly, doing odd jobs for most of the time. Got bored a week ago and I headed to Tetj," Danny admitted. "I thought I would be safer up here and farther out of Lady Jirocha's range, out of the family's reach. Been lucky to this point."

True or not, Wulf and Matthew found Danny's exaggerations and yarns fascinating. As they sat and talked some more, Nellie kept fresh mugs coming.

Near midnight, Wulf and Matthew watched the half-elven rogue or master thief depart the tavern, then disappear into the empty streets as if a ghost. The cleric steadied himself on the table as he stood. "Quite a history."

Wulf gazed at Matthew, trying to bring his double vison into focus. "Maybe it's the ale talking, but I believe him. He seems dangerous, almost reckless. I admire those qualities. He seems willing to take risks, take chances. Would you cross him?"

Matthew laughed, putting his arm around Wulf, attempting to balance them both. "No, Wulf Blackhawk, I would not want to cross him."

Chapter Twenty

531, Age of the Arch Mage

A bright sun cascaded past worn curtains, aggravating bloodshot eyes. Aching heads and a cotton mouths reminded Wulf and Matthew morning arrived way too soon. Swaying back and forth like sailors at sea, they dressed, shouldered their packs, then plodded down the stairs to the barroom. The bitter aroma of brewing coffee brightened their mood. They found Nellie and Merle in the bar washing dishes and sweeping the floor. Nellie paused her chores. "Coffee and breakfast?"

Wulf and Matthew nodded hopefully. Nellie poured them each a cup, then ambled into the kitchen. Seated at a table near the window, they watched the folks hurrying from place to place along the busy street. Vendors pushed wooden carts painted in bright colors filled with vegetables, fruits, and sacks of grain. Ox-drawn wagons carried crates and boxes. Fancy horse-drawn carriages transported affluently dressed passengers deeper into the city.

"I could not live like this," Wulf admitted, breaking the quiet. "You know what I mean?"

"Oh yeah," Matthew cracked. "Fighting orcs and giants is so much safer than working and living in a city."

Wulf narrowed his eyes and grunted.

Nellie arrived carrying two heaping plates of eggs, ham, and potatoes, and a pot of fresh coffee. The haze clouding their minds dissipated as they each consumed two platefuls. They paid their tab and said goodbye to Nellie and Merle, then headed for the stables.

◊ ◊ ◊

The driver pulled hard on the reins and shouted for his horse team to halt outside Parker's Coach Service. The noise awoke Danny from his ale-induced slumber. He sat on the edge of his bed until the room stopped spinning. Danny tried twice to stand, and each time he fell back onto the bed. He found success on the third try. On shaky legs, Danny teetered to the window swearing to himself. He peered down onto the street below. He wanted to examine the travelers disembarking from the coach, hoping to find fresh prey. This morning a single passenger stepped off.

Danny leapt back from the window. *Paddy Staggs! Is Kyric close as well?* He did not hesitate. He put on his clothes, grabbed his weapons and pack. Danny slipped from his room, then down the stairs. His mind whirled, anticipating the worst. *How did he find me here?* He crept out a back door and into the alleyway behind the boardinghouse. *Well, Paddy is the best tracker.* Danny felt a sudden surge of pride as he hurried to the stables, sticking to the side streets and narrow lanes. *At least they cared enough to send Paddy.*

◊ ◊ ◊

Wulf and Matthew departed the Blue Mule around midmorning. Wulf spotted Cleon and a mix of wayward boys and errant men loitering close by. From their shabby appearance, Wulf assumed they enjoyed meager success in their current occupation. None stood over six feet tall and they all seemed young except for Cleon. Wulf tapped Matthew on the shoulder and pointed. "Wave to our adoring fans."

Wulf and Matthew provided an inappropriate hand gesture before entering the stables. They dawdled, tacking their horses and securing their gear onto the saddles, expecting Cleon and his thugs would be lingering. The goons were waiting when they exited. Wulf hoisted himself into the saddle, pointed Maggie toward the hoodlums. "Beautiful morning, Cleon. You and your boys have a great day."

Matthew laughed. "A thoughtful gesture."

"Agreed," Wulf responded.

Cleon and his hooligans advanced, hurling swear words and drawing their weapons. Wulf let go of the reins. Maggie snorted, pinned her ears back, and bared her teeth. She gnashed her teeth and thrust her front hooves, scattering Cleon and his thugs.

"That blasted horse always seems to amaze," Matthew muttered, shaking his head.

Wulf chuckled. "She did the same to the stray dogs in Shallow Cross."

◊ ◊ ◊

Paddy Staggs arrived in Tejt around midmorning. A pile of thick gray clouds lumbering in from the west toward the city promised to overtake the morning sun soon and deliver welcome relief from a rare fall heat wave. Four days bumping along a dusty road had fouled his mood. The driver reined his draft team to a stop outside the Parker's Coach Service office. Paddy stepped from the coach and stretched aching muscles. "Any recommendations on where to stay in this lovely town?"

"The Blue Mule," the coach driver responded. "Two blocks from here, across from the stables. Best vegetable beef stew this side of midtown."

"Thanks." Paddy handed the driver five gold pieces, shouldered his pack, and wandered down the street. A pair of constables gave him an odd look. *I guess halflings are a rare sight in Tejt.* He strolled by the closed taverns, gambling parlors, and pleasure houses, each one awaiting dusk when they would spring back to life.

◊ ◊ ◊

Danny hid himself in an alley near the stables and watched Wulf's horse scatter Cleon and his thugs. He delayed until Wulf and Matthew disappeared from his view. *They saved me once. Maybe I should ride with them?* Danny picked the lock, then slipped into the barn via a side door. Once inside the stalls, he saddled the first horse he found. *Hope you're a good one.* Danny froze near the door. He spotted the halfling entering the Blue Mule. *Too close.*

Danny waited, his eyes fixed on the Blue Mule. *What are you doing, Paddy?* A minute passed, then two more. No further sign of Paddy. Danny eased himself and the horse from the stable into the adjacent alley. The rogue paused again and stifled a laugh, watching Cleon and his thugs race south on horseback. *Well, you all are dumber than I thought.* He glanced about, ensuring he remained alone and unseen. He climbed aboard, then pushed the stolen horse into a gallop. *I can help them.*

◊ ◊ ◊

Wulf and Matthew traveled through town, passing shops, homes, and markets built along the main street. Tejt was a decent-sized city—a mix of rundown and modern. They noted several militia patrols who gave them a quick glance, but nothing more.

Broad streets ran parallel to smaller secondary streets which intersected side roads and alleys. Folks scurried to complete their daily business and vendors driving their horse-drawn wagons clogged the streets. People paid scant attention to them—strangers were an everyday occurrence in the city. Gray clouds rolled in from the west and sporadic rain greeted them as they cleared the southern outskirts of Tejt.

◊ ◊ ◊

A fine mist fell as he entered the Blue Mule. The tavern was empty except for the old man wiping down the bar and the rotund barmaid sweeping the floor. The man stopped his chores and grinned.

"Well, well. Nellie, come and take a gander at this," the old man summoned. "Welcome, Master Halfling. Been ages since a Greenes' folk graced these doors. Name's Merle. This here is my Nellie. What can we do for you?"

"Thank you, Merle. Nellie," Paddy greeted, his manner charming. "My momma called me Paddy. Merle, I have not slept in a bed or chugged a mug of cold ale in four days. Sure hope I am in the right place?"

"A room?" Merle asked while pouring Paddy a mug. "Of course."

Paddy slid five gold pieces across the bar. "Please. One having a bathtub. You know, your finest accommodations."

Merle grinned at his good fortune, set the mug on the bar, and pocketed the gold. "Nellie, take Master Paddy to room number one."

Paddy gulped down his mug, then plodded behind Nellie. Although not to his customary standards, Paddy found the room adequate. He unpacked, taking care to hang up his custom-tailored clothes. Next he soaked himself in the tub, washing away four days of dirt and grime. He changed his attire, then moseyed back to the tavern for another cold mug and hot food.

◊ ◊ ◊

A mile south of town, Danny caught Cleon and his gang. "Cleon!"

Never being one not to return a favor, Danny slid from his horse and settled in the center of the road. "Hey, dumbass, let's end this now."

Cleon threw up his hand and reined his horse to a stop. He turned and spotted Danny. Cleon roared and spurred his horse towards Danny. *I was wrong. You are a moron.* Danny let fly an arrow, clipping the thug leader in the shoulder and laughed as Cleon howled. A flurry of arrows winged four more and scattered the rest.

Danny watched Cleon and his thugs flee north. He remounted the horse and turned him south, chuckling to himself.

Chapter Twenty-One

Fall 531, Age of the Arch Mage

Four miles out of town, the rain turned to a drizzle and then to a fine mist. Matthew glanced at Wulf. "You realize we are being followed?"

Wulf grinned. "Yeah. They are not very good at it."

A mile farther on, they heard pounding hooves coming from behind them. Matthew peeked over his shoulder. "You don't suppose—"

"Nah," Wulf interrupted. "Even those morons aren't that stupid."

"True," Matthew stated. "Then who is this?"

Wulf reined Maggie around and stopped. The rider, cloaked and face shrouded within the folds of a cowl, slowed to an easy trot. Wulf cocked his head and studied the rider as he neared. "All those idiots were slovenly. This guy has a slender build."

"You going to just sit there?" Matthew inquired, his eyes focused on the rider.

"What do you want me to do?" Wulf smirked.

"Blast!" Matthew swore, yanking his mace from his belt. "You almost killed three men who tried to steal Maggie. And now you won't defend me."

"Do you need me to protect you?" Wulf chuckled.

"At least appear threatening."

Wulf contorted his face and growled.

"Hilarious," Matthew quipped. "You should have been a court jester."

The rider halted a few yards short and pulled the cowl from his head.

"You still want me to shoot him?" Wulf questioned.

"Yeah," Matthew demanded. "He's dangerous. The others were nuisances."

"Not sure why you want to shoot me," Danny Caldwell questioned. "I ambushed Cleon and his goons a mile back. They won't be bothering you anymore."

"Thanks, I guess," Matthew offered, his expression somewhere between grateful and embarrassed.

"Sure," Danny said. "So where are you headed?"

"Highpoint," Wulf admitted, urging Maggie south.

"What for?" Danny asked, squeezing his horse in between Matthew and Wulf.

"Some princes there want us to do something somewhere," Wulf explained, as he looked past Danny to Matthew. "Ride along. We could use a thief possessing your ability. Right, Matthew?"

Matthew rolled his eyes. "Sure."

"That's master thief to you," Danny corrected. He eyed Wulf and Matthew for a minute. "This will not be a suicide mission, will it? I am kind of fond of self-preservation."

Wulf and Matthew glanced at Danny, then at each other, and grinned. Wulf leaned over the saddle. "I am convinced it will be. So, you in?"

Danny peered over his shoulder and rode for a few moments, considering their offer. He had blown his cover in Tejt and Highpoint was a large city. He could blend in there for a while. Danny knew Paddy well. When the halfling pursued a target, he would not stop until he finished the mission. Danny decided having some added protection was prudent. "Yeah, I'm in. I guess."

"Welcome aboard," Wulf stated. "So why the large iron skillet?"

"Oh, this old thing? My mother used it for Sunday dinners. She said it was lucky," Danny confessed, his grin awkward and thin. "I find it useful for cooking and the occasional makeshift weapon."

◊ ◊ ◊

The tavern was still empty when Paddy reentered. He paused near a picture window, watching the rain fall in sheets, turning the dusty streets into a muddy river. He hoisted himself onto a barstool and waited for either Merle or Nellie to return. Paddy drummed his fingers on the bar until Merle appeared from the kitchen. Merle wanted to impress the wealthy halfling. He did not ask—he took it upon himself to pour Paddy another ale. Paddy pulled a long, satisfying draw. "Merle, the coach driver told me the Blue Mule serves the finest vegetable beef stew in Tejt."

Merle stood somewhat taller, his grin steeped in pride. "Yep, Nellie's famous for her vegetable beef stew and homemade bread. Getcha bowl and loaf? Hot and fresh."

"Sounds great," Paddy replied, ensuring his tone remained friendly. He sipped on his ale and stared out the window until Nellie delivered his food.

Nellie smiled as she set the bowl on the counter. "Enjoy, and there is plenty more."

Paddy shoveled Nellie's stew and fresh bread into his mouth as if his last meal had occurred four days ago. In between bites, he engaged Merle in small talk to learn more about the city and Caldwell's whereabouts. While Paddy devoured his meal, they discussed the war beyond Tressel's northern border, local politics, the weather, and the wizard who burned down the Motsslyn Inn. He feigned interest as Merle prattled on about Nellie, their children, and their grandchildren. Every few words, Paddy bobbed his head, showing he was paying attention. Paddy sopped his bread in what remained in his bowl and emptied his mug.

"Merle, refill on the mug, please," Paddy requested, while dabbing at his mouth. "Say, Merle, I am looking for a friend of mine. We were supposed to meet here in Tejt two days ago. I got delayed in my travels and I hope I did not miss him."

Merle set the fresh mug on the bar. He wiped his hands upon a soiled apron and he leaned back into the counter. "Get lots of travelers in here, Master Halfling. Gotta description?"

"Well, a tall lanky fellow," Paddy began. "Blond hair, blue eyes. Elvish in appearance, having pointy ears similar to mine."

Merle stared at the floor and rubbed his stubbled chin for a brief minute. He raised his eyes to meet Paddy's. "Yes, a fellow matching that description came in here last night to avoid some local hooligans chasing him."

"Hooligans chased him?" Paddy responded. He took a drink, scanned the room, trying to visualize the scene. *Last night. I'm getting closer.*

"Yeah, three of them, but a couple of strangers, big outlander-looking types, came to his rescue and mine," Merle related. "They sat over there, closed the bar down just after midnight."

"Came to his rescue?" Paddy inquired, faking concern. *You're worth nothing to me dead, Caldwell.* "Did you catch his name?"

"Nah, never even asked," Merle confessed.

Paddy endured Merle's rambling narrative about the previous night for the next ten minutes, catching but a few bits and pieces of the story. Paddy was done, his tolerance exhausted and his mug empty.

"Merle, you're right. Those outlanders are heroes," Paddy lied, forcing a thin smile. "Have you seen my friend since?"

"No," Merle answered.

Paddy's expression went blank. His eyes hardened, causing Merle to recoil.

"Merle, you must tell me the hooligans' names and where I can find them," Paddy commanded, his words measured, his tone irritable as he lied again. "I am concerned about my friend's safety."

Merle wrung his hands and cleared his throat while attempting to evade Paddy's icy stare. "Cleon, JoJo, and Hugo. They should be easy to find, owning them busted up faces. Try Pinky's. It's a dive bar two blocks down the street."

The halfling grinned and slapped five gold pieces on the bar as he slid from his stool. He caught Merle staring at him when he turned.

"Thanks, Merle," Paddy fibbed once more. "Be back soon for another helping of Nellie's delicious stew and bread."

Chapter Twenty-Two

Fall 531, Age of the Arch Mage

Paddy Staggs tramped out of the Blue Mule, his mood soiled, his thoughts coarse. He had been gone nearly two weeks, yet he already pined for South Hampton. A fine mist replaced the rain as he wandered down the street, avoiding the mud and water puddles. Paddy revealed his true character as he smirked in devious delight watching a group of men struggle to liberate a draft team and a loaded wagon from the muck and mire.

Paddy located Pinky's—Merle had provided accurate directions. The halfling heard the laughter and boorish talk spilling out onto the streets. He paused outside and peered through a window clouded by smoke and grease to get a feel for the bar. To his surprise, Pinky's was half-full. The patrons fell quiet, all eyes focused on him as he stepped into the haze-filled rathskeller. Paddy lingered just inside the door, surveying the room. He detected another entrance along the alehouse's back wall and two windows set into the south wall. His eyes flitted across the faces, trying to determine which of the men were Cleon, Hugo, and JoJo. He recalled Merle saying all three wore busted-up faces. He observed a lone bartender working behind the bar. Five men sat at the counter nursing their mugs, and three more sat at a table along the wall. *Nine in all.* From what he could see, each man carried at least one dagger and a pair of long knives.

"Hey, little boy," the bartender shouted over the hush. "Your momma's calling for ya. She wants you to come home so you don't get hurt."

The jeers and insults meant nothing—he had endured them before. *Keep right on talking, tough guy.* Paddy beamed, swaggering to the bar. As one, the men rose from their seats. Like a pack of wolves, they growled, stalking to impede his path. Brave and confident, each one underestimated him. *Grave mistake.* Too many men in the past had made similar errors, and they paid a high price in blood for their foolishness. Paddy held his ground, studying them, searching for anyone having a busted-up face. He chuckled and pointed. Three wore bandages, their faces marred and swollen. *Gotcha.* Men matching Hugo's, JoJo's, and Cleon's description stood at the front of the mob. *Too easy.*

Emboldened by the pack, Cleon sneered and strutted toward Paddy, his stench unbearable and his breath as hard as torch oil. "You were told to go home, little boy."

The pack hooted and hollered, showing their approval. They cackled, urging Cleon to continue his taunting. As he began circling the halfling, Paddy drew his long knife and buried it into Cleon's thigh. Cleon screamed and bent at the waist, grasping for the hilt. Paddy grabbed the back of Cleon's head and drove his knee into the wounded man's nose, spraying blood and snot. Bones fractured and cartilage gave way as Cleon crumpled onto the wooden floor.

Clumsy and slow, the men lumbered for Paddy. Before they reached him, Paddy chucked a pair of daggers, removing JoJo and the man standing next to him as threats. JoJo staggered, clutching at the dagger impaled in his kneecap. The other dropped to his knees, stunned by the sharp pain shooting into his side. Paddy kicked JoJo in the face.

They reeled back as Paddy leapt forward. He yanked a long knife from beneath his jacket. Full of fury, his eyes narrowed. The men faltered—their courage failed. In a crouch, he scanned the room. He saw their apprehension, smelled their fright, observed their growing doubts. Paddy pressed his advantage and padded towards Hugo. Wide eyed, Hugo back-peddled, almost tripping over JoJo. Movement from behind the counter caught Paddy's attention. The bartender leveled a light crossbow at the halfling. Paddy snatched a mug from the table and hurled it. The mug struck the bartender in the head and shattered. The bartender careened backwards, covering his face with his hands, and slammed into a shelf lined with bottles. Shelf, bottles, and the bartender toppled to the floor in a loud crash.

Paddy returned his focus to Hugo as he backed him into the wall. He heard the front door open, he counted their footsteps as the men fled, leaving their wounded compatriots behind. Now only he, Cleon, JoJo, the unconscious bartender, and Hugo remained.

Paddy did not speak. Instead, he glowered at the terrified man. Paddy paused and lowered the long knife. He held the blade near his side, waiting for Hugo to crack. It did not take long. Hugo was a weak-minded fool.

"Hey, man, meant no harm," Hugo whined. Like any other bully, he was a coward minus the pack. "We was just funnin' ya."

"Real funny," Paddy spat. "What is your name?"

"H-hug-go," he stuttered.

"I see." Paddy scanned across the tavern, letting Hugo suffer the silence.

"W-what you want, m-man?" Hugo sniveled. "Ain't got no money."

"I do not want, nor do I have need of your money," Paddy seethed. "I possess plenty of my own."

"Then what, man?" Hugo moaned.

"Hugo, you do not possess an ounce of respect," Paddy fumed. "You call me 'man' one more time and you go home a eunuch. Understand, *man*?"

Hugo winced, grabbing his groin.

"Sit," Paddy demanded. "Tell me what I want to know and you walk out of this place unscathed and in one piece. Understand?

"Yes, sir," Hugo murmured while lowering himself into a chair.

Paddy drove the long knife into the table and adjusted his jacket. He sat down and leaned in close to Hugo. "What happened to your face?

"A big outlander," Hugo groaned.

"Last night at the Blue Mule?" Paddy pressed.

"Yes, sir," Hugo mumbled, staring at the floor.

"Looks like an arrow wound on your neck?"

Hugo grimaced and rubbed the injury.

"You're having a great week." Paddy snatched the long knife from the table and ran a stubby finger down the blade. "I seek a half-elf. Blond hair, blue eyes. A scammer like you."

Hugo grinned and raised his gaze to Paddy. "Yeah … I mean yes, sir. I seen him this morning. He ambushed us south of town while we was chasin' them two hulking outlander types."

Sullen, Paddy asked, "Left? Where? What two men?"

Fidgeting under Paddy's hardened stare, Hugo cringed and looked away. "He rode south along the road leading to Leeds. I guess with the same two oafs who roughed up JoJo, Cleon, and me in the Blue Mule last night."

Leeds? Paddy paused his questioning and allowed his brain to process Hugo's information. "What's in Leeds?"

"Nothing, it's a shanty border town," Hugo grumbled. "Poor and rundown."

Why Leeds? Why would he head there? And who were these men? Paddy exhaled loudly. "What city lies south of Leeds?"

"Highpoint," Hugo said.

"If you lied, Hugo, I will hunt you down and kill you," Paddy advised. "Get."

Paddy cackled, seeing Hugo scramble out of Pinky's like a frightened goblin. He sat for a moment longer, thinking. *Highpoint, that makes more sense.* A smug smile tugged at his cherub face as he admired his handiwork. There was satisfaction watching Cleon writhe on the floor in pain and listening to the bartender groan. Paddy wanted to avoid the authorities, so he slipped out the back door, disappearing into the alley. He let any thought of Danny Caldwell fade for the moment and hummed an old halfling drinking song as his musings turned to ice cold ale and another bowl of Nellie's stew and bread. He was not lying.

Paddy paused as a single thought entered his mind. One not considered until now. Cleon and his thugs blew Caldwell's cover when they chased him into the Blue Mule. Petty criminals embellished their successes and lied about their failures. And they did not forget anyone who cheated them out of money. By now, Cleon had described Caldwell to his fellow goons, and as of this morning, Caldwell was now known within Tejt's criminal element. Paddy knew this. Again, Caldwell made an unexpected mistake and as a half-elf, he did not blend into Tejt's general populace easily. Paddy also knew this. *Getting sloppy, Caldwell.* It made sense, Paddy thought to himself, for Caldwell to flee to a larger city and start anew. The cold ale and Nellie's stew would have to wait a few minutes longer.

A quick stop at Parker's secured Paddy a seat on tomorrow morning's coach to Highpoint. The idea of spending more time bouncing along a dusty road in a horse-drawn coach exasperated the halfling. So he wasted the rest of this day drinking from one tavern to another. Maybe half-drunk or hungover would make the trip palatable. Tracking Danny Caldwell could wait one more day.

Chapter Twenty-Three

Fall 531, Age of the Arch Mage

Amid a cool fall evening, Targinn Mirth strutted down Welcome's torchlit streets flanked by six of his devoted Myrmidons. He beamed, soaking up the attention heaped on him by those who passed by. Tonight, cutthroats and pirates weighed down by the gold coins in their pockets would overrun the town. Welcome offered them a reprieve, a haven from those seeking their demise. They desired drink, altering substances, card games, and sins of the flesh, anything to distract them from their drudgery for a few fleeting moments. By tomorrow morning, the money boxes across the village would overflow with gold—a plentiful bounty for his tax collectors to harvest and more coins to line his own purse.

Targinn failed to sense the presence of danger as he and his Myrmidon protectors reentered the Crypt of Belhaaz and reacted too slowly. He reeled as a sharp pang pierced his neck. Targinn clutched at the dart, trying to remove it from his skin. A burning sensation spread through his body and sent him to his knees. Harsh voices echoed in his ears as he lost consciousness. "Bring him."

When he awoke, shadows striped the room. He discovered his vision blurred and his brain fogged. His head throbbed and every muscle in his body ached. Targinn panicked. Iron shackles bound his arms behind his back and secured him to the chair. As he struggled to free himself, the bonds tightened and gouged his wrists. He identified his own fear and soiled clothing. Targinn tasted the metallic tang of his own blood as it trickled from his mouth and pooled in his lap. He stamped his feet, trying to clear his mind and to determine what had happened to him. Targinn scanned over the candlelit room. It was familiar. He recognized the fireplace, the paintings on the wall, and the imported furniture. Dread replaced panic when Targinn realized someone held him captive in his own home.

"Over here, Targinn Mirth," Deemos growled, setting Je-Hong's Alchemy Guide on the table next to him. He gazed about the room. "Nice place. I love the décor. The paintings and tapestries are exquisite. I applaud your gaudy taste. It really works."

Targinn's mind raced as he tried to comprehend his dire situation, and his eyes widened as things became clearer and more abhorrent. It was distasteful enough that Deemos himself was here, but he gawked in horror at the four menacing Odjahary mercenaries flanking Deemos as well as the drow female hovering nearby.

"Did you know some believe you can change lead into gold?" Deemos asked. "Seems like a lot of work, don't you think, Targinn Mirth? It's easier to just take what you want."

"No," Targinn answered. "Why are you here?"

"I think you know why I am here, Targinn Mirth," Deemos said.

"No. N-no," he whimpered. Targinn moved his head from side to side. His thoughts jumbled, further words stuck in his throat. He saw six of his Myrmidons sprawled on the floor, lying in puddles of blood.

"Come on, Targinn Mirth," Deemos scoffed. "You are a smart man, figure it out."

Targinn closed his eyes, slumped his head to his chest.

Infuriated, Deemos leapt to his feet and stomped to Targinn and grabbed him by the hair. Targinn yelped as Deemos yanked his head back.

"The kobold, you egotistical bastard," Deemos jeered, laying a dagger to Targinn's throat. "Where is Aeros, Targinn Mirth?"

Deemos removed the blade but kept ahold of Targinn's hair. Targinn stared into Deemos's heartless eyes, endured the malice, the evil, the hatred.

"I don't know," Targinn sniveled. "He has not returned."

Disgusted, Deemos released Targinn's head. Deemos positioned himself in front of Targinn and bent to the man's level. "Was he sober when he left, Targinn Mirth?"

Frantic to avoid Deemos's callous glare, Targinn glanced away. "No."

Deemos slapped Targinn hard across the face, bloodying his cheek and nose, tearing his eyes.

"You are a cleric of Belhaaz," Deemos raged, stepping back. "You understand the master's fury at those who do not accomplish his bidding. Aeros failed, Targinn Mirth. He and his dragon riders killed the master's heir."

"I swear I tried to—"

Deemos struck Targinn again, using the back of his hand. Deemos stormed to his own chair and sat down. Without speaking, he sat glaring at his captive. He let the moment linger. Deemos reveled in torturing others, gained pleasure in Targinn's agony and terror. Deemos leaned forward.

"Targinn Mirth, I have every right to kill you," Deemos warned. He leaned back again into his armchair and crossed his legs. Deemos opened the book once more and flipped a few pages. "Yet I am a compassionate man, so not tonight. But should you ever fail the master again, you will die by my hand. Understand?"

Targinn's head bowed, his eyes centered on the stone floor.

"Good. Targinn Mirth. Now give me the name of a competent bounty hunter who will not let the master down," Deemos ordered, his eyes never leaving the book.

"Essa Jaragua," Targinn whispered.

"And where do I find this Essa Jaragua, Targinn Mirth?" Deemos demanded, flipping another page.

"The Silver Toad w-when in t-town. Y-you can find h-her and her crew there relaxing," Targinn moaned.

"Is Essa Jaragua in town, Targinn Mirth?" Deemos queried, raising his gaze.

"I-I don't know," Targinn whined.

"Unfortunate," Deemos countered, coming to his feet. He scowled as he stood in front of Targinn once more. "It appears you have disappointed once more, Targinn Mirth."

Deemos plunged his fingers into Targinn's chest and crushed the man's heart in his hand. Deemos wheeled about, grabbed the book and stormed out, followed by the drow maiden and his Odjahary mercenaries.

Chapter Twenty-Four

Fall 531, Age of the Arch Mage

Bored out of his mind and feeling useless, Seth fretted over his inability to ride on the patrols. An errant orc arrow had caught him in the left leg, removing him from combat duty two weeks prior. The naturopaths had applied their salves and tonics and bandages. He summoned his own healing magic, but it did not possess Kiah's power, so the injury persisted.

Despite the limp, Seth remained determined to join Jonathon's patrol this morning. Seth groaned on each hobbled step as Western Union followed him from the corral. Pain shot up his left leg as he set his foot into the stirrup. He gripped the saddle horn as if his life depended on it and hoisted himself into the saddle. Seth's face contorted and twisted in anguish, his left leg throbbing as he nudged Western Union into a trot.

Seth arrived as the patrol assembled near the Mulford River. The troopers hooted and hollered their excitement to have the ranger among them once more, but Jonathon frowned.

"No. Go home and rest your leg," Jonathon exclaimed, his exasperation obvious. "Blast. You are a stubborn ass, like your brother."

Seth grinned like a Highlander mule. He considered the comparison a compliment. "Thanks."

"I did not give you a compliment," Jonathon clarified, his arms folded across his chest.

"Oh, I thought it was," Seth admitted, feeling some heat rush to his cheeks. "Anyway, I am good. Let's go."

"Prove you are fit. Dismount," Jonathon demanded. "Hurry, Seth, we have to depart."

Blast. Seth grinned and steadied himself as he swung his right leg over the saddle. He clamped down on the inside of his lower lip as he eased himself to the ground. He muzzled a yelp, releasing the saddle horn. "See, fit for duty."

"Okay, now mount up," Jonathon ordered.

Blast. Seth wanted to avoid placing his injured left foot into the stirrup. He slipped under Western Union's neck and vaulted from his good right leg while swinging his left over the saddle. Once settled, he offered Jonathon a tightlipped grin at the cheat he used to win the challenge. "See, I'm healed. Let's ride."

"No, Seth," Jonathon barked. "You're still hurt. You will not ride today. Rest the leg, ranger."

Blast. Seth fumed as Jonathon and the troopers splashed into the Mulford River and galloped north. Frustrated, Seth reined Western Union toward the stables when an idea struck him. W*hy did I not think of this earlier?*

He slipped to the ground, avoiding his left leg. Seth removed the saddle from Western Union's back and set it in the dirt. He stowed his book and charcoal into his satchel. Seth hugged her neck. "I don't need a saddle."

Seth made a subtle gesture using his hand. Western Union knelt. Seth grimaced, easing onto her back. Once he settled in place, she rose. *No pain.* Seth looked north and found the patrol out of sight. *Blast.* He knew he could chase after them but did not want to further anger Jonathon.

Seth released the reins and guided Western Union using his knees as they traveled onto the grassy plains east of Raphine. Before noon, they crossed Bison Creek north of the Horse Tribe outpost. He paused on the creek's east bank. He smiled, recalling the last time he and Raniyah stood here. Seth urged Western Union forward. Another two hours passed and they arrived at the Hebrum River. Loitering along the banks, Seth stared into the Blackhawk Territory. *Home.* Seth leaned over Western Union's neck. "Are you thinking what I am?"

She threw her head in agreement. Seth located a crossing point where they could ford the river. A flood of memories swept over Seth as Western Union climbed the bank. He was home. Seth felt his father's calming presence, sensed Kiah's guiding hand upon his shoulder as he and Western Union rode deeper into Blackhawk. *Wish you were with me, Wulf.*

Seth glanced over his shoulder as if his mother lurked somewhere behind him unseen. He patted Western Union's flanks. "Oh, don't tell Mom."

She snorted. His secret remained safe with her.

Seth closed his eyes as Western Union gracefully traversed the forest. Though other parts of Blackhawk had been ravaged by orcs, including his home village, these ancient woods remained unspoiled by man and war. Pines and oaks soared high into the morning sky like sentries guarding a king's palace, noble and honor-bound. The occasional ribbon of sunlight penetrated their sprawling limbs and boughs to touch the forest floor. The air smelled earthy and damp, perfumed by rotting leaves and decomposing trees. Shadows performed a dance in rhythm with the mild breeze rustling through the leaves. A series of hills, rises, draws, and vales crisscrossed the landscape.

As a ranger, Seth held a druidic connection to the earth. It felt good to be here—he belonged in these woods, the forests of his native land. Seth had lingered in the company of men for far too long. He wanted to work alone, by himself, and unafraid. He cleared his mind, enabling his senses to search out what he could not see, hear, or smell as Kiah had taught him, like he had practiced for hours on end.

Locating twenty-one orcs three miles away and near the far edge of his range disturbed Seth. His eyes snapped open. Seth detected more. He reined Western Union to a halt and cocked his head. Humans, eight of them, trailed the orcs. Seth drew four arrows from his quiver. He set one into the bowstring while grasping the others in his right hand.

Seth continued northeast for another half hour. He possessed no knowledge of this area within Blackhawk, but he suspected Fairbriar was nearby. One more time he freed his senses. On this occasion, he confirmed the orcs plus the humans still moving in his direction. The orcs, two miles to the northeast, maintained a southwest course. The eight humans tracked off to his right. *They're closing.* Seth eased from Western Union's back, wincing as he put weight on his left leg. He slipped the bridle from her head, hung it on a limb, and pulled her close. "Stay here. Be back soon."

Chapter Twenty-Five

Fall 531, Age of the Arch Mage

Seth tugged his cowl over his head, then blended into the forest, disappearing among the thick underbrush. He took measured steps, slow and methodical. He became the hunter, unseen and unheard, stalking his way toward where he detected his prey. Seth used the terrain to mask his movement, kept himself veiled by traveling in the draws and dry creek beds.

He felt their presence ahead of seeing or hearing them. Concealed behind a tree trunk, Seth slowed his breathing, closed his eyes, and spread out his senses. The orcs traipsed southwest, their armor clinking and clanking on each plodding step. *That's not chain.* He heard their labored breaths. They worked hard, traversing the forest in bulky armor. Seth crept forward from his hiding spot. He took several additional steps when he spotted the orcs fifteen yards from where he stood.

Something inside Seth snapped at seeing the orcs. A savage rage consumed him and roiled through his blood. His ability to judge right from wrong cowered as his fury grew. For a second, his mind transported him back to his family's farm. Orcs attacking his mother and setting his home on fire flashed before his eyes.

He shoved aside the pain and let his feral instincts assume control. Seth drew the bowstring tight to his check, sighting in on the lead orc, noting the metal plates protecting the chest and shoulders. Exhaling, he let the arrow fly. Pierced through the neck, the orc fell dead. For the moment, Seth held the advantage and released another missile. *Two dead.*

Seth dashed ten feet to his left, attempting to confuse the orcs, to prevent his detection. The orcs howled and jerked their swords from their sheaths. Angered by the ambush, they rushed for Seth's previous position. Seth pressed himself into a tree and closed his eyes, waiting for them to pass. *Ugh, the stench.* He unleashed his senses once more. *Other than these, no more orcs. The humans are sprinting and closing fast.* Seth sucked in a quick breath, set the arrow onto the bowstring, and emerged from behind the tree.

Undaunted, he waded in, ignoring his wounded leg and the fact his prey outnumbered him. The orcs spun about and realized their mistake too late. Enraged at the callous thinning of their ranks, they swarmed towards Seth. The young ranger held his ground. He discharged a burst of arrows, cutting the orcs down. When half their number was dead, the orcs fled. Seth gave chase—the adrenaline numbed the burning pain in his leg. Up and down hills the orcs ran, seeking cover. Some stripped off their armor, trying to outdistance the cloaked figure pursuing them. A few, the brave ones, mustered their courage and spun about to fight. Nothing worked. One after another, the orcs died by his bow.

Lathered in sweat, Seth knelt beside a dead orc. He pulled his book and charcoal from his satchel and started writing. This orc suffered the hoggish face, and the low, sloped brow typical of orcs. *Why does it seem bigger?* It appeared even taller and broader than the orcs he had fought in the Border Lands. First, he examined their armor. He noted its composition, a series of overlapping metal plates similar to dragon scales. *Scale mail.* He noticed the mark of the enemy emblazoned on their chest plates. *No surprise.* Yet the five diagonal blood red stripes now appeared applied by a professional artist, not the crude smears he had seen in the past. Next, Seth picked up the sword by the hilt. Unlike previous orc short swords, it appeared balanced and sharp, forged by a skilled metalsmith. He ran his finger down the serrated edge near the hilt, then along the blade to the hooked tip. It looked wicked, a weapon for killing and instilling fear in the enemy. He examined the orc's sword in his hand once more. He glanced over at the dead orcs, studying them a bit longer. Seth hoisted the orc sword over his head and hesitated. *These bastards continue to evolve.*

In a rage, he brought the sword down and severed the dead orc's hand from the wrist. Seth snatched a dagger from the orc's belt and hobbled to the closest tree. He drove the dagger through the orc's hand and pinned it to the tree.

His leg throbbed. He had overexerted himself. Seth closed his eyes—he sensed the humans neared, heard them speak in hushed tones, listened to their heavy footsteps crushing branches and fallen leaves. He hid near a towering oak and waited.

◊ ◊ ◊

Cade Badeaux raised his right hand, bringing his companions to a sudden halt. He armed his bow, and the others followed his lead.

Cade gazed over the dead orcs, each executed by a single arrow. He knelt next to one, lying face down, and examined the arrow. The missile had exploited a gap in the armor and pierced the orc's heart. Only an expert archer could have made the shot. He snapped the arrow in half and studied the fletching. *Turkey feathers.* Cade could not detect any distinguishing marks, but he knew a skilled fletcher had handcrafted it. He threw the arrow aside, turned to face his companions, and shrugged. He brought a finger to his lips, then motioned his patrol forward. Every few yards he discovered additional dead orcs, all slain in the same manner. At the last dead orc, Cade paused. He had counted twenty-one deceased orcs. Was this all the orcs he and his patrol tracked?

He felt a tap on his shoulder and turned. Trinity DeKyser stood next to him, her eyes as big as an owl's and her mouth agape. "Ambush?"

"I think so," Cade admitted. "And by a single assailant."

"One?" she exclaimed.

Cale glared at her. Trinity clapped her hand over her mouth.

"All the arrows are the same," Cade whispered. "And each shot found a gap in the armor."

◊ ◊ ◊

The minutes passed at a miserly slow pace as he listened to the humans follow the trail of dead bodies. Seth silently drew his cowl up, covering his head. He laid an arrow into his bow, drew it tight to his cheek, and did not make a single sound emerging from behind the tree.

"Go no farther and stay your weapons."

Startled at his sudden presence, they reeled back a step or two. Their wide eyes flitted from Seth then to each other. Caught, they complied and lowered their weapons. Seth assessed the humans standing rooted in front of him, six men and two women. Their leather armor bore the markings of the Blackhawk Brigade. Their weapons varied, but each carried a bow. He noted they were not much older than he. "Who are you?"

Again the brigade members looked at each other uncomfortably. They had no reason to trust him and said nothing.

"I will not ask again," Seth warned as he shifted his aim to the youngest brigade member.

Cade Badeaux stepped forward cautiously, his gaze fixed on Seth.

"Easy, I think we are on the same side," Cade stated. "I am Lieutenant Cade Badeaux and these are my companions. Did you kill all the orcs?"

He could smell their fear, see their trepidation. It was visible in their eyes and body language. Seth ignored the question, relaxed his draw, but kept the arrow set against the string. "Where are you from?"

"Fairbriar," Cade responded, his eyes never leaving Seth.

"The orcs overran Fairbriar," Seth hissed.

"Correct. Many seasons past." Cade frowned. He could discern nothing—height, weight, or age—about the hooded figure standing in front of him. The figure faded in and out of focus. He blurred at the edges.

"Where do you live these days?" Seth queried.

"Turkey Foot," Cade expressed. "It's in southern Blackhawk, out of harm's way at the present."

"Why did you track the orcs?" Seth questioned.

"They were a patrol out of Fairbriar," Cade explained. "Their mission was to probe the Horse Tribe defenses in and around the Mulford River."

Seth leaned forward. *Could this be true?* His brown eyes locked on Cade. "How are you sure?"

"We captured an enemy soldier a week ago. A human soldier," Cade informed him. "We got him to talk."

"How many orcs in Fairbriar?" Seth pressed.

Cade shrugged. "Unsure. The orcs, hill giants, and their human allies control all of Blackhawk north of the Rappacion River."

"I see," Seth murmured. Although unfamiliar with southern Blackhawk, he knew, like Shallow Cross, Turkey Foot was a river town and it sat on the banks of the Rappacion. He shifted his attention from Cade and looked into the eyes of the others. Bandaged and scarred, they looked like hardened veterans, not teenagers. "Who defends the Rappacion?"

"The remnant of the Blackhawk Brigade," Cade declared with a touch of pride in his voice.

"I see." Seth turned and began the return journey to Western Union.

Dumbfounded by Seth's sudden departure, Cade and his companions watched him take a couple of steps.

"Hey!" Trinity DeKyser uttered, her voice unsure and unsettled. "Cade answered all your questions. We have some for you."

Seth stopped and faced about. His eyes, callous and unforgiving, met her gaze.

Trinity recoiled a step under his rigid glare. "Who are you?"

Seth pivoted and resumed walking.

"Seth Blackhawk," he announced without looking back.

Chapter Twenty-Six

Fall 531, Age of the Arch Mage

Cade Badeaux and his companions gaped in disbelief as Seth disappeared into the forest.

"Seth Blackhawk. He wiped out the entire patrol by himself," Trinity DeKyser mumbled to herself as she noticed the dead orc missing a hand. She looked at the tree next to her and gulped.

"He was like the wind," Silas Kerwin commented. "We could see the effect, but he was barely visible. He is a wraith."

"Legends say he and his brother stalled the orc invasion outside Shallow Cross," Pyam Tice added.

"All right, enough hero worship." Cade grimaced, knowing the inaccuracy of Pyam's statement. "Let's move out."

"Cade!" Trinity pointed at the orc's hand pinned to the tree.

"Blast," Silas whispered.

Cade glanced at the orc's severed hand, then over his shoulder and shook his head. *I think he let us see him.*

◊ ◊ ◊

By midafternoon, Seth found Western Union right where he left her. She whinnied as he approached. Seth threw his arms around her neck and clung to Western Union as the fury ebbed from his body. He trembled, sensing the adrenaline fade and feeling the pain in his leg roar back. He slipped the bit back into her mouth and buckled the throat strap. He motioned for her to kneel. Once he was aboard, Western Union came to her feet. Seth looked back over his shoulder one more time. *Blackhawks still fight.*

The day's sun was a distant memory when Seth and Western Union forded the Mulford River. Seth located his saddle lying in the grass. He hoisted the saddle onto his left shoulder and limped for the village as Western Union walked at his side. Seth mulled through his encounter with the Blackhawk Brigade remnant. How many remained? Who led them? The notion they continued fighting brought him some hope. Seth heard Jonathon yelling his name as he neared the stables. *Blast.* Seth mustered his charm and faced Jonathon wearing a guilty grin. "You called?"

"Seth Blackhawk, where have you been?" Jonathon blurted out. "I have searched the entire village for you."

Seth showed him the orc sword.

"Where did you get this?" Jonathon muttered, his eyes riveted on the blade.

"Blackhawk," Seth responded, wondering if the sword distracted Jonathon enough to keep him from further trouble.

"What were you doing by yourself in Blackhawk?" Jonathon demanded.

"Hunting," Seth confessed.

Jonathon scowled at Seth, then considered the orc blade. Jonathon's scowl contorted into a frown.

"I ambushed an orc patrol somewhere southwest of Fairbriar," Seth resumed.

"Ambushed orcs?" Jonathon snarled. "Fairbriar? Blast, Seth."

"They wore a lighter version of plate mail," Seth provided, ignoring Jonathon's renewed anger. "Our enemy keeps evolving."

"Scale mail?" Jonathon inquired. "You—"

"Jonathon, there's more," Seth interjected. "The orcs were heading southwest when I caught them."

"Come, my father needs to hear this," Jonathon ordered. "He will want to see the sword as well."

Seth glared at Jonathon. *Blast.*

◊ ◊ ◊

"Blackhawk?" Asa shouted, holding the orc sword in his hand.

Seth nodded and held his tongue, ready to endure Asa's ire. Asa inspected the sword, allowed his gaze to take in the blade's full length. "Blast!"

"Father," Jonathon cut in. "You need to hear Seth out. There is more."

The three men stood on the porch as Seth detailed his foray into Blackhawk. He described his ambush of the orcs and his subsequent encounter with Cade Badeaux and his companions. He conveyed that the enemy controlled most of northern Blackhawk, but a remnant of the Blackhawk Brigade defended the Rappacion River and Turkey Foot.

"Chief, they informed me the orc patrol headed for Raphine to explore weaknesses in our defenses. It reminds me of what they tried several seasons past," Seth relayed. "Once again we may face additional forces originating from Fairbriar."

Asa pondered the sword for a moment. His mind churned at the implications. With their forces spread so thin already, he knew Beth Amen could not endure a two-front war. He peered back at Seth.

"This is disastrous news." Asa commented, settling into a chair.

"Chief, I think I have a solution, or at least the start of one," Seth hinted.

"What?"

"Let me go to Jacob's Forge," Seth requested. "Blackhawk refugees live there, who I am sure can and will fight."

A crooked smile crept over Asa's face. "What are you proposing?"

"We can unite with the remnant of the Blackhawk Brigade," Seth suggested. "We can strike at the orcs in Fairbriar. Keep them off balance. Get them chasing us instead of invading Beth Amen."

Asa altered his gaze from Seth to Jonathon.

"It could work," Jonathon conceded, offering a shrug. "Maybe Seth could buy us time until we are ready to attack."

"Maybe," Asa agreed. He paused, staring off into the distance. Was he willing to lose another Blackhawk to a fool's mission? He wanted to say no. He desired to put an end to this inane discussion. But he held his tongue. The ranger's proposal held merit and he should not discount it. "Okay, Seth, make it happen. A wagon train leaves for Jacob's Forge in the morning. You can provide security."

Seth hobbled down the porch stairs. As he limped off, he heard Asa call his name. Seth stopped and pivoted to Asa.

"Seth, stay in touch. Please," Asa appealed. His words sounded like a plea, not a request. "And stay safe."

Seth nodded and resumed walking.

◊ ◊ ◊

As the sun slipped under the rim of the western horizon, Cade and his companions traversed a rope bridge spanning the Rappacion River and entered the fortifications, a series of earthworks and battlements surrounding Turkey Foot. Here on the banks of the Rappacion, people from all over the Blackhawk territory assembled in the days, weeks, and months following the orc invasion. All the towns and villages north of Turkey Foot were under enemy occupation, including Cache Creek, their citizens dead, exiled, or enslaved. Compelled to survive day to day, the refugees dwelled in tents, lean-tos, and shanties. They endured a brutal first winter as starvation, disease, and illness swept through Turkey Foot, killing hundreds. Nothing the healers tried could save them or lessen their pain, but spring's long-awaited arrival had delivered new hope.

From this scattered remnant, resistance fighters, men, women, and teenagers, arose from the destruction to refill the ranks of the Blackhawk Brigade. Over five hundred strong, they fought back, refusing to succumb to the orc domination. Led by the Territorial Governor Ezra Blackhawk, the Brigade stalled the orc onslaught along the river a season ago. The Blackhawk Brigade mounted a succession of vicious counterattacks and hurled the orcs back to Fairbriar before summer.

Today Cade and his companions had covered twenty miles on their return trek to Turkey Foot. Tired and hungry, Cade sent his footsore troops to the chow tent as he sought his captain. Cade ran over the events of the day in his mind, ensuring he presented accurate facts and details from the mission. His patrol had picked up the orcs near mid-morning, twenty-one in all, as they departed Fairbrair tacking southwest. Cade had explicit orders—track the orcs west and gather as much information as they could. Nothing more. The day had progressed without incident until they discovered first one dead orc and then another and another, the entire band spread across several acres, each slain by a single arrow. And then the stranger, cloaked and brooding, appeared from out of nowhere.

He located his captain, Ilai Blackhawk, seated at a table outside the officers' mess. Amid the torches, Ilai consumed his dinner alone. Cade considered Ilai Blackhawk for a moment. Large and muscled, no more than twenty-five years old. His deep brown complexion matched his eyes and long hair. He had fought in the early days of the war as a member of Fairbriar's Reserves the morning the orcs invaded Blackhawk. Wounded and thought dead, the Fairbriar defenders left Ilai outside the village as they fled south. His body bore the scars as proof. He had trudged for miles through orc-held territory ahead of arriving at Turkey Foot.

Ilai waved for Cade to join him.

"Welcome back," Ilai sputtered, shoveling another spoonful of wild game stew into his mouth. "Sit. Tell me about the mission. Hungry? There is plenty of chow."

"I will eat later," Cade replied and sat down on the bench opposite Ilai. He provided his report, a succinct summary of their actions. Cade did all the talking as Ilai ate, offering an occasional grunt between bites and gulps of ale. Cade hesitated to conclude his account, causing Ilai to pause.

"Is there more?" Ilai inquired, refusing to lift his eyes from his food.

"Yes," Cade answered. "About four miles from the Hebrum River, we discovered the entire orc patrol wiped out. Each killed by a single arrow."

"What?" Ilai garbled with his mouth full of stew. "Horse Tribes?"

"Not sure, but a single cloaked man caught us by surprise. Captain, he appeared out of nowhere." Cade related. "He asked us many questions yet did not admit to killing the orcs."

Ilai drained his mug and wiped his mouth using his shirt sleeve. "Did you at least get his name?"

"Seth Blackhawk."

Ilai leaned back on the bench. His eyes brightened as a satisfied smile broke over his rugged face.

"Do you know him?" Cade wondered.

Ilai delayed his response as the name rolled around his brain.

"Huh? You mean personally? No," Ilai admitted. "His and his brother's reputation? Yes."

"Is this a good thing?" Cade asked.

"Yes!"

Chapter Twenty-Seven

Fall 531, Age of the Arch Mage

Two hours ahead of sunrise, Seth dressed and packed. He removed a faded banner tacked to his wall. Frayed at the edges and battle-worn, the black flag bore the Second Battalion's unit crest, a yellow hawk. Seth considered the standard for a minute, a modest piece of cloth carried by his grandfather in the Goblin Wars. He reverently traced his finger around the hawk's outline, its significance on the aging banner not lost on him. *How many men fought and died under this pennant?*

Carefully he folded the flag and placed it into his pack. He took a step and grimaced. Seth hobbled out the door, swearing under his breath each time his foot struck the ground. Jeribai waited for him on the porch, his back resting on the wall. The king's presence startled Seth.

"A rare occasion when I can sneak up on a ranger," King Stockton admitted, his smile wide and prideful.

Seth did not respond—heading to Blackhawk preoccupied his thoughts.

"They forced me to slink out of my own quarters," King Stockton chuckled. "The Home Cavalry are relentless. It is infrequent when I get a moment to myself."

Seth stared but did not speak.

"I understand you are leaving?" the king inquired, his smile now forced and reluctant.

"Yes, your majesty. This is something I must do," Seth admitted, not sure how to answer.

"Drop the 'majesty' crap, Seth, there is no one here except you and me," the king insisted. He handed Seth a piece of parchment. "Here, take this."

Seth glanced at the parchment, then back at the king.

"Read it," Jeribai urged.

Seth unfolded the paper and read its contents. He grinned at the king's gesture—a dozen pack mules, weapons, and armor would go a long way. "Thank you. This means a lot."

"I wish I could do more," King Stockton said. He considered the young ranger standing before him. A child in any other nation, but now a seasoned combat veteran by age sixteen. A trooper, fearless and lethal. *War, what a waste.* Jeribai winced at the thought of losing another Blackhawk from his ranks. Both natural leaders, consumed with purpose and strength. So similar to Wulf in many ways, yet so entirely different.

Seth nodded as he took his leave. Jeribai tarried on the porch until Seth disappeared from his sight. He closed his eyes and mouthed a prayer.

◊ ◊ ◊

Seth and Western Union met the wagon master near the horse barn. Dressed in a hefty mottled cloak, a long sword hung from his belt. His dark hair peppered gray, his facial features were typical for a man of the steppe, brown and leathered. He looked middle-aged, short and stocky, and his hands possessed an iron grip.

"Decent to get you along on our expedition, Lieutenant," the wagon master drawled. Grinning, he extended a beefy right hand. "They call on me as Sergeant Quinn."

Seth chuckled at Sergeant Quinn's accent and his odd choice of words. Although all Horse Tribesmen spoke the common tongue, the usual idioms spoken by those hailing from southeastern Beth Amen always amused Seth.

Twenty empty wagons and their draft teams waited in an organized single file column and ready to depart. Sergeant Quinn climbed onto the seat of the lead wagon. He turned his head. "Forward!"

Creaking and groaning, the wagon train pulled out of Raphine, heading south.

For those who were awake, the first notes were faint but familiar. The Highlander war horns blared from somewhere in the nearby Goodthread Pass, the clarion call announcing their approach. Seth grinned as the low mournful notes shattered the dawn's hush. *Barbarians!* The ranger's grin spread into a broad smile as he visualized the troopers' response to the barbarians' triumphant entry.

◊ ◊ ◊

Raphine slumbered. Only the troopers manning the defenses moved about, as King Jeribai Stockton strolled to his quarters. He pondered the young ranger's self-imposed mission while he rambled along the empty pathway. Could Seth protect Beth Amen's eastern border? he wondered. Could he unify the Blackhawk remnant? He chuckled to himself. *Yes, of course he could.* Jeribai found the Blackhawk brothers headstrong to the point of becoming unreasonable when they decided on a course of action. *Stubborn as a Highlander mule.*

He wavered on his next step and cocked his head. Jeribai shut his eyes and listened. He heard the horns peal, their inspiring tones washing over the sleeping village like a gentle spring rain. *Barbarians!* He pivoted about, a broad grin pulling at the edges of his mouth.

Jeribai raced over the footbridge spanning the river. He navigated the array of barriers and barricades protecting the northern approaches to Raphine. He had dashed a hundred yards onto the open plains before his startled troopers realized their king had rushed past them. Jeribai stopped and scanned the western horizon. There was no possibility of containing his joy. He beamed. He danced. Jeribai laughed aloud. Hope poured over him like a bucket full of water as all the painful decrees and all the gut-wrenching decisions washed away—at least for a moment.

◊ ◊ ◊

Like each trooper in Raphine, the Highlander war horns awakened Captain Yosi Vandermoff. He dressed, grabbed his weapons, and hurried to the king's room. He acknowledged the two Home Cavalrymen posted outside as he knocked on the door. Captain Vandermoff hesitated, then knocked once more. He waited for the king to respond. A minute passed and no answer. He eased the door ajar and peeked in. The bed was empty, the window opened. Embarrassed at losing his king, Captain Vandermoff became frantic. Furious, he dispatched his Home Cavalry to sweep the entire village as he sprinted for the defenses.

Captain Vandermoff located his king, surrounded by Asa and dozens of troopers standing a hundred yards north of the defensive positions. Exasperated, he shook his head, yet thankful at the same time his king was unharmed. Jeribai Stockton behaved nothing like his father Beracah. This made Jeribai the most difficult to protect. As he had aged, Beracah had enjoyed the comforts of the palace and the grounds and never ventured beyond the gates by himself.

Jeribai acted quite differently. He bristled at the pomp and circumstance his father had embraced. Jeribai refused to conform to the strict royal rules of conduct enacted by his father. He often stole away from the palace during the evening hours. The Home Cavalry would happen upon him in the barracks drinking and playing cards with the troopers, eating dinner among his people in a local tavern, or enjoying a troupe of traveling bards performing in the city square. No matter how hard he protested, Captain Vandermoff understood he could never alter Jeribai's behavior.

To reach his king, Captain Vandermoff elbowed his way through the throng. King Stockton shrugged, his expression embarrassed when he noticed the captain standing at his side. King Stockton put his arm around his frustrated captain's shoulder and hugged him. "Barbarians!"

"Yes, my lord," Captain Vandermoff acknowledged. Despite his best effort, Yosi smiled at the king's uncontained excitement.

◊ ◊ ◊

Seth sat next to Sergeant Quinn when he detected their presence before he saw them. Forty-one riders heading north. He perceived the protective aura surrounding the riders. He recognized the same aura in Matthew. Half an hour later, the riders came into view.

"Do these aged eyes of mine deceive?" Sergeant Quinn exclaimed.

"Who are they?" Seth asked.

"War clerics called the Canons of the Dawn," Sergeant Quinn answered. "Fought with us at the Mulford. Ain't seen them in near twenty years."

"Where are they headed?" Seth inquired. He wondered if they possessed the same powers as Matthew.

"To the king, I suppose." Sergeant Quinn handed Seth the reins. He grabbed the back of the seat to steady himself and stood as the first clerics drew abreast. "Master Canon, what is your path?"

"To the king, wagon master," Azmaveth declared. "May the Maiden's blessing rest upon you and your men."

Seth studied them as they rode past the wagon trains. They traveled in a column of twos clad in chain armor the color of the dawn. Their shields, bearing the Maiden's symbol, and helmets glistened in the sun. Other than their leader, the Canons looked young. The ranger watched them until they disappeared over the horizon and wondered how the troopers would react.

Sergeant Quinn sat and stared straight ahead. His eyes gleamed and the wide beam splashed across his leathered face showed his joy. He snatched the reins from Seth and blew out a breath. Seth peeked over at the wagon master. "Is their arrival good?"

"Ha!" Quinn snorted. "Lieutenant, them Canons fight like demons. Ah, yes, their arrival is good. Very good, indeed."

Seth allowed his smile to match Quinn's broad beam as he imagined Jeribai's reaction. He removed his book and charcoal from his pack and scribbled some notes, then sketched a picture of the Maiden's emblem—the rising sun.

Chapter Twenty-Eight

Fall 531, Age of the Arch Mage

The two Highlander war horns, each with a distinct sound, blared throughout the morning, announcing their imminent arrival. The sun shimmered off iron helmets and weapons. The earth trembled under each heavy footstep. Amid a detachment of Home Cavalry, Jeribai and Asa gawked in amazement as the massive barbarians neared.

◊ ◊ ◊

Dao Chauinard, the half-orc commanding the orc army, felt the ground shudder beneath his feet before he heard the two separate war horns blaring into the morning. Two distinct war horns meant two barbarian hordes had arrived to bolster Raphine's defenses. He knew in an instant the scales had tipped toward the Horse Tribes. *Barbarians, cursed barbarians.* Dao slapped his forehead and screamed. At that moment, he realized the barbarians would have killed or scattered the forces he sent to block Goodthread Pass. From experience, Dao considered the scrappy Horse Tribesmen a nuisance and not easily defeated, but the hulking Highlanders were deadly. Little scared Dao Chauinard, but the barbarians terrified him. Dao grabbed the orc closest to him and hoisted it into the air. "Do you know what this means?"

The trembling orc did not reply. Dao screamed again and threw the frightened orc to the ground. Dao turned to one of his lieutenants. "Find me the number of barbarians. Now!"

◊ ◊ ◊

"Wait for me here," King Stockton ordered. He locked his eyes on Asa and Yosi, the smile on his face gone.

King Stockton marched west fifty yards, leaving Asa and his Home Cavalry behind. As King of the Horse Tribes, he bore the responsibility to greet the Highlanders first. A booming voice ordered the horde to a halt. A lone barbarian strode forward. He stopped short of King Stockton, offering a respectful bow.

"Blessings upon your tribe, master barbarian," Jeribai declared. The barbarian looming over him by a foot awed him. "Who leads this noble horde?"

"King Stockton, lord of the Horse Tribes, I am Asger Bynjar, Chief of the Waraxe Tribe," Asger affirmed, his massive two-bladed war axe resting across his broad shoulders. "Bjarke Halvard, Chief of the Hilltopper Tribe, trails close behind. My queen, Siobhan Petra, Empress of the Barbarians, sends her regards."

"Welcome, Chief of the Waraxe. It is an honor to stand shoulder to shoulder among our Highlander brothers once more," Jeribai announced. He motioned for Asa and Captain Vandermoff to join him. "Let's get them settled."

"The honor is ours as well," Chief Bynjar acknowledged.

Side by side, Asa and Jeribai watched the two barbarian hordes cross over the Mulford River and assume their positions inside Raphine's defenses. Jeribai peeked over at his brother. "Hope?"

"Maybe?" Asa returned, his face masked with relief.

◊ ◊ ◊

Furious at the interruption, Asa stormed towards his brother's tent. Captain Vandermoff and the four Home Cavalry troopers guarding the entrance stepped aside, allowing Asa access. He saw his brother sitting at a table with a leather folder under his hands.

"You summoned," Asa snapped. "I have—"

"Oh, don't get yourself in a snit," Jeribai scolded. "I am still the king. Sit. Ale?"

"No." Asa sat and studied his older brother for a minute. Something was amiss. *Still the king? What did he mean?* He did not detect the normal confidence his brother exuded. The eternal hope he always expected from him seemed a distant memory. For the first time Asa could recall, his brother looked tired, beaten down and threadbare. A few hours ago, his brother danced at the barbarians' arrival and now he appeared subdued and old. This seemed unusual behavior for Jeribai, the eternal optimist.

Jeribai opened the folder and removed a piece of parchment. Haunted eyes met his brother's. "Asa, even though the barbarians stand among us, I am not sure we survive."

Surprised by Jeribai's somber admission, Asa furrowed his brow. "What are you saying?"

Jeribai handed the parchment to Asa. "Read this."

Jeribai rocked back and forth in his chair, watching his brother's eyes as they skimmed over the document. Asa set the parchment on the table and stared at Jeribai in disbelief. "Are you serious?"

"Yes," Jeribai vowed.

"You realize what you are doing?" Asa pressed further. He wanted to think Jeribai was joking.

"Yes," Jeribai insisted, his eyes locked on the parchment. "I am abdicating the throne. I have no other choice."

"Once you sign this, there is no going back," Asa reminded him. "Plus, she is a Blackhawk now, not a Stockton. Jeribai, knowing my daughter, she will not yield her surname."

"I know," Jeribai affirmed, his gaze now fixed on Asa.

"Stocktons have sat on our throne for a century," Asa reminded him. "Are you willing to concede this?"

"Yes," Jeribai pledged. His conviction did not waver. "If I do not, it won't matter what last name sits in Stirling Hill. Can she handle this?"

"Yes, and you knew the answer prior to asking," Asa sighed. Maria was no longer a little girl in his mind. His daughter was a woman, strong and independent like her mother and every other Horse Tribe woman he knew. "She is stronger than we think."

"In accordance with our laws, I will exercise my right to retain generalship over the army," Jeribai added. "After the war, my fate for future service will rest in her hands."

Asa nodded. Jeribai had decided and no one could change his mind. Asa came to his feet. "Anything else?"

"Yes. One more thing," Jeribai frowned, as he rose from his chair. "Minus one platoon, I am transferring the remaining Home Cavalry to serve under my command. They will answer to me. I have no legal right, but we need them here."

"The queen has every right to their protection and their service as she sees fit," Asa stressed.

"You're correct," Jeribai concurred, his voice weary and hard. He looked down at the parchment and exhaled aloud.

Asa studied his older brother for a long minute. This matter concerned his daughter's safety. Yet he knew Jeribai was desperate to gain his approval.

"Your point is valid," Asa agreed, trying to shroud his reluctance. "She will be safe in Stirling Hill. I agree with your decision."

Jeribai sighed and stood a little taller. It seemed someone had lifted an enormous burden from his broad shoulders. "Thanks."

"Good day, General Stockton," Asa smirked, walking out of the tent.

Jeribai grunted and made an obscene gesture with his hand. A second later, Captain Vandermoff reentered the tent. Jeribai faced his loyal guardian and removed his royal crest.

"You are to dispatch a platoon of Home Cavalry to Jacob's Forge within the hour," Jeribai ordered. "Maria Blackhawk is to be given this crest and letter. She will be our queen. Under the royal banner, the platoon is to escort the queen to Stirling Hill and serve at her pleasure. Yossi, this second letter is for Joseph Locklynne. Ensure it reaches him prior to the queen's arrival. This is my final edict as king."

King Stockton grasped the quill pen and signed his name to the document before he could change his mind. Dumbfounded, Captain Vandermoff stared at his former king in complete disbelief. "My king, this is—"

"You will refer to me as General Stockton," Jeribai informed him, cutting off his captain. "The rest of the Home Cavalry, including you, are now under my direct authority."

"My place is beside you, General Stockton," Captain Vandermoff affirmed, his expression avowing his loyalty.

◊ ◊ ◊

Asa departed Jeribai's tent and hustled to find his son. Colonel Stockton had set his left foot into the stirrup when he heard his father shouting his name. Jonathon stepped down and turned to see his father approaching. Asa stopped short and motioned for Jonathon to join him. Jonathon saw the frown and halted. "You don't appear happy."

"I am not," Asa admitted. He paused for a second and sucked in a deep breath. "Your uncle has abdicated the throne."

Jonathon stared and offered no response as he contemplated his father's announcement.

"Did you hear what I said?"

"Oh, I heard you," Jonathon confessed, his expression blank.

"That means your sister is now the queen," Asa stated.

"I know."

"And?" Asa asked.

"And what?"

"You have nothing to say?" Asa wondered.

"Maria will do a great job," Jonathon proclaimed, his smile broad. He patted his father on the shoulder and climbed into the saddle. "We are in capable hands."

Asa spoke no further. He stood in place, mouth agape, and watched his son ride off with his patrol.

◊ ◊ ◊

For days they had ridden north across broad plains flush with winter grasses and through villages large and small. Southern Beth Amen remained pure, untouched by battle and orcs. A late afternoon sun burned bright in an azure western sky. After yesterday's wind and icy rain, Azmaveth soaked in the soothing warmth. He looked over at the young lieutenant riding at his side. Dust clung to her face, hair, and armor, making it difficult to guess her age. Her patrol had intercepted them several hours ago, and she offered to escort his Canons to Raphine. They had talked for a while and then their words trailed off. Azmaveth found Lieutenant Synane's story similar to the other maidens he had encountered on this journey. Sorrow fell upon him when he considered the heartache and destruction the war had brought to this land.

Dusk ushered in a dazzling assortment of purples, oranges, and cobalt onto a darkening western sky when the Canons and their

Horse Tribe maiden escorts reached Raphine. As they approached the barricades and redoubts, they noticed the troopers seemed more dour than usual and a nervous buzz droned among them. Lieutenant Synane halted her patrol and the Canons when a trooper walked up to her.

"Ma'am, have you heard the news?" he inquired.

Synane shook her head.

"The king has abdicated the throne," the trooper informed her.

"What? When?"

"It's true," he assured. "Our sergeant read us the message this afternoon. King Stockton is now General Stockton."

Synane cocked her brow and shot Azmaveth a concerned look. Azmaveth shrugged and flashed her a thin smile. Synane peered down from her horse. "Who rules the realm?"

"Chief Stockton's daughter, Maria Blackhawk."

"We have a queen." Synane chuckled at the notion and ran a gloved hand through her dusty hair. She turned in the saddle. "Did you hear that, ladies? We have a queen!"

The Horse Tribe maidens in the patrol hooted at the news and shouted, "Hail to the Queen of the Horse Tribes!"

Synane leaned over the saddle, her gaze fixed on the trooper. "Azmaveth and his Canons are here to join our fight against the orcs."

"Proceed, ma'am."

Inside the fortifications Lieutenant Synane dismissed her patrol and turned to Azmaveth. "I guess I am leading you to the General's quarters instead."

"We will follow you, lieutenant," Azmaveth replied. As they rode deeper into Raphine, he struggled with the idea of Jeribai as General Stockton. Many seasons had come and gone since he last spoke to Jeribai. Following the Battle at the Mulford River, they had each settled into their own lives. *King or not, I look forward to seeing you once more.*

Troopers stopped and stared at the odd column riding along Raphine's roads. Azmaveth chortled to himself as the troopers pointed and whispered to each other. To these troopers, the Canons were nothing more than a long-overlooked footnote in Beth Amen's history. Azmaveth wanted to change their perception. The Horse Tribe troopers needed to regard the Canons as allies, not strange clerics living behind protective walls.

A frenzy of memories assaulted Azmaveth from each direction. Two decades past, he rode these same streets. He gazed into the eyes looking back at him. He saw the same fear and worry reflected on their faces as the troopers he had fought alongside twenty years ago. Azmaveth saw the dead and injured. Suffered the dead's silence and the pleading cries from the wounded. The battle itself remained a blur. A blessing for those who survived.

Azmaveth and his fellow Canons had occupied the center where the fiercest fighting occurred. From dawn to dusk, the orcs and goblins hurled themselves at the soldiers manning the defenses built along the Mulford River. And each time, the defenders repelled the orcs and goblins. Azmaveth heard the Highlander war horns erupt and as one the nations surged forward. Swords and axes hewed flesh and rent armor. Thousands of arrows filled the sky. Horses charged into the fray. Iron-shod hooves trampled the earth, orcs, and goblins. When the battle ended, the Southern Realms had emerged victorious, but at a tremendous cost. The losses were staggering. An entire generation of men and horses lay dead, their blood staining the soil. Everywhere he looked, bodies littered the grasslands. In a single brutal encounter, he had lost a lifetime's worth of friends, including Zelek.

The lieutenant reined her horse to a stop outside a tent near the village square and climbed down from her horse. She approached the Home Cavalryman standing guard. "Azmaveth Jakkes is here to see General Stockton."

One Home Cavalryman disappeared into the tent. A few seconds later, Jeribai and Asa exploded from the tent. Jeribai scanned over Azmaveth and the Canons. "By the Maiden."

"Yes, General, you are correct," Azmaveth confirmed. "By the Maiden."

"First the Highlanders," Asa beamed. "And now the Canons. Welcome, Azmaveth."

Chapter Twenty-Nine

Fall 531, Age of the Arch Mage

Fresh off the hunt, Essa Jaragua and her crew spent the evening at the Silver Toad enjoying the spoils of their labor. In celebration of their latest success, Essa bought drinks for everyone in the tavern and continued wasting their earnings into the early morning hours.

Tonight, Essa relished the attention she often shunned. Her fame among the assassins and mercenaries had reached new heights. Surrounded by a dozen admirers, she reclined in a lounge chair, sipping on a fourth glass of wine. She was gorgeous. All the other women paled in comparison. Essa was willowy, owning soft features, and amber eyes that caused people to stare. Elven in look, her aura was evocative and mysterious. As a dark elf, Essa Jaragua's parents reared her in the manner of a ranger, a deadly huntress adept at stalking prey. She was a drow maiden born and bred to kill.

She felt the heat extending over her cheeks, a slight numbness in her hands, and a clouding around the edges of her eyes. Essa waved away those gathered around her and closed her amber eyes. A thin satisfied smile spread over her face as she reflected on their last assignment. The job took months of planning and surveillance, but once she and Naszea had slipped past the guards, killing the senator was easy. Even their—

Her eyes snapped open. She sensed a presence, an evil one. She shuddered, reaching for her blades.

"What's wrong?" the drow sitting next to her asked.

"An evil, Scribe," Essa admitted, her voice a whisper above the din. "An evil I have not perceived since ..."

Scribe rose from his chair, conjuring a spell as he scanned the dim torchlit tavern. Debauchery inundated the room, unsavory types filled every inch of space. He glanced at Essa. Her eyes were wide and her body tense. She was ready for a fight. "Where?"

"I don't know," she admitted, her voice still a whisper. "I can't pin it down."

She percieved someone hovering prior to the hand touching her shoulder. In one instantaneous movement Essa was on her feet, gripping a pair of long knives, then she relaxed and smirked as she recognized Rhent Dubois. Arms outstretched and palms up, Rhent recoiled a step, staring at the long knives in her hands. He shared her dark elf features, her aura. Tall and strikingly handsome, his eyes were the color of coal.

"A man upstairs has a job offer for us," Rhent exclaimed.

"What man?" she scowled, her tone showing her irritation at the interruption.

Rhent pointed at the balcony. "That one."

Essa followed Rhent's arm to the man glaring at her from above. She shrugged off the man's frosty stare and studied him for a moment. He loomed over average men, his shoulders hunched. A leathered face and gray hair suggested he had passed middle age. Essa shuddered. "Lead the way."

Essa and Rhent maneuvered through the crowded tavern toward a staircase. They reached a closed door at the top of the stairs. Essa knocked and waited. No one responded. Evil dwelled beyond the door. She peered over her shoulder at Rhent.

"Open it," she murmured, her hand resting on a long knife.

Deemos sat in a large leather chair nursing a mug and reading a book when Essa and Rhent entered the private room on the Silver Toad's second floor overlooking the bar.

"Your blade will not benefit you, drowess," he warned, without looking up from his book. "You both will die before it clears the sheath."

Deemos remained seated and motioned for Essa and Rhent to sit. He flipped another page and looked up at the drow maiden. "Did you know alchemists combine spiritualism, science, and philosophy in their pursuits to create a better world?"

Confused by the old man's odd question, Essa and Rhent shook their heads.

"Me neither. Anyway, I am not here to discuss alchemy with you, Essa Jaragua," Deemos admitted as he shut the book and set it on the table. He leered at Essa. There was no denying her beauty. "Targinn Mirth recommended you, Essa Jaragua. He guaranteed me you and your crew were the best before his unfortunate passing."

Essa glared at Deemos, her eyes reflecting the rage roiling inside. She stood and snatched Rhent's cloak and wrapped it around her, then sat again. "I am not a simple bar strumpet here for your enjoyment, old man."

Deemos's expression turned frigid, devoid of any emotion. Essa and Rhent cowered under his unrelenting scowl. Her confidence ebbed, her arrogance drained away like a fleeting moment in time. She fought the urge to flee the old man's presence. Essa summoned every ounce of courage she possessed to remain in the room.

"Dear Essa, I take what I want when I want," Deemos announced, then took an extended draw from his mug. "Once you understand that, we will get along just fine. Understood?"

At a loss for words, Essa managed a slight nod while gripping Rhent's hand in her own. She understood his discreet but icy threat. As a drow, it required a lot to frighten her—she recognized evil. But this old man exuded a malevolence beyond any she had encountered before.

"Good. I will pay you a handsome fee," Deemos offered. "Say, twenty thousand gold pieces. Half up front."

Rhent snuck a quick peek at Essa. Her eyes had glazed over from the lingering effects of the alcohol, or maybe even from fear. Essa caught herself and refocused on Deemos. "Who is the target?"

Deemos smirked, knowing he had the drow bounty hunters right where he wanted them—afraid. He drained his mug, then wiped his mouth on a cloth napkin. "A kobold, a Wyvern Charmer. He goes by the name Aeros Askin."

Essa and Rhent kept silent, held their breath, staring into the face of pure wickedness.

"Aeros failed my master. Bring me his head," Deemos demanded. "He wears an amulet. A talisman permitting him to control black dragons. I covet it as well."

Essa nodded.

"His last known location was Prosper inside the Stowan Freeholds," Deemos stated, rising from his chair and picking up the book. "You have thirty days from today to complete the task or I will place a price on your pretty head so high every bounty hunter this side of Highpoint will come for you. Do you get what I am saying?"

Too afraid to speak, Essa nodded once more.

"Do not fail me," Deemos threatened as he exited the room. Upon reaching the door, he spun back. "I will wait here for your return."

Essa blew out a breath and rested her head on Rhent's shoulder once Deemos departed.

Chapter Thirty

Fall 531, Age of the Arch Mage

Essa rose and met the coming dawn sober, almost. Thin strands of sunlight, bright and cutting, snuck around the curtains, irritating her bleary eyes. Her mind remained fogged from the liquor and the meeting with the old man. Essa slid from beneath the covers and hurriedly dressed. She gathered her weapons and pack, then departed for the harbor.

Welcome lingered in an inebriated stupor as Essa hastened down quiet streets. The saloons, gambling parlors, and pleasure houses were closed and attempting to recover from a night of debauchery. She retched. The town reeked of flat ale, vomit, and urine. She passed a half dozen sots sprawled in the dust, sleeping off their drunkenness on her way to secure passage to Prosper.

Her mind worked again as she devised a plan. Her search for Aeros would begin in Prosper. Essa swore in frustration. All she knew was the village sat on the banks of the Ossabow River inside the Stowan Freeholds. Essa hated working this way. Rushing into the unknown forced errors and bred mistakes. She desired time to study and think through each detail. She sighed—she did not possess the luxury of time. Essa needed a map to orient herself. Even a rudimentary chart would suffice for now.

She halted near the docks. Her eyes flitted over the ships tied pier-side and riding anchor in the harbor. A ship of the line, the heaviest of the sea-faring vessels, was too large. She required one with a shallow draft to navigate the river. A small vessel, fast and agile, was essential.

Essa located a little two-masted dhow dubbed the *Scamp* bound to the dock. A dozen shabby sea dogs toiled topside. They ceased their chores and leered as she climbed the gangplank to the main deck. Her eyes narrowed as they swept across the deck, seeking additional threats. A sailor sneered as he approached. His clothes hung from his body, lean and wiry. His skin possessed a deep brown, darkened and leathered from the sun.

"Missy, what ya doing?" he slurred.

Essa let him enjoy the view for a second then kicked him in the groin. He fell to his knees, gasping for breath. Then in one swift motion, she drew a pair of long knives from her belt and prepared to battle the rest.

"Where is your captain?" Essa hissed. "I seek transport."

Unsympathetic, the other tars laughed and pointed at the injured sailor kneeling near Essa. A door flung open, silencing the deck hands. His massive frame filled the companionway. His muscles rippled, his appearance intimidating as he strode onto the main deck. Familiar with his unforgiving demeanor, the sailors scurried back to their labors. She noted his brown skin and bald head, a white beard pure as cotton covering harsh facial features. In his massive hands, he gripped a kilij. The long-curved blade gained her immediate respect. Essa retreated a step as he approached, not out of fear but to create maneuver space. He paused a yard from where she stood, surveying the injured sailor ahead of lifting his gaze to Essa. His face remained expressionless as he spoke in a distinctive Emirates accent. "Your handiwork?"

She did not respond. Essa glanced down at the moaning sailor kneeling nearby, then back to the massive man standing in front of her.

"Why?" he growled.

"To make a statement," she conceded.

"I see," he acknowledged, permitting a faint grin to spread over his bearded face. "What do you intend, drowess?"

"Only to the captain will I speak," Essa stipulated.

"I am he," the captain countered. "State your business or depart my vessel before I allow my crew to have their way with you."

Essa smirked, sheathing her long knives. *I will remember your threat.*

"I seek passage to the Stowan Freeholds," Essa glowered, her eyes indignant and glacial. "My crew and I must depart this morning."

"I am a wanted man in the Freeholds," the captain bragged. "Will cost you—"

"Five thousand up front with no questions asked and I am in charge," she interrupted. "Five thousand when we finish."

He glanced about his ship and observed his crew looming close enough to hear and see what happened next. The captain appreciated that they watched for him to show weakness, to fold to the demands of this brazen drow. He studied Essa, admiring her beauty. Her tenacity fascinated him. The captain noted the short swords and longbow slung across her back, the three long knifes tucked into her belt, and the brace of daggers across her chest. He was convinced she hid additional blades somewhere on her body, which he would enjoy uncovering when he took her prisoner.

Essa laughed—she understood his intent. She sensed their presence, discerned Rhent and the rest of her companions neared. Essa pulled a gold coin from the sack attached to her belt and flipped it into the air. She caught the coin and tossed it once more, the smile never leaving her face.

"What are you doing?" the captain demanded, bemused by her behavior.

"Buying time," she retorted.

The captain motioned his hand, his tolerance of her antics exhausted. "Time's up."

As the sailors came for her like rabid dogs, Essa closed her eyes, allowing her senses to reach out. She whipped two daggers at the closest ones. Both fell as her drow blades pierced skin. Essa listened as the kilij rose, heard the captain's accelerated breathing as she hurled the long knife. Her eyes snapped open in time to see him clutch at the knife buried hilt deep in his neck. She flashed an acerbic smile, watching his life drain from his body. *I don't forget a threat.* Essa spat on his dead body as she drew the short swords from her back. Swords, one in each hand, blurred in a flurry of slashes and swipes—drow steel ruining flesh. Essa drove the sailors towards the bow. She cut and sliced her attackers with the grace and dexterity found among the elven kind.

Rhent Dubois sprinted for his mistress. His chain mail was silent, muted by dark elf magic. His longbow hummed as his arrows rained down on the crew. As they died, the drow fighter raced up the gangplank, attaining the main deck in four easy strides.

The drow wizard strode down the docks, his black robes billowing, his long silvery hair splayed by the ocean breeze. From the pier, Scribe Everclay peppered the *Scamp's* crew with a slew of fiery missiles leaping from his outstretched fingers.

The duergar, cheerless in demeanor and gray in appearance, pounded the dock with each weighty step. Brothers Knot and

Packus hustled behind Rhent as fast as their stubby legs could carry them.

The dark gnome assassin slipped unnoticed from the morning shadows. Crossbow in hand, Naszea Jaryne aimed and squeezed the trigger, propelling the bolt into the sailor rushing toward Essa.

Overpowered and outmatched, the remaining crew members dropped their weapons and raised their hands. They surrendered after watching half of their shipmates die in a matter of seconds. Essa grinned, a wicked smile reflecting the evil in her heart as she surveyed the dead and wounded strewn about the deck. She scowled at Packus and Knot. "Kill the wounded, then toss their bodies overboard."

As the duergar brothers executed her grisly orders, Essa approached the remaining sailors. She noted the hatred for her mirrored in their eyes. She breathed in their fear. "Where is your first mate?"

They pointed to the tar she had kicked in the groin, still writhing on the deck.

"Perfect." she laughed. "Rhent and Naszea, cut us loose."

Essa steadied herself, feeling the dhow drift from the pier. She waited for the sailors to get the first mate to his feet. She lingered, allowing her rage to pervade her mind, body, and soul. Essa placed her sword along the first mate's neck, permitting him to experience the cold steel pressed to his skin. Essa fought the impulse to plunge her blade into his heart, to exact revenge. She stayed her hand, knowing she required his nautical expertise.

Chapter Thirty-One

Fall 531, Age of the Arch Mage

"You miserable sea rats will refer to me as captain," Essa barked. "Prepare to sail for Ragged Point."

The sailors stood unmoving, their eyes shifting between their first mate and Essa. The first mate groaned, bending over from the waist.

"You heard the captain," he moaned. "To the oars."

He stood, his eyes refusing to meet hers.

"Your name?" she seethed.

"First Mate Chara El-Asante."

"To your post, First Mate El-Asante," Essa demanded.

El-Asante staggered to the wheelhouse and grabbed the railing to balance himself. In a steady rhythm, the sailors rowed the meager dhow from the docks and into the middle of the harbor.

"Raise the sails," El-Asante ordered.

A western wind billowed the main and mizzen sails, propelling the *Scamp* out onto the open sea. Captain Essa stood at the stern near Chara El-Asante, her reluctant first mate. So far, so good, she thought. Rhent, Naszea, and Scribe loitered near the main mast watching the sailors expertly crew the little ship. Lathered in sweat, the sea dogs glided over the deck, trimming the sails, tightening and loosening ropes. Knot and Packus leaned along the port railings, staring into the East Sea's crystal blue water, enthralled by the waves and mist splashing over their arms and faces. Chara El-Asante manned the tiller, barking out orders to his crew while skillfully guiding the *Scamp*.

"Why Ragged Point?" El-Asante inquired, risking his new captain's ire.

"Why not?" Essa answered.

"Mistress, I am a skilled sailor and tillerman. Been at sea my entire life," El-Asante provided. "There is nothing worth plundering in Ragged Point unless you are seeking slaves."

"I am no slave trader, First Mate El-Asante," she spat, disgusted by his accusation. "If you must know, our final destination is Prosper."

El-Asante fell quiet. He glanced over at what remained of the crew, checked his compass to confirm their course heading. "Captain, if I may?"

Essa nodded, trying to contain her temper.

"You realize Prosper is a backwater village? Nothing except poor fishermen and farmers," El-Asante explained. "Worse than Ragged Point."

"And?" she inquired. "What is your point?"

"Mistress, the more information you provide," El-Asante resumed, "the better I can assist you in your endeavor."

Essa laughed as she faced him. Her eyes were now frigid, her voice monotone. "Why would you do that?"

"Maybe a chance to keep my, I mean this, ship," El-Asante suggested.

Essa sighed, allowing her irritation to wane at his boldness. Though she held little faith in chance, so she did not blame him for wanting to keep the ship.

"Fair enough. On the slim chance you keep my ship," Essa indicated, making sure he understood she decided who lived or died, "I seek a kobold, a dragon rider and a bounty hunter. His last known location was Prosper."

"Aeros Askin," El-Asante muttered.

"You have heard of him?" Essa snapped.

"Yes, Mistress," El-Asante admitted, knowing he'd just increased his chances of keeping the *Scamp* as his own. "I am aware of him and his black dragon riders. They own a reputation as vicious and successful bounty hunters."

"There are others?"

"Three," El-Asante confirmed.

"It is my understanding three are dead," she announced.

"News to me."

Essa and El-Asante spent several minutes bantering back and forth like swordsmen thrusting and parrying rapiers. Sensing El-Asante may prove valuable beyond his skill as a sailor, Essa described her task without alluding to Deemos. El-Asante strived to strengthen his position by feeding Essa small pieces of information about Aeros and his dragons.

"Captain, I am a simple sailor," El-Asante proclaimed. "However, I understand black dragons and lizard folk seek swamps for their lairs."

"Go on," Essa insisted.

"If I may?" El-Asante requested.

"What?" she demanded.

"The former captain kept maps in his quarters," El-Asante stated. "Can I show you?"

Essa let El-Asante suffer her hardened glare. "Now."

El-Asante summoned another tar to replace him at the tiller prior to leading Essa to the companionway located midship. El-Asante gripped the ladder and slid down to the deck below. Essa caught Rhent's worried, or perhaps his jealous, gaze as she followed the first mate into the captain's quarters. She held her breath and watched El-Asante take his time unrolling the map. The intricate details inscribed on the chart fascinated her, each country, major city, fishing village, bay, inlet, the coastline, and islands annotated on the pirate's map. She loved maps, especially old ones. A map gave her direction and allowed her to plan. They provided a sense of discipline to her life. Essa savored the ink and parchment's smell. For some unexplainable reason, she enjoyed the scent of old maps, acrid with a hint of vanilla.

El-Asante waited for her approval to begin. He watched her study the chart, taking the moment to soak in her beauty. Essa nodded for him to start.

"Mistress, we are here," El-Asante explained, pointing at the map. "South of Welcome. Ragged Point is here. Prosper sits here atop the Ossabow River."

"Swamps?" she queried, following his fingers as they traced the map.

"Yes, swamps cover the Freehold, especially in the south," El-Asante answered. "If Aeros hides here, then these swamps are too small to conceal a black dragon for long."

"Then where?" Essa requested, her voice a whisper as her eyes flitted over the map.

"Here, Mistress," El-Asante replied, pointing to a large isle off the Emirate's southeast coast. "Myre Island. The entire south side of the island is swampland."

"Large enough to hide a black dragon?" she questioned, lifting her eyes to meet his.

"Yes, Mistress," El-Asante grinned.

◊ ◊ ◊

Essa spent the next two days sequestered in the captain's quarters, studying the maps and developing her plan to kill Aeros. She applied her full attention to her task and did not tolerate any distractions. She worked this way ahead of each mission. She gave each detail careful consideration, every angle covered, and nothing left to chance. Her reputation and her success relied on her planning. Now her life and her crew's life depended on it. Her mind drifted to the old man, Deemos. She shuddered at the memory of their encounter. His touch, icy and callous. His eyes, frigid and cruel.

"Enough!" she shrieked, returning to the map. As she focused her thoughts on Aeros and his black dragon, Essa ran her finger slowly around and around the island's coastline as if already searching each cove and inlet for their location. A kobold was an easy kill. The dragon could prove challenging.

A tap on the door interrupted her concentration. Angered by the disruption, Essa hurled a vase at the hatch. "Don't disturb me."

"Mistress, begging your forgiveness," El-Asante pressed. "We have Myre Island in our sights."

Essa gathered her composure and opened the door. "Have someone clean up this mess."

"Yes, Captain." El-Asante bowed as she passed by.

Essa caught Rhent's gaze when she reached the main deck. She motioned for him to join her as she followed El-Asante to the prow. The ocean water misted over the bow, leaving a salty film on her arms and face. Essa saw the island rising above the southern horizon. El-Asante handed her the spyglass.

"Where do you recommend we go ashore?" she asked El-Asante, peering through the spyglass.

"Mid-island windward side," El-Asante answered.

"How soon?" Essa inquired.

El-Asante checked the sun's position, then scanned south. "Just after noon."

"Similar to us, kobolds and dragons possess night vision," she said, almost to herself. "Leaving us no advantage when the sun sets."

Rhent nodded.

"Rhent, gather the others," Essa ordered. "Meet me in the captain's quarters."

Rhent smirked, walking away. Essa stared out over the bow, counting the remaining days. If all went well on Myre Island, she would have plenty to spare.

"First mate, prepare both long boats and sufficient manpower to row my team ashore," Essa ordered. "You will join me."

"But—" El-Asante began protesting until her wintry stare shut him up.

He shook his head. Once the long boats departed, only four crew members would remain aboard. A dangerous situation in perilous waters prowled by pirates. How ironic, he thought. *Pirates concerned about other pirates.*

Essa's crew awaited her arrival. She surveyed the room, took an inventory of her crew. They had accumulated significant wealth and a reputation as well-respected mercenaries under her leadership. *Maybe gold could buy loyalty.* First, Scribe Barclay, he had been with her the longest. He seemed bored, leaning against the bulkhead picking at his fingernails. Maybe even indifferent, nothing new. Next to Scribe stood Packus and Knot. Skilled fighters, ruthless killers who could be head-faked by an anvil. Contrary to ancient conflicts and long-held hatreds between duergar and drow, she found the dark dwarf brothers' dedication to her almost unnatural. Then onto Naszea Jaryne. The dark gnome grinned her way, knowing the time neared when his feet would feel solid ground, when his weapons would draw blood. Then Rhent Dubois, his face stoic, his gaze hardened and focused. Essa suppressed a smile. They were ready.

"Myre Island is our destination," she started. "The southeast side comprises swampland large enough for Aeros and his dragon to hide."

She paused, making sure they followed along.

"We take long boats ashore," she resumed, pointing at the map. "Land here, then move inland."

Midafternoon neared and rain clouds gathered in the west. Essa stood close to El-Asante while he guided the *Scamp* into a sheltered inlet. The deck droned with activity as the crew readied the longboats and the equipment required for the shore excursion. Five hundred yards from the coast, El-Asante ordered the sails lowered and secured. He let the *Scamp* decrease her speed almost to a stop before dropping the anchor. Essa stepped away from El-Asante and made her way to Packus and Knot. "Remove the ship's tiller and bring it along."

She permitted the duergar to take a step. "Don't break it."

They gave her a dismissive shrug while El-Asante shot her a murderous glare, which she disregarded.

Ahead of the approaching storm, the inlet's waters were still calm as the long boats descended and the bright blue was flattening to gray shades of sapphire. Although a dark elf, Essa was a ranger, and she enjoyed the simple beauty of nature. She sucked in a deep breath and held it. It smelled fresh and clean and left a salty taste on her tongue. Colorful fish, big and small, and in all shapes and sizes, darted in and out of the coral reef. A lone sea turtle lazily swam by, its flippers pulling it effortlessly through the water. Without ceasing, gentle waves rolled across the inlet and tenderly lapped against the beach.

Minutes later, the sea dogs rowed Essa and her crew for shore. Near the land, Essa closed her eyes and allowed her senses to reveal the kobold and the dragon. A sneer spread over her thin lips. *They are close.*

Chapter Thirty-Two

Fall 531, Age of the Arch Mage

As they stepped ashore, Essa sent Naszea to scout ahead. Essa moved near El-Asante as his sailors hauled the long boats onto the sand. "I will hunt you down if you leave me stranded here."

As they stepped ashore, El-Asante nodded. He held little interest in facing her wrath again. *Hope the dragon wins.*

"Packus and Knot, grab the oars," she ordered.

Essa fired a murderous glance at El-Asante as she wandered into the woods, followed by Rhent, Scribe, Packus, and Knot. A hundred yards off the beach, they found Naszea waiting for them in a clearing. Packus and Knot hid the tiller and oars underneath the brush.

"I'm no ranger, Mistress," Naszea murmured, wide-eyed. "Hard to miss the damage here."

Essa flashed a hand signal, telling Naszea she understood. She stalked the glen, absorbing the sights, sounds, and scents emanating from the swamp while the others waited and watched. The smell of death, rot, and stagnant water hung heavy in the humid air. Insects buzzed while the birds fluttered through the air and treetops, singing their songs. Lizards and snakes slithered along the ground and coiled around the trees. She noted the broken limbs, the matted grass, and the clawed footprints embedded in the mud. However, it was the bones scattered throughout the clearing, gnawed and pitted, that caught her attention. Kneeling next to the bones, she examined a femur. Running her hand along the bone, she felt the teeth marks, picked up the latent odor of acid.

The drow ranger closed her eyes, slowed her breathing, and blocked out the distractions. Focused on the dragon and the kobold, Essa freed her senses to seek her prey. A sated grin crept over her face when she located them two miles away. A wave of her hand sent her companions onward.

Traveling single file, Essa and her crew traversed the swampland in silence. A persistent mist drifted down from thick gray clouds hanging over the fen, coating clothes and weapons and terrain in a watery sheen. Occasionally, she would halt her companions, allowing an opportunity for her senses to disperse across the swampy terrain. Essa guided them along unmarked trails, around quicksand and bogs.

She felt the danger lurking, sensed the ominous presence as they cleared a bend in the trail. Rain replaced the mist, silencing the swamp as she brought them to a halt. She shuddered when her senses detected the dragon and the kobold looming close.

Naszea lingered near her side, waiting for Essa's order. She pointed to her left, then motioned for him to move. Naszea skulked off, hidden from everyone's view but hers. Another gesture sent Rhent right. She watched the drow fighter slip into the jungle unheard until he vanished from her sight.

Essa drew four arrows from her quiver. She set one into the bowstring while holding the others in her left hand. She peeked behind, finding Scribe and the duergar brothers awaiting her orders. Essa knew they could not pass undetected as a ranger did. They would need her help. She mouthed the words that would mask their steps and mute their movement. She signaled for them to stay close behind.

Essa relied on her intuition as she maneuvered her way through the heavy jungle with the grace of a lioness. She wore a contented grin as she progressed. She was at peace, taking pleasure in stalking her prey. Essa was in control, a drow maiden on the hunt.

Essa paused and eased behind a tree—something was out of place. Closing her eyes, she released her senses again. The dragon remained fixed a hundred yards away and unmoving. Naszea and Rhent neared, attempting to flank the dragon. She detected him lingering above. She found Aeros perched on a limb ten feet above the ground. Essa slowed her breathing, pulling the bowstring tight to her cheek.

She exhaled. Her arrow leapt from her bow, striking the kobold in the shoulder. Aeros squalled, plummeting to the ground. The kobold snapped off the arrow shaft and scrambled to his feet, gripping his long knife. Crouched, he scanned the jungle in desperation for his attacker.

Resilient, Essa mocked, nocking another arrow. She drew the string taut, then waited. She let him suffer, let him dwell on his pending death. Essa loved this part of the game, which was her way. She let the arrow fly when Aeros reached for the talisman hanging around his neck.

Essa knelt near the dead kobold, admiring her handiwork. Two arrows pierced Aeros, one in the shoulder and the other in the neck. She claimed his weapons as her prize and stowed them in her pack. Essa saw the charm that hung around his neck, suspended from a silver chain. She observed the black dragon crafted from tourmaline, the ruby eyes. Essa snatched the talisman, breaking the chain, and slipped it into a pouch hung on her belt. She froze. The dragon's menacing roar echoed through the jungle, the ground trembled under each footstep.

Essa spun around to see Scribe, Knot, and Packus come into view.

"Scribe, come along," she directed. "You two cut off the kobold's head, then wait for our return."

Essa sprinted in the dragon's direction as Scribe trailed behind. Another roar erupted from the dragon, this time closer. The trees groaned, swaying back and forth as if blown by the wind. Essa slowed her pace and motioned for Scribe to seek cover. She armed her bow as the dragon crashed through the trees ahead of her. His enormous body snapped tree trunks and shattered limbs.

His deafening roar, his massive presence, sent a wave of panic over her. She gathered her determination and stood her ground, drawing the bowstring tight. Essa thrust her senses beyond herself. She located Naszea and Rhent rushing to her location. Scribe kept his eyes on Essa and summoned a white energy that formed and grew along his arms.

The great winged lizard bared rows of teeth, jagged and sharp. Skeletal in appearance, his broad head covered in spikes, curved horns were affixed to each side. Asp advanced, each menacing step shuddering the ground. His narrow eyes reflected hate. The black scales encasing his enormous frame resembled plate mail armor. They glistened in a thin sheen of rain. Steam bellowed from flaring nostrils, acid dripped from a forked tongue. Asp fixed his foreboding glare on Essa.

Essa sensed Rhent and Naszea close by. A slight hand motion showed she wanted them to keep their distance. Essa listened to her instincts. She relaxed her draw, permitting the arrow to fall on the ground. Her hands signaled for Scribe to remain vigilant. She removed the talisman from the pouch. Essa heard Asp's deep rumble as she showed him the charm.

He scared her, yet Essa shoved the fear aside as she stepped closer. Asp recoiled, his growl deep and threatening. She pressed forward, gaining confidence with each step. She knew certain dragons could speak and possessed the ability to communicate in the common tongue.

"Aeros, your master, is dead, and I possess the charm," she declared, her tone now confident.

Asp snaked his head back and forth, his eyes never leaving Essa.

"What do I call you?"

"Asp," the dragon answered, his voice low and gravelly. "Aeros was a drunken fool."

"Yes, he was," Essa agreed, taking another step. "Where are the other dragons?"

"Dead!" Asp bellowed. His voice shattered the air and shook the trees.

Essa stopped and held out the talisman. "Are you enslaved to the talisman?"

The dragon recoiled at her question. His face twisted as he snarled and spat a stream of acid onto the ground. Essa watched the acid burn the grass, then looked back at Asp. Somehow Essa swore she saw a hint of sadness behind the dragon's piercing glare.

"Asp, I release you from the talisman's bondage. You are free," Essa declared.

In an instant, the black dragon's leathery wings lifted its massive frame into the air. Asp circled Essa prior to disappearing from her sight.

Essa exhaled sharply while returning the talisman to her pouch. She forced a grin, watching Naszea, Scribe, and Rhent approach. Essa peeked an additional time skyward, then turned to her companions.

"Why did you let him go?" Rhent challenged. "He was worth a fortune."

"And do what? Keep him?" Essa seethed. "Sell him as a slave? Don't permit your greed to wash away your past."

Rhent stared at the ground, avoiding the anger flaring in her eyes.

"Look at your wrist, Rhent," Essa insisted, stomping towards him. She grabbed his wrist and pulled up his sleeve. She fixated on the brand. He did not earn the symbol for bravery or wear the marking as a family tribute. Slavers had seared the numbers into his flesh to identify him as their property. She shoved his arm into his face. "Remember! A number, Rhent, that's all you were to them."

Rhent held his tongue, hoping to sidestep her wrath. She did not relent. Her fury boiled to the surface.

"I am vile to my core," she fumed. "Yet I am not a slave trader and under no circumstance will I become one."

Chapter Thirty-Three

Fall 531, Age of the Arch Mage

From over the horizon, the rising sun painted lithe spindles, pink and orange and yellow, upon a deep blue canvas. A fall chill permeated the air. Winter waited around the corner. The morning elapsed into mid-day as the wagon train journeyed over a rutted dirt road snaking across broad flat grassy plains that dominated the landscape for miles. This region of Beth Amen remained pure and tranquil, unscathed by the orcs and the horrors of war. Seth spent the days riding in each wagon for a couple of hours at a time, wasting away the time talking and laughing with the drivers. Dusk neared when the wagon master brought the train to a halt and circled the wagons. Campfires were lit for cooking and keeping the frosty air at bay. Night came and withdrew into the west, devoid of trouble. A thin frost sheen embraced the grass, trees, and wagons as the train set out for another day.

The days and nights repeated themselves for three additional boring and dusty days. Near mid-morning of day four, Seth recognized them before they came into his view. He knew they must be Horse Tribesmen this far south. Seth let loose his senses to see if she rode among them. Seth smiled. *Raniyah.* He watched them advance from the west, a squad-sized unit comprising Horse Tribe maidens closing at a gallop.

The patrol leader slackened their pace as they approached. "For the horse."

"For the rider," the wagon master returned.

"Honorable wagon master, I am Lieutenant Cathay," she announced. "It would be our pleasure to escort you and your companions into Jacob's Forge."

"Lieutenant, the pleasure will be ours," Sergeant Quinn responded.

As the troopers flanked the wagon column, Seth watched Raniyah Lo'Cain. He smiled at her and waved. She brought her mount beside Seth and Western Union, a sly grin spread over her dusty face. "Ranger."

"Druid."

Raniyah whooped, then leapt from her horse onto Western Union's back. She hugged Seth tight and kissed his cheek. All the wagon drivers and troopers turned and stared at the ranger and druid. Seth chuckled as a wide smile spread across his face. This was Raniyah, wild and free, and no one would ever change her. Raniyah shrugged, then waved. "What?"

The others' reactions showed a mix of embarrassment and amusement. Lieutenant Cathay steered her horse toward Seth and Raniyah. "Sergeant Lo'Cain, I'm going to assume you know the lieutenant?"

"Yes, ma'am!" Raniyah announced without hesitation and kissed Seth again.

"Think we could save the reunion until we are off duty?"

"Uh. Yeah, I guess," Raniyah replied. She squeezed Seth one more time, then returned to her own horse.

Lieutenant Cathay shook her head, then urged her horse for the head of the column.

"Seth, what are you doing this far south?" Raniyah quizzed.

"Headed for Jacob's Forge," he disclosed, avoiding her piercing green eyes.

Raniyah shot him an odd glance, letting him know she suspected he had more to tell her. He shrugged. "Long story, Raniyah."

"Well, we have at least an hour until we attain Jacob's Forge," she retorted. "Is that sufficient time?"

Over the next hour, Seth did most of the talking. She nodded only a couple of times to let him know she was listening. As they rode, he related his tale and the reason behind his journey. Raniyah stared at him for a minute when he concluded and pondered his narrative. "So, you plan on assembling a fighting force from the Blackhawk refugees in Jacob's Forge?"

"Yes," Seth responded.

"Interesting," she muttered. Raniyah remained quiet for several minutes. "You know you will have need of a druid."

Seth chuckled. "I am sure of it. Got anyone in mind?"

He laughed, she did not. Raniyah snorted and glared—he did not amuse her.

The wagon train and the troopers passed beyond the fortifications constructed north of Jacob's Forge after mid-day. Seth sighed, thankful the trek had ended.

"We will see each other soon, Seth Blackhawk," Raniyah giggled, her eyes reflecting a hint of mischief. She reined her horse left and pushed him into a gallop to join her fellow troopers heading for the stables.

He smiled at the thought. "Counting on it."

Seth bade Sergeant Quinn and the wagon drivers farewell, then headed for the village. Seth and Western Union halted and he dismounted, entering the village. Wagons and people crowded the dusty road, bisecting Jacob's Forge as he worked his way south. He felt out of place and uncomfortable as folks pressed in on him. The village seemed to be twice Raphine's size, and some buildings stood three stories tall. Aromas from fresh-baked breads and smoking meats wafted in the air. He passed inns and taverns painted in bright colors, waiting for dusk. Next came the specialty shops, their shelves stocked with hats, armor, and jewelry. Close by, a large general store selling clothes, leather goods, weapons, and more, occupied an entire block.

Seth stopped a Forge Volunteer foot patrol near the village center. "Sergeant, I'm looking for my mother, Helen Blackhawk. Any idea where I can locate her?"

Their mouths fell open and the young troopers did not reply. They gaped at Seth and elbowed each other like they stood before the king.

"Blast," one exclaimed.

"Is this Wulf or Seth?" another whispered to his companion.

"Well, Sergeant?" Seth asked, ignoring their admiration.

"You are Helen Blackhawk's son?" the sergeant inquired, his expression somewhere between joy and admiration.

Seth sighed. "Yes."

"Sergeant, ask him—"

The sergeant waved his hand, shutting up the trooper. "Troopers, look at his rank insignia. This is Lieutenant Seth Blackhawk, the ranger."

"Whoa!" the teenaged troopers shouted in unison. "The ranger!"

"Gentlemen, please," Seth stated. "I am a trooper like you—"

"No way, sir," the sergeant interrupted. "You're a hero!"

"Okay," Seth said, his voice reflecting his frustration. "Troopers, I have completed a long journey and want to find my mother."

"Oh yeah, sure, Lieutenant," the sergeant replied. "Take a right at the next street. You will find her living near the Chieftain's home, a two-story spread. Can't miss it. She shares the house next door with Chief Stockton's wife and daughter."

"Thanks."

Seth ignored their further mumblings as he walked away. Seth and Western Union strolled down a side street until he arrived at a modest one-story home. Once he removed Western Union's tack, he left her to graze on the grass in the front yard and climbed the stairs to the front porch. Seth opened the door and stepped in. A familiar smell greeted him, the sweet aroma of a baking cherry pie. The scent reminded him of home. He recognized the voices. Maria, Louise, and his mother were laughing in the kitchen.

"Momma!"

Chapter Thirty-Four

Fall 531, Age of the Arch Mage

Rain clouds tarnished the sunset as dusk neared. Lightning streaked the sky in thin white threads and thunder boomed deep and low all along the western horizon. A soup-like brume rolled over the plains as the late afternoon air cooled ahead of the pending storm. Riding under Beth Amen's royal banner, Lieutenant Luc Tylee and his platoon of Home Cavalry attained the barriers protecting the northern approach to Jacob's Forge. They had ridden hard for three days from Raphine, only stopping for a few hours to rest and water their horses. Fatigue wore on his troopers and their mounts, and Lieutenant Tylee was eager to shelter in Jacob's Forge before the hard rain fell.

Lieutenant Tylee scanned the village, bathed in a soothing glow from the torches and candles. He knew somewhere tucked inside dwelled his new queen, an unsuspecting young woman who did not know he came to see her. He wondered about her reaction to the news he carried as he patted the satchel slung over his shoulder for the hundredth time. Inside the leather pouch sat the small royal crest, a single silver horseshoe flanked by gold leafing, and a letter from General Stockton.

A fine mist clung to their cloaks, armor, and mounts as they passed unchecked through a series of barricades and obstacles. Lieutenant Tylee and his men's arrival minus King Stockton troubled the Forge Volunteers manning the defenses. Despite their inexperience, they understood the Home Cavalry did not travel without the king except in dire circumstance. They murmured and whispered, their words fearful and morbid.

Empty streets greeted Lieutenant Tylee and his platoon when they entered the city. The shopkeepers had closed their businesses for the day as a peaceful hush fell over Jacob's Forge. He brought his men to a halt when a four-man Volunteer patrol approached. The patrol leader stepped forward. "Your presence minus the King is disturbing, Lieutenant."

"Disturbing times, Sergeant," Tylee replied. "Please know, King Stockton is well."

Amid the torchlight, Luc Tylee noted the Volunteer's relieved expression. "I need your help."

"Sure, Lieutenant," the sergeant responded.

"First, direct my men to the stables and barracks," Tylee requested. "Next, tell me where I can find Chief Jenga Hodge."

"Can do, Lieutenant," the sergeant ensured.

Tylee dismounted and sent his horse with his platoon. The sergeant dispatched two of his men to lead the Home Cavalry platoon to the barracks and stables while he and another Volunteer escorted Lieutenant Tylee to Chief Hodge's residence. A short walk later, Lieutenant Tylee stood outside a simple two-story home. Tylee thanked and dismissed the Volunteers.

Lieutenant Tylee wandered up a torchlit path, climbed the stairs to the veranda, and knocked on the door. A minute passed, then the front door opened, and a large man stepped onto the porch. His eyes flitted from Tylee then into the shadows. Tylee recognized the concern painted on the man's face.

"Lieutenant," the man stammered. "Is the king nearby? No one informed me of his arrival."

"No, the king is not here," Tylee declared. "Are you Chief Hodge?"

The man fidgeted and pulled at his long beard. "Yes. Then why are you here?"

"First, the king is alive and well. He dispatched me on an errand," Tylee explained. From his satchel he produced a sealed envelope. "Chief, send riders to Stirling Hill in the morning and ensure they deliver this dispatch to Joseph Locklynne."

Chief Hodge removed the envelope from Tylee's hand. "Yes, of course. But I don't—"

"Chief, I am not at liberty to discuss this matter now. Perhaps in the next day or so I can provide you a proper explanation," Tylee said, interrupting the chief. "Please tell me where I can find Maria Blackhawk."

"What do you want with Chief Stockton's daughter?"

Lieutenant Tylee did not answer. He tilted his head and scowled.

Chief Hodge let out a harsh breath and pointed to the house adjacent to his. "She and her mother live in the house next door."

"Thank you," Tylee said. Luc strode down the stairs, leaving Chief Hodge perplexed and angry.

Jenga Hodge stood outside his home clutching the envelope and watched Lieutenant Tylee as he first paused in the yard. *What message was he preparing to deliver to them?* He thought Tylee looked pensive, even as climbed the stairs to where Maria and Louise lived. When the lieutenant finally entered the home, Jenga stepped back into his own.

"Something is wrong," he grumbled. He locked the door, already drafting in his head a missive to Joseph Locklynne. Jenga Hodge was the chief of Beth Amen's largest town and he considered himself the monarch's equal. Other village chiefs sought his advice and Jeribai should as well. He leaned against the door and folded his arms across his chest. *Bah, Jeribai. Your father Beracah always consulted me.* To Jenga, information was power and not knowing what the lieutenant intended with Maria Blackhawk left him venerable. Jenga felt slighted by the lieutenant's cryptic manner, and he would articulate his concerns to the realm's steward. He slammed the envelope down on a table and stormed off to bed.

◊ ◊ ◊

Lieutenant Luc Tylee lingered in the mist, staring at the house. He stood near the porch stairs, rehearsing his words one more time. He sighed, attempting to steady his nerves. The last thing he wanted to do was scare the future queen. Tylee paused and considered his last thought and frowned. "Don't be so dull. Of course she will panic. The news I carry will alter the entire course of her life."

Candles burned in the windows, and he heard voices and laughter. He inhaled the comforting aromas of a home-cooked meal as he ascended the steps. Beneath the overhang, he hesitated a moment before knocking.

◊ ◊ ◊

They had gathered for dinner, Helen, Louise, Maria, Seth, and Raniyah, a rare reunion during trying times. The scents of herbed pot roast and fresh baked bread filled the kitchen. The sink overflowed with dishes and there was no rush to clean them. Two empty wine bottles sat on the table, and they were working their way through a third. Regardless of their recent circumstances, they laughed and smiled as they talked, grateful to enjoy one another's company.

Only Raniyah knew of Seth's pending mission to Blackhawk. He wanted to wait for the right opportunity to tell his mother, and tonight seemed like the perfect time. A rap on the front door interrupted Seth's news. After exchanging odd glances among themselves, Seth stood. "Kind of late for visitors."

Seth hurried towards the door. He drew a dagger, palmed it in his hand, then peered out the window. By the uniform, Seth knew the man on the porch was Home Cavalry, but the shadows hid his face. *Why is the king in Jacob's Forge?* Seth moved to the front door and opened it.

Chapter Thirty-Five

Fall 531, Age of the Arch Mage

Speechless, the two men stared at each other until Seth broke the silence.

"Luc Tylee, what are you doing here?" Seth exclaimed. He stepped onto the porch, letting the door shut behind him. "Where is the king?"

"Seth!" Luc shouted. "Um, I am here on other business."

"What other business?" Seth demanded. "Is the king okay? Asa? Jonathon?"

"Seth, stop! Give me a chance to explain," Luc insisted.

"Yeah, sorry."

"Seth, the king is alive and well. So are Chief Stockton and Colonel Stockton," Luc clarified. "I am here to see Maria Blackhawk. Is she present?"

"Maria?" Seth quizzed. He cocked his head, his mind swirled to connect the dots. "What does the Home Cavalry ... Oh, really?"

"Yes. Seth, please, I need to speak to her," Luc persisted.

"Of course, follow me."

Seth and Luc heard the women laughing when they walked into the house. Seth entered the kitchen first, followed by Luc. An eerie silence fell over the women as they gaped at the unexpected presence of the Home Cavalry. Helen clasped Louise's hand in her own and Raniyah put her arm around Maria. Dread and fear consumed Louise and Maria, each convinced something horrible had befallen Asa or Jonathon or both.

"The king, Asa, and Jonathon are alive and well," Seth assured them. He watched their apprehensive expressions evaporate. "Maria, Luc is here to talk to you."

Maria stared, her ebony eyes wide. "Me? What does the Home Cavalry want with me?"

"My lady, I am Lieutenant Luc Tylee," Luc started, as he opened the satchel. He retrieved a small wooden box and the parchment and presented them to her. "My lady, these are for you."

Maria's nervous glance flitted between her mother and the articles in Luc's outstretched hands. "What are they?"

Luc gestured for her to open the box and read the parchment. Maria's hands trembled as she grasped them. She lifted the lid and gasped. She lowered herself into a chair, her eyes riveted on the royal symbol resting atop a piece of purple cloth. Maria lifted her gaze to Lieutenant Tylee. "What does this mean?"

Luc took a knee in front of her, took her hands in his.

"My lady, you are now the Queen of Beth Amen," he announced, his voice gentle. "Queen of the Horse Tribes. My platoon of Home Cavalry is in your service, your life is in our hands, and we will ensure you arrive in Stirling Hill unscathed."

Raniyah and Seth stared at each other in stunned silence. Astonished, Helen shook her head. The words Luc spoke sounded absurd. Louise stifled a laugh—this news did not surprise her in the least. She suspected this would occur when Jeribai evacuated the civilians from Raphine. Her brother-in-law desired a trooper's life, not a king's. Maria shifted her eyes to her mother. "I don't want this."

"Maria, you know I can't ascend the throne," Louise reminded her, noting the anxiety in her daughter's eyes. "I am Stockton by marriage, not blood."

Helen touched Luc's shoulder. "Luc, give us a minute. Please wait outside."

Luc hesitated, questioning the request. Forever loyal, the Home Cavalry did not leave a royal unprotected.

Seth noted Luc's reluctance to leave the new queen. "It's okay. She is safe."

Luc nodded, then departed for the front porch. No one spoke or moved. A hush fell over the room, with their eyes riveted on Maria. Helen waited until she heard the door shut, then sat next to her daughter-in-law. Maria looked at Helen, her eyes begging for an explanation. Helen grasped for Maria's quivering hands. "The king has his reasons, I am sure. You are strong, Maria, and you can do this. You will be a great queen."

"But I am a Blackhawk, not a Stockton," she protested.

"By marriage, Maria," Helen countered. "You are Stockton by birth. The king made the only and obvious choice."

"You sound like Wulf," she chuckled, forcing a thin smile. "I am scared, Helen."

"I know," she consoled. "Do you want me to read the letter?"

Maria nodded in agreement, staring at the royal symbol resting in her hands. Helen broke the wax seal and removed the parchment from the envelope.

"Dear Maria, please forgive me. You too, Louise. Maria, I realize the heavy burden I am placing upon your young shoulders. There have been few decisions I regret more than this one. Our nation faces a determined enemy bent on eradicating our people. And it is with this knowledge I relinquish the throne into your capable hands. I cannot prosecute a war and reign over our land at the same time. I am asking you to lead the nation while I command our brave troopers. As I abdicate my duties as king, I exercise my right according to our laws to retain my title and position as commander of the Beth Amen Army. I also confess I have overstepped my bounds in transferring all but one platoon from the Home Cavalry to serve under my direct authority. My act is illegal, and I will answer for my actions once we rid our land of this current menace. My queen, many dedicated and loyal advisors stand ready to serve you on your arrival at Stirling Hill. Always faithful, Jeribai Stockton, General."

Maria stood and dabbed at the tears forming in her eyes. She gave her mother a pleading look. "You will come as well? You will join me?"

Louise smiled, removed the pin from Maria's hand and pinned it to her daughter's shirt. Louise stepped back, wearing a proud smile. "Of course, my daughter, my queen."

Helen left the others in the kitchen and found Luc waiting on the front porch. Helen smiled. "She will be fine. Thanks for your patience."

"Sure," Luc acknowledged. "What now?"

"Give her a day or two to let all this sink in," Helen advised. "We will protect her in the meantime."

"Okay, ma'am. I am counting on you," Luc agreed, his tone reluctant. "Please tell Queen Stockton I will check on her in the morning."

"First piece of advice," Helen encouraged. "Refer to her as Queen Blackhawk."

"Well, that may prove difficult," Luc admitted. "I will try, and I will pass the word to others. Don't want to be on the wrong side of a Horse Tribe woman."

"Correct," Helen agreed, placing her hands on her hips. "Get some rest, Luc. You look exhausted."

"Good night, ma'am," Luc said, then walked away.

"You too, Luc." Helen lingered on the front porch until Luc vanished into the rain and gloom. She had only one thought in her head. *What would Wulf think of this?* She laughed out loud at the notion. *My son, the consort.*

◊ ◊ ◊

The following morning Lieutenant Tylee paid another visit to Chief Hodge. Luc ascended the stairs and rapped on the door. Jenga opened the door and stepped onto the porch.

"More ambiguous news?" Jenga spat.

Luc ignored Jenga's contempt. "Did your riders depart for Stirling Hill?"

"Yes," Jenga huffed. "How much—"

Luc held up his hand. "Jeribai Stockton abdicated the throne. Maria Blackhawk is now our monarch."

"Blackhawk?" Jenga raked his hand through his hair and looked past Luc. "Why?"

"Not my job to know," Luc retorted as he turned to leave. "Ask the queen."

"Blast." Jenga lowered his frame into a chair. He put his hands behind his head and leaned back. "What have you done, Jeribai? You just placed the fate of the realm on a mere girl's shoulders. Blast."

Jenga stood and gave a bitter laugh. "Absurd."

Chapter Thirty-Six

Fall 531, Age of the Arch Mage

An uncomfortable hush fell upon Jacob's Forge wondering why a Home Cavalry platoon was present without the king. Hearsay and speculation spoke of King Stockton's death. To quell the gossip, Chief Hodge finally issued a decree dispelling the rumors of the king's demise and introducing the new queen. The young queen's presence among them generated excitement within the village. Town criers stood on street corners and in the public squares to ring their hand bells and shout the news. "Hail to the queen! Long live Queen Blackhawk!"

Chief Hodge's proclamation furthered the villagers' curiosity. Everyone, young and old, men, women, and children, all wanted to have a peek at the new monarch. They swarmed around her house until the Home Cavalry and the Forge Volunteers could usher them away.

Seth rested on the front porch, enjoying a peaceful morning. He sipped on a mug of coffee, appreciating the cooler temperatures fall brought to the region. He determined today would be the day he told his mother about his plans for returning to Blackhawk. How would she react? He did not have a clue. Over the last few days, he and Raniyah had recruited fourteen others to their cause, and they planned to leave at week's end. A visit to the quartermaster to gather supplies and the pack animals remained the last piece. The creaking of the front door opening interrupted his musings.

Maria carried two tankards in her hands. She smiled, handing him one.

He laughed. "A little early?"

"It's good to be queen," she quipped. Maria sat down and pulled a draw from her mug. "Seth, is he okay?"

"Of course," Seth assured her. "Wulf is too stubborn not to be."

She giggled and took another drink. She scanned her surroundings. "Where are the onlookers and well-wishers who won't leave me alone?"

"I called in a favor to keep them from bothering you."

"Aren't you out of favors by now?" she asked.

"Not when your sister-in-law is the queen," he chuckled.

"Seth, thanks for keeping the Home Cavalry at bay for a couple of days."

"I thought you needed the time."

"I did," she admitted, her voice steady and confident. "I am ready now."

"Do you want me to have Lieutenant Tylee come see you?"

"Yes," Maria answered. She gazed at Seth as she selected her words. "I am sending him back to Raphine."

"Why?"

"He is a trooper, not a nanny," she stated. "He belongs at the front with my uncle."

"Who will—"

"Don't fret," she interrupted. "I have spoken to Lieutenant Cathay. She and her platoon will be my Home Cavalry. No, I'm going to call them the Queen's Cavalry."

"Are you sure?" he asked. "They are not—"

"I know. They will figure it out like I will." She went quiet for a moment, staring off into the distance. "Seth, what do I do?"

Seth considered her question prior to responding. He could think of many answers to provide her. The simple response was more troopers and additional mounts and supplies. But 'allies' kept spinning in his mind. Why allies? He had often overheard Jeribai, Asa, and Jonathon express their concern over a lack of allies willing to stand with Beth Amen. "Allies, Maria. Allies we can trust to fight alongside of us."

"Will you be one of those?"

"Yes," he vowed. "I will do everything I can to protect Beth Amen and you, my queen."

She stood and looked at him. "I expect nothing less."

In that instant, he realized Maria would be great. He drained his mug, then shut his eyes. Her courage was unmatched, and she may be braver than all of them. Seth rose to his feet and stretched. For the first time in over a month, his leg did not hurt. He opened the door and stepped into the house. "Momma."

He found his mother reading at the kitchen table. She peered at him over her book and smiled. "It is nice to have you here, even for a short time."

Seth returned her smile and sat down.

"When do you head for Raphine?" she asked, closing her book.

"I'm not," he confessed. He saw her expression go everywhere between relief and concern. "I'm going to Blackhawk."

"Blackhawk?" Helen quizzed. Her voice mirrored the confusion on her face.

"Momma, a few days ago I ..." Seth caught himself. Ambushing the orcs would be his and Western Union's secret for now. "I ventured into Blackhawk somewhere southwest of Fairbriar. I happened upon a patrol. They said they belonged to the Blackhawk Brigade based in Turkey Foot."

Seth paused and waited for a reaction that did not come. She sat unmoving, her stare blank and distant. Seth resumed his tale and in a few brief minutes, he had summarized his journey. He then recounted his conversation with Jonathon, Asa, and Jeribai. Seth concluded his story by telling her how he and Raniyah had gathered fourteen others to accompany them. "So?"

Helen smiled and patted his hand. "When do we leave?"

"What?"

"What?" Helen shot back.

"What do you mean?"

"I'm going as well," she declared.

"But your people are here," Seth blurted out.

Helen snorted and gazed over the empty kitchen. She shrugged. "Yes, you. Maria and Louise head for Stirling Hill. There is nothing for me here."

"But—"

"Oh, stop fussing," Helen demanded. "I will not fight. That's your job. But I can contribute in some way."

Seth stared at his mother. Now his expression was somewhere between relief and concern.

"So I ask again," Helen stated, coming to her feet. "When do we leave?"

"In three days," he mumbled.

"Well, then," she laughed, ambling out of the room. "I need to pack."

Seth sat at the table, his eyes fixed on the kitchen wall, not sure if the conversation went well or not. It certainly did not go the way he thought it would. He expected tears and anger, not another travel companion. A rap at the kitchen door interrupted his thoughts. He looked at the door and saw Raniyah. He motioned for her to enter.

"Did you see a ghost, ranger?" she cackled, her smile and eyes bright.

"I told my mom our plans for going to Blackhawk," Seth admitted.

"Oh. And?"

"She is coming as well," Seth uttered.

Raniyah laughed so hard her eyes teared. "I love your mom!"

"W-what?" Seth stammered in disbelief. He noticed a pattern among the women in his life. Unpredictable.

"Come on, ranger," Raniyah insisted, dabbing at the tears in her eyes. She kissed him on the cheek. "Since you did such a good job informing your mother, you can help me tell my parents."

"Yeah, a great job," Seth replied sarcastically. "But I need to find Luc first."

Chapter Thirty-Seven

Fall 531, Age of the Arch Mage

Maria Blackhawk, Queen of the Horse Tribes, and Louise Stockton, Royal Advisor to the Queen, sat on the front porch enjoying a crisp fall day. Maria saw him and four Home Cavalry troopers near. She stood, waved, and called his name. Lieutenant Luc Tylee returned her greeting. He positioned two troopers at the front gate and strode to the porch. He stopped at the stairs and saluted. "My lady."

Maria motioned for him to join her and Louise. "Afternoon, Luc. Please come and sit."

He left the other troopers at the bottom of the stairs. He climbed the steps and sat near Maria. Luc detected a complete change in her manner and her expression. She smiled, confident and composed. She exuded a simple dignity that defied her age.

"Luc," Maria hesitated. "Or do I call you Lieutenant?"

"Either works, my lady," he admitted.

"Okay," she stated. "I don't want to violate protocol."

"My queen, be yourself," he advised. "You will learn, and we will adapt."

Maria shrugged her shoulders and grinned.

"Luc, this is my mother, Louise Stockton," Maria introduced. "She will serve as my advisor. You are free to discuss any matter in her presence."

Lieutenant Tylee nodded and smiled. "Ma'am."

Louise said nothing and returned his smile.

"Luc, I am ready now," Maria professed. "Thank you for your patience."

"Of course, my lady."

"Luc, I am sending you and your platoon back to General Stockton," she announced, leaning forward in her chair. "You are fighters and belong at the front, not in Stirling Hill."

"But who—"

"Not your problem anymore," she assured, cutting him off. She had decided it required no further discussion. "I have a plan. Now please summon Chief Hodge and Lieutenant Cathay to join us."

Lieutenant Tylee wanted to protest further, but her stern demeanor warned him to keep his opinions to himself. He came to his feet and saluted. He spun about, then marched off. Luc paused at the gate—he could not wipe the smile from his face. He and his men wanted nothing more than to return north.

◊ ◊ ◊

Louise greeted Chief Jenga Hodge, Lieutenant Rebekka Cathay, and Lieutenant Luc Tylee at the door when they arrived. "Welcome. Queen Blackhawk awaits your arrival."

"Queen Blackhawk?" Chief Hodge asked, his tone a blend of confusion and acrimony.

Louise smirked at his discomfort. "She is married."

"Hm," he muttered. "So the Stockton line has—"

"For now," she interrupted.

"Strange. Louise, I have sought an audience for days," Jenga complained, his voice low and raspy. "Each time she rebuffed me."

"Oh, Jenga, don't think you are special," Louise chided. "She has avoided everyone, including her Home Cavalry."

Louise ushered them into the kitchen, where Maria sat waiting. Each one offered a respectful bow. Maria smiled, then motioned for them to sit at the table. "Thank you for coming on short notice."

Observing them seek a favorable seat amused her. These were the subtleties she would have to learn or dismiss as ridiculous. Luc sat on her right and Rebekka to her left. Jenga seated himself in front of her.

"I won't waste your time any longer than necessary. I will be blunt and to the point," she declared. "Chief Hodge, I request the transfer of Lieutenant Cathay and her platoon from your authority to mine. I want them to serve as my Queen's Cavalry so I can send Lieutenant Tylee and his troopers back to General Stockton."

Hodge glanced over at each lieutenant and Louise, then back to Maria. Thinking he could intimidate Maria, he narrowed his eyes and fixed his gaze on her. "I worry about the orcs."

"If the orcs breach the defenses at the Mulford," she explained, her glare meeting his, "they will roll over Jacob's Forge with or without Lieutenant Cathay and her platoon. The orcs won't stop until they stand outside Highpoint. We all know this."

Stalling, he rubbed his bearded chin. "Queen Stock ... I mean Queen Blackhawk, this is a most unusual request. I will need some time to—"

"Chief!" she interjected, her voice stern and steady. She ignored his intended snub and allowed her eyes to portray her anger. "I have little patience for being tested or my authority being questioned. I leave in a few days and have no time for delays, so I expect your answer now."

Louise grimaced. Jenga Hodge was a seasoned chieftain who would not tolerate his authority being challenged in public. Gruff in manner and appearance, he cast an imposing shadow over normal-sized men. His eyes became hard and unforgiving. Hodge was an effective leader, calculating and impatient. Under his tenure as chieftain, Jacob's Forge matured from a village into a vibrant city. It rivaled Stirling Hill. She studied her daughter and fought back a grin. She had not seen this side of Maria, steadfast and determined.

Maria did not blink or back down. Her ebony eyes locked onto his. Luc and Rebekka eased their hands to sword hilts while absorbing the pending confrontation. They peeked at each other, knowing the queen faced her first challenge.

Her blatant request flustered him. He hesitated, deciding on a response to her request. Hodge wanted to say no. He was a politician, there must be negotiations, offers and counteroffers. Then he thought otherwise. Quarreling with the young queen may not be prudent considering her uncle's, father's, and brother's popularity among the citizens. In the end, it would be a quarrel he would lose. He exhaled in frustration. "Of course, my queen. As of right now, they are in your service."

"Thank you, Chief Hodge. Our business is done," Maria smiled, coming to her feet. "Luc and Rebekka, you have work to do. Thank you for coming."

Chief Hodge and the lieutenants rose and followed Louise to the front door. She opened the door. "Good day."

Red-faced, Hodge dithered on the porch until the lieutenants walked out of ear- shot. "Louise, I was not—"

"Jenga, I advise you to quit while you are ahead," Louise suggested. "Go. I will talk to her on your behalf."

He frowned, then trudged home.

Louise leaned against the porch column and watched him depart. She chuckled to herself. *Jeribai, you magnificent bastard, you made the right choice.* She spun toward the door and jumped. She had forgotten about the two troopers guarding the entrance. "Blast. I will have to remember you are here."

Chapter Thirty-Eight

Fall 531, Age of the Arch Mage

Essa's return journey from Myre Island was effortless. Calm seas and prevailing winds propelled the meager dhow back to Welcome. Essa and her crew arrived in port in the late afternoon, having plenty of days to spare.

She had recovered the talisman and possessed the kobold's head as Deemos demanded. Essa allowed El-Asante to keep possession of the *Scamp*. His talents and experience had proved invaluable to her success. In the end, she respected Chara El-Asante, and she would work alongside him again.

Welcome had shrugged off last night's stupor and was coming awake. The village stood ready for another round of debauchery. Essa and her crew tramped into the Silver Toad and stopped at the front desk. She requested the clerk deliver four wine bottles and pails of hot water to her room. Essa wanted nothing to do with crowds. She planned on spending the rest of the day alone.

"We will meet down here at noon tomorrow," Essa announced to her crew. She did not wait for them to answer, climbing the stairs to her room.

Essa shut and locked the door. She yanked the thick curtains closed and lingered, soaking in the dark. As a drow, she should find comfort in the dark, yet often she did not. For the first thirteen years of her life, Essa had lived in darkness. This darkened room reminded her of the Belowground, painful memories she sought to forget. Her sire, or at least she thought he was, instructed her in the ways of a ranger, how to track, heal, and to move unseen and unheard. He taught her how to fight using the sword, bow, and long knife, and with her hands. At an early age, employing cunning and speed, she bested her older and stronger brothers. Her sire stressed planning and study. Rash and negligent behavior got you killed. Her sire was a cruel teacher, and she suffered physically and mentally under his tutelage. She endured his wrath for the slightest mistake and her back bore the evidence. Even in success, his praise was critical. Only perfection will keep you alive, he screamed.

As cruel as her sire was, her mother, Mallas Jaragua, surpassed him. As a proper drow matron and a devoted acolyte of the spider queen, Mallas showed no affection for her children or her children's sires. Mallas governed her sprawling estate with an iron scepter. Essa grew up in a house filled with hate and suspicion. She learned at an early age to trust no one but herself. Each female child born into the house became a status symbol that Mallas paraded around the village streets for all to see. Mallas used her children as a statement of her own youth, beauty, and fertility.

Essa swatted away the memories like they were gnats. She lit a single candle. Essa sat on the bed, staring at the candle flickering in the darkened room. Shadows from the flame whirled and twirled across the walls, floor, and ceiling. Her musings drifted to the *Scamp*...

A sharp rap on the door snapped her back. Essa unlocked and opened the door. She permitted the chambermaids to pour buckets of hot water into the tub and spread buckets of embers into the cast iron heat box beneath it. Essa relocked the door, popped the cork, then drew a long drink from the bottle.

She shed her dirty clothing and slipped into the tub and closed her eyes. The hot water soothed her aching muscles and washed off layers of grime. Essa was unsure of how to proceed. Despite her success, she did not want to face Deemos again. She despised him, every fiber in her body hated him. No one had ever frightened her as he did. Deemos possessed an inherent evil she had not encountered in her life, and she had met plenty of evil beings in her past, including her mother and sire. She gagged at the notion of Deemos's knotty hands touching her skin. She kept reminding herself she was deadly, a drow maiden, lethal and malicious. Essa repeated the words out loud over and over, trying to convince herself it remained true. A skilled assassin, ranger, and mercenary, yet Deemos lingered in her head for reasons she could not explain. His fierce glare terrified her, sapped her confidence. It ripped the scabs off memories she'd buried years ago. Essa rubbed her left wrist, touched the ugly raised scars.

Essa drained the wine bottle, then shut her eyes once more. Her village occupied a lightless cavern a few hundred yards below Gaiand's surface. She had celebrated her thirteenth birthday the day before they came. Essa's mother had made a spectacle of her youngest daughter coming of age and Essa's formal entry into the service of the spider queen. The slavers assaulted the village from the east as dawn neared. Hundreds strong and bearing torches, they swept through the village, pillaging, burning, and killing. Shouts from the men and the screaming from the dying and wounded drow echoed in her mind. Although the drow warriors fought with unmatched bravery, the raiders outnumbered them. They rounded up the survivors, men, women, and children, and chained them together.

To this day, she could see their leader, a necromancer, tall and imposing, similar in so many ways to Deemos. He hid his face inside the cowl of his ashen robes. The end of his staff emitted light, brilliant and grim. Essa remembered him and his lieutenant strutting down the line of prisoners. He would pause and study the females. His hands, calloused and gnarled, lifted their faces to meet his soulless gaze. Essa shivered. His touch to her skin felt cold and heartless.

They herded them from the village to the surface like cattle. The snaps from their cruel whips kept the drow in line. On the surface, the sunlight, harsh and bright, burned her eyes and skin, sapped her strength. For days, they marched onward—no food, water, or rest. When a drow fell from exhaustion or injury, they left them to die. Half of the prisoners survived the journey to the slavers' camp. They forced the drow into a single file inside narrow chutes for processing. From her place in line, she heard the shrieks, smelled the searing flesh. It took two slavers to restrain her. She tried to scream, but it stuck in her throat. Essa's eyes went wide as the brand, glowing orange and crimson, neared her left wrist. She felt the ...

"No!" Essa yelled. She shot up in the tub, gasping for breath. She clutched her left wrist. Essa felt the brand pressed into the palm of her hand. Her eyes flitted over the empty room. She put her head in her hands for a long moment, trying to regain control. She leaned back against the tub and exhaled. Essa grabbed another bottle, popped the cork, and chugged it half empty. She continued soaking and drinking the rest of the night and into the early morning. The alcohol eased her pain, erased her fears, at least for the moment.

Essa missed her meeting with her team and shunned them while waiting for the days to pass. Only Rhent appeared bothered by her reclusive behavior. She expected this. He had always wanted more from her than she desired to give him. Some day? Maybe? The others could care less. They enjoyed the down time, wasting away the hours and their money in the taverns and gambling parlors.

◊ ◊ ◊

Essa and Rhent sat in an empty candlelit room waiting for Deemos's arrival. Her stomach churned, consumed by dread, and she fought back against the nausea. She trembled and grabbed Rhent's hand when Deemos strolled into the room. Deemos neglected Rhent and fixed his lecherous gaze on Essa. She endured his leering, his lustful gape.

"Well?" Deemos jeered, lowering himself into a chair.

Essa handed the talisman and the bag holding the kobold's head to Rhent. The drow fighter stood and placed the items on the table. Deemos pocketed the dragon charm. He smiled, then laughed, peering into the bag. He had the kobold's head and controlled the talisman. I should kill her now, he thought for a fleeting second. Instead, he stayed his hand. He saw a hatred in her dark eyes that mirrored his own. The drow maiden possessed the skills and experience he might exploit in the future. Deemos set two sacks on the table.

"Payment in full," he pronounced.

Essa pointed at the sacks. Rhent nodded and removed the sacks from the table. Deemos stood, his gaze still fixed upon Essa.

"Take this, Essa Jaragua," Deemos ordered as he set the Scrawlstone on the table. "Carry it with you at all times. There will be further work for you. Additional fame, glory, and wealth await you. More than you can imagine."

"What is it?" she queried. Her voice quivered as she stared at the stone.

"A Scrawlstone," he answered. "It allows me to communicate with you even when I can't see your lovely face. When I call, you answer."

"No!" Essa blurted out. "No more working for you."

"Come now, your success will please my master," he chided.

"Forget your master!" Essa yelled.

"Ah, you have no choice, my dear," Deemos responded, his tone and expression mimicking his depraved heart. "I own you now. I speak your language, Essa Jaragua."

"Which is?" she demanded.

Deemos cackled, low and eerie, moving for the door. "Money and power. I will be in touch."

"Does this stupid rock have instructions?" Essa yelled.

Deemos paused and peered back. Madness and wickedness ruled his thinking. A scowl formed on his face, his eyes glared at her with a cruel intent. "Trust me, drow maiden, you are not as clever as you think."

Essa fought the urge to scream as Deemos exited the room.

Chapter Thirty-Nine

Fall 531, Age of the Arch Mage

At week's end, they assembled at the stables—seventeen in all. Wrapped in heavy cloaks, they completed final preparations. They tightened tack and saddle bags and strapped their weapons and quivers in place. A final check ensured the equipment carried by the pack animals was lashed tight to the packsaddles. Horses and mules snorted and pawed at the ground. A thin layer of frost clung to the earth and plants and the air, sharp and cold. Sunrise gathered in the east. Shards of scarlet, orange, and pink streaked a dawn blue sky. A promising start for a long journey.

As Seth formed them into a traveling column, Helen Blackhawk trotted up astride Salmista. Seth chuckled at her. His mother wore a chainmail shirt, a cavalry saber and quiver strapped to her saddle and the longbow slung across her back. He knew she had a pair of long knives hidden somewhere on her body. "I thought you were not fighting."

"Hush, child," Helen chided, sticking her nose in the air, her eyes and smile mischievous. "I am a Blackhawk matron raised among the Horse Tribes. My weapons are a part of me."

Raniyah and the others laughed at Seth's expense as Helen rode by.

Seth ignored their chiding as he considered those assembled. His mother—well, Helen Blackhawk was as tough as horseshoe nails and no one would underestimate her strength and prowess. Then there was Raniyah Lo'Cain, who was as free as her wild auburn hair and untamable spirit. She was a druid, a protector of nature and a devout follower of the Maiden. The rest were an assorted collection of young men and woman, each one seeking adventure and maybe a small measure of revenge. The eldest, Band Dollor, was twenty-two and the youngest, Fynn Skinner, fifteen. The others fell somewhere in between. Together they would return home to rid Blackhawk of orcs.

"Mount up," Seth ordered.

"Lieutenant Blackhawk."

He paused when he heard his name called. Seth glanced over his shoulder and viewed Maria, Louise, the Queen's Cavalry, and the Home Cavalry. He chuckled—it was quite the spectacle to say goodbye to a seventeen refugees returning home. "My queen."

Maria dismounted and stood before Helen and Raniyah. There had been too many goodbyes of late and she hated the thought of this one. She embraced both with a long hug and forced smile as she released them. "I will always need both of you."

She turned to Seth, her expression now serious. She pulled him close and kissed him on the cheek. She locked her eyes onto his and clutched his hands in hers.

"Win, Seth Blackhawk. Whatever it takes, win," she whispered. "Protect my border and rid Blackhawk of the evil that walks your land."

"I will," he vowed. He climbed onto Western Union and urged her into a trot.

For a few minutes, Maria stood and watched Seth, Helen, Raniyah, and the others ride off. A sadness crept into her. It was a similar feeling she had while watching Wulf ride away. Her emotions were confused and jumbled. She would miss them but desperately needed them to succeed. She possessed limited knowledge of military tactics, yet she knew that Beth Amen could not fight a two-front war. *May the Maiden bless every step you take.* She remounted her horse and glanced at Luc Tylee.

"Ride north, Lieutenant," Maria commanded. "And thank you."

"My queen." Luc bowed his head. "Home Cavalry, forward."

She sat motionless and mouthed a silent prayer as Luc and his men galloped north. Maria sighed, knowing it was time to head for Stirling Hill.

"I am in no mood to face Chief Hodge," Maria confessed. She smiled, looking at her mother and Rebekka. "Let's sneak away before the village wakes up."

◊ ◊ ◊

Out onto the plains northeast of Jacob's Forge, Seth and his company rode. The morning sun, a brilliant yellow orb, broke over the horizon, bathing the landscape in a welcoming golden hue, warming the air and driving the chill west. For a better part of the morning, they rode in quiet speculation on a course that would lead them into southeast Blackhawk and home. Seth peeked over at

Raniyah and then his mother. He was thankful for their companionship, and, at the moment, content.

The days and nights, five in all, passed incident-free. This area of Beth Amen was far enough removed from the war fronts it remained unscathed and unscarred. The plains on which they rode were broad and flat, and occasionally interrupted by buttes and escarpments. Over those days, Raniyah directed their attention to every variety of plant, bug, bird, and animal they encountered, her explanations in depth and, at times, exhausting. Shaggy-haired buffalo herds roamed the vast tracts of grasslands that dominated the nation's eastern side. Pronghorns, white-rumped and wearing their winter fur, were migrating south seeking warmer climates as the mating season neared. Hawks and eagles, their wings spread wide, soared on the wind currents, seeking their prey.

On the afternoon of day six, Seth brought his little band to a halt. They stood on the banks of the Hebrum River. Before them lay their homeland. Seth glanced over his shoulder. Fifteen smiles greeted him in return. He snuck a quick peek at his mother. He could not read her expression. Her lips formed a distinct line. Seth was not sure of her reaction, sorrow or joy, or maybe both.

"Momma, lead us over."

Helen's grin back to Seth was quick and determined. She urged Salmista ahead. The black stallion plunged forward, his powerful legs churning the chilled water. Reaching the other side, Salmista ascended the riverbank in four graceful strides. Helen guided him into the forestlands and reined the stallion to a halt. She gazed about. In all the seasons away, Helen did not imagine she would see Blackhawk again. Memories flooded her mind. Teddy, Wulf, and Kiah. Her garden, home, horses, and friends. All forever branded in her heart. Helen pursed her lips. She did not want to cry, yet the enormity of the situation swept over her. It was a spring flood of emotion. Finally turning back to survey her companions, a knowing sigh escaped Helen. No one, including her stoic son, had dry eyes.

Raniyah drank in the forest air and let it fill her lungs, wet leaves, damp wood, and the smell of rot all blending to create an earthy scent. Birdsong, skittering squirrels, and chirping bugs satisfied her senses. As a druid, as a child of nature, this was where she belonged. It was here, above all other places, she desired to be.

Single file, they rode into the coming dusk. The late afternoon sun languished in the west, keeping temperatures tolerable. Thin threads of nearly horizontal sunlight snuck between the tree trunks and striped the ground in narrow shadowy bands. Seth kept them tacking northwest. He knew Turkey Foot lay along the banks of the Rappacion River. An hour farther on, they reached the Rappacion and Seth turned them due north. Seth brought up his hand, signaling for them to halt. He slid off of Western Union, pulled up his cowl, and pointed at Raniyah. "Stay."

"Woof." Raniyah rolled her eyes and dismissed him with a rude hand gesture.

Seth disregarded her sarcasm and scurried off. In a matter of seconds, he vanished.

Helen peered at Raniyah. "Am I the only one who finds what he just did a little disturbing?"

"Nope," Raniyah droned. "Creeps me out every time."

Seth slowed his pace and cast out his senses. He located thirteen humans trudging east less than a mile away. Unheard and unseen, he sprinted, navigating trees and brush. Each movement, every footfall, silent. His route placed him ahead of the patrol. Seth eased behind a tree. The humans were loud as they neared. Crunching leaves, cracking twigs, their breathing, and the stench of their sweat gave away their location. Seth inched from the tree and into their path. He jerked the cowl from his head and raised his hands in the air. Seth watched as they faltered at his sudden appearance. They scrambled, drawing their weapons and arming their bows. Seth laughed and dropped his hands—he recognized their patrol leader. "Cade."

◊ ◊ ◊

Torches blazed in the waning day, their flames an act of defiance. The defenders of Turkey Foot wanted the invaders to see the light boldly burning in the pending twilight. The flames, like their fighting spirit, would endure. Escorted by Cade Badeaux and his patrol, Seth, Helen, Raniyah, and their small company entered Turkey Foot. The curious villagers lined the dirt streets as the procession rode by. Voices, nothing more than a whisper, wondered who these strangers were. Some said prisoners while others mourned the arrival of additional refugees. Captain Ilai Blackhawk stopped in the center of the road. His hands were on his hips and a scowl disfigured his face.

"By the Maiden," Ilai roared. "What do we have here, Lieutenant Badeaux? More refugees?"

"No, sir," Cade responded, his smile sly. He gestured to Seth. "Captain, I give you Seth Blackhawk and his company."

Seth beamed at the recognition. Raniyah raised her eyebrows and wrinkled her nose.

"What did he call us?" Fynn asked Band quietly.

"Seth and company," Band answered.

"When did we agree to that name?" Fynn said with a half-smile.

"We didn't," Band confirmed with the other half of the smile.

"I thought this was a group collaboration?" Fynn inquired. "You know, each of us having our own specialty."

"I wish they had consulted me on the title of our group," Band confessed, barely containing his laughter.

"It just hurts," Fynn admitted, just loud enough for Helen to hear.

Helen cocked her head and glared at Fynn and Band. "Hush! If anything, it's my company."

Ilai tilted his head to one side and lifted an eyebrow. Seth halted Western Union, dismounted, and strode toward Ilai. He stuck out his hand and grinned. "Seth Blackhawk, Captain."

"Welcome home!" Ilai roared. He shook Seth's hand, then wrapped him in a massive bear hug. Mid-embrace, Ilai looked past Seth's shoulder and lowered the ranger to the ground. He nudged Seth aside and reached for her hands. "By the Maiden, Raniyah Lo'Cain.

"Helen, Helen Blackhawk!" A booming voice shattered the din. "Do my aging eyes fail?"

Helen pulled back her cowl and raven colored hair spilled from beneath. She wiped the strands from her eyes and smiled. "Ezra."

Chapter Forty

Fall 531, Age of the Arch Mage

Daybreak loitered in the east, sunrise tarried below the horizon and a waning full moon bathed Ripley's Keep in an unnatural orange luster. A brume, thick and heavy, rolled over the barren landscape, seeping into the cracks and crevices. The mist swirled about the scrub and rock outcrops, cleaving to them like a cloak, mottled and torn. A thin sheet of frost blanketed the terrain and kept the ground from thawing.

In the predawn, Colonel Espen Asbyorn, accompanied by Major Dag Einar and the half-orc Skrabb, paused near the edge of their encampment.

"Was the poison Gambier provided distributed and applied to the bolts and blades?" Asbyorn inquired, the disgust dripping in his words.

Einar frowned and spat on the ground. "Yes, cowards use—"

Asbyorn held up his hand. "Under normal circumstances, yes. These are not normal circumstances, Major."

Major Einar did not offer a response. He thought less of this mission with each passing minute. Colonel Asbyorn ignored his brooding major as he studied the ancient bastion lofting above the plains. His limited knowledge of the fortress worried him. He possessed no idea what lurked inside the walls. The Keep's stone walls, drab and somber, rose twenty feet high. There were no towers, turrets, or a gatehouse. A lone road led to a wooden ironbound gate. Guards absent from the ramparts concerned him. What lay hidden behind the walls, he wondered to himself? Shadows draped about Ripley's. Not a single torch or candle burned. From here, the Keep appeared undefended. His assessment seemed consistent with the information he had received prior to departing Udontawny.

"Seems Gambier provided correct information."

"Agreed," Major Einar concurred.

Colonel Asbyorn turned to the half-orc standing on his right.

"You may begin your attack," he instructed. "Skrabb, the prince is to be captured, not killed. If there are others, I don't care what you do to them."

Skrabb grunted, then strode off.

"Major, prepare our soldiers," Asbyorn directed. "In the event the orcs fail."

Major Einar saluted, then marched away.

◊ ◊ ◊

The first wave of orcs surged forward, emerging from the morning's murk and haze, their chain mail armor and sword sheaths clanking on each step. The lead ranks lugged the siege ladders and the climbing ropes for scaling the walls. Behind them marched the crossbowmen and archers, reinforcements, and the orcs bearing the battering ram. Skrabb ascended a rock outcrop to observe the assault. A sneer, content and cruel, spread over his deformed face as his orcs clambered up the Keep's wall unopposed.

◊ ◊ ◊

Kheel reacted first, hearing their taunts and curses, the scuffling of their boots as they traversed the courtyard. Conjuring his magic, Kheel flung open the front door. Fiery orbs exploded from his hands, consuming the orcs nearest to the house. Kheel dove for cover behind the door, avoiding a barrage of orc crossbow bolts. Coming to his feet, he detected two orcs scrabble into the house. In an instant, lightning arced from his hands, ripping into the attackers.

Awakened by the screams from the dying orcs and Kheel's shouts, Francis and Mora sprinted from their bedroom to the front of the house. Mora entered the living room as Kheel unleashed another lightning bolt. The arcane energy leaping from his hand tore into the orcs' chainmail, searing flesh, enveloping them in a killing white light.

Mora froze, her mouth agape as she watched her son. He should have been afraid, yet she did not notice the slightest hint of fear. To her surprise, she saw anger. Kheel's magic, raw and savage, pulsed unconstrained, like the blood flowing in his veins. He was at a tipping point, almost out of control.

Francis headed for the open door, confident this was nothing more than a rabble of orcs seeking to pillage the Keep. Surely, three arcane casters should be able to dispatch them with little effort. He stepped outside into the coming dawn and froze. Francis gasped at the sight and changed his mind. Orcs moved all over the courtyard. He conjured the wind in his outstretched hands. Motioning his arms, he brushed aside the additional orcs approaching the house. Calling forth another cantrip, Francis scattered the dawn's early brightness in a brilliant flash of white light, blinding the orcs for a few seconds and illuminating the courtyard.

Kheel bolted after his father. Kheel swept his arms in a wide arc, blanketing the courtyard with fiery shards flying from his hands. Ablaze, the orcs screamed and howled in agony while the flames devoured them. Kheel pivoted right. He pitched a fireball, slaying the orcs racing for the stables. The blast shredded the enemy like scarecrows, spraying rock, dirt, and dust the full breadth of the Keep. Over and over, he threw out scythes of fire slicing into the orcs. After clearing the courtyard, Kheel rushed to the wall, his father trailing close behind.

Francis grabbed Kheel by the arm as they reached the rampart stairs. "Use your magic as a shield,"

"How?"

"The way you did all this," Francis answered, pointing at the dead.

"I just thought about it," Kheel confessed.

"Do that then." Francis spoke the words and summoned his arcane shield, then bounded up the stairs.

Kheel repeated his father's words and felt his arcana wrap itself around him in an invisible shield, then climbed the stairs. Kheel and Francis peered west, observing hundreds of orcs positioned for another assault. Francis scanned to the north, south, and east and found that the orcs surrounded Ripley's Keep. *Trapped.*

◊ ◊ ◊

Mora cursed her arrogance. They should have set wards around the Keep to warn them of unwanted intrusions. She stared at the dead orcs. Five red slashes emblazoned their armor. Their markings looked familiar. She had seen them before but could not remember when or where. This was not a roving band of orcs, this was an army. At that moment, Mora panicked. She gazed about—fleeing became her sole thought. She and her family used their magic for study and gaining knowledge, not fighting.

"Francis and Kheel, come back," she yelled. "We can tele—"

The windows behind Mora shattered, spraying glass fragments and splinters into the living room. She ducked and raised her hands to protect her face. The broken glass peppered her body, slashed exposed flesh, and ripped her clothes. She recoiled when the bolt grazed her left shoulder, drawing blood. The orcs swarmed into the house through the broken windows. Mora staggered to her feet, calling forth her spell. A second bolt pierced her thigh, breaking her concentration and sending her to her knees. The orcs advanced on her, jeering and brandishing their swords. Mora ignored her injuries and focused her mind. She sent forth white hot slivers of energy. Lightning leapt from her hands, slicing into their bodies, scorching skin and melting armor.

"Belhaaz," Mora murmured. "The markings are of Belhaaz ..."

Her words slipped away as she struggled to concentrate. *Why?* Troubled by her notions, she glanced about, wondering if someone had betrayed them. *Who?* As the adrenalin from the fight waned, she felt the searing pain running up and down her arm and leg, perceived a numbness spreading in her body. Her mind fogged, then her knees buckled. She reeled back. Her hands reached for the wall to steady herself. Mora gasped for breath as she lowered herself to the floor. *Poison,* Mora concluded, as her consciousness faded.

Chapter Forty-One

Fall 531, Age of the Arch Mage

Another wave of orcs swelled onto the battlements as Francis and Kheel readied themselves. Francis raced north along the ramparts. Sleet and hail emitting from his hands buffeted the invaders. Wounded and blind, the orcs lost traction and plunged to the ground. Francis summoned the wind once more. Francis moved his hands back and forth, releasing a ferocious squall that removed the siege ladders and climbing ropes from the entire length of the west wall. Kheel proceeded south. He unleashed a flurry of fireballs, sweeping the orcs from the battlements. Afire, the orcs died in place or jumped to their deaths trying to extinguish the flames.

The impact from the battering ram slamming into the gate shook the wall. Kheel caught himself and peered over the battlements as the ram collided into the gate once more. The gate groaned from the impact, its wooden planks cracking and splintering. Kheel raised his hands above his head and called forth his spell. He stomped his foot and thrust his hands down. He focused his arcana on the dirt path. The incantation buckled the road, opened deep fissures in the ground, rendering it unpassable. A score of orcs and the battering ram tumbled into the fractures and crevices. They perished beneath a torrent of rock and stone. The remaining orcs hesitated. Kheel hurled two more fireballs into their thinning ranks. Their valor failed. In unison, the orcs quit and fled.

The morning sun embarking on its daily journey sat low in the eastern sky when Francis and Kheel repelled the initial assault. They watched in grim vindication as the orcs abandoned the attack. Francis scanned the Keep. It lay in ruins. Dead orcs littered the courtyard, ramparts, and the ground beyond the walls, the earth and walls scorched and streaked. Pungent odors from burnt skin and blood hung in the air.

He paused and looked at the house. *Mora.*

◊ ◊ ◊

Skrabb, dejected and furious, remained atop the rocks many yards west of the Keep. Twenty minutes earlier, his orcs had swarmed over the walls without resistance. Explosions, followed by the screams, crushed his confidence. He was helpless, watching the two magic-users repel each wave of the attack. With fire and ice and wind, the wizards swept the orcs, ladders, and ropes from the walls. Then the earth in front of the gate buckled and rolled. A fissure in the ground opened. Twenty orcs perished and the battering ram was lost beneath rock and stone. His orcs faltered, their courage evaporated. In minutes, the wizards killed over half of his force. Everywhere he looked, the orcs were dying. Two more fireballs exploded in their midst and panicked the rest of his orcs. As one, the rest of his force fled.

◊ ◊ ◊

Francis left Kheel to defend the walls and sprinted for the house. Francis entered the house by the front door, calling for Mora. Shattered glass and six dead orcs lay scattered over the stone floor. Shredded and singed, the curtains fluttered in a scant breeze blowing in from the broken windows.

When he discovered her, Francis thought her dead. She did not stir as he neared. Mora slumped against a wall, her eyes closed and her skin ashen. She sat in a pool of her own blood. It had splattered across her face, clothes, and arms. Blood flowed from deep lacerations on her face, hands, and legs. He grimaced seeing the bolt in her thigh. He whistled in relief as she snatched a couple of ragged breaths. Francis grabbed a waterskin and a dagger. He cut cloth strips from his cloak. She stirred as Frances set the wet cloth to her forehead. Mora coughed, then groaned as a fresh wave of pain slammed into her body. Mora opened her eyes. She noticed his expression, panicked and distressed. A smile, thin and feeble, crept over her bloody face. Grateful he was here, she stroked his cheek. Francis let her take a few sips of water.

"Poison," she whispered.

"Hold on," he implored, getting to his feet.

Francis rummaged around in the kitchen until he found two small flasks, then hustled back to Mora's side. He knelt close, removed the cork, and placed a flask near her lips. She drank deep, allowing the healing elixir to wash inside her battered body. Mora jerked, her face contorted. She stared into Francis's tender brown eyes and gagged. "Ugh, the stench."

"The orcs?" Francis asked.

"No, the potion," she retched. "Gallego's recipe?"

"Yes, my dad's," Francis chuckled, pulling the cork from the second flask. "Take my hand. This will hurt."

Mora squeezed his hand and shrieked—her body convulsed as Francis poured half of the elixir over the bolt wound. She cried out in pain as he carefully extracted the bolt from her thigh and tossed it onto the floor. Francis soaked a strip of cloth in water and dabbed away the blood, then applied the remaining elixir to her injury. "The potions will help, but you need a healer."

"Kheel?"

"He's fine," Francis assured her, rising to his feet. "I need to go."

"Wait," she pleaded. "Did you notice the markings on the armor?"

Francis glanced at the markings. They meant nothing to him. "Five red slashes. So?"

"Belhaaz."

He looked at the dead orc, then back at Mora. "Belhaaz? You mean the banished demon?"

"Yes."

"Why?"

"I don't know." Mora shut her eyes again and leaned her head into the wall. "Francis?"

"Yes."

"Keep our boy safe," she beseeched.

"On my life."

Francis rushed from the house. He stopped halfway across the courtyard. His eyes swept over the dead. During the fighting, he had not noticed all the orcs bore the markings of Belhaaz. It made no sense. *Why would Belhaaz attack Ripley's Keep?* Francis took a step and paused. *How would Belhaaz know someone occupied the Keep?* He lifted his gaze to the walls. He found Kheel right where he had left him minutes ago. *Why would Belhaaz care?* He shook his head in frustration and hurried to join his son. He stopped once more and looked back at the house. *Mora.*

Chapter Forty-Two

Fall 531, Age of the Arch Mage

Colonel Asbyorn and Major Einar stood at a distance, observing the assault unfold. Smoke, thick as pitch, roiled from the compound into a cloudless morning sky. Epsen Asbyorn was a battle-worn soldier and an accomplished commander. He had endured all the hardships associated with a military career spanning twenty-five years in the Palagian army. He expected to endure death, destruction, and injury in this line of work. Bold and aggressive, he climbed the ranks, bypassing those more senior and pinning on the rank of colonel in under twenty years. Firm and fair, he was a dedicated leader to those he led, and in turn, they remained loyal to him.

This, however, was an unfamiliar experience. Nothing he had done in the past could have prepared him for this assignment. Leading orcs seemed like binding a banshee using string, almost impossible. He found them lazy, unruly, and cruel. Their half-orc commander was not much of an improvement. Colonel Asbyorn decided early on the orcs under his command were disposable, fodder replaced with little effort. He would employ them as shock troops to soften up the Keep. He held his human soldiers in reserve until the orcs spent themselves.

Less than thirty minutes earlier, he had sent the orcs forward. They stormed over the walls using ladders and ropes to penetrate the Keep's battlements. He and Major Einar heard the blasts, followed by the screams of the wounded and dying. They saw the fiery explosions catapult debris and bodies into the air. Major Einar contorted his face in frustration and swore under his breath. Colonel Asbyorn remained expressionless, watching the two arcane casters fend off the attack, repelling the orcs using their magic. He ignored the remaining orcs fleeing the onslaught as they sprinted past his position. Asbyorn glanced over at his dejected major.

"We were told there was one magic user," Asbyorn stated.

"Correct, sir," Einar replied. "What shall we do about the orcs?"

"Let them go," Asbyorn directed. "Send in our soldiers."

Einar nodded and stormed away. He hated the orcs as much or more than his colonel did. Useless, he concluded.

Asbyorn stood motionless, his expression blank and his eyes devoid of emotion, as Skrabb drew near. He knew from the half-orc's bearing his failure humiliated him. Skrabb stopped short, his head bowed. Asbyorn did not flinch. He drew his sword and plunged the blade into Skrabb's chest. "I will not tolerate your failure."

◊ ◊ ◊

Dusk loomed in the west. The sky clouded, the air chilled and swathed the world in gloom. When the sun settled below the horizon, the horns signaled retreat. Francis peered over the wall and watched the human soldiers withdraw, taking their dead and dying with them. In the distance, he watched the campfires flare to life, tiny flickering dots washing the desolate landscape in an eerie glow.

During the day, Francis recalled, the identical gruesome scene played out many times. Again and again, the soldiers had hurled themselves at the Keep, and each time Francis and Kheel threw them back. Their combined magic had prevented the enemy from attaining the walls.

Francis contemplated their fate, taking another somber look at the forces massed against the Keep. He understood this was not over. Their attacks would persist until they captured the Keep. He shivered as the sweat on his skin cooled. Francis gazed at his arms and clothes, torn and flecked in blood. He bit his lip to prevent himself from screaming out in frustration. Mora's wounds ended their opportunity to flee using a teleportation spell. Their survival rested on his and Kheel's shoulders.

Exhausted, he leaned on his staff. He felt worn, his magic spent. Francis was a wizard, not a sorcerer like Mora and Kheel. The arcana did not flow inside him naturally. He required sleep and study to relearn his spells. He peeked over at his son. Kheel stood resolute on top of the battlements, silent and unmoving. Fury burned in his eyes, his face and arms streaked with sweat and blood, his clothes tattered and soiled. Francis was in awe of his son's arcane power, raw and feral. Just fifteen, Kheel never asked why. He just fought. Francis put his arm around Kheel's shoulder. "I must rest or I am useless for the next fight. Can you stand watch?"

Kheel did not answer. His eyes locked on the burning campfires.

Francis descended to the courtyard, leaving Kheel to man the ramparts. He paused in the middle of the courtyard.

"Belhaaz," he said. "What am I missing? How could he know Mora's location?"

His mind churned, pursuing answers he knew he would not find. In recent years Auroryies had abandoned Ripley's Keep, deciding the ancient bastion no longer possessed any value. Few of the serving princes knew of its location, and even fewer comprehended its historical purpose. He was positive no one other than the high prince and the senior princes knew of their whereabouts. *Could they betray...* He could not complete the notion—it was full of treachery and betrayal. *Yet it was...*

◊ ◊ ◊

Kheel stood guard when the enemy renewed their assault near midnight. There was no need for surprise and stealth. There were no flanking movements to attack from the north or south and no intent to deceive. This time, they intended a direct assault from the west. He listened as the bugle rang out, high-pitched notes calling them to arms. He heard them marching east. Regimented and precise, these were human soldiers, not orcs. Their boots pounded the earth in unison, their armor clanking in precise rhythm on each disciplined step. He watched as they emerged from the gloom, their weapons, shields, and helmets glistening in the moon's glow.

Wrapped in a shimmering arcane shield, he waited. When they were in range, Kheel raked them with a barrage of fireballs, stalling the attack for an instant. Flames lit up the early morning sky, igniting everything caught in its blast. Fueled by wrath, Kheel called upon his arcane power once again. He perceived it coursing along his body, down his arms and amassing in his hands. Spreading his fingers, he uttered the phrase, sending forth a bright burst of energy. Slender threads of lightning ripped into the soldiers, rendering their armor useless and searing flesh.

Archers assailed him from a distance—their arrows shredded his arcane shield, leaving him defenseless. As he conjured another spell, an arrow ripped open his side. He staggered, the pain almost driving him to his knees. Kheel fell into the wall and attempted to evoke his magic. He slapped his forehead, trying to clear the fog and haze from his mind. Another arrow clipped his shoulder, wrecking his concentration. His vision blurred and his consciousness withered.

The soldiers fractured the main gate using their second battering ram. Explosions woke Francis from a fitful sleep. A few hours of study and a brief rest had restored his spells. He leapt to his feet and rushed out the front door. Terrified, he watched the soldiers spill into the Keep. Francis called upon his magic. He extended his arms and motioned them back and forth. His sleet and hail pummeled the invaders once more. His spell slowed their advance, bought him time to hide Mora.

"Mora, they've breached the gate," Francis yelled, scooping Mora into his arms. "Get into the tunnels."

"What?"

"Now, Mora. We are out of time," Francis persisted, carrying her to the hatch. "We can't win this. The heir of Gallantry must survive at all costs."

"Kheel? Where is Kheel?" she cried, struggling to free herself from his grasp. "Francis, where is my boy?"

"The tunnels, Mora," Francis implored. "I will find Kheel. Go!"

Mora fought him, begged him to release her.

He set her down and grabbed her by the shoulders. He stared into her gray eyes, eyes filled with pain and fear. "I can't lose you! Gaiand can't lose you."

Francis shoved her into the tunnel and sealed the door with his magic. He set a hand to the door and spoke. Once his cantrip was complete, the door blended into the wall. He heard her cursing his name and pounding on the door. Francis whispered a silent prayer and raced for the wall. He heard the soldiers in the house.

Trapped.

Chapter Forty-Three

Fall 531, Age of the Arch Mage

Wulf, Matthew, and Danny rode on, forgoing the dingy roadside inns dotting their route, choosing instead to sleep under the stars. The road led them onto the desert plains that dominated southern Tressel. Bleak and cheerless, the landscape reminded Wulf and Matthew of the Border Lands.

An unhappy collection of shacks and lean-tos, looking like forgotten children's toys left to rot in the sun and rain, revealed themselves as the trio neared the outskirts of Leeds. They snaked their way along the lone road winding through town. Dust hung thick and heavy in the humid air. The dilapidated town was in spitting distance of the Highpoint border, teasing the occupants with a better life a short journey away.

In a past life, Leeds was probably a decent small town. A place where a man could earn a decent living and provide a life for his family, but today it stood as nothing more than a squalid border town filled with fading memories from better days. Many of the buildings sat on stone foundations wrapped in wooden siding. Each structure yearned for a fresh coat of paint and cried out for a new roof. Seedy brothels, taverns, and gambling halls occupied the buildings where businesses and homes once thrived. Metal bars covered the windows, preventing people from entering or exiting.

The town folks stared, their hollow eyes and gaunt appearances exposing their forlorn situation. Grubby-faced children clad in filthy, threadbare clothing trotted alongside their horses begging for a few copper coins. Wulf and Matthew absorbed the scene in dismay. Privation like this did not exist among the Horse Tribes villages.

Not Danny.

Leeds reminded him of the slums and shantytowns languishing on the outskirts of South Hampton. He had witnessed poverty similar to this, more than he would care to admit. Memories of hunger, fear, and loneliness washed over him like waves pummeling the shoreline, relentlessly beating the sand into submission. The condition of the men and women did not bother

Danny as much. They could decide to improve their lot. The children were stuck, forced to live with their parents' poor life choices. They tugged at his heart.

Reaching into his saddlebags, Danny retrieved a small coin sack. He reined his mount to a stop, then dismounted in the street. Intrigued by his sudden action, Wulf and Matthew halted their horses. At once, a dozen pleading children surrounded Danny. He saw and comprehended the desperation written on undernourished faces, heard it in their thin voices. Danny knelt in the dust to get on their level. He handed each child a gold piece. The smiles on their grimy faces provided Danny some redemption and closure for past sins. Danny climbed back into the saddle and looked straight ahead. "Something I needed to do. We can go now."

Wulf studied Danny for a few moments as they resumed their ride. He appreciated what Danny had done for the children. *Maybe this master thief is more than a heartless assassin.*

A mile south of Leeds, they happened upon a run-down shack. Clad in a ragged Tressel army uniform, a disheveled man stumbled out the door, gripping a jug. He grabbed at an empty sword sheath and staggered onto the road. He tottered carefully, placing the jug down into the dirt. His rumpled uniform barely contained him. It strained and screamed for mercy at each seam. A bulging belly spilled over his belt, the buttons on his shirt appeared as if they may give out at any moment. The soldier peered at them through blurry eyes, then waggled a beefy finger at Wulf, Matthew, and Danny.

"Halt, what be your business in leaving, uh …" he stammered, as he lost his words.

"Tressel?" Wulf suggested.

"Why, yes. Tressel," he slurred. "Thank you."

"May we proceed?" Matthew prompted.

"Oh, well, I guess you can," he garbled. "Please close the door behind you."

They watched the drunken soldier pick up his jug, drink a long swig, then careen back into the shack, slamming the door behind him.

"Tressel's finest," Matthew laughed.

A noon sun slipped in and out of wisps of white clouds as the trio rode past a large 'Welcome to Highpoint' sign featuring faded words painted in fancy script. Matthew pondered the sign's condition. *Faded words. Seems appropriate for Highpoint.*

Situated a hundred yards south of the border, they encountered a succession of barricades, battlements, and crossbow platforms extending a mile on either side of the road. A twenty-foot-wide gate blocked the way. Soldiers manned the defenses, their weapons and bronze-colored plate mail glinting in the sun. A scowling soldier emerged from behind a barrier and motioned for them to stop. "Tell me your business here at Highpoint."

"Prince Singjeye summoned us," Matthew replied. "I bear his token."

Matthew produced the token from his saddlebag and presented it. The soldier removed the token from Matthew's hand. He eyed Matthew suspiciously at first, then he smiled. He examined it, flipped the symbol back and forth in his gloved hand. "I won't delay you any longer. I am sure he is expecting you."

"Yes, this day," Matthew answered.

He looked first at Matthew, then shifted his gaze to Danny and Wulf while handing the token back to Matthew. "Are these your friends?"

"Yes."

"Enjoy Highpoint, it is beautiful this time of year," the soldier said. "Open the entrance. They carry Prince Singjeye's token."

Danny glanced over at Matthew and then at the soldier. *Hm. Strange.*

From five miles off, Wulf, Matthew, and Danny had detected the first signs of Highpoint looming above the southern horizon. Buildings, some over four stories tall, came into focus as they neared the city. Danny glanced at Wulf and Matthew. "Ever been here?"

"No," they answered in unison.

"Me neither, but I have heard stories of the city's greatness, all legends and lore," Danny admitted. "Rumors tell that a powerful sorcerer founded the city centuries ago. I heard they store ancient and dangerous artifacts in sealed vaults deep below the fortress. They maintain knowledge from Gaiand's earliest days in massive libraries and archives. Supposedly, they train wizards in the ways of the arcane here. I am told magic users rule the city. You know, a magocracy."

"A mago ... What?" Wulf questioned.

"Come on ... ruled by magic users, wizards, necromancers," Danny chuckled. "Everyone knows that."

"Maybe I should have left you in Tejt," Wulf growled.

Wulf, Matthew, and Danny attained Highpoint's outskirts as the sun settled into the west. They smelled the ocean breeze, felt the salt air coating their skin. The dirt road transitioned to cobblestone streets as they ventured deeper into the city. On they rode past bakeries, tanneries, three inns, two banks, and a general store. Townsfolk moved in and out of the multi-colored businesses, homes, and shops built along broad tree-lined streets. They hustled about their daily lives, ignoring the trio as they passed by. Wary of any constabulary force, Danny peeked at the soldiers patrolling the streets. He admired their sharp white uniforms and armor even as he noted their weapons, long swords and crossbows.

Wulf and Matthew soaked in the sights, smells, and sounds. Highpoint was massive and the city awed them. Unlike South Hampton, Danny noted the clean streets and well-maintained buildings. Near the city fountain, they turned left onto East Street and discovered it was another crowded broad avenue. Torch tenders were kindling the streetlamps where East Street transitioned into Knowledge Road.

They rode into a broad swath of gardens that fronted the Citadelle and past gray statues that lined the side of the road. As they neared the walls, they came upon a monument pond. This statue appeared larger, more ornate than the others, its gaze transfixed on the Citadelle.

Past the larger statue, they observed four Sentries approaching. Their white plate mail and helmets gleamed in the fading sunlight, their tabards and white shields bore the mark of Auroryies, a gold key and burning torch crossed atop a white oak tree.

Wulf, Matthew, and Danny halted as the Sentries neared. The Sentries stopped short of where the trio stood. Each one appeared young, haggard, and wary. One stepped forward. "State your business."

Matthew extracted the token from his saddlebag.

"Prince Singjeye gave me his token," Matthew explained, presenting it to the Sentry. "He claimed it would allow entry. He is expecting us."

Grasping the token, the senior Sentry examined it. "You are?"

"I am Matthew Jakkes, accompanied by Captain Wulf Blackhawk. We hail from Beth Amen, the realm of the Horse Tribes," Matthew provided. "This is our companion, Danny Caldwell. I did not get your name."

"Sergeant DeIeva." The Sentry momentarily studied Wulf and Danny, then returned the token to Matthew and smiled. "You have traveled a long way. Come with me."

Danny studied Matthew's interaction with the Sentry. He watched the Sentry's haggard look and frown fade away. *It just happened again.* While Matthew talked with Sergeant DeIeva, Danny leaned into Wulf and pointed at Matthew. "Have you noticed the effect Matthew—"

"Yes," Wulf answered, his eyes fixed ahead.

"What is—"

"I don't know, but never speak of it again," Wulf cautioned.

"Oh?" Danny asked "Why—"

"No reason. I just wanted to sound mysterious," Wulf chuckled.

Danny's head fell to his chest and he muttered a blasphemy to himself.

Matthew and Sergeant DeIeva led the way, talking to each other, followed by Wulf, Danny, and the other Sentries. Several times, Danny saw Matthew and DeIeva laugh and slap one another on the back.

The Citadelle of Auroryies rose in front of them. A stone wall and a series of towers, turrets, and battlements protected the bastion from those who intended her harm. Sentries, armed and armored, paced atop the ramparts and occupied the gatehouse. Danny noticed a burly dwarf clad in plate mail eyeing them from the wall, saw the great axe gripped in his right hand. Danny dropped back to one of the tailing Sentries. "Who's the dwarf?"

"Captain Groshek, the Captain of the Citadelle Sentry Corps," he answered. "Don't cross him."

"Ah, thanks," Danny murmured.

"Open the gate," Sergeant DeIeva shouted when they reached the gatehouse. He turned to Matthew. "Nice meeting you, Matthew. We must finish our rounds."

"Same here. Your mother will be in my prayers." Matthew shook Sergeant DeIeva's hand. "May the Maiden's blessing rest upon you."

Chapter Forty-Four

Fall 531, Age of the Arch Mage

An iron-reinforced wooden gate creaked and moaned as it rose into the archway. The Sentry motioned for the trio to enter the Citadelle. He stopped and faced them. "Dismount and accompany me."

They lowered themselves from their saddles, and Wulf removed Maggie's bridle. The trio trailed the Sentry into the Citadelle and the aura within the ancient bastion felt sober and melancholy. Everyone Wulf, Matthew, and Danny encountered wore a frown. Without speaking, the Sentry led them on a winding torchlit gravel path bisecting the inner grounds. Poplars, willows, and oaks towered over the commons, their green leaves fading into a collage of golds, russets, and oranges. They trooped by swaths of green grass and sprawling gardens meticulously maintained, the fall flowers in full bloom. A chill hung in the air as the day's heat escaped into the coming night.

"Hold here," he instructed when they arrived at a covered pavilion. "I will inform Senior Prince Singjeye of your arrival."

Danny scanned their surroundings. Except for patrolling Sentries, the grounds were empty. He raised his gaze to the towers. He detected two black-robed figures staring at them from a balcony. *Odd.*

◊ ◊ ◊

Obscured in the folds of their black robes, the messenger and the envoy peered onto the inner grounds as if they were vultures eyeing a decaying carcass. The messenger cackled to himself. "So this is the best Beth Amen can offer?"

"Oh, this may work out better than I expected," the envoy crowed.

"Come," the messenger ordered. "I want to congratulate Prince Singjeye on a job well done."

The envoy delayed an extra second to enjoy the view. A satisfied sneer washed over his leathered face as he pivoted to join the messenger.

◊ ◊ ◊

"Well, I imagined they would be as friendly as Sergeant DeIeva," Danny exclaimed.

Wulf and Matthew bobbed their heads in agreement. They tarried beneath the pavilion, expecting Prince Singjeye's immediate arrival. The minutes came and passed and Singjeye was nowhere in sight. Wulf removed Maggie's saddle, freeing her to dine on the grass. Wulf wrapped himself in his cloak, laid his head on his saddle, shut his eyes, and fell asleep. Tired of Singjeye's tardiness, Matthew and Danny followed his lead.

Maggie whinnied and woke Wulf from his slumber. He squinted from one eye and noticed a young robed man and two Sentries draw near the pavilion. They stopped short of where the trio lounged.

"What are you doing?" the robed man screeched, placing his hands on his hips.

"Knitting," Wulf growled and shut his eyes again.

"Get up," he ordered. "Get off the grass."

"Easy, governor," Danny chortled. "It's not like we are vagrants."

"Then stop acting like one," he demanded.

Wulf, Matthew, and Danny dawdled coming to their feet. The man who confronted them bore a sober expression on his pallid face. His arms were now crossed over his chest and his cheeks flushed with anger. His robes, white and trimmed in purple, hung like drapes from a scrawny frame. They were clean and neat, recently laundered and ironed. His flaxen hair touched narrow shoulders, his chin veiled in a sparse beard.

"You are late, Matthew Jakkes," he declared, his voice high-pitched and grating.

"Yep, a minor war going on north of here delayed our arrival," Matthew pointed out. "Maybe you heard?"

"I am Prince Sheldon IV," he proclaimed, brushing aside Matthew's sarcasm. "I shall be your escort during your brief stay here. Private Arckos and Private Billings will tend to the horses while I usher you to the guest quarters."

"Great," Matthew acknowledged. "We are here to see Prince Singjeye. Where is he?"

"Matters you cannot fathom detain Prince Singjeye," Sheldon countered, doing nothing to mask his disdain.

"I tend to my horse," Wulf snarled. "Show me to the stables so I can take care of her."

Sheldon exhaled out loud and rolled his eyes. "I must—"

Wulf narrowed his eyes and took a step towards Sheldon. "Is that a problem?"

"Have it your way," Sheldon snorted, wanting nothing to do with the menacing outlander. "Privates, lead our esteemed guests and their mounts to the stables. Bring them to the guest house when they finish. Gentlemen, we have a tight schedule to keep, so please be quick."

Trailing behind the Sentries, Danny scanned the tower. The figures had disappeared. *Strange.* He centered his attention on the Sentries. He studied them as they walked to the stables. They looked young and seemed inexperienced, or even new recruits. Danny maneuvered his way in between the two Sentries and turned on his roguish charm. "What's Shelly's deal?"

"What do you mean?" Private Arckos asked.

"Why so arrogant?" Danny inquired. "And what's with the attitude?"

Arckos shrugged.

"Most of them act that way," Private Billings declared, jumping into the conversation.

"Hm, wonder why?" Danny continued, hoping to draw out further information.

"Because they are pompous asses," Billings exclaimed, trying to suppress a smile. He wanted to say more but held his tongue. Disparaging the princes was a punishable offense. "We have talked enough, and we are here. Stable your horses so we can lead you to your quarters."

While Wulf and Matthew tended to their horses, Danny sat on the partition between the stalls. His brain churned. First, why didn't Shelly's disposition toward Matthew change? And second, how could he further annoy Shelly?

Matthew glanced at the rogue. "What are you doing?"

"Dithering. I dislike Shelly, so I'm going to irritate him as much as I can," Danny confessed, his smile and eyes puckish. In an instant, his expression became sober. "Don't you think there is something strange about this place?"

"The stables?" Wulf grinned, scratching Maggie's ears.

"No, not the ... Hilarious." Danny frowned. "No, be serious."

"Yes," Matthew admitted. "Betrayal and duplicity live inside these walls. I felt it as we neared."

They completed caring for their horses in silence, each dwelling on Matthew's admission. When they finished, Wulf, Matthew, and Danny headed for the guest house. Crimson-faced, Sheldon was pacing outside when they arrived.

"The first three rooms are yours to choose from," Sheldon fumed, tossing each a key. "You will meet me here in thirty minutes and I expect promptness since you are joining a senior prince for dinner. Do what you deem—"

"Oh, which one?" Danny inquired, cutting Prince Sheldon off mid-sentence. "Can I guess? Uh, can I? Can I? I love guessing games. All right, give me a clue."

"Senior Prince Singjeye!" Sheldon shrieked. "Do what you deem necessary to ready yourselves and leave your weapons behind."

"All of them?" Danny continued, his face now serious. "Or just certain ones? Because some people don't think of a dagger as a weapon. I personally—"

"All!" Sheldon exclaimed, his voice a high-pitched shrill. He whirled on his heels and stormed off.

Danny turned to Wulf and Matthew with a broad beam plastered over his face. Matthew smirked. "Think you irritated him?"

Danny winked. Wulf laughed.

They took more time than allotted them. Sheldon traipsed back and forth, muttering to himself and shaking his head, when Wulf, Matthew, and Danny exited their rooms. He paused and scowled. "You are late. Follow me."

"Wait," Wulf pronounced. "Is my cloak clasp straight?"

"No. The horseshoe is upside down," Matthew answered. "Here, let me fix it."

"Thanks."

"Of course. You can't meet a distinguished prince appearing all disheveled," Matthew declared, repressing a grin.

While Sheldon simmered, Matthew spent a minute adjusting Wulf's clasp.

"Hey, how's my hair?" Danny snickered, running his hands through his hair. "It gets unruly at about this time each day, especially in the salt air, and I want to make a good impression on Prince Sentay."

"What?" Sheldon shouted. "His name is Senior Prince Singjeye."

Matthew stepped in front of Danny and examined his hair. "Let me—"

"Enough!" Sheldon protested. "No more delays."

In a huff, Sheldon stormed down a torchlit passageway. Delighted by their own tomfoolery, Wulf, Matthew, and Danny trailed behind without speaking. Not through tormenting Sheldon, Danny winked again at his companions. He sauntered beside Sheldon and placed his arm around the prince's shoulder.

"So, Shelly, are you a wizard? I mean, a real wizard?" Danny quizzed. "What I really mean is, are you a full-fledged wizard or just some common lackey who tends to guests on behalf of the other princes? I got to know so we can take our relationship to the next level."

Sheldon cut short his next step, removed Danny's arm, then spun to face the rogue.

"You will address me as Prince Sheldon, nothing more and nothing less. Understood?" he seethed. "Yes, I am a wizard, a full-fledged wizard. I am saddened that my current duties are to attend to the likes of you. All of us must bear distasteful burdens from time to time."

"Easy, Shelly," Danny grinned, cognizant of the nerve he struck. "I mean Prince Sheldon, your princeness. Meant no offense."

Flushed with anger, Prince Sheldon resumed his harried pace while Wulf and Matthew struggled to contain their amusement.

Chapter Forty-Five

Fall 531, Age of the Arch Mage

Sheldon and the trio wound their way over torchlit pebble paths until they came to a covered walkway draped in flowering vines. The minutes crawled by as they strolled on, eventually ending up at a wooden door. Sheldon opened the door and gestured for Wulf, Matthew, and Danny to go inside.

The soft glow of candles and lanterns welcomed them as they set foot inside a giant, opulent chamber. A fire burned in a massive granite hearth, its heat removing the chill from the dining room. Ornamental paintings and tapestries depicting Auroryies' glorious history decorated the stone walls. A feast of roasted meats, cheeses, vegetables, and loaves of fresh bread sat atop an enormous banquet table dominating the center of the room. Two elves stood talking beside a keg and a third hovered nearby.

Captain Roan Ambrose surveyed the half-elf and the two humans as they walked in. The elven ranger immediately sensed a calming effect. Roan caught sight of the talisman affixed to a silver chain that hung around the man's neck. He recognized the icon, an emerging sun sculpted from sapphire. *A cleric serving the Maiden.* Roan took a drink from his mug and zeroed in on the last man to enter. He wore a Horse Tribe uniform yet did not look like any of the steppe folk Roan had met in the past.

Wulf paused—the elves intrigued him. On rare occasions, elves had ventured into Shallow Cross to buy, trade, or sell merchandise. His mother had spun stories about their prowess using the longbow during archery lessons. She believed they imbued elven magic upon their weapons, making the bows stronger and the arrows fly truer.

They resembled Danny, yet they were different. Their slender, graceful appearance and fine features were striking compared to humans. One wore forest green robes and a slender silver band adorned his head. Another wore a military uniform and a scarlet cloak. The third appeared aloof and shy. His manner showed his discomfort in this setting. He stood an inch taller, appeared a little stockier, and his skin tone looked a shade or two darker. His mottled cloak and clothes reminded Wulf of his Uncle Kiah. Like the other elves, he wore his hair long except it was black instead of blond. Wulf studied the elf a few moments longer and recalled Kiah describing an elf like this one. Kiah said they hailed from Graywild, a remote location within Evergreen, and they had a reputation for producing the finest rangers in all Gaiand.

Sheldon left Wulf, Matthew, and Danny near the door and headed straight for the elves. He bowed, mindful of Wrayer's standing as elven royalty. He motioned for Wulf, Matthew, and Danny to join them.

"Let me introduce Prince Wrayer Tytonidae, Captain Roan Ambrose, and Lieutenant Naphtali Lacchi," Sheldon announced, his beam broad and condescending. "They hail from Evergreen, the land of the elves."

When the introductions were complete, Sheldon's eyes flitted to the clock on the wall. It showed Singjeye ran late.

"Prince Wrayer, I am sure important proceedings delay senior Prince Singjeye," Sheldon announced, flashing the elven royal a nervous smile.

Wrayer's nod set Sheldon at ease.

"Uh, we can eat while we, uh, await his arrival," Sheldon stammered. "So please, fill your plates and top off your mugs."

"Way to take charge, Shelly," Danny commended, his tone sarcastic. "I mean Prince Sheldon."

"Here, here," Matthew and Wulf chimed in.

Embarrassed, Sheldon discarded Danny's insult and sat down at the table. The ensuing dinner conversation stayed lighthearted and diplomatic. A strange apprehension filled the room when Prince Singjeye made his grand entrance. Arrogant and pious, he resembled a he-goat strutting into the room.

Decked out in princely attire, Singjeye carried a large leather-bound tome in his hands. He placed the book on the table, smoothed and adjusted his robes. Singjeye combed graying hair using his fingers. He frowned and faced Matthew. "You are late, Master Cleric. We postponed this mission on account of your tardiness."

Impassively, Matthew ignored Singjeye's displeasure.

"Who are these two?" Singjeye challenged.

"Wulf Blackhawk and Daniel Caldwell," Matthew responded.

"Pleasure, your princeness, to make your acquaintance," Danny exclaimed. "Call me Danny. All my friends do."

Singjeye rolled his eyes, snubbing Danny, and fixated on Matthew.

"Um, 'Captain' Wulf Blackhawk," Wulf interjected. "Horse Tribe Trooper."

"Sorry," Matthew mumbled. "Should have included the captain part."

"Ah, no worries," Wulf remarked.

"No, really," Matthew insisted. "Meant no—"

"I summoned you, not them," Singjeye interrupted, as his patience waned with their antics. "These two are not welcome."

"I think they will serve a useful purpose," Matthew professed, his eyes locking onto the aging wizard. "You send them away, I go as well. You choose."

Singjeye fumed. He was indignant when those beneath him questioned his authority. It furthered his disdain for the uncivilized outlanders. His arrogance compelled him to say no and let the cleric and his companions depart. But without them, he knew the elves would leave as well. This would jeopardize the plan to retrieve Francis and the artifacts. How would he explain to the high prince if all of them left? It was not a risk he wanted to assume.

"If you insist, Master Cleric," Singjeye acquiesced, choking down his pride. "I approve of their presence."

Singjeye browsed over the room, buying himself a minute to gain his composure and allow his anger to abate. "Gentlemen, on behalf of the high prince, High Prince Xavian IV, welcome to the Citadelle, home to the Princes of Auroryies. Prince Sheldon and I will be your hosts during your brief hiatus here."

Danny shot a side glance at Wulf and Matthew. *That's the second time they have said 'short or brief stay.' Why?*

Singjeye filled a goblet, then sat at the head of the table. He sipped the wine from his chalice, perusing the chamber once more. "I will be concise. A determined enemy opposes us. We all know this. Orcs to the north and marauders menacing the coasts. You will start your search for Prince Francis and the relics at Ripley's Keep."

"Ripley's Keep?" Roan queried.

"Yes, Captain Ambrose," Singjeye confirmed. "An ancient bastion deep in the Border Lands abandoned years ago. Auroryies once used the Keep to train our war mages, Sentries, and Lancers."

Wulf snuck a questioning peek at Matthew. The cleric shut his eyes, offering a wordless prayer to the Maiden for wisdom and discernment. *Help me parse truth from lies.*

"How do we get there?" Wulf probed. "Horses?"

"Well, it would be foolish to walk," Singjeye ridiculed, his sneer patronizing. He gave Wulf a dismissive wave. "It would take you months."

Wulf slammed his fists onto the table, spilling glasses and upsetting plates. His chair sailed into the wall behind him as he leapt to his feet. Matthew grasped Wulf by the arm. Singjeye's eyes went wide. He recoiled and almost fell from his chair. Wulf snarled at Singjeye, then at Matthew.

"Do I kill him now, or do I kill him later?" Wulf growled. "Either way, I am going to kill him!"

"How about later?" Matthew suggested, releasing his grip on Wulf. "Now sit back down."

Danny muted a laugh. Not sure what to do, Naphtali and Wrayer fidgeted in their seats. Sheldon cringed at Wulf's outburst, then made a quick recovery. He rushed to assist the senior prince. Singjeye gestured him away. He adjusted his robes and straightened in his chair. Roan did not flinch. His eyes, callous and piercing, narrowed.

"Captain Blackhawk asked a fair question. Now answer," Roan insisted. His voice was taut, his expression blank. "How do we get to the Keep?"

Singjeye cleared his throat and drank from his goblet. "Horses, uh, would work best."

Sheldon jumped into the conversation, granting Singjeye time to compose himself. "And we will provide you with a map."

"I see," Roan stated, masking his annoyance. "What is so important about this Prince Francis?"

"We wrongly accused and convicted him for crimes he did not commit," Singjeye answered, averting his eyes from Roan.

Wulf, Matthew, Naphtali, Danny, and Wrayer sat stationary and silent, their attention on Roan.

"You have your own military," Roan commented, never removing his eyes from Singjeye. "Why not use them to retrieve him and the relics?"

"Our Sentries and Lancers are defensive in their mission," Singjeye justified, his voice clipped and tight. "They do not possess the equipment or the training for an assignment like this one."

Not quite accurate, Matthew concluded. *There is more than we are being told.* "What are these artifacts?"

"The Hammer and Helm of Valaaham," Singjeye droned. He crossed his legs and spent nervous energy smoothing out his robes again.

"Who is Valaaham?" Roan pressed. "And why these particular relics? What powers do they possess?"

"Valaaham was a cruel cleric in the service of Belhaaz," Singjeye admitted, peeking at Wulf. The outlander scared him and his threats frightened him even more. "Heroes of old banished Valaaham centuries ago. We do not comprehend why someone stole these specific artifacts or the true extent of the Hammer's and Helm's powers."

"Who is Belhaaz?" Roan continued.

"An ancient demon exiled at the same time as Valaaham," Singjeye revealed. He stood, signaling the meeting was over.

Roan paused and studied the senior prince. Singjeye's answers were brusque and nebulous. He hid something. The look on Matthew's face confirmed what Roan believed. "Stop, I have more—"

"Captain Ambrose!" Singjeye cut Roan off mid-sentence. "Are you paying attention? We know only what I have told you."

A strained hush fell over the room. No one spoke or moved. Roan blinked. When he opened his eyes, they bored holes into the senior prince. Singjeye tugged on his sleeve and peered at the clock on the wall. Danny and Wulf kept their eyes on Roan and shifted their hands to the long knives hidden in their boots. Naphtali and Wrayer exchanged worried glances. Sheldon froze, his pallid face even paler.

"King Longpine said you would provide the answers," Roan stated, his voice edgy. "Do you have the answers I require? Are we speaking to the correct prince? Is there another who could better explain?"

Singjeye's face flushed several shades of crimson. His eyes flared in rage.

"This is getting us nowhere," Matthew protested, breaking the tension.

"Concur," Singjeye acknowledged, thankful at least the cleric remained reasonable. He ignored the others and spoke to Matthew.

"Then we agree," Singjeye declared, hoping to leave the room with some semblance of his dignity intact. "You depart at dawn tomorrow."

"Dawn?" Roan exclaimed, coming to his feet. "No, this is too soon."

"Why?" Singjeye replied, his voice tight.

"We need time to prepare and to gather supplies," Roan explained. "I need to study a map."

"No," Singjeye snapped. "You have tonight to ready yourselves. Provide Prince Sheldon your requirements. He will fulfill them."

Roan fixed his eyes on Sheldon. "I need a map, horses, food, and water."

"Shell ... I mean Prince Sheldon, I don't need a horse," Danny declared. "Stole one in Tejt."

"We brought our own," Wulf barked, pointing at Matthew. "But I will need arrows."

"Hey," Matthew said, looking at Wulf. "What about those things your mom made for us that one time?"

"You mean the cherry pie?"

"Yeah. That was so good."

Wrayer and Naphtali stood close by in stunned silence, each wondering if they would survive this adventure alongside Danny, Wulf, and Matthew. Sheldon turned to Singjeye for consent. Singjeye nodded in approval. Singjeye pivoted and stormed out of the room, his robes fluttering with each step. Roan smirked as the door slammed.

Singjeye, Roan concluded, was a moron. He was a puppet, minus the strings. Every word he uttered was almost an outright lie. Singjeye's hesitation, his eyes, and his body language betrayed him. Matthew's expression said he agreed as well. This whole thing seemed nothing more than an elaborate charade, a fool's errand. Now Roan felt conflicted. Wisdom screamed for him to liberate himself from this whole affair. To walk away and return to Evergreen. But would his sense of duty and honor allow him to quit? And, despite the lies and deception, intrigue held him captive, his curiosity now piqued. Why? Roan knew the truth remained beyond his reach here in Auroryies. A venture to Ripley's Keep was required, and perhaps elsewhere, to discover the truth. Even then, he might not find what he sought. Was he prepared? Was this disparate bunch capable? And he hoped Wulf, Matthew, and Danny possessed a serious side.

Sheldon rose and headed for the door. Roan snatched him by the collar of his robe. "You and I are not done. Sit."

Sheldon gulped as he rubbed his neck then sat.

Roan jerked a long knife from his boot and set it on the table in between himself and Sheldon. He extracted a leather-bound book from his satchel and a slender piece of charcoal. He turned his icy gaze toward the arrogant prince. "Describe Francis."

Sheldon hesitated as his mind swirled, staring at Roan's long knife. They were supposed to be unarmed—he wanted to flee. The crazed elf and the others frightened him. He considered the half-elf uncouth and unbearable and the outlanders boorish. Roan slammed his fists on the table as he rose and pointed at Wulf. "See the big trooper over there?"

Sheldon tore his eyes from Roan and gazed at Wulf.

"I don't think he likes you much. Any excuse to bash your head in, he would welcome." Roan sat back down, opened his book, and picked up his charcoal. He snapped his fingers to get Sheldon's attention. "You and Singjeye have exhausted my patience with your deceptions and half-truths. Now, describe Francis."

"Dark-skinned. His beard and hair are gray," Sheldon described. "Tall and lean."

"What do you mean by dark-skinned?" Roan asked. "Suntanned or like Captain Blackhawk's?"

Sheldon peeked over at Wulf and nodded.

"Go on," Roan demanded. "Give me more. Eyes? Limp? Scars?"

"Nothing else," Sheldon admitted. "I rarely interacted with him."

"I think you lie, Shelly," Danny whispered in the prince's ear. The rogue winked at Roan. "Let Wulf kill him?"

Roan held up his hand. "Soon."

Sheldon screwed his face and squirmed in his chair.

"The Helm and Hammer. Describe them," Roan commanded.

"The Helm is crafted from gold and adorned with black ram horns on each side," Sheldon stammered. "Leather wraps the Hammer's handle and it's head is forged from platinum."

"Good enough." Roan scribbled a few more notes. "Tell me about the Keep."

"I don't know," Sheldon confessed. "They abandoned the bastion before I arrived in Auroryies."

"Find one, Sheldon. Find me a description," Roan seethed. "I want you to deliver the information to my quarters within thirty minutes. Understand?"

"Yes."

"Go."

Chapter Forty-Six

Fall 531, Age of the Arch Mage

A full moon, bright and orange, bathed the Citadelle in a foreboding glow. Matthew gazed at the sky trying to sort the source of his hesitancy. A thousand distant stars set against an ebony backdrop appeared to signal a warning, a proposal that their pending journey would end in failure. Roan, too, sought to discern if any truth lay hidden in the scripted declarations of the nervous princes as he peered into the gloom. Shadows cast from the torches danced in the darkness, mocking him and the other five men trudging for their quarters, each locked in their own haunted speculation.

Considering his companions, Roan understood his elven countrymen were raw and untested. Their inexperience concerned him. He perceived the power, the inherent wisdom, and the calming aura within Matthew. Nevertheless, the cleric was young, perhaps twenty-five in human years. Wulf seemed reckless, yet he carried himself with noble purpose. Roan saw every battle Wulf had fought reflected in his eyes, the scars on his cheek and neck and armor offered as proof. The half-elf was boisterous at first and now quiet. His reticence caused Roan to wonder which extreme might be closer to the half-elf's true character. Roan sighed—he concluded they had little chance of success.

A Sentry shifted his weight from one foot to another as he loitered near the guest quarters clutching an envelope intended for a Captain Ambrose. He froze as he observed six men emerge from the murk. He stuck out his hand. "This is for Captain Ambrose"

Roan retrieved the envelope from the Sentry's hand. "Thank you. Please, carry on."

Roan gazed at the package for a moment and wondered how Prince Sheldon had gathered the information so quickly. "Matthew, I discern you have suspicions. You have past dealings with the princes?"

"Yes, sadly," Matthew lamented, sitting down on a stone bench. "Singjeye told partial truths, which is the prince's way. He hides the entire story. There is more to this tale than he disclosed."

"Agreed," Roan admitted. "Our king's confidence in the princes erodes."

"Wise," Matthew commended. "I am convinced our village chieftain and King Stockton would second your king's opinion."

"Gents, we have just met, so I will not attempt to speak for anyone but myself," Roan stated. "I own little confidence in the success of this endeavor."

"I concur," Matthew added. "Too many unknowns, too many deceptions."

"Unknowns and deceptions be damned," Wulf declared. "I am going."

"Why?" Danny asked, puzzled by Wulf's immediate reaction.

"For my family, for my country," Wulf confirmed. "Duty and honor. For times such as these. We have the power to protect those who cannot defend themselves and the power to shorten the war."

"Seems a little naïve," Wrayer chimed in. "Could cost our lives."

"It is a risk I am willing to take," Wulf vowed.

Naphtali stepped next to Wulf. "I'm with Wulf."

"Ten minutes ago you threatened to kill Singjeye," Matthew reminded Wulf. "Are you sure about this?"

"I am going to kill him," Wulf confirmed. "Yes, I am sure. We set out to shorten the war. I will at least try."

Matthew faced Roan, his eyes narrowed, and his mouth set in a hard line. "Despite my better judgment, Wulf is correct and the Maiden prompts that I must continue on this path."

"What do I have to lose?" Danny declared, his tone of voice reflecting his doubts. "Count me in."

Roan looked at Wrayer. "Well, your highness?"

Wrayer did not answer immediately as he considered his companions for a moment. He barely knew them, even his own countrymen. The outlanders and Naphtali appeared determined and so did the half-elf to some extent. He looked back at Roan hoping to decipher the ranger's thoughts. Roan wore a blank expression. *Did it suggest he did not care either way?* Wrayer finally nodded. "We go."

◊ ◊ ◊

When the conversation had ended and the decision decided, the others shuffled to their quarters. Near a table, Roan lingered in the torchlight. There was work to do. He opened the envelope and found a map and parchment describing Ripley's Keep. Roan grimaced as he smeared wet ink on the map and parchment while trying to read it. *Someone just made this.* Roan sucked in a gulp of air and resumed. Ripley's comprised four walls, one gate, and three buildings and nothing more. *Simple.*

Next he unfolded the map and placed it on the table. He grabbed four stones and set them on each edge of the map. Wulf stopped at the entrance to his quarters and gazed back. He watched as the ranger leaned over the table. Wulf walked over to Roan and stood near him. Roan paused his study and looked at Wulf. "Captain Blackhawk."

"Captain Ambrose," Wulf acknowledged. "Can I assist?"

"Yes."

Roan returned to the map. He found it more of an unrefined drawing than a cartograph. Wulf bent close and squinted. He struggled to recognize key landmarks and villages within Beth Amen, the Highlands, and Blackhawk. "Not very accurate from what I can see."

"No, not at all," the ranger sighed. He gestured at the map. "The eastern portion is wrong. Oakrun is not this far south."

Roan and Wulf barely slept during the night and into the early morning. Roan scribbled notes in his book as they spent their time pouring over the map, studying every detail. Wulf smiled to himself—a ranger is a ranger. Roan and his book reminded him of Kiah and Seth's methodical nature. They read and reread the parchment attempting to glean information that could aid them in their journey.

"Ripley's is here." Roan pointed to a circle north of Maguana. "Suggestions?"

"Avoid cities as much as possible."

"Concur."

"Tressel and southwest Beth Amen are untouched by orcs," Wulf asserted. "As troopers, Matthew and I can guarantee safe passage, and there are villages where we could rest and resupply."

"Good."

Wulf looked at the map, then at Roan. "Maguana? No clue."

"Understood," Roan acknowledged. He sat down and grabbed a fresh piece of charcoal from his satchel. "I say we track northwest once we cross into Tressel. We bypass Kenly and Tejt and traverse Beth Amen up to the Highlands border?"

Wulf nodded in agreement.

"What about the Highlands?"

"Staunch allies but hate visitors," Wulf stated. He grimaced, recalling his run-in with Kodiak and the Ironhand Tribe. "Especially unannounced."

"Firsthand knowledge?"

Wulf nodded again.

"Okay," Roan chuckled. He looked down at the map. "We hug the border, then cross the North River into the Border Lands."

"I don't see any other options," Wulf stated.

Sometime following midnight they agreed on a general route. Roan scrawled a few more notes, closed his book, and stretched. "Thanks."

"Sure. See you in a few hours." Wulf strolled to his quarters and disappeared behind the door.

Roan folded the map and placed it and his book into his satchel. He scanned his surroundings. The Citadelle slept. *Was it peaceful?* Roan doubted it. Too much discord and controversy inside the walls. He saw the elongated silhouettes of the Sentries posted atop the ramparts, their clanking armor and heavy footsteps intruding on the quiet. He glanced into the early morning sky. The moon, amid a thousand stars, trawled west at a steady clip. A stiff breeze blew in off the Sea of Marhgot, salting the air that clung to his skin. *What would the coming weeks hold for him and his new companions?* This was a question he could not answer.

He slung his satchel over his shoulder and entered his quarters. Roan laid down on the bed, shut his eyes, and fell asleep.

Chapter Forty-Seven

Fall 531, Age of the Arch Mage

Colonel Asbyorn and Major Einar had marched for Ripley's Keep ahead of the coming sunrise. The dead orc and human soldiers littered the grounds in front of the ancient bastion. The road leading up to the gate was rent and buckled. Einar wavered a second before entering the courtyard, the scene before him gruesome and disheartening. This was a novel experience for him, and he could not conceal the horror on his face. He retched at the pungent smell of death and burnt flesh suspended in the unmoving air. Blood streaked the walls and pooled on the ground. Lifeless orcs and humans lay strewn throughout the courtyard, their bodies broken, scorched, and disfigured, their armor melted and ruined. Death reigned over Ripley's Keep.

Asbyorn paused midway between the gate and the house. Expressionless, he surveyed the Keep. The loss of life appalled him. He knelt near one of his soldiers and placed a gloved hand on the man's forehead. *I hope your sacrifice will not be in vain.* He closed the soldier's eyes and mouth, then rose to his feet. Asbyorn motioned for a soldier standing outside the front door to the house. "Where is your captain?"

"Dead, sir," the soldier answered. "His body is in the house."

"Who's in charge?"

"The lieutenant," the soldier replied.

"Take me to him," Asbyorn ordered.

Colonel Asbyorn trailed the soldier into the house. As the colonel entered, a lieutenant approached. The colonel held up his hand. Asbyorn glanced over the room. More dead, soldiers and orcs. The fighting had ruined the room—windows shattered, walls charred, and blood stained the stone floors. He focused on the two unconscious prisoners, wrists and ankles shackled by iron restraints, lying near the hearth. "They are alive?"

"Yes, sir," the lieutenant confirmed.

"Are there others?" Asbyorn wondered.

"No," the lieutenant responded. "We have scoured the house, barn, storage building, and found no others."

"These two men are the cause for all this death and destruction?" Colonel Asbyorn asked.

The lieutenant had been puzzled as well when their search yielded no one else. He shrugged, "Seems so, sir."

"Load the prisoners into the wagons," Asbyorn ordered. He masked his fear in a thin smile. "Withdraw your men, lieutenant. We depart for Udontawny in an hour."

◊ ◊ ◊

Francis jolted awake, discovering his wrists and ankles bound by iron shackles. He stared at the shackles in frustration. Francis lay on a wooden floor in a rolling cage and listened to the steady beat of horse hooves striking the ground. The hooves, wagon wheels, and the soldiers' boots plodding along the trail formed low-hanging clouds of sand and dirt. He choked on dust so thick it only permitted slender ribbons of sunshine to penetrate the haze. Francis could not determine the time of day, adding to the confusion clouding his mind.

Francis was desperate to clear his throbbing head, to regain his concentration. He needed to get his bearings to find out where he was and in what direction he traveled. Francis felt the weight of the shackles dragging on him like an anchor. He saw his own blood streaked down his forearms. It spilled onto the wooden floorboards from the jagged iron edges tearing into his skin. He ached, and the jostling wagon added to his misery. France almost blacked out from the pain screaming through every fiber of his body as he attempted to pull himself to his feet.

Francis forced the pain deep down into his body, then tried to speak, to call out to Kheel, but his parched throat prevented him from uttering a sound. A sharp wind blew cold. Icy fingers bore through his torn clothes and ripped at his exposed flesh. Dust clouded his vision. It blurred the soldiers marching alongside his cage. Wagons creaked, men shouted, and boots stomped—he sorted each sound in the noise of a troop on the move but could not discern his son.

Francis examined the cage holding him captive. He saw the heavy bolts securing it to the wagon. He noted the thick metal bars and the huge iron lock that fastened the door. With his strength depleted, exhaustion won. He slumped against the bars and closed his eyes. He felt hopeless to do anything to free Kheel and himself from their captors.

He panicked as his worry raced to Mora. His last memory was shoving her into the tunnels running beneath the Keep. *She must be safe.* Despite his fears, he forced himself to believe she was safe and undiscovered.

◊ ◊ ◊

Mora stirred in the unlit chamber hidden ten feet beneath the main house. Her body throbbed but she lived. She held her breath and listened. An eerie hush permeated the Keep. The terror that forced her into this place seeped back into her mind. *Francis! Kheel!* She set her feet on the stone floor and rose from the cot. She snapped her fingers. In an instant, a soft white light glowed in her palm. Mora raised her arm and gazed at her surroundings. She shivered. The room resembled a tomb, cold and void of life. It smelled of dust and mold. Mora wrapped herself in the old cloak she had found and used as a blanket and moved to the door. She removed the iron bar from the bracket. Metal scraped the rough stone as she dragged the door open.

She extended the light in front of her and plodded down the corridor to a spiral staircase ascending to the main floor above. Mora groaned with each step to the top. She paused and slowed her breathing, then placed her ear against the wall. Silence. Mora whispered the words to remove Francis's spell. She extinguished her light and pushed open the door.

Mora gasped. Her hand shot to her mouth and muzzled the scream that leapt from her lungs. A nearly full moon's light revealed a ghastly scene. Cadavers littered the house, their bodies stiffened from time and the cold. There was no sign of Francis or Kheel. No sign of the living. Only death lingered here. Mora trembled. Sidestepping the corpses, she eased her way carefully to the front door and peered out into the courtyard. Additional dead, orc and human, lay strewn across the grounds. Mora limped to the gate.

Mora leaned against the gate frame and stared across the darkened expanse spread before her. She peered into the nothingness, alone and afraid. Mora contemplated Belhaaz for a long moment. She knew the name and shuddered. She knew of the demon her father had battled and banished. Mora brushed at the air in an effort to dismiss the thoughts.

Her husband and son were not here and that was her primary concern, not some ancient demon. She perceived her son—he lived. Still weakened from her injuries and the poison, she did not trust her senses. She could not detect Francis—could he be dead? Mora knew the limits of her power. She could only identify sorcerers, not human wizards. *Might he still live also?* A moment passed. Mora felt helpless, vulnerable, and there was nothing she could do—hope faded as quickly as she had attempted to conjure it.

-- He lives --

"He does?" she asked.

-- Yes --

"How do—"

-- Trust me. I know --

Mora closed her eyes and wiped at the tears. Knowing Francis lived was more terrifying than if he were dead.

A long pause ensued. His presence lingered. She felt his touch on her shoulders.

-- It's time, Mora --

"No, not now," she hissed and pulled away. "I am a wife and mother."

-- When? --

"I don't know."

◊ ◊ ◊

Kheel opened his eyes. Once his vision cleared, he saw thousands of shining stars filling a clear black sky. A breeze, raw and chilled, blew in from the north. He smelled burning wood, heard the crackle from the campfires, and out of the corner of his eyes glimpsed the flickering flames.

He was cold. The sweat and blood had dried on his skin. His body hurt everywhere. He found it difficult to move. Kheel labored himself into a sitting position by leveraging the heavy metal bars holding him captive. He stared at the shackles binding his wrists and ankles, aware he did not possess the means to free himself from their biting grip. Kheel perceived the warmth of fresh blood that trickled along his hands, seeped down his arms and feet. He heard voices—some words he understood, the others sounded foreign, harsh and guttural. Kheel observed the gray outlines of the human soldiers moving among the fires. Amid the haze of smoke he saw another cage secured to a wagon a couple of yards behind him. He pulled himself to his feet, using every ounce of strength his damaged body possessed. Kheel clutched the metal bars, preventing himself from collapsing, sucked air into his burning lungs.

"Father!" Kheel shouted. "Where are you?"

Kheel's captors hurled rocks and jabbed him with the blunt ends of their spears, trying to silence him. He resisted their beatings, fought back the best he could. Kheel glared at them, his eyes bloodshot and consumed by hatred. He gripped the cage bars tight, defying their attacks and disregarding their orders.

"Kheel, I am here!" Francis pleaded. "Keep the faith, son. I promise you we will get out of here."

Above the soldiers' yelling, Francis begged for Kheel to reply. Unhurried, the minutes passed, one after another. Kheel said nothing. The shouting subsided and gave way to a low drone. Francis hung his head. Kheel never responded.

Three additional harsh days passed in agony for Francis and Kheel as they bounced in the wagon cages, further aggravating their wounds and creating new ones. Minus food and water, their battered bodies were pushed to a breaking point. Many times Francis felt death's icy grip reaching for him, clutching at him, whispering his name. He resisted, struggled to break free and to stay awake.

Relief, so to speak, came when the column slowed its pace. They attained an outpost tucked into the south side of a mountain range. Francis opened his eyes and glanced at his surroundings. The landmarks were unfamiliar. Craggy snowcapped peaks soared into the sky on one side. Rugged and ominous, they loomed over the landscape. On the other, a dense forest. Leaves of gold and russet rustled over the ground. The tree trunks held a dusty, ashen color, suggesting they were sick and dying. *Could the torturous journey be nearing its end?*

Chapter Forty-Eight

Fall 531, Age of the Arch Mage

Colonel Asbyorn and Major Einar rode at the head of the column. For days they traveled over barren terrain, dusty and broken. Warmed by the sun's heat, the days were bearable. The nights were crisp and chilled, especially when the north wind blew. He had lost half of his men during the assault on Ripley's Keep and all the orcs. Losing orcs did not matter, they were expendable. But he found the needless slaughter of veteran soldiers to capture two men hard to reconcile. He hoped their sacrifice would somehow fit into the overall picture. He felt some satisfaction and a little relief when Udontawny came into view.

◊ ◊ ◊

Francis's cage on wheels rolled over dusty streets, past bedraggled buildings desperate for repair, and into the slums surrounding Udontawny. Monsters he could not identify rushed at him, hissing and snarling, their clawed hands groping for him through the iron bars. Eyes full of hate glared at him, their breath hot and foul. They howled in frustration as the human soldiers shoved them back.

As the day faded away, burning torches replaced the setting sun. An unwelcome breeze sweeping down the streets added to his misery. The column exited Udontawny, heading north into an open field. Francis peered through the bars keeping him captive and strained to see where the odd procession headed. He saw the fortress looming ahead, dull and bleak. Towers and parapets rose above stone walls bathed in the glow of torches. Soldiers illuminated by the torches patrolled the ramparts and manned the turrets. The fortress reminded him of Ripley's Keep. Francis heard their shouts. They were human voices calling for the gates to open.

Whoever ordered his capture waited for him there. Why? He did not know. Francis's mind, his best asset, remained fogged from his deteriorated condition. It prevented him from thinking. Drained from his efforts, Francis slumped back into the iron bars. Suffering from dehydration and starvation and blood loss, Francis closed his eyes, letting his head rest on his chest.

Francis was barely conscious when the soldiers hauled him from the cage. Too weak to walk, they half dragged him, but even as his head lolled about, he commanded his eyes to search for Kheel, but he could not locate his son. He almost fainted from the agony searing through his body as they dragged him away from the wagon, and the soldiers steadied Francis between them. Francis shut his eyes and tried to push the pain away. He felt the dirt transition to stone beneath his boots. The soldiers stopped. He opened his eyes and lifted his head.

Silhouetted by the torches, a diminutive man shrouded in black robes stood in front of him. Thin wisps of graying hair covered his balding head, his smile errant and insincere. The man stared at Francis, his beady eyes hidden beneath a wrinkled forehead.

"Prince Francis, I am Zim Patok," he gloated. "Welcome to Demonstaug. I will be your host during your brief stay here. So glad you and your boy could join us."

Francis used what remained of his strength and spat at Patok. A sharp blow from a soldier's elbow into Francis's rib cage drove him to his knees. Francis gagged and coughed blood. He raised his gaze, focused his eyes on Patok.

"Take him and the boy to their cells," Patok ordered and motioned for the soldiers to pick Francis off the ground. "In the morning, I want them cleaned and fed. They must be presentable for Valaaham."

Valaaham. Francis's world faded to black.

Kheel awoke sore and his body ached. He opened his eyes. He found his surroundings ashen and dour and unfamiliar. Kheel remained disoriented, his mind cobwebbed. Hunger and thirst gnawed at him and added to his misery. The air, damp and stale, caused him to shiver. A single torch hung on the stone wall, illuminated the small cell holding him captive. He rose from the straw mat, his restraints gone. Kheel rubbed his wrists and found them raw and bruised. It required his eyes a minute or two to adjust to the gloom. He took unsteady steps toward the cell gate. Not surprised, he found it locked and the bars secured to the stone floor. Kheel tried summoning a spell that would open the door. On each attempt, he failed. Despair grabbed at him until he heard a familiar voice. Kheel gripped the iron bars of his cell and looked to his right. He spotted his father in the cage next to him.

Francis coerced a weary smile, finding his boy alive. He reached between the bars and clung to Kheel. He tried to speak, but the words stuck behind a lump in his throat. Just knowing his son lived would suffice for now.

"Where's Mom?" Kheel cried, his eyes wide and his voice cracking.

"She's all right," Francis answered as calmly as he could. He was trying to console Kheel and convince himself at the same time. Francis hoped he sounded confident because he wasn't. He remained unsure whether Mora was safe.

Kheel lowered his head, his eyes affixed to the stone floor. "Why are we here?"

"I don't know," Francis admitted. His mind flashed to Valaaham. What did he and Kheel have to do with a banished cleric? He tried to focus. Francis failed, his brain would not cooperate.

"I can't summon my magic," Kheel complained.

"Me either," Francis replied. "The poison lingers."

Francis heard the metal doors clang and the plodding of boots. He motioned for Kheel to stay quiet. Zim Patok emerged from the shadows, followed by eight soldiers.

"Back away from each other," a soldier ordered. "Keep your hands visible."

Francis complied and gestured for Kheel to do the same. While their companions aimed their crossbows, two soldiers entered each cell. They slapped iron shackles on to Francis's and Kheel's wrists. Once they were bound, Patok entered Francis's cell.

"You will not speak," Patok sneered. "Your boy will die if you do. He is expendable. Nod your head if you understand."

Francis nodded. The soldiers roughly hauled Francis and Kheel to their feet and led them to another room. An hour later, eight soldiers escorted Francis and Kheel back to their cells. Their captors had brutally scrubbed their bodies raw, days of dirt and blood washed away with soap, brushes, and cold water. Incompetent healers applied healing salves and bandages to their wounds. Their ragged, soiled clothes were replaced with fresh black robes. When Francis and Kheel returned to the dungeon, they found their cells cleaned and the straw removed. Small beds replaced the straw and slop buckets were placed in the far corners. Exhausted from their ordeal, Francis and Kheel collapsed on their beds. Guards slipped a tray of food and a bowl of water under a narrow slot in the cell doors minutes later.

Francis rested on his back, staring at the ceiling. He rolled to his side, watching his son. Ravaged by hunger and thirst, Kheel ate everything on the tray and gulped down the water. Francis returned to his back and closed his eyes. To put together the pieces, he needed to think. He narrowed his thoughts to a few questions, a trick Kysellah had taught him as a child. He fought against the poison lingering in his body, strained to free his mind. Francis relaxed, slowed his breathing. Bit by bit, the fog lifted and his thinking became clear and focused.

Patok had mentioned Valaaham. Francis knew the name and connected it to the missing relics. At one time, they had belonged to an evil cleric serving Belhaaz. *Belhaaz?* Soldiers and orcs bearing his mark had assaulted the Keep. *How did the orcs and soldiers find me?* His mind strayed, and his concentration failed. He shook his head. *Focus, one thing at a time. The Helm and Hammer.* The assembly had convicted him for stealing them. And Gambier's disappearance. Gambier and the relics. Francis repeated the thought several more times. He groped around in his mind for the answers to his own questions. *Gambier and the relics. Are they connected? Could a fellow prince ...*

His eyes snapped open. *They are!* A sickening notion revealed itself. One so vile, so repulsive he could not bring himself to say it out loud.

Chapter Forty-Nine

Fall 531, Age of the Arch Mage

Dawn's approach, a broad blush of cobalt, pink, and crimson, peeked over the eastern horizon. Roan, Wulf, Matthew, Danny, Naphtali, and Wrayer exited their quarters and discovered new leather packs and four arrow quivers placed outside their doors. Singjeye had kept his promise. A hasty inspection revealed each one contained food, water, and other necessary equipment required for their mission.

"Nice touch," Danny declared. "And you all said we could not trust the princes."

Wulf grabbed the new pack and dumped its contents onto the table. He set his own pack onto a chair. The others stood and stared in stunned silence. He sifted through the contents. Wulf removed the iron rations and water skins and placed them in his pack and left the rest. He picked up a coin bag and opened it. He looked at his companions, smiled, then poured the gold coins onto the ground.

"Guilt money," he snarled. "Guess my life is only worth fifty gold pieces."

Wulf shouldered his pack, grabbed a quiver of arrows, and strolled to the stables.

"He always like this?" Danny whispered.

Matthew raised an eyebrow and shrugged. Roan chuckled to himself and left his new pack on the ground. The others followed Wulf's lead and trailed him to the horse barn.

◊ ◊ ◊

He stood alone and unseen on the balcony, peering down into the torchlit courtyard. The trees swayed and their leaves rustled in a south breeze coming in off the harbor. They cast ghostly shadows that whirled and twirled in the early morning. He wrapped his black robes around his body as protection against sharp and damp air. He smiled, meager and bitter. It satisfied the messenger that his plans were unfolding as expected. Gambier and the relics were in Udontawny. The bothersome brothers, Francis and Tralderonn, no longer sat within the assembly, and they could not interfere anymore in his plans. Francis stood accused and imprisoned in Ripley's Keep for crimes he did not commit. No, he corrected himself. Francis should arrive in Udontawny soon. He gave a mirthless laugh. *And Mora and Kheel dead. Mora dead. What a pleasant thought.*

"And Tralderonn." Just speaking the rebel prince's name enraged him. He gripped the iron railing tight. The bounty hunters had him in their hands, the messenger assured himself, and soon Tralderonn would join his brother in Udontawny as well. Finally, the elves and outlanders were departing on their forlorn rescue mission. Six against the abominations stalking the Border Lands? Their failure all but guaranteed. He laughed at the notion. Yes, all was going according to plan. *The master will be pleased, and I will gladly assume all the credit.* A sharp rap on the door interrupted his musings.

"Enter," the messenger grumbled.

The door creaked and moaned as the proxy entered the messenger's darkened quarters. He halted in the dimness and waited.

"What?" the messenger croaked.

"The Lancers have not returned from Ripley's Keep," the proxy declared, his countenance blank.

"Why would I care?" the messenger snapped.

"Thought you should know," the proxy admitted.

"Now is not the time for ill news." The messenger waved his hand. "Come."

The proxy stepped onto the balcony and stood next to the messenger.

"The last piece." The messenger pointed to the elves and outlanders exiting the Martial Gate. "All is in order."

"So it seems," the proxy stated.

◊ ◊ ◊

Singjeye watched from afar as the six rode out of the Martial Gate. Singjeye removed the cowl from his head and wiped his brow. A satisfied sneer slithered over his face. He spat on the ground. "May death find you, elf and outlander."

A figure skulked from the gloom and loitered near a tree. His body was shrouded by his robes, his face concealed beneath a cowl. Singjeye noticed and approached the figure. He offered a respectful bow.

"It is done?"

"It is," Singjeye answered.

"As discussed?"

"Yes," Singjeye assured.

Without another word, the figure slunk back into the shadows.

◊ ◊ ◊

Just as the sun blended into the colors of dawn, they rode over empty torchlit streets. None spoke, only the rhythmic clacking of horse hooves on stone pavers disrupted the silence. Highpoint slept, unaware of their presence. Their journey, Roan had informed them, would consume at least a week, maybe longer. Wulf glanced at the ranger. The cobalt eyes focused straight ahead, the brow furrowed. A sense of urgency had fueled his speech and actions. Roan was in a hurry and Wulf concurred. The sooner they departed Auroryies, the better.

They crossed the Tressel border as the sun cleared the eastern horizon. A mile outside Leeds, Roan veered northwest and, a day later, turned due north. The days grew shorter and the weather colder as they rode north. Winter was prepared to make its presence known. They set a steady pace, and the ensuing two days and nights passed without incident.

◊ ◊ ◊

After another bumpy and dusty coach ride, Paddy reached Leeds. The driver halted the team, climbed down from the seat, and peered at Paddy. "A quick stop to water the horses."

Paddy stepped from the coach and took a quick look around. He removed a rag from his vest pocket and wiped the sweat and dust from his face. "What a dump."

Paddy disregarded the people staring and pointing as he strolled along the dirt streets, stretching his legs. Paddy stopped a few feet from a group of young boys leaning against a dilapidated building. One of them flipped a gold coin up in the air, then caught it. *How does a child in this shabby village have a gold coin?*

He stepped a little closer and waited. When the boy tossed the coin again, Paddy snatched it out of the air.

"Hey!" the boy squealed. "That's mine."

Paddy ignored the child and examined the gold piece. *South Hampton gold.* A broad grin spread across his cherub face. "Where did you get this?"

"An elf," the boy spat.

"Hm. About this tall?" Paddy asked, standing on his toes. "Pointed ears like mine?"

"Yeah, I guess," the boy answered. "Give me my gold."

"Oh. Yes, sorry," Paddy muttered as he handed the boy his gold. The halfling reached into his pocket and pulled out another gold piece. "Here. For your trouble."

"Hey, thanks," the boy said and showed the piece to his friends. "Look what the little elf gave me."

Paddy spun about and headed back to the coach. "Getting closer, Caldwell."

◊ ◊ ◊

On the dawn of day three, the six companions left Tressel and passed into Beth Amen. Over broad grass plains stretching from horizon to horizon, they rode. The sun burned bright against a cloudless sky, its warmth dissipating last night's chill. It was late afternoon when they observed large herds of cattle grazing on the last of fall's grass. Thirty more minutes elapsed until they caught sight of buildings rising from the plains.

Dusk clung to the west when they entered a small village built along a stream. A lone waterwheel creaked and moaned as it turned. The sign outside the village said Cowpens and the companions' noses agreed. The inquisitive peered out their doors to get a glimpse of the riders. Candles burned in the windows as they passed homes, a stable, a general store, and an inn. Three men congregated outside the inn and recognized Wulf and Matthew as troopers.

"Georgy, go see what they want," one suggested.

"By the Maiden," Georgy declared, his beam wide and friendly as he stepped from the porch. He looked back over his shoulder. "Fritter and Clipp, we got troopers and elves in our village!"

"Well, it's been a minute since I have seen me an elf," Fritter chuckled.

Wulf reined Maggie to a stop and climbed out of the saddle. He noticed their weapons—sword scabbards strapped to their belts and their bows leaned against the building. "Gentlemen, I am Captain Blackhawk, and these are my companions."

"Captain, what brings you to our little corner of the kingdom?" Georgy inquired.

"On an assignment from the king," Wulf replied. "Won't be staying but the night then moving on. You got room for us and stalls for the horses?"

"A cold mug and a warm meal?" Matthew added.

"Sure. Troopers and their friends are welcome here." Fritter motioned for them to come inside. "I sure miss seeing you boys around here."

"Yeah," Clipp chuckled. "Ain't nothing around here but old folks and youngsters these days."

"And cows!" Fritter laughed. "Smell 'em for miles, you can."

"All gone north?" Matthew asked.

"Yep," Clipp answered. "Colonel Aseph and his entire regiment."

"Even took our Volunteers," Fritter added. "Said they're needed around Jacob's Forge and Stirling Hill."

"We ain't bellyaching, though," Georgy chimed in, patting the scabbard strapped to his hip. "We're all old troopers anyway.

"Any news from the front?" Clipp inquired. "Ain't seen a messenger here in months."

"King Stockton and the army were holding along the Mulford when we departed," Matthew offered.

"Got the limp and lost a couple of fingers at the Mulford," Georgy whooped. "Miss 'em sometimes."

"Stables over there," Clipp pointed. "While you're tending to your mounts, I will rustle up some chow."

After Wulf, Matthew, Roan, Danny, Naphtali, and Wrayer groomed, fed, and watered their horses, they spent the evening eating, drinking, and swapping stories with their hosts. It seemed at one point the entire village crammed into the inn to peek at the elves and their peculiar ears or to enjoy some stories. Somewhere around midnight, the crowd thinned and the companions headed for their rooms. If they had been asked, the villagers would say they slept better knowing the troopers and elves were there.

Chapter Fifty

Fall 531, Age of the Arch Mage

When the sunrise came, the companions were an hour northwest of Cowpens. For two days, their path led them north across Beth Amen's northern plains. They stayed in Early Branch that night and the following in Amosville. Rested and resupplied, the companions passed over the Maguana border ahead of the next sunrise. The rugged Highland mountains, majestic and snow-covered, stood proudly on their right as they traveled. On occasion, they heard the blare, low and mournful, from a lone barbarian war horn echoing down the valleys and ravines. On the morning of day eight, the six companions forded the North River and passed into the Border Lands.

"It's good to be home, Maggie," Wulf declared, running his hand down her neck, his tone sarcastic and his smile impish.

Maggie snorted and threw her head.

Wrayer leaned to Matthew. "She understands?"

"Yes, every word," Matthew answered.

"Oh," Wrayer said. "Well, okay."

The terrain was a vast barren plain stretching out before them for as far as they could see. Rocks fractured and weathered, and windswept trees littered the entire landscape. Rolling hills loomed to the north and snow-covered mountains farther beyond. Roan kept them tacking north along a well-worn dirt trail. Boot prints, horse hooves, and wagon wheels rutted the earth.

"Someone recently traveled this trail," Roan stated, peering over at Wulf. "You ever see roads in the Border Lands?"

"No," Wulf replied.

"I don't recall a village or outpost shown on the map."

"Me neither." Wulf shrugged. "Remember, it's not accurate."

"I know." Doubt crept further into Roan's mind. Was the map mis-drawn on purpose? The thought added to his mistrust.

An hour farther on, Roan noticed the vultures circling. He projected his senses, searching the broken terrain. Other than the flying scavengers, the ranger detected nothing. Three miles later, Roan brought his companions to a halt and retrieved his book from his saddlebag. In front of them lay human bodies, stripped and broken, and the rotting carcasses of their mounts. The attackers had plundered weapons, clothes, and tack and left nothing behind. A foul stench wafted in the air, causing Danny, Wrayer, and Naphtali to retch. Dried blood stained the ground and grass. The corpses were bloated and pallid. Flies droned, and other insects crawled in and out of the remains. Roan and Wulf dismounted and scattered the vultures.

Roan strayed twenty yards north, stopping occasionally to peruse something he saw on the ground. A set of footprints intermingled among paw prints, a piece of fur, a drop of blood. Each one a clue.

Roan paused and scanned the surrounding terrain. Rolling hills flanked the trail. He worked his way back to his companions. Danny stood atop a small rise. Wulf knelt near a dead horse and Naphtali roamed among the corpses. Wrayer and Matthew traipsed east, pointing at the ground as they went.

"See anything?" Roan shouted to the rogue.

"Footprints and claw marks," Danny yelled. "Nothing else."

"Okay." Danny's discovery confirmed Roan's hunch—the orcs had ambushed the humans. He halted near the dead.

Roan found foot and paw prints all around. The footprints he knew belonged to orcs, the others required further study. He knelt in the dirt and traced his finger along the edge of a paw print, wide, broad pads and claws embedded into the ground. *Worgs.* Worgs produced these prints. He knew them well. Many times his bow and blades fought them in the past. Akin to wolves, the worgs possessed a massive head and a body the size of a pony. Slender muzzles contained long rows of teeth sharper than pikes. Dark eyes sat under a furrowed brow, narrowed and consumed by a feral hatred. Gray and black, their coats were wiry and thick. Roan stood and moved to a dead human.

The ranger knelt near the body. Most of the flesh was gone, picked clean by bugs, birds, and other scavengers. He recognized the broken orc arrows lying near the corpses.

Wulf stopped near one horse. Its head and neck bore sword slashes. Broken arrows lay near the body. Wulf examined the crude fletching—he had seen it before. A large chunk of flesh was missing from the horse's flank and hindquarters. He bent down. The area around the wound appeared ripped and torn. Wulf was not familiar with injuries like these.

Roan stood and resumed his gruesome examination. He knelt again. A glimmer near the body caught his attention. He picked up the object and studied it for a moment. It was a bronze belt buckle with 'Lancer' engraved on the metal. He grimaced and came to his feet.

Wulf moved to a second dead horse and observed similar wounds. "Roan, look at the wounds."

Roan stepped to Wulf and tossed him the buckle. He paused near the dead horse. "Worgs."

Wulf nodded. He recalled Kiah's stories concerning the giant wolves and their orc riders. He considered the buckle, then handed it over to Matthew. "Highpoint Lancers."

"Yes," Roan agreed. He pointed east. "Orcs ambushed the Lancers. From what I can piece together, they never expected the attack."

Roan climbed into the saddle, removed a leather-bound book from his bag, and began writing.

"What were Lancers doing this far north?" Matthew wondered.

"Not sure," Roan admitted. "Other than tracks, the orcs left us no clues."

"Does it matter?" Danny chimed in.

"Not really." Roan surveyed the area again, then scribbled a few notes in his book. More intrigue, fewer answers.

"How long have they been dead?" Naphtali inquired with a notable sadness in his tone.

"A week? Can't say for sure," Roan answered. "The scavengers and decay make it difficult to estimate."

"This whole affair gets stranger by the day," Wrayer stated, fidgeting in the saddle. The sight of the lifeless soldiers disturbed him.

And deadlier, Roan concluded.

Chapter Fifty-One

Winter 532, Age of the Arch Mage

Tralderonn awoke in the early morning hours soaked in sweat, his muscles tight and his back sore. Weeks had passed since his fight with the bounty hunters and the calendar now showed 532 Age of the Arch Mage. He sat up and placed his bare feet on the cold stone floor. Tralderonn struggled to his feet and limped to the window. He drew aside the thin curtains. A full moon and stars shone bright against a cloudless sky. He stared over the sleeping city. A quiet hung over Tetj as the city prepared for the coming day. Tralderonn placed his hand upon the window and felt the frosty morning air. Fall had passed and winter eagerly replaced it.

His thoughts went straight to Carjlin. He missed her bright blue eyes and sincere smile. Restored and recommitted into the Maiden's service, she had departed for the seminary in Beth Amen two days ago. He counted her as a friend, he concluded, and with time, it could have been more. *In the near future? Maybe? When this was all over? Curious.* He dismissed the ridiculous idea, but not her.

His mind drifted to his mother. Her calming presence, her infectious charm and warm smile thawed his frozen heart. Again, he wondered how he knew she had died. His old professor and friend, Prince Hura, had taught him, for reasons unexplained, a sorcerer's natural magic bound them to other sorcerers. He chuckled to himself at the notion. He did not know he was a sorcerer until he came to Auroryies. Hura instructed him that sorcerers came by their arcana naturally, where wizards must learn and study their magic. Hura said sorcerers inherited their magic, passed down from one generation to another.

Tralderonn paused his musings for a moment. He cocked his head and set his other hand to the window. If this was true, then it meant his mother was a sorceress. *Curious.* His mother told him tales concerning his grandmother's magic, but he never considered his mother a sorceress. This time, Tralderonn laughed out loud. *Could she* ... He could not finish the thought. A wave of guilt replaced his laughter as he realized he had not afforded himself the opportunity to grieve. He closed his eyes and let the tears come.

Tralderonn slumped to the floor and leaned his head against the wall. The rage combined with the magic consumed him. It ruined his health and gnawed at his soul. His mind clouded, Tralderonn found it difficult to think. He rubbed his chin and touched the rough stubble of three, maybe four, days of growth. He ran his hand over his bald head. It felt the same. His eyes snapped open and he scanned the room. Tralderonn was alone, yet he perceived a distant voice cutting through the murk inside his head. *Curious.* He closed his eyes once more and heard the voice again. This time, it was clearer and recognizable. He climbed to his feet and faced the window once more.

-- I am sorry -- she whispered. -- Kysellah is dead --

I know.

-- Traldy, someone murdered your mother -- she declared.

Murdered? Why? Who? He felt his anger and magic stir.

-- I am not sure -- she confessed. She possessed strong suspicions, but it was not the time to share them. Tralderonn was unstable, physically and mentally.

My father?

-- He lives -- she confirmed. She omitted the fact that Elaire's ward protected him. -- He remains safe within Evergreen --

Tralderonn struggled to his feet. *I am going to Prosper.*

-- For what? -- she inquired. -- Vengeance? --

Yes. He snapped his fingers and watched the flames dance in his palm.

-- Do no such thing -- she demanded.

Why not?

-- I need you -- she implored.

For what?

-- Francis and Kheel are gone -- she admitted, her voice frail and scared. --Taken by the forces of Belhaaz --

He dismissed the flames and set his head against the window, felt the cold glass on his skin. His mind churned. Francis and Kheel gone? Belhaaz? He had so many questions but fumbled for the words. He lifted his head and exhaled. Tralderonn stared into the frosted pane. His reflection surprised him. The frown and his eyes, sunken and hollow, bothered him. He looked older than his age. Death's grip closed about him. He sensed its fearsome presence. *Do you know where they are?*

-- No --

Then how do I—

-- Come to Ripley's Keep and we can figure this out together --

For a long minute, he let their conversation lag while languishing in silent speculation. His thoughts scattered everywhere at once. Revenge for his mother's killing. Locating his father. Saving Francis and Kheel. In the end, he decided revenge and his father could wait. Francis and Kheel could not. *I will leave soonest.*

-- Thank you --

Tralderonn sensed the relief in her voice and prayed she would not regret placing her hope in him. *Mora?*

-- Yes --

Are you the—

-- Soon -- Mora vowed. -- Soon, Tralderonn --

And then, like a candle in the rain, her voice faded. He smiled and for a moment, Tralderonn felt an inner peace he had not enjoyed in decades. Tralderonn scanned the simple yet comfortable room where he had lived for the past month. He would not forget the Matron Sister and her clerics' grace, kindness, and hospitality. He dressed, stowed what few possessions he owned, grabbed his staff, and shouldered his pack. Wisdom told him it would be best to depart Tejt ahead of sunrise. Tralderonn paused when his eyes caught sight of the leather satchel hanging on the chair next to his bed. He had forgotten about it.

Tralderonn sat on the corner of his bed and studied the bag for several minutes. He recalled snatching it from the dead bounty hunter's hands as he fled his room at the inn. Tralderonn grabbed the satchel from the chair and held it in his lap. Did he want to know its contents? *Curious.* His fingers fumbled over the buckles. He lifted the flap, stared inside. What was he afraid of? The truth? He dumped the contents on the bed. An envelope and a coin bag tumbled out. He grasped the coin bag—it was weighty and poured out gold. He picked up a piece and held it near the candle. It was unmarred and shiny, most likely minted a few months ago.

Tralderonn grimaced at what he saw. The coin bore the likeness of High Prince Xavian. He flipped the coin over and read the word Highpoint engraved on it. Two hundred gold pieces lay in a pile. His life was only worth two hundred gold pieces? *Curious.*

Tralderonn removed two pieces of parchment from the envelope, one a letter and the other a map. The letter looked neatly written, each pen stroke precise. The writer appeared educated and a skilled scribe. A prince, he concluded. He read and reread the letter. The author mentioned him by name, along with a detailed description of his appearance. The words written in the last paragraph chilled him.

Take him to a man named Milton. You will find Milton at the Troll's Head in the city of Udontawny. Milton will pay you the other half of your fee.

"Four hundred gold pieces," Tralderonn smirked. "That's better."

He examined the map. It was crude but useable. He located the city deep inside the Border Lands. He dwelt on the letter. "Why would they take me to Udontawny?"

"Udontawny," Tralderonn whispered. He stood and stepped to the window. He felt betrayed, that his life resembled an elaborate charade. *Curious.* Tralderonn paused his musings and looked at the map. He repeated Udontawny over and over, trying to assemble the puzzle. "Of course, Udontawny."

His gut told him Francis and Kheel were there. He shut his eyes. His sense of fleeting peace dissipated in an instant. He felt his grandmother's magic, his mother's magic roiling inside him scorching and able, freed from ethics or logic. *Mora.*

-- Yes --

Udontawny is where I will find Francis and Kheel.

-- Are you sure? --

Yes. I am going to find them!

A long silence passed until she spoke again. -- Use restraint --

I am a model of restraint.

-- You lie --

◊ ◊ ◊

The Matron Sister knelt in the chapel. Only the soft glow from a single candle scattered the darkness surrounding her. This was her time to spend in undisturbed prayer as the dawn hovered below the eastern horizon. She cherished these moments in the Maiden's presence. In the middle of her prayer, an ominous feeling hammered her. The Matron Sister gasped and her eyes flew open. There was rage, unfettered and savage, inside the Cathedral. She took a deep breath to calm herself and rose. "Forgive me, my Maiden. I must go to him."

The Matron Sister hustled through darkened corridors. Worry and concern etched her face. Out into the empty courtyard she trotted, each breath clear in the chilled air. A fading full moon hung low in the western sky, the stars erased from view. Barren trees swayed back and forth, their leaves rustling over the ground. The damp and brisk breeze chilled her skin. She saw him exiting the stables as she neared. She slowed to a walk, then stopped.

Tralderonn hesitated when he caught sight of the Matron Sister. He felt a twinge of regret and embarrassment for sneaking off. He had wanted to find her to say thank you and goodbye, but his courage failed him. And now here they stood, facing each other.

"You are not ready to leave," she stated, her elven features drawn tight, her eyes pleading. "I cannot protect you beyond these walls."

Her pained expression intensified his remorse. Tralderonn shifted his eyes from her gaze.

"I must," he admitted, his voice cracking as he spoke. "My brother and nephew need me."

She stepped to him and took his hands in hers. "There is too much rage."

His eyes met hers. "It may save my life, and theirs."

"Please stay."

"I can't." Tralderonn drew her into his arms. He felt her strength, her conviction, and in the raw morning air, it offered hope. A hope he wanted. A hope he needed. "Matron Sister, let me go with your blessing."

In his embrace, she perceived the fury roiling within him. It scared her. Tralderonn stood on the brink—one step either way and he could lose himself or save himself. In the end, it would be his choice, salvation or damnation.

"And the Maiden's," she whispered. She eased from his arms and kissed him on the forehead. "I pray you find the peace you seek."

Tralderonn smiled. Neither had anything else to say. He turned from her and strode for the gate, then climbed into the saddle. A Canon opened the gate and Tralderonn rode out of the cathedral grounds, never looking back.

Keerrin Feeallah, the Matron Sister, lingered in the cold early morning as a sense of significant loss swept over her. She knew in her heart Tralderonn would never grace these grounds again. The Matron Sister hustled to the gate and leaned against the wall. She watched him ride away into the torchlit streets. She kept her eyes fixed on him until he rounded a corner and disappeared from her sight. The Matron Sister dabbed at the tears welling in her eyes. "May the Maiden shine upon you, Tralderonn."

Chapter Fifty-Two

Winter 532, Age of the Arch Mage

The companions resumed their ride north, leaving the dead Lancers behind. Morning passed into afternoon and the terrain and weather changed. Flat plains gave way to mountains. Peaks, snowcapped and rugged, dominated the skyline. A raw and cutting north wind sailed down the slopes, penetrating clothes and armor, chilling exposed skin. Crooked scrub trees, deformed and bare, groaned, defying the breeze. Roan led them into a canyon wide enough to fit a wagon. Sheer rock faces rose hundreds of feet on either side. Roan bristled at the lack of maneuver space. It would prove difficult fighting in close quarters. Ugly memories of the Belowground crept into his mind.

On the wind, Matthew detected a noise, feeble and distant. Perhaps a hymn of praise or a limerick recited in honor of a hero. He closed his eyes and heard it again. This time it was louder with a tinge of sorrow. It was no longer a song or poem but a mournful wail, like a mother lamenting the loss of a child. Matthew hesitated and then heard it a third time. Curses, profane and blasphemous, emerging from the abyss assailed his soul. Screams and shrieks stabbed at him. He recoiled to avoid the attack. From a nightmare, the creature materialized and came toward him. Coarse hair stood along an arched spine. Eyes, red and narrowed, locked onto his own. The creature stood upright on two legs, its height akin to a barbarian's. The maw, long and narrow, was ajar, revealing hooked fangs. Jaws snapped angrily at the air. It swung a bloodied muzzle at Matthew, baring all its teeth. Icy claws borne on the wind swiped at him. Matthew feared the beast. This was unfamiliar territory for him. He clung to his faith, embraced his beliefs. He threw his head to clear his mind. *No! By the Maiden, flee from my presence!*

The cleric's eyes flew wide open. His hands shook. The beast was gone. He felt the sweat rolling down his back and forming on his brow. He peered over at Wulf. Matthew exhaled—his friend was unaware.

Onward they trudged, ignoring the weather. By midafternoon, the canyon widened into a broad valley. The wind abated, and the sun broke free from the clouds, warming the air. Another hour passed until they viewed the ruins emerging from the canyon floor, a ragged collection of stone spires, walls, and buildings decayed by the elements and forgotten by time.

"Stop!" Matthew demanded. His companions obeyed and focused on the cleric. "An ancient evil lingers in those ruins."

Roan nodded and placed a finger to his lips. He closed his eyes and freed his senses. Out they stretched, seeking unseen threats his eyes could not see and his ears could not hear. His eyes snapped open. He detected thirteen giants loitering inside the shattered city. Another presence dwelt among the ruins, elusive and ethereal. His wariness piqued as he perceived the evil. It was one he did not recognize, a thread twisting in the wind, an apparition lacking form and substance. Roan signaled for his companions to stay put and leapt from his horse. He tugged his battle mask up, armed his bow, and sprinted west. Matthew moved his mouth in silent petition beseeching the Maiden's protection. In a breath, the Maiden shielded them.

The ranger hastened his pace—they could not afford even a brief delay. On each step, the evil flourished, growing stronger as he neared. He felt its weight bearing him down as he ran. A mile later, Roan entered the ruins. Only collapsed archways, crumbling buildings, and deteriorating statues remained. He scanned his surroundings. He stood amidst a snarl of dilapidated structures constructed by an ancient civilization long dead and forever gone. For a second, he thought he caught sight of it, a wisp of black, a puff of smoke unworldly and intangible. And then it was gone. He scurried on through debris-filled streets searching for the giants. He found them foraging among the wreckage and rubble near the city's center. Lumbering and slow, each giant taller than the largest barbarian, they grunted and snorted, picking at the fragments, seeking trinkets and food. Despite their dull nature, they possessed immense strength and could kill a man using their hands. For a second, he considered attacking. He drew the bowstring to his cheek and sighted in. Quickly, Roan decided he could lead his companions around the west side of the city undetected. There was no need to fight unless they must. He let the giants alone and scampered back.

An hour remained in the day when Roan found his companions where he left them. As one, they rose to greet him.

"Thirteen giants occupy the ruins," he disclosed.

"The evil?" Matthew inquired.

"It is there. Keep praying. I am not sure bows and blades will protect us," Roan admitted. "Come, I will lead us around the giants."

With Roan in the lead, the companions set off again. The day's sun was easing below the western horizon when they reached the city's outskirts. Roan paused and gathered them around him. "Stay close. I can mask our movement. The hill giants will not see or hear us."

Roan spoke a few Elvish words. In an instant, he cloaked and muted their presence. He wanted to cast out his senses but knew he could not conceal them and search for threats at the same time. He hoped the giants still lingered near the city center. Roan beckoned his band forward. Melting into the dimness, they crept around the western side of the city. Matthew cringed when an evil as old as Gaiand revealed itself. A voice called to him, a menacing murmur across the forsaken landscape spoke into his head.

-- Cleric of the Maiden-- it whispered, so only Matthew could hear. --The darkness will consume you. There is no victory for you--

The cleric kept pace alongside his companions. He did not waver. *I will forever win.*

-- Not today --

Yes, he avowed, his tone confident and sure. *The dawn's light forever wins over darkness.*

The voice did not speak further.

Fifteen minutes passed—they were halfway through. The six companions shuddered. With each footfall, the evil assailed, filling them with doubt and tearing at their faith. Roan looked over at the cleric. Matthew's lips moved, his words unheard as he continued his appeal to the Maiden. The others did not know what was happening in the spiritual world, but Matthew's shield glimmered in its blue hue, so they were assured the Maiden marched by their side. Their faces reflected what they could see, hear, and smell. A blessing, Roan concluded.

Like a worg, it stalked them at a distance. Gathering its scattered form once more, it sprang forth from the dusk. It was visible to Matthew now, frightening and murderous. Muscles coiled tight rippled on each step. Anticipating the kill, eager to consume flesh and taste blood, its tongue curled over jagged teeth. Claws raked the earth as it padded on a parallel course, searching for a gap to exploit. Eyes, piercing and red, flashed with hate. It was a demon, or a fiend, Matthew determined. This time, Matthew did not fear the beast. He resolved the Maiden's protection would suffice. The beast leapt for the cleric. Bathed in the dawn's blue light, the shield rose to meet the beast. Light exploded as the shield and beast collided. The beast howled in anger, yelped in pain as it staggered from the blow. Back on its feet, the beast snarled, low and enraged, in frustration at seeing its prey escape. Matthew looked at his companions. They held no knowledge of what had just happened.

Fifteen more minutes elapsed until they reached the west side. The sun was setting in layers of pinks, scarlets, and purples above the gray clouds when they cleared the ruins. Roan did not curtail their rate of march. Now was not the time to tempt fate. Besides, tangling with thirteen hill giants and an unseen specter could prove time-consuming and deadly. Time was not a luxury they possessed. He dispelled his masking magic and discharged his senses. The giants and the baleful apparition remained in the city and no other threats revealed themselves. They had passed out of danger for the moment.

Over the next three miles, they marched into the coming night. The moon surfaced in the east, stars emerged onto a black canvas. The day's warmth was long gone, and frosty air supplanted it. An hour came and went before Roan halted them five miles beyond the ruins. He allowed them a quick rest for a sip of water and a couple of bites from their rations. They caught their breath, drank, and ate in a tenuous silence. None of them dared to speak out loud. Roan eased from his saddle and scoured the immediate area. The road was gone and the giants they avoided in the city had formed the only tracks he discovered. He yanked the map from his satchel. The city, the road were nowhere on the map. Doubt endured, uncertainty nagged with each mile they traveled.

After ten minutes, they climbed into the saddle once more. Roan led, trailed by Danny, Wulf, Matthew, and Wrayer. Naphtali secured the rear of their six-man single-file column. Beyond the city, the landscape transitioned to a wide expanse of rolling hills. Through the dusk and the night, they progressed north at a rapid pace. With each passing hour, the temperature dropped. The moon and stars peeked in and out of the clouds. The air was damp and adhered to their clothes, weapons, and armor. They stopped every two hours for a brief respite for them and the horses.

Thick clouds spoiled the sunrise and threatened rain. The hills were behind them, and they found themselves amidst a tangle of rock formations stripped bare by weather and time. Roan scrambled atop an outcrop of boulders and tugged the map from his satchel. He scanned the barren landscape, then looked at the map. Ripley's Keep should be close. A dense fog blanketed the terrain, obscuring his view. Closing his eyes, Roan concentrated on the Keep, visualized the ancient bastion in his mind. He permitted his senses to reach out, sweeping the Border Lands' vastness. *Nothing.* What he sought was beyond his range or not there at all.

A hundred yards ahead, the rock formations ended, and another barren plain assumed its place. The terrain offered no clues, no evidence he could pursue. His instincts urged him to proceed east. Roan exhaled—his exasperation was apparent. Roan climbed down to where his companions stood. "I can't sense the Keep."

Can't sense the Keep. Roan's admission amazed Wulf. Kiah and Seth could perceive danger and live creatures, not inanimate objects. He could not recall Kiah or Seth possessing the ability to mask others. *What kind of power did this elven ranger possess?*

Wulf glanced at Matthew, hoping the cleric would have an answer. Matthew shrugged. The ranger confounded him as well.

"According to the map, the Keep should be within five miles of here." Roan balled the map in his hand and tossed it away.

Chapter Fifty-Three

Winter 532, Age of the Arch Mage

Eastward they marched, traversing the desolate and broken terrain. The mist and clouds persisted into late afternoon, soaking their clothing. Windswept scrubs, blunted and misshapen, reminded Roan of the duergar or the dark dwarves, gray and dour. The small company could see for miles in each direction trooping amid wide open plains. The landscape offered no cover to mask or conceal their movements. They trudged on alone and exposed.

Roan scoured the eastern horizon and frowned. Two miles ahead, he detected the landscape abruptly transition from flat sweeping plains into a snarl of rocks and boulders extending for miles north and south. From this distance, he could not determine if the horses could navigate the terrain. Roan closed his eyes, his senses leapt out seeking what he could not see, hear, taste, or smell. He sighed, shaking his head. Francis, the relics, and the Keep remained beyond his range. But the pack of orcs astride worgs was not.

"Worgs and orcs tracking us from the west." Roan yanked his battle mask up over his face. "The rocks ahead may provide protection. I will distract them."

"Find a passage through." Wulf was adamant. He looked at Roan and lifted a hand to signal his intent. "Maggie's faster."

Before Roan or anyone else protested, he reined Maggie around and urged her into a gallop.

"Wulf—"

"Let the Orc Slayer go, Roan," Matthew interrupted. "He knows how to fight. He may be reckless, but he is not stupid."

Roan knitted his brow and frowned. Eight minutes later, they attained the rock formation.

"Danny, ride south no more than a mile," Roan ordered. "I will go north. Wrayer, Naphtali, and Matthew, keep an eye out for Wulf."

Roan turned his horse north. He rode less than two hundred yards when he found a breach in the rocks, one wide enough to accommodate a horse. He leapt from his horse and scampered into the formations. Fifty yards in, he determined this would be their path. Too narrow to ride so they would have to lead the horses through. Roan pivoted, sprinted to his horse, and exited the rocks.

"Naphtali," Roan yelled. He motioned for the others to join him.

◊ ◊ ◊

Maggie cantered free and easy, her iron shoes tearing into the terrain. Her breathing was effortless, her gait smooth and flawless. Now six years old, she was just inside her prime and no longer considered a filly. Maggie possessed a simple grace uncommon among trooper mounts. Her strength and power defied her average stature, her endurance and dexterity unmatched. Fiercely loyal and spirited, she was fearless in combat. Her mind was sharp. No one could find a smarter horse. Full of surprises, Maggie never ceased to amaze, and sometimes she knew what Wulf intended to do before he did.

They shared an uncharacteristic bond—it was an uncommon attachment between horse and rider. Faithful? Yes. Devotion? It was undeniable. An unconditional love for each other? Of course. And like his, her body bore the scars from countless skirmishes and battles.

Wulf slowed Maggie to a trot and scanned west, seeking the worgriders. He peeked over his shoulder—his companions neared the rock formations. They only needed a few more minutes. Wulf brought Maggie to a halt and ran his hand down her neck. "You sense them?"

She whinnied and pawed the ground. He had his answer. Although beyond his vision, Maggie felt their presence. They lingered in place until Wulf observed a handful of worgriders crest a slight rise. Maggie did not wait for Wulf to urge her into battle. She pinned her ears and exploded into a gallop. Wulf released the reins and nocked an arrow. He tightened his grip on his bow and applied his draw. Sound faded to a dull drone and his vision narrowed. Wulf exhaled and released the string. The arrow hissed as it took flight. Unseen, the missile streaked through the gray mist on a deadly path. The worg stumbled for another stride, then crashed to the ground, crushing the orc rider under its weight.

Maggie wheeled hard right then back left while Wulf's bow loosed death on the worgs and orcs. Claws raked at unoccupied space and maws snapped at empty air. The worgs roared in frustration and the orcs cursed as Maggie zigzagged just beyond their reach. As the last worg sucked in its final breath, Wulf gazed west. The rest of the worgriders were coming into view. Wulf grabbed the reins and steered Maggie east to reunite with their friends. He leaned over the saddle and Maggie found another burst of speed.

◊ ◊ ◊

They gathered near the gap. Roan directed a glance west to check on Wulf and Maggie. He could see them, trooper and his ardent mount, racing towards him. Roan cast out his senses. The orcs and worgs advanced, their pace increasing. "Danny, lead them through. Naphtali, take my horse."

Roan scampered onto the rocks and surveyed the plains. Wulf and Maggie neared, less than a minute out. Roan spun to his right. Wrayer stood next to him. "Got an idea."

The ranger smirked. "Okay."

"Let the orcs get within a hundred yards," Wrayer demanded.

Wulf reined Maggie to a halt and slid from the saddle. He removed her bridle and hung it on the saddle horn. "They're closing fast."

"I know," Roan replied with a wry smile. "And with five fewer in their ranks."

"Find Matthew." Wulf patted Maggie on the butt, and she walked into the breach. Wulf joined Roan and Wrayer on the rocks. "We running or fighting?"

"Not sure at the moment," Roan admitted.

"More like a delaying action," Wrayer added.

The three companions watched the worgriders come into view. Wulf set an arrow onto the string and winked at Roan. Wulf drew the string taut and sighted in. A hush fell over him. He slowed his breathing, felt his grip tighten on his bow. He delayed his shot, allowing the worg and orc to come a few steps closer. The arrow leapt from the string. The missile buried into the worg's chest, sending it and the orc tumbling. Wulf snatched another arrow from his quiver and rearmed his bow. He shifted to his left and released the string. A second worg collapsed.

In rapid succession, Roan fired twice, slaying two more worgs. When the worgs were in range, Wrayer traced an arc over the rocks using his staff. He clapped his hands and spread his arms wide. A wall-sized barrier of fire erupted from the ground in front of the worgs. He spun about to face his surprised companions. "We should go."

The lead worgs and orcs reacted too slowly. They plowed into the flames, catching fur and flesh on fire. Screeching and yelping, they spun and fled. The remaining orcs snatched at the reins, desperate to avoid the flames. Roan, Wulf, and Wrayer jumped from the rocks and dashed into the breach.

Chapter Fifty-Four

Winter 532, Age of the Arch Mage

Their pace slowed to a near crawl as the companions and the horses picked their way through a maze of stone formations, split and jagged. The clouds broke as the sun began its slow descent into the west. Lizards, snakes, and skinks basking on the warm rocks hissed their displeasure when the six companions disturbed their slumber.

The rocks and stone trapped and absorbed the sun's warmth, raising the temperature inside the maze. They emerged from the labyrinth near dusk, drained and soaked in sweat. A stiff wind blew in from the north and, minus the cloud cover to retain the day's heat, the companions faced a chilly night. Pinks, grays, and yellows had washed over the western sky when Roan brought them to a halt. They stood on a narrow rock ledge just wide enough for the horses.

Roan scrabbled atop a stone formation for a better view of his surroundings. The minutes passed and their chances of escaping the worgriders waned as the daylight receded. In less than an hour, the Border Lands would fade to black. He perceived the orcs loitering near the breach. The hunt was on and soon the worgs would pick up their scent. They could not camp here for the night. Hurriedly, he studied the terrain sprawling out ahead of him, seeking a path to safety. Mountains to the south and north flanked a wide vale a hundred feet below. Trees lined a stream snaking its way along the valley floor.

Roan shut his eyes, and he released his senses, searching for the Keep, seeking any hint of Francis or the relics. Nothing, yet he believed they proceeded on the correct course. He scowled and cursed under his breath. Roan stepped to his left and located a game trail descending into the valley. The path was not ideal, especially for Wulf and Matthew. The elves and the half-elf benefitted from night vision, a natural ability to see in the dark. Wulf and Matthew did not, and it left them at a disadvantage. It was a risk, but one worth taking. It would get them off the ledge and farther away from the worg riders. From his perch, Roan spun west. "Worg riders!"

A roar, angry and loud, shattered the coming dusk.

"Naphtali and Matthew, take the breach," Roan shouted. "Wulf, you have the north flank. Danny, you come with me. Wrayer, keep watch over the horses."

Naphtali dashed into the breach, anticipating the attack. Years of tedious practice and decades of mundane drills had sharpened Naphtali's skills and fueled his confidence. Combat and death's sting had eluded him during those years. Today this would change. Naphtali tightened the grip on his sword and shield, watching for the worgs to emerge inside the breach. A quick flick of Naphtali's head propelled the helmet visor down. The visor clanked into place, covering his boyish face. Naphtali spun the long sword in his right hand and sprinted forward. The Watchman threw back his head and allowed the elven war cry to erupt from his mouth.

Matthew peered skyward and let a prayer pass over his lips. His shield radiated a soft blue light. He felt the Maiden's divine presence washing over him and his companions. The cleric trotted after Naphtali, wielding his mace and grasping his shield.

Roan nocked an arrow, sprinting atop the rocks, each stride silent, each footfall sure and steady. He could see Naphtali and Matthew down in the breach. Roan saw Wulf to his right, keeping pace. He sensed the orcs riding the worgs advancing. Roan swore they must end this fight fast. They could not afford any further delays. He needed to get his companions and the horses off the ledge prior to sunset. The ranger caught sight of three orcs skulking over the boulders. He did not slow. Three rapid shots killed the orcs.

Danny followed Roan onto the rocks. He angled several yards southwest and then turned west, putting some distance between the ranger and himself. Danny considered his companions, appreciating he was a thief and an assassin, not a soldier. Fighting in this manner unnerved him. This was nothing more than an alley brawl between two rival gangs. Danny was a hunter, always working alone, patient and deliberate. He studied and stalked his prey sometimes for months before killing them when they least expected. Violence and death were familiar to him. He had killed many times in the past, although from a distance, it was nothing new. Killing up close and personal, that was another story. Soldiers and mercenaries fought that way, not assassins. To his left, he saw the two orcs negotiating the rock and boulders. Danny slowed and armed his bow. Pulling the string tight, he selected his target. The missile struck the orc in the neck. The second orc hesitated, then raised its bow. With skilled precision, Danny set another arrow onto the string and let it fly. His arrow punctured the orc's heart.

Wulf armed his bow and raced west. He saw a worg and rider inching east through the breach. His first shot removed the orc from the saddle. Wulf set two arrows against the bowstring and maneuvered to the edge of the breach, closing the distance to his target. He drew the string tight and released the arrows. They pierced the worg's neck, ending its life. Wulf pivoted to his right. He detected three more orcs slinking in his direction. His bowstring hummed as he cut down all three in quick succession.

Naphtali vaulted the dead worg. He landed in a crouch in front of another. The worg howled, its massive maw biting at the air. The Watchman dodged fangs and claws as he advanced. He coiled, then erupted. His shield hammered the worg's jowl up, snapping its neck. Naphtali disregarded the rider and propelled himself off the breach wall onto the dead beast's back, then leapt clear to the ground. He stood face to face with the next worg. He swung his shield upward, breaking teeth and shattering the jaw. Wounded, the worg tottered on its feet. Naphtali plunged his sword into the worg's chest. The orc tumbled from the dead worg and landed at Naphtali's feet. A swift slash to the neck decapitated the orc. Wetted with worg and orc blood, Naphtali sought his next target. Two more worgs and riders died on his blade and shield before the others fled.

Matthew struggled to match Naphtali's quickness and speed. The elf showed an amazing combination of power and dexterity. The cleric stood in awe. Troopers hacked and slashed. The only gracefulness in their fighting style was their horses and even they were brutal most of the time. In a stunning sequence of nimble, refined leaps and bounds, Naphtali elegantly slayed the worgs and orcs unfortunate enough to be in his path.

The remaining orcs and worgs broke and ran, realizing their quarry was stronger than they expected. Wulf, Roan, and Danny killed three more as the orcs and worgs raced west. Frustrated, Naphtali flipped up his visor and frowned as the worg riders fled. Not sure how to handle the adrenaline still coursing through his body, Naphtali shook with excitement. Naphtali looked to his left, then right. He stared at the dead worgs and orcs littered about the ground. He gazed upon the blood and earth soiling his once pristine armor. Clanging his sword against his shield, Naphtali arched his back and shouted the elven war cry once more. He had found his purpose.

Chapter Fifty-Five

Winter 532, Age of the Arch Mage

Roan stood atop the rocks, watching the worgriders flee west. He checked the sun's position. Thirty minutes of daylight left. "Head to the horses. We must get off the ridge before sundown."

Wulf, Naphtali, Matthew, and Danny hustled for Wrayer and their mounts as the ranger took a quick moment to survey the dead. There was nothing unusual about these orcs and worgs. He knelt next to an orc Danny had killed. The skin appeared swollen and bright red near the puncture wounds. Roan yanked the arrow from the dead orc and studied it. He winced at the pungent odor of poison. He ran his hand down the fletching and determined a master fletcher had handcrafted the arrow. *Drow.* Roan removed his book from the satchel slung over his shoulder and jotted a few notes, then placed the drow arrow in his quiver. He screwed his face, then trotted to join his comrades.

They waited for him near the ledge.

"There is a trail a few yards east of here," Roan announced. "It will take us to the valley and put some distance between us and the worgs, should they return."

"Let Maggie and me lead," Wulf suggested. "The other horses will follow her."

"Concur," Roan agreed.

Wulf stepped to the trail and descended. Maggie followed. Next came Roan, Danny, Matthew, and Wrayer. Naphtali protected the rear. Down they went, the six companions and their mounts picking their way over rock, pebbles, and debris. Man and horse toiled to keep their footing on the initial steep descent,. Midway into their endeavor, the companions entered a mountain forest. Under and around aspen, cottonwood, and pines they meandered. Tree limbs whipped and cut exposed skin. Finally the trail transitioned to a gradual slope near the valley floor.

Man and horse emerged from the trail bleeding and worn. Darkness spread over the vale, the sole light coming from moon and stars. Roan released his senses. Out they went, sweeping the valley. He did not detect any threats, they were alone. They walked another mile until the ranger selected a suitable site near the stream for them to rest for the night.

As they settled into a makeshift camp, Wulf glanced over at Naphtali. The elf wore a satisfied grin. His once pristine armor now bore the scars of combat, blood and gore. Naphtali had proved himself in battle.

"You fought well," Wulf commented, removing his saddle. "I have never seen a shield used that way."

Naphtali acknowledged Wulf, his grin proud and satisfied.

"The Keep remains elusive," Roan frowned. "We will continue east and resume our search in the morning. Naphtali, you got the first watch."

Naphtali waved, then moved off.

"I got the second," Danny volunteered.

"Then I have the third," Roan stated. "The other of you get some sleep. I am not sure what we will face in the morning."

Matthew studied the rogue for a few moments. A frown marred his face, his eyes downcast. The cleric sat next to Danny. "You okay?"

"Yeah. I'm fine," Danny lied.

Matthew smiled as he stood and gripped the rogue on the shoulder, then walked away. He paused and faced Danny. "You destroyed evil today to protect friends. There is nobility in your actions."

"Something to consider," Danny replied. The rogue moved off by himself, his thoughts adrift. His killing days were supposed to be done. Yet again he killed. He considered Matthew's declaration and maybe the cleric's words held some wisdom. Danny balked at the notion, wondering how many more lives he would take in the coming days. He choked down a couple of bites from his rations, then rolled into his cloak and fell asleep.

Roan found Wulf and Maggie in a clump of trees. Wulf leaned against a trunk, cleaning one of his long knives, Ill Wind, his bow, and quiver within arm's reach. Maggie whinnied as the ranger neared. Roan ran his hand down Maggie's neck. "Even our finest horses don't compare to this mare."

"I hear that a lot," Wulf chuckled. "She still surprises me sometimes."

Roan sat across from Wulf. "The two-arrow shot was impressive. Who taught you that?"

"My mother," Wulf acknowledged, his voice full of pride. "We practiced it all the time. But it is only effective at short range."

Roan nodded in agreement. "We?"

"My mother, younger brother, and me," Wulf disclosed. "Seth is a ranger like you."

"I see." Roan uncorked his waterskin and sipped.

Wulf sheathed his knife, then drew the one from his right boot. He glanced at Roan. "You are from Graywild, right?"

"Correct," Roan smiled, crooked and amused. "How did you know?"

"My uncle was a ranger also," Wulf revealed. "Kiah spoke of the Graywild rangers often."

"Two Blackhawk rangers," Roan declared, as he stood. "You are full of surprises, Captain. Get some sleep. I am convinced we are going to need your bow again."

Wulf Blackhawk will lead us someday, Roan thought to himself, walking away.

◊ ◊ ◊

Naphtali scanned east into the valley as the sky faded from blue to gray and then black. A restlessness settled over him as he paced along the stream banks. He ran the day's battle over and over in his mind as Wulf's words echoed in his head. Near the mid-point of Naphtali's watch, clouds rolled in, threatening rain and obscuring the moon and stars.

A fine mist crept in like a wraith during Danny's slumber. He felt the damp, heard the dripping water hitting the ground near where he lay, bringing him awake. Danny reached for his bow and stood. He slung his quiver over his shoulder, then picked his way to Naphtali. He shivered—something was amiss. He did not possess a ranger's or a cleric's or a mage's insight, but as a child of the streets he could sense danger. Drawing his cloak tight against his body, Danny sat near Naphtali. Danny turned to the Watchman. "Anything?"

"Nothing," Naphtali responded with a tinge of regret in his voice.

The mist turned to rain as the elf and half-elf stared off into the dimness, neither one needing to talk. Around midnight, the rain abated as the storm edged east. Naphtali stood and stretched. "The watch is yours."

Danny nodded. He sat still, listening to the unfamiliar sounds of the Border Lands. A mournful howl echoed across the vale. A piercing screech caused him to flinch. His mind drifted as he reflected on his life fleeing the Jirocha family. Danny was a hunter who was now the hunted. *Odd.* It was a feeling, a sensation he could not remember. Three horses whinnied, and a couple snorted, breaking his concentration on the past. They perceived danger. A glint of metal and motion to his right caught his attention.

◊ ◊ ◊

Roan's senses roused him awake. *Bugbears!* He grabbed his bow, slung his quiver over his shoulder, and sprinted for the threat. Concealed within the gloom, the ranger became a specter, silently pursuing his prey.

◊ ◊ ◊

Danny came to his feet and advanced, his vision focused. He counted four creatures, massive and fearsome. He heard their grunts and guttural breathing. They were loud, their movements lumbering and clumsy. His companions stirred awake behind him and, in seconds, they would rush to his aid. Danny decided there was not time to determine if they were friend or foe. Everything he had encountered so far in the Border Lands intended to kill him. He allowed Daniel Caldwell, the assassin, to assume control. He could adapt—he must. There was no going back. South Hampton was nothing more than a dimming memory.

Danny set the arrow against the bowstring and drew it taught against his cheek. He exhaled, sighting in. He released the string. Into the dark his arrow flew, undetected and accurate. Seconds later, he listened to a high-pitched squeal, followed by the sounds of an enormous body crashing to the ground. He nocked another arrow and let it fly.

Two died before he alerted his companions to the threat.

All were dead when his friends arrived.

"Dead?" Naphtali asked, the disappointment apparent in his voice. "Any more?"

Wulf laughed and placed his arm over the elf's shoulder. "I am convinced there are more things out here that need killing."

"Hope so," Naphtali mumbled. Disheartened, the elf wondered off, cursing under his breath in elvish.

◊ ◊ ◊

Roan remained at a distance, observing. Danny had just killed four bugbears—not an easy feat. He freed his awareness to search the valley in a wide, sweeping arc, seeking additional hazards. They were alone.

Chapter Fifty-Six

Winter 532, Age of the Arch Mage

They awoke drenched and with aching muscles. The six companions readied themselves to move ahead of the sunrise. The day broke dappled and somber. A damp chill clung to the skin and crept into the bones. Fog veiled the sun, shrouding the valley in a cloak of mist and clouds. The mountain ranges defending the north and south flanks protected the vale from the harsh conditions plaguing most of the Border Lands. Unlike the barren plateau they traversed yesterday, the air here felt clean and fresh. Winter had forced fall's surrender. The valley grass resembled a patchwork of pale greens and russet browns. Trees, stripped of their leaves, wore only dull and gray.

Roan ventured from the campsite as the others prepared for the day's journey. He located the four bugbears slain earlier in the morning. He noted a single drow arrow piercing each throat, and the red irritated skin surrounding the wounds. *An assassin's kill, lethal and precise.* He opened his book and jotted a few notes.

Similar to a large goblin, bugbears stood as tall as a barbarian. Fierce and ruthless in appearance, they wore a mix of hide and leather armor over thick tan fur. He strolled back to the campsite mulling over his discovery, deep lines etching his face.

"Danny, you killed bugbears earlier this morning," Roan stated.

"Oh," Danny smirked. "Is that good?"

"Definitely." Roan grinned at the rogue's question. He tugged his mask over his face. "Where there are bugbears, you will find goblins. Don't let your guard down. Despite a bugbear's mass and clumsy gait, they are agile and crafty."

Single file, they rode east, paralleling the river. The clouds wandered away, blown south by a northern breeze. Clothes dried and spirits lifted as the sun spread its warmth over the vale's breadth and length.

Near noon, Roan stopped for a break inside a grove of willows hugging the riverbank. He stepped away from his companions and closed his eyes. His instincts told him the Keep lay to the east. He sucked in a breath and gradually released it. Freeing his awareness, he sought threats that might impede their search for Ripley's Keep. East through the valley, his senses dispersed. Around trees and rocks, they hunted. At the end of the valley, he felt the terrain change. Gone were the vale's lush greens and winding streams. Browns and drabs filled his mind. Over broken and barren landscape, his senses fanned out. The ranger smiled. Amidst a ghostly haze, he found his elusive prey. *Ripley's Keep.*

Midafternoon ushered in another abrupt change in the landscape. The friends exited the valley and traveled into a vast nothingness, windswept and cracked. Shades of ugly dulls and flat drabs replaced the fading greens. Over the eons, a harsh sun had baked the terrain into brick. The air felt stale and unmoving. Scattered rock projections and boulder outcrops supplanted grass and trees. Farther on, they noticed a broad flat mesa emerge from the stark terrain. Large black bodies soared high above, their wings spread wide, catching the wind currents.

Roan stared across the emptiness, caught sight of the vultures circling above. He closed his eyes, dispersing his senses across the worthless terrain. Roan searched for Francis, the relics, and the Keep. He detected the Keep sitting atop the mesa. It sat right there in front of him, but Francis and the relics still eluded him. Death lingered ahead—Roan felt it clinging to the air. The ranger slowed his breathing and resumed his pursuit. He opened his eyes. *A battle occurred here.* His nose detected the decaying bodies, his tongue endured the metallic tang of blood carried on the wind. Roan pivoted to his companions and pointed. "Ripley's Keep."

The ancient Keep, stark and colorless, loomed ahead, rising several hundred feet above the Border Lands. Three miles from the Keep, Roan slowed their pace and the six companions spread out to better investigate the area. They located a residual encampment. Abandoned fire pits, discarded weapons, and trash spoiled the area. Hundreds of boot prints intertwined among hooves and wagon tracks that crisscrossed the terrain. Roan dismounted and knelt in the dirt. He removed his gloves and traced the indentations. *Orcs and humans. Horses, oxen, and wagons.* Next he noticed a set of tracks heading north and away from the Keep. The tracks revealed a disciplined military unit, regimented and organized, that had marched away from the Keep.

Despite the cool air and weak winter sun, the reek of bloated bodies intensified with each step as they resumed their trek toward the Keep. Roan detected additional boot prints, hoof marks, and wheel ruts latticing the dust. When they reached a rutted dirt road, Roan knelt once more. He determined the men and orcs executed a carefully planned and coordinated attack, not just a simple raid. Someone threw a small army at the Keep. *Did they come only for Francis? What about his wife and son? Did they capture the artifacts?* He stood and frowned. Too many questions and not enough answers.

Roan shut his eyes and let his senses go once again, allowed them to reach out. Except for the dead orcs and human soldiers, the Keep was empty of life. His eyes snapped open and he looked west. Lingering at the fringes of his range, he detected goblins advancing in their direction. *We have become the hunted.*

Still afoot, Roan alternated his gaze between the tracks in front of him and the mesa above. He proceeded to the bottom of a narrow road and his eyes followed the army's boot prints leading up the mesa to the Keep. He wandered among the dead, orc and human. Roan counted eighty-seven remains scattered over the landscape, their bodies twisted and stiff, their flesh burnt, their armor seared and torn.

"Wrayer, what do you think?" Roan inquired.

The elven wizard dismounted and bent down first near a human soldier then next to an orc dead. Wrayer studied them before responding. Few roaming Gaiand possessed enough energy to inflict this type of damage. "Fire and lightning."

"A wizard?" Roan inquired. He knew the answer but held some hope Wrayer would not say sorcerer.

"No. Only a sorcerer wields this kind of power," Wrayer confirmed.

Roan grimaced, knowing the rarity of sorcerers. "We cannot underestimate Francis's power."

"Their armor bears the five diagonal blood red stripes," Wulf declared. "These are the same markings we saw in Blackhawk and Beth Amen."

"I am not familiar with these," Roan admitted.

As Roan and Wulf discussed the markings, Danny got off his horse and stepped over the dead littering the road and worked his way towards the gate. Gashes, deep and cleft, marred the road, making it almost impassable. Near the top of the road, he hesitated for a moment. Danny shuddered and glanced around for any sign of life. Among the hundreds of boot prints, a pair of drag marks caught his eye. Danny knelt and studied the tracks, running his fingers along the outline. "Roan."

"Watch the west," Roan ordered, stepping off for Danny. "Goblins approach."

Roan knelt close to Danny and examined the marks. "Seems they dragged at least two individuals out of here."

"I don't think they struggled," Danny added.

"Correct, a grown man and a boy." Roan rose and stared at the walls. His eyes scanned the ramparts and shattered gate for any sign or clue. Something baffled him, something seemed out of place. He swore. An obscure presence lingered beyond the walls, but it eluded him. Roan could not lock it down or determine if it was good or evil. *Did magic mask it? Did arcana cloud his senses?*

Chapter Fifty-Seven

Winter 532, Age of the Arch Mage

Afoot Roan led the way, followed by Danny. Wulf, Matthew, Wrayer, and the horses trailed while Naphtali brought up the rear. Roan circumvented the fractures in the road, avoiding the dead littering the narrow rocky trail. Ripley's Keep, formidably stoic from afar, could not hide its scars up close. They reached the shattered gate, finding merely splinters hanging from the iron hinges. Roan paused and stared at the ground. Intermingled with the other tracks, he found a set of boot prints smaller and shallower than all the rest, close to the edge of the gate. Did the wife remain? His senses had failed to detect a living person. Roan scanned about the Keep, again wondering if magic impeded his senses.

More death and destruction greeted them as they entered the Keep. Charred orcs and humans lay slaughtered amidst the courtyard, their armor scorched and rent, their flesh burnt and blistered. Ripley's Keep resembled a battlefield—as if two armies had engaged in a deadly contest for days. The stench of death struck at Danny, Wrayer, and Naphtali. Unlike Roan, Wulf, and Matthew, they had never endured such a foul stench or heard the flies buzzing around the dead. Danny and Wrayer stemmed the nausea, fought the sickening repugnance until Naphtali retched and vomited, causing them to empty their stomachs as well. Wulf, Matthew, and Roan eyed their companions with sympathy. You never got over the pungent odor of death.

The corpses and their stench had little effect on Maggie and Matthew's mount—death was a familiar occurrence. The other horses shied away from the dead and gnawed at their bits. A sharp snort followed by fluttering sounds escaped their flared nostrils and eyes went wide as they trotted toward the safety of the stables.

Roan posted Naphtali and Wrayer at the gate, then directed the rest to the main building that occupyied the center of the compound. They discovered the front door torn off, and the windows smashed—tattered curtains flapped in the breeze. They pressed their backs against the stone walls, and Roan, Danny, and Wulf armed their bows. Matthew prayed for the Maiden's protection over them. Roan motioned for Danny to enter first.

Danny nodded, then stepped inside the building. The room looked like the rest of the Keep, wrecked, its stone walls spoiled and covered in a heavy layer of soot and residue. Dead human soldiers and orcs lay upon the floor, their twisted bodies scorched and charred. The room reeked of death, an unpleasant malodor of blood hung thick in the air. Danny gagged—the bile burned the back of his throat. He coughed and spat onto the floor. He shrugged, then worked his way along the walls, scanning the area for the living, for any lingering threat, for any sign of Francis and his family. The rogue found none, not a single trace. Danny moved into the rest of the house as Roan tracked behind.

The house sat empty, each room damaged beyond repair and anything of value stripped and plundered. Only the dead, maintaining their silent vigil, lingered here. Disappointed, Roan gathered his companions in the main room.

"None of this makes sense. The princes told us three people lived here, and we found three sets of tracks," Roan hissed through clenched teeth. "Where is the third person? We need to explore the rest of the Keep. Matthew and Danny, check out the stables. Wulf and I will scout the storehouse."

Matthew and Danny proceeded to the stables as Wulf and Roan headed to the storehouse. Roan led, releasing out his senses as they moved. He still detected nothing, which added to his irritation. *There must be someone here. There must be some clue.* A door lay near the entrance as they approached. Roan peered in and saw a small empty room. No other doors or windows. Roan gestured for Wulf to stay outside, then stepped in. He found more tracks, orcs, human, and the woman's imbedded in a thick layer of dust, but nothing else. The ranger moved the dust away from the center of the room until his boot hit the stone floor. He knelt and ran his hand over the stone, looking for a seam that might reveal a door. Roan wiped away more. Nothing. He stood inside the empty room and swore under his breath. Overall, his investigation proved fruitless. No signs of life. No sign of anything. Doubt crept into his mind, and he wondered if this was even Ripley's Keep. "Wulf, there is nothing here."

Wulf glanced at Roan as they walked back to the house. He noted the pursed lips and the furrowed brow etched on the ranger's face. "Roan, are we in the right place?"

"I wonder the same thing," Roan said with a loud frustrated sigh. In the next instant, Roan sensed the danger. He felt the threat emerge from behind him.

Before Roan could react, he heard a forceful voice call out, raspy and female. "Don't take another step."

Roan grabbed Wulf's arm as they halted. Roan perceived the arcana, frightening and powerful, flowing from the woman.

"Tell your friends to stay where they are," she commanded.

Wulf and Roan wavered, neither sure what to do.

"Do it now!" she insisted.

"Naphtali, Matthew, and Wrayer, stay where you are," Wulf yelled.

A disturbing silence ensued. Roan and Wulf heard a hiss.

"Tell the one in the stables to come out," she demanded. "And don't ever underestimate me again."

"Danny!" Wulf shouted. "Show yourself."

"Lower your weapons, then ease about," she ordered.

Wulf and Roan lowered their weapons and turned. A small human female stood in front of them. Tangled hair, matted to her head, rested on her shoulders. Deep cuts and dried blood laced her fawn-hued skin. Soot and dust covered the tattered clothing cleaving to her slight frame. She gripped a staff in her right hand—flames consumed the left. She scowled at Roan and Wulf, her eyes callous and angry as she took several unsteady steps, then halted.

"An elf and a human. Who are you?" she insisted. "Why are you here? Who sent you?"

"I am Captain Roan Ambrose," Roan responded, trying to prevent his voice from cracking. He cleared his throat. "This is Captain Wulf Blackhawk."

"And?"

Roan balked at providing an answer. He did not know her or trust her. Sensing her power, he knew she could produce all the death and destruction in and around the Keep. He recognized she commanded enough magic to kill him and his companions before they could even think to defend themselves.

Her eyes, heavy and hollow, shuttered. "I will not ask again."

Roan realized her patience waned and time ran short. He could not stall much longer. "We seek Prince Francis and his family, a wife and a child, and some stolen relics."

"There is more," she shrilled, stepping closer.

Roan sighed. He was out of options. His eyes flitted between her piercing gaze and the fire burning in her palm. "The Princes of Auroryies dispatched us here."

Her eyes narrowed in annoyance, her glare piercing as she studied them. Her eyes had an ashen gray hue, disturbing and intimidating to those who dared to meet her gaze. Their eyes met hers. They could not get past her hardened stare. It laid them bare and stripped off their defenses. They were powerless in her presence. In that instant, their confidence failed—she terrified them.

The seconds passed slowly as Roan and Wulf endured her cruel glower. They did not move, fearful to breathe. They watched her relax. The fire in her left hand dissipated, the grip on the staff lessened.

"So, the high and mighty princes are checking up on their prisoners," she mocked. "How thoughtful, how considerate. Look around, boys. As you can see, we are fine, just fine. Nothing is wrong here. Please share this when you return to Auroryies."

Wulf and Roan glanced at each other, unsure what to do next. They wanted to be certain the small woman would not blast them with a fireball or turn them into newts, but they were not entirely sure yet.

"So, you are Francis's wife?" Wulf muttered.

Her face grew grave. She gave a slow nod but did not otherwise respond.

"And Francis?" Roan inquired. "Is he here?"

"Gone," she mumbled, her gaze distant. "Both Francis and my son, Kheel."

Two bodies dragged from here. It made sense now, Roan concluded.

She staggered and leaned on the staff, which kept her from hitting the ground.

"Your injuries need attention," Roan said. He peeked at Wulf, then took a wary step toward her. "May I?"

She nodded. Roan got to her as she collapsed. He steadied the woman until Wulf scooped her up in his arms.

"Let's get her into the house," Roan urged.

Chapter Fifty-Eight

Winter 532, Age of the Arch Mage

She felt weak and fragile, nothing more than a wisp of a cloud in Wulf's arms as he trailed Roan to the house. Roan summoned Matthew to join them. The cleric removed his cloak and spread it on the stone floor. With Matthew's help, Wulf laid her on the cloak. Matthew knelt by her side and placed his burly hands on her battered body. A soft glow enveloped his hands as his mouth moved in silent supplication. She winced as the cleric's healing energy flowed through her body, repairing abrasions, mending bones, and erasing bruises.

Then he hit a wall. Something he could not identify hindered his ability to complete the healing. Matthew pulled back for a moment and wiped the sweat from his brow. When he resumed, he focused on the bolt wound in her thigh. He discovered a strong toxin enhanced by a dark arcana lingering near the injury. He renewed his efforts and removed what he could of the poison. Her body would have to filter out the rest.

Matthew mended the physical pain, but he knew he possessed no cure for the mental and emotional anguish she endured. Except for her shallow breathing, she laid motionless. Matthew grabbed for his waterskin and a rag and gently washed her face and arms, removing dried blood and grime.

Mora felt a calming presence emitting from this man. He held favor with his Maiden. She slowly opened her eyes and let her gaze meet his. "A cleric serving the Maiden of the Dawn."

"Drink some water," Matthew suggested, offering her a water skin. "Do you have any food left?"

Mora shook her head. As she struggled to her feet using her staff, Matthew protested and reached for her. Her head snapped toward him. Her eyes issued an angry warning. Matthew flinched at her fierce gaze.

"Touch me no further," she ordered.

A couple of unsteady steps later, she lowered herself onto the stone hearth. She held her face in her hands for several moments. Her head lifted, and she exhaled. She surveyed the damaged house, then fixated on Roan, Matthew, and Wulf. "I am Mora."

"I am Matthew Jakkes," Matthew furnished. "You have already met Roan and Wulf."

"We made our acquaintances," Mora expressed, forcing a thin smile.

Matthew shrugged.

"Well, leave it to the esteemed princes to send mere boys deep into the Border Lands to check on an imprisoned prince and his family," Mora sneered. "Still afraid to get their hands dirty. Figures, the sniveling cowards."

Roan, Matthew, and Wulf nodded but chose not to speak. They perceived the anger and the betrayal dripping from her words.

Mora examined them, studied them, reading them like an open a book laid out on the table. She sensed they feared her, and they should.

"Francis and Kheel fought for a day or two. I don't really know for sure," Mora sighed. "I lost track of time after Francis locked me in the tunnels."

Mora paused her tale, considering her next words.

"I believe they attacked us on purpose," she resumed. "They knew my husband's location."

Roan, Matthew, and Wulf did not speak. They eyed Mora, not knowing what to say or do.

"Who attacked you, Mora?" Matthew requested, breaking the hush.

Mora ignored Matthew's question. "You mentioned some relics."

"Yes," Roan acknowledged. "Prince Singjeye stated someone stole two powerful ancient relics from the artifacts vault. He referred to them as the Helm and Hammer of Valaaham. Are they here?"

"Are they here?" she smirked. "Seems an obscure question for an elven ranger from the Tribe of Graywild. Did you sense them here?"

"No. How did—"

Her dismissive wave cut Roan off. "Not important. I am hungry."

Matthew dug into his pack and removed a tin of iron rations, then handed them to Mora.

Mora swallowed two bites and grinned at Matthew.

"This is terrible," she chuckled, putting aside the rations. "Where are the other three? I want to meet them."

Naphtali, Wrayer, and Danny stepped into the room several awkward minutes later.

"Mora, this is Wrayer Tytonidae, Naphtali Lacchi, and Danny Caldwell," Matthew introduced.

"I see. A Tytonidae Prince, an officer from the Scarlet Watch, and a half-elf assassin," Mora deduced, as she noted the physical similarities between Wrayer and his father, Isaiah. "Quite the ensemble."

Danny, Naphtali, and Wrayer exchanged stunned glances.

"Okay, let me get this straight," Mora proceeded, shaking her head. "So the princes dispatched three elves, a half-elf, and two humans deep into the most dangerous place on Gaiand to retrieve my family and the relics."

"Yes," Roan confirmed.

"And you agreed!" Mora laughed. "Are you stupid or naïve?"

"A little of both," Matthew admitted sheepishly.

Returning to Roan, Mora grinned. "Any threats nearby, ranger?"

"Goblins tarry near the extent of my range," Roan declared, no longer amused by her insight.

"Good. We have some time to talk," Mora announced.

Amidst the dead and the debris, the six companions lingered. Mora sipped on a water skin and choked down more bites from the rations.

"Let's start with my Francis," Mora began. "Someone framed and convicted him for murdering two Sentries, stealing the relics, and Prince Gambier's disappearance. Despite his innocence, the princes imprisoned him here."

She took another sip of water and gazed over at her captivated audience.

"Next, the relics," Mora continued. "Mighty heroes of old expelled Valaaham, a wicked cleric serving the demon Belhaaz, from Gaiand following the first war against Belhaaz. His Helm and Hammer are malevolent and powerful and dangerous. After his expulsion, the princes stored them in the relics vault for safekeeping."

"Why not destroy the artifacts?" Roan asked.

"Fair question," Mora admitted. "Unfortunately, I don't have a satisfactory answer."

Mora hesitated, staring at the stone floor. A handful of minutes passed until she raised her gaze, her eyes vacant, her expression flat.

"Who is Belhaaz?" Matthew inquired.

"A vile demon banished to the Outer Planes centuries ago by the same heroes," Mora provided. "The dead in the courtyard bear his markings."

"How did he return?" Matthew challenged.

"I don't know," Mora admitted, her tone stiff and bitter. A prolonged pause ensued, generating an uncomfortable air within the room. Wulf, Wrayer, Naphtali, and Danny fidgeted near the front door as Mora, Roan, and Matthew had done the talking. Finally Roan spoke again, shattering the unpleasant pause.

"You said they knew of Francis's location." Roan stated. "Are the missing relics and your husband linked?"

"I think so," she replied, shaking her head. "Although I am not sure. Francis was familiar with the relics in the vault. All the princes knew the vault's contents as a precaution. Only a handful of princes possessed unfettered access to the vault and the details of each relic. Marcelinus and Gambier served as the keepers of the vault."

"And Gambier is the missing prince," Roan inquired, regretting the question the moment he asked.

"I already said that," Mora scoffed, rolling her eyes. Her voice trailed off for a second as she collected her thoughts. "He disappeared at the same time the relics did."

"Is there a connection?" Roan wondered.

"I suspect," she consented. Her expression went blank, her eyes shut. "But I am not sure. I do not possess any evidence, only speculation."

The conversation wavered again, and a hush refilled the room. Matthew glanced at Roan. He seemed lost in silent conjecture. His companions loitered near the front door, absorbing the conversation. Next he gazed over at Mora, her countenance now vacant and distant.

"Any idea where they might have taken your son and husband?" Matthew blurted.

Mora stared blankly at Matthew for a few fleeting moments. Forcing herself to think, Mora closed her eyes and slumped against the stone hearth. Exhaustion from her ordeal threatened to overtake her. Mora's mind was as empty as her look at Matthew, and she found it hard to concentrate. Somewhere in her head, surely, she possessed the answer to his question, yet it eluded her. It concerned

Tralderonn, but she could not recall how. Mora exhaled in despair—she could not find the answer to his question. "No."

Surprised at her response, Roan and Matthew exchanged quick looks. They expected a different answer. 'No' would not suffice. Roan dropped his head onto his chest as he fought exasperation. The words uttered by his king resonated in his mind. *If this is a fool's errand, come home.* Roan needed more. His mind churned, trying to fit pieces together. So far, this endeavor seemed a failure. Now they were no closer to finding Francis or the relics. He required additional information to finish this mission.

"Do you—"

Without opening her eyes she bade them go with a weak wave and let her hand drop limply back into her lap.

"No more questions!" Though her movements seemed slack, her tone left no room for doubt on further conversation. "I am tired. Leave me be."

Chapter Fifty-Nine

Winter 532, Age of the Arch Mage

Without speaking, they filed out of the house and gathered near the gate. Matthew glanced at his companions in the fading daylight.

"I repaired her the best I could, but there remains damage that is beyond my ability to heal. I detected a potent poison inside her body. She should be dead," Matthew declared. "The wounds Mora suffered should have killed her."

"Then how did she survive?" Danny wondered.

"I can't explain it," Matthew admitted. "There must be something more to her than we see. I sense no evil in her. Anger, sadness, betrayal, yes, but no evil."

"I agree," Roan added. "No evil, but she wields tremendous arcane powers."

Wrayer thought through Roan's and Matthew's assessments.

"Her powers are far beyond anything I can comprehend," Wrayer conceded. "I think she may be more powerful than Prince Singjeye. We need to consider the possibility the princes view her as a threat."

"Interesting," Matthew stated, rubbing his chin. "Something I had not thought about."

"If she is so powerful, then why didn't she and her family leave?" Naphtali queried. "They could have used their magic and fled."

"Yeah, why not?" Danny queried.

"Well," Wrayer started, then stopped. He considered Naphtali's question for a moment prior to starting again. "If Mora and Francis sustained wounds early on, especially a strong poison, then they might not have been able to flee or use their magic. I am not sure. Just a theory."

"What about the boy?" Danny asked.

"Yeah. Could he have caused all this damage?" Naphtali added.

"Perhaps," Wrayer offered. "There is a good possibility he possesses similar powers to his parents."

"Makes sense," Danny replied. "I guess."

"Can we trust her?" Naphtali inquired.

"Maybe?" Wrayer answered, his gaze focused on Matthew and Roan. "Right, Matthew? Roan?"

Roan and Matthew looked at each other and nodded in agreement.

"Are you sure?" Naphtali challenged. "We just met her."

"I trust her more than the princes," Matthew avowed. "They deceive and twist the truth with their words. Mora does not. She is blunt and direct."

Matthew peeked at Wulf. Wulf stared at the ground, the toe of his boot rearranging the dirt. Matthew knew his thoughts and recognized the determined look on his friend's face. Wulf had decided. He was already on his way to rescue Francis, Kheel, and the relics. Tenacious was the perfect word to describe him. Or maybe just stubborn.

"Okay, enough debate," Wulf interjected. "What do we do?"

"I can't sense Francis, Kheel, or the artifacts," Roan confessed. "They are beyond my range."

"They have at least a two-day head start," Danny proclaimed. "We have no allegiance to anyone here. Seems kind of pointless to press on."

"What?" Wulf barked in disbelief.

"Wulf, the situation is hopeless," Danny expressed, his eyes consumed by doubt as he grabbed Wulf's shoulder. "We did our best, but there is little to no chance we recover Francis, his boy, and the relics. It is time to go home."

"I agree," Wrayer chimed in.

Roan was tempted to concur. He could not discount Danny's and Wrayer's opinions. Matthew stood unmoving and said nothing.

Naphtali remained silent, weighing both opinions. Wulf stared at Matthew, his brown eyes pleading. The cleric shrugged and offered no words.

"No!" Wulf stated, his manner steadfast and unyielding. "Let's do what we agreed to. We have our horses and can move faster than those who captured Francis and his son. Roan, you can track them."

"Of course." Roan chose not to take offense. A blind man could follow the trail the caravan left. The question that troubled him was, would a smart man track them?

"Well?" Wulf asked, his patience abating. "I am going after Francis and the relics, with or without the rest of you."

Wrayer shook his head. "You can't go by—"

"Don't," Matthew interrupted, his voice calm. "Once the Orc Slayer sets his mind, there is no changing it. He is as obstinate as a Highlander mule."

"I am with Wulf," Naphtali announced. "Our honor is at stake."

An awkward silence ensued for a minute or two as the others decided how they wanted to proceed. Matthew kicked a rock across the compound. "By the Maiden, Wulf Blackhawk, you are going to be the death of me."

"Captain Blackhawk," Wulf beamed.

"Oh, all right," Danny stated.

Wrayer could not believe Wulf, Naphtali, Matthew, and Danny were serious. He looked over at Roan. The ranger nodded his head in a final decision. Wrayer blew out his breath. "Okay."

"It's settled, then. We go," Roan declared, his tone rather reluctant. "Naphtali, you have the first watch. The rest of you get some sleep. We leave ahead of dawn."

◊ ◊ ◊

Mora was aware the troop retreated from the room, and she felt herself sinking into a slew of despondency. Death had surrounded her. The dead bodies did not disappear even though her eyelids blocked them from her vision. *What can possibly happen now?* Hollow minutes passed. Then she remembered. Her eyes opened wide. Tralderonn. Udontawny. *Yes, that's it.* Tralderonn headed for Udontawny to find Francis and Kheel. She rose and hobbled for the front door.

◊ ◊ ◊

Halfway to the house the companions detected Mora. Propped against the doorframe, she waited for them. She leaned on her staff and took an uneasy step.

"Boys, if you are going after Francis and my son," Mora said. "I need to tell you about Tralderonn."

"What is a Tralderonn?" Wulf let slip.

"Not a 'what,' trooper, but a 'who,'" Mora grinned. In the next moment, the smile vanished. "Complicated characterizes him best. Tralderonn is a sorcerer, a former Prince of Auroryies, and Francis's younger brother."

The companions stood unmoving, their attention focused on Mora.

"He is ..." Mora faltered. She grimaced, chasing the correct words. "Unstable. Maybe unhinged right now."

The companions held their breath, not sure they wanted to hear any more.

"Anyway," Mora restarted, "he is on his way to Udontawny to find Francis and my son. So ... use caution when you find Tralderonn."

She pivoted and limped for the house.

"Wait," Roan demanded.

She spun back. Her eyes locked on to Roan's. "What?"

"Where is Udontawny?"

"You're a ranger," she stated flatly. "Follow the tracks."

She turned and disappeared into the house. Roan was stung but managed not to flinch. Speechless, they remained where they were, all but Wulf and Naphtali regretting their decision.

◊ ◊ ◊

While the others moved to the barn to tend to the horses, Naphtali whistled as he strode across Ripley's Keep toward the open gate, mulling on the day. The dust swirled around his feet, clung to his leather boots. The sun had already dipped below the horizon and dusk was upon them, closing another day. He enjoyed the cool northern breeze that blew over the Border Lands as clouds laden with rain gathered to the northwest. Naphtali rested his back on the shattered gate frame, taking in the cheerless scenery, miles of scrub and blasted rock. The bleakness of the scenery stretching out before him left Naphtali longing for the beauty of Evergreen's forests and glades, everything green and full of life.

He looked down at his armor. Once polished to a glistening sheen, his gray plate mail and shield were dirty, soiled and splattered with blood. Naphtali grinned in satisfaction. He drew his sword and admired his disheveled appearance in the steel. Like himself, his elven blade had prevailed in their first taste of combat. Together, they had proven their worth in battle.

Content, he sheathed his sword and stared out into the dying light. Footsteps from behind him ruined his concentration. Roan raced for the stairs leading to the ramparts, cursing in elvish.

Chapter Sixty

Winter 532, Age of the Arch Mage

"Naphtali, stay alert," Roan barked. "Goblins rushing in from the west."

Eager for another fight, Naphtali donned his helmet. A flick of his head brought the visor down. He drew the long sword, spun it in his right hand, and tightened the grip on his shield. Naphtali positioned himself in the middle of the open gate and steeled himself for an attack he hoped would come.

Roan bounded up the staircase, reaching the ramparts in four strides. Roan seethed, his ire directed at himself for getting wrapped up in Mora's story and not paying attention. Roan closed his eyes, freeing his mind to locate the threat. *Goblins. No bugbears.* He was familiar with goblins. Roan had fought them on many occasions in the past and he despised these dull, orange little creatures. As cruel as orcs, goblins were vicious scavengers, raiding and plundering those weaker than themselves. Their eyes, yellow and full of malice, their wiry bodies wrapped around small muscular frames. Fangs adapted to rip and tear flesh filled their mouths. Standing near four feet tall, they clothed themselves in grubby leather armor and animal skin. Emboldened when attacking as a pack, yet the lone goblin was a coward at heart.

They advanced east, skulking toward Ripley's, sixty of them slinking like hyenas seeking to pillage and plunder someone else's hard work. Roan opened his eyes—the goblins would arrive in ten minutes.

"Goblins inbound. To the gate!" Roan yelled.

Roan pulled his battle mask over his face, drew four arrows from his quiver while keeping his mind focused on the goblins. He placed an arrow into the bowstring, holding the others in his right hand. Roan sensed the goblins had stalled. They kept to the shadowy side of the mesa, waiting for deeper dusk to settle over the Keep above them.

Danny scampered atop the wall opposite Roan while Matthew and Wulf joined Naphtali in the open gate. Wrayer bounded up the stairs, positioning himself near Roan. The ranger grinned beneath his mask, pleased how they had deployed themselves.

"Wulf and Danny, kill the biggest goblin you find!" Roan shouted. "His death might break up the attack."

Danny nocked an arrow and scanned for any movement. On the ground, Wulf did the same, earning a bemused look from Naphtali. "What are you doing?"

"Nocking an arrow. Why?" Wulf gaped at Naphtali's question.

"You carry a great sword. Why don't you use it instead?" the Watchman teased.

"Momma always told me to use the bow first, then the sword," Wulf bragged, his beam wide and proud.

Naphtali laughed. "What? You listen to your mom?"

"If you knew my mother," Wulf retorted, "you would too!"

"Focus!" Matthew snapped, tightening the grip on his mace and shield. "You don't talk this much before a fight."

The troop heard a chorus of grunts and growls erupt from the goblins. The goblins outnumbered their prey and sensed victory. Similar to the other elves, Danny possessed dark vision, allowing him to see at night. It was an innate ability that served him well in his previous life. He watched the goblins slink through the gloom. Their weapons dimly reflected the yellow glow from their eyes. Their hatred was palpable as they skulked up the path to Ripley's Keep.

Roan's observations mirrored Danny's. The goblins acted skittish, unsure of what awaited them once they attained the Keep. Their greed and desire to scavenge outweighed their cowardly nature. It drove them onward. Wulf squinted, trying to discern the goblins from the shadows. He drew the bowstring tight, sighting in on the dim figures creeping his way. Naphtali bounced, fidgeting with nervous anticipation.

Matthew, like Wulf, struggled to differentiate the goblins from the murk. A glimmer of illumination was all he and Wulf needed. Matthew's prayer bathed his shield in a pale blue glow. He set his gaze on the slinking figures while thrusting his mace heavenward. In a breath, fire descended from the sky in a fiery column. His wilkenfire exploded into the goblins, tore through their ranks, scattered burning bodies, rock, and stone.

All but Wulf wavered for a second. His bowstring thumped in a steady rhythm as his arrows cut down the goblins. The companion's eyes darted between Matthew and the devastation below them. They stood unmoving and stared, mesmerized and astounded by cleric's power.

"Whoa!" Naphtali shrieked, stricken with amazement. He reeled back a step, his night vision blurred.

Danny, his mouth agape, relaxed his draw and let the arrow slip from his hand. His mind could not process what he had just witnessed. There were wizards in South Hampton, and he had heard tales concerning their strong connection to the arcane. He recalled being among a crowd of onlookers when a troupe of street magicians performed simple tricks and gimmicks in a local park. He found Wrayer's use of magic against the orcs and worgs impressive, but nothing like this.

Even the veteran ranger appeared amazed, and it took him a moment to refocus.

Wrayer shook off the astonishment. He moved his fingers in an ordered sequence and mouthed the words to call forth a spell. He concentrated on the remaining enemy creeping up the road. Immediately a mist seeped from the ground, enveloping the goblins in a green, repulsive haze. Sickened and blinded by the toxic cloud, they reeled away in confusion.

In the next instant, the goblins fled, their resolve broken. Arrow upon arrow leapt from Wulf's and Roan's bows until their targets evaporated like specters escaping from the dawn. Wulf nocked an arrow then trod down the road, searching for movement, for any sign the goblins lingered.

"Wait," Matthew ordered. He strode to Wulf's side, ready to face any remaining goblins.

Wulf looked at Matthew. The cleric's demeanor surprised him. Something seemed different about him. In the past, Matthew's shoulders slumped and his eyes shuttered after using the wilkenfire. This time, he appeared alert and unaffected. *What changed?* Wulf shrugged and resumed tromping down the road.

"See anything?" Wulf called out a dozen yards past the main gate.

Roan and Wrayer scanned the landscape below them. The goblins were gone.

"No," Roan shouted.

"No! What do you mean, no?" Naphtali hollered. "No more goblins? The fight is over? They didn't get close enough for me to swing."

Frustrated, Naphtali removed his helmet, revealing an odd look somewhere between disbelief and anger smeared over his face. He tipped his head to one side, raising his sword and shield in outstretched arms.

"Things move pretty fast around here," Roan chided, slapping Naphtali on the shoulder as he passed. "You need to keep up."

"Maybe your momma should have taught you how to fire a bow," Wulf yelled back. "It's not too late to learn."

"I thought all elves learned how to shoot a bow?" Matthew continued to roast, his voice booming.

"I do," Wrayer announced, with a hint of pride in his voice.

Wulf, Roan, and Matthew resumed their descent, leaving Naphtali to wallow in self-pity. Wulf and Matthew fanned out to the right and left near the bottom of the path, looking for survivors. The burning fires threw a portentous glow, cast eerie shadows over the terrain. Nothing moved, dead goblins, arrow-pierced and scorched, littered the ground. Roan reached out, letting his senses travel through the night air, searching for a threat, for any sign of a new danger.

"They're gone," Roan confirmed. "Let's get back to the Keep."

Danny had not recovered his composure. He leaned over the wall, absorbing the destruction. He scanned the landscape. His mind swirled, trying to process Matthew's sheer power. In a blink, the cleric splintered the attack and annihilated dozens of goblins. He shut his eyes to clear his mind. Mystified, Danny walked down the stairs to join his companions.

Mora waited for them when they returned. Her presence unsettled them as she locked her eyes on each one of them.

"Quite an impressive display," she chuckled.

Mora cackled and limped her way back into the house. Matthew, Roan, Wrayer, and Danny followed Mora into the house, leaving Naphtali and Wulf standing near the gate. Naphtali glared at Wulf, then ambled off mumbling elvish curse words.

◊ ◊ ◊

Naphtali stepped inside the house and motioned for Wrayer. The Watchman led the wizard around the house and paused.

"Wrayer," Naphtali said, kicking at rocks. "Can you, uh, teach me how to shoot a bow?"

"Teach you what?" Wrayer said way too loudly.

"Shh, not so loud," Naphtali hissed. "Can you show me how to shoot a bow?"

"Really, you're asking me?" Wrayer cocked an eyebrow.

"Yeah, you said you knew how to shoot a bow," Naphtali said.

"Why don't you ask Wulf, Roan, or Danny? They are the experts."

Naphtali looked at his toes. "I tried to pull the string on Wulf's bow when he wasn't looking."

"And?"

"I couldn't budge it."

Wrayer laughed.

"Will you show me or not?" Naphtali demanded.

"Well, I read a book on archery for athletics studies."

"Y-o-o-o-ou read a book?" Naphtali stuttered, already regretting that he asked Wrayer for help.

"Do you want me to teach you or not?" Wrayer huffed, his arms folded across his chest.

Naphtali sighed and stared at his toes again. "I am not so sure now."

"Ah, come on. This will be fun." Wrayer could not contain his excitement. "I'll find a couple of discarded bows."

A minute later, Wrayer returned with two bows and a handful of arrows lifted from the dead soldiers and handed half of them to Naphtali.

"If I remember the diagram on page twenty-seven correctly," Wrayer stated. "You stand with your legs spread like this."

Naphtali gripped the bridge of his nose and exhaled.

"What?" Wrayer blurted.

"Nothing, please continue," Naphtali mumbled.

"Anyway, stand with your legs like this." Wrayer stopped and looked at Naphtali. "Well?"

Naphtali, feeling self-conscious, mimicked Wrayer.

"That looks right. Now grip the …" Wrayer stopped again. "Are you right or left-handed?"

"Does that matter?"

"No, but I think Roan shoots with both hands," Wrayer declared.

"Right-handed," Naphtali murmured.

"Now grip the bow and apply your draw," Wrayer instructed.

"What about the arrow?" Naphtali inquired.

"Oh, yeah, set the arrow on the string," Wrayer blushed. "And apply your draw."

"Apply my what?"

"Apply your draw."

"I don't understand what you are saying."

"It means apply your draw," Wrayer insisted. "I can't make it any simpler."

"Can you at least try?"

Laughter from nearby interrupted the archery lesson. Wrayer and Naphtali both whipped around to face the source of the laugher. Matthew tried to compose himself and offer encouragement. "It looked like you were doing quite well."

Danny and Wulf doubled over, tears streaking their cheeks. Even Roan found it funny, a slight grin forming at the corners of his mouth. Naphtali snapped the bow over his knee and stormed off.

"Naphtali? Is the lesson over?" Wrayer wondered, watching Naphtali stomp away.

Naphtali did not reply.

Chapter Sixty-One

Winter 532, Age of the Arch Mage

Roan stood atop the ramparts alone and brooding during the last watch, his musings hellish and haunting. His days fighting the drow in the Belowground clouded his thoughts. Tunnels deep inside Gaiand, twisting and curving, festooned with traps and wards. Endless miles of caves and caverns carved into the earth and far from the sun's penetrating light. Places so black you could not see your hand in front of your face. It was in the Belowground where he had sharpened his skills, learned to employ and trust his senses. Roan winced. The recollections ripped off scabs, laid bare memories he considered buried deep inside himself. Next came the skirmishes and battles. With sword and dagger, drow and elf tore into each other with a vicious fury. Brother elves locked in a bitter and pointless war, each bent on the mutual destruction of the other. The fighting at times so intense he could smell the enemy's breath upon his skin, taste their spilled blood on his tongue. Roan closed his eyes. The screams from the wounded and dying still echoed in his ears, never muted or forgotten. He opened his eyes and swiped at the images like they were gnats.

Roan peered at the terrain stretching out before him, a land broken and treacherous. His anger regarding the current circumstances resurfaced as he brooded about buying into Wulf and Naphtali's naïve bravado once more. He cast his gaze all around. A grim nothingness filled his vision.

He exhaled into the crisp dawn air, trying to calm himself. He looked west one more time as a new day loomed behind him. Unprepared, he would lead his companions deeper into the Border Lands to retrieve Francis and Kheel. The relics? He did not know. Roan grimaced at the notion. No plan, no map, and no time to prepare. It forced him to pursue Francis and Kheel following days' old tracks—at least his time-honed instincts were intact, one tiny glimmer of...*well was that really even enough to constitute hope? What will we encounter? Orcs, goblins, and bugbears? Demons and devils?* The orcs, goblins, and bugbears were easy. Demons and devils—well, they could prove challenging.

Roan watched Mora emerge from the house as his five companions filed around the corner of the house, stoic and determined, leading their horses. Wulf brought up the rear with Maggie and the ranger's tacked-ready mount in tow. Their demeanor, their surety of purpose, bolstered his flagging spirits. Striding down the stairs into the courtyard, Captain Roan Ambrose vowed to lead them to the extent of his abilities. He pledged he and his new friends would prevail—they must. Their honor was at stake.

"Here," Mora stated. Roan recoiled as she shortened the distance between them. She chuckled at his expense. "Relax, ranger. I will not smite you."

He shrugged, his reddened cheeks betraying him.

Mora placed a blue amulet affixed to a silver chain into his hand. "A Location Stone. Keep it on you at all times. Francis knows how to use it."

"But what if—"

Raised on tiptoes, she put a finger to his lips, and kissed him on the cheek. "Don't doubt. You are Graywild, a ranger of renown. Trust your instincts, Captain Roan Ambrose. You will find Francis and my son. They are alive."

Roan nodded and slipped the chain around his neck. They climbed into the saddle and rode for the gate.

Out the gate and down the road they went. Roan glanced back over his shoulder. First at Mora and the keep then at his friends. *Six warriors on a fool's quest.*

◊ ◊ ◊

From the gate, Mora watched until they disappeared from her sight. Awash in renewed hope, she smiled and limped to the house. Her job now was to rest and heal. Roan and his companions might require her magic to bring them, her husband and son, back.

-- He is your hope. The one who will bind them all together --

The ranger?

-- No. Blackhawk --

How can you be sure? He is a reckless boy. The trooper has no power. He does not command magic. How?

-- Do not doubt --

I must. I deal with logic and reasoning.

-- Your magic is based on neither --

I don't—

-- Trust your heart this time --

Mora let his words linger and offered no response.

◊ ◊ ◊

Dawn entered the day hazed and gloomy. Clouds veiled the morning sun and the air, sharp and biting, hung heavy with mist. For two uneventful days and nights, they followed the tracks north. Rest for man and horse came infrequently, mere minutes to snatch a few bites of rations and sips of water. Sleep became sporadic, no more than four hours a night. The wasteland they traveled was fragmented and fractured. Boulders, crags, and rock outcrops littered the earth. It looked like a giant's playground. From horizon to horizon, the landscape appeared steeped in browns, umbers, and beige.

On the morning of day three, the tracks skewed west. Roan knelt in the dirt. He traced the impressions using his finger. They appeared less than a day old, only twelve hours. The ranger stood and smiled. They were gaining on their prey. Roan gestured his companions forward. Morning gave way to afternoon as they entered a canyon. Mountains, serrated and scraggy, soared skyward on either side, blocking the sun. Clouds obscured the summits, snow concealed the slopes in a white blanket. Tendrils of fog rolled over stones and rocks, roved in and out of crevices and fissures. As dusk conceded to the night, Roan led them on. Stopping in the canyon to rest was not an option.

◊ ◊ ◊

He sat at the foot of a tree. What type did not matter to him. The day was almost done, dusk succumbing to night. Slender stripes of scarlet, pink, and yellow streaked across a cloudless western sky, the sole reminder of the day's presence. Without the clouds, the night would be cold and damp.

Tralderonn felt exhausted, everything hurt, and his mount shared his fatigue. For his whole life, he'd heard tales concerning the Border Lands—a region of mystery and evil. The stories were wrong. This broken landscape was worse, a world scorned by hell. For almost two weeks he traveled, driven by emotion and sustained by his magic. During that time, he had crossed barren plains, fought goblins, rode over rolling hills, and traversed mountains.

Ten more miles, he concluded, and he would be in Udontawny, if the map was correct. Tralderonn did not have days to complete his journey. Maybe hours at best. He willed himself to rise and resume his journey. His mind pretended to be willing, but his body would not comply.

Tralderonn shut his eyes and shivered. He pulled his cloak around himself to preserve his waning body heat. He sucked in a sharp breath and gagged. Tralderonn stank to the point he could not endure his own stench any longer. He was quite certain he smelled worse than the roving goblin bands he had battled progressing north. He retched as he recalled the foul odor of their burning flesh after he incinerated them with a fireball or two. What was the plan? He did not have one. *Curious.* Perhaps his anger and magic would be enough. Doubtful, he decided.

Tralderonn exhaled. A plan, he thought. *I need a plan.* A minute passed, then another, and one more. Nothing. Then his mind completely jumbled—every thought poured in at once. The princes and betrayal. Cornell. His mother's death. His father. Tejt. Bounty hunters. The mob seeking retribution. The Matron Sister. Anything and everything but Francis and Kheel. He balled his fists and clenched his teeth. *Focus.* Then Mora graced his musings. *Curious.* He lingered on Mora for a moment. She was a sorceress. She admitted it. He always suspected but never confirmed. Could she be …? He let the notion hang unanswered.

Next came Carjlin. Her bright blue eyes, her beam. He grinned at her memory. Tralderonn owned no interest in religion. Did not give it a second thought. He preferred logic and reason. Scholarly pursuits and facts always preferable to hope in an unseen deity. Yet he found the clerics of the Maiden intriguing. Their faith, their convictions appealing. He wondered how and what Carjlin was doing. He wanted to believe her safely inside Beth Amen and restored as a priestess to the Maiden. Steeping herself in her studies and preparing to take her oath of devotion. Did she think of him? He hoped so. Then he frowned. Not at her memory. It wasn't at her beauty. Not her kindness. But at what might have been. *Curious.*

He opened his eyes and found himself shrouded in near darkness. The moon shone bright, the stars flickered in a raven-hued sky. He was alone, but not an unfamiliar experience for him.

He had spent most of his life alone. Even when surrounded by people, including his family, he always felt alone. Yet here, deep within the Border Lands, it seemed like he was the last living soul on Gaiand. For some strange reason, he felt a rare longing for companionship. A moment or two enjoying his mother's company. A scholarly debate with his old teachers Hura and Dhansi. A few minutes talking to the Matron Sister. Or strolling across the cathedral grounds with Carjlin on his arm. *Curious.*

Tralderonn peeked at his mount. She slumbered on her feet. He heard the rhythmic sounds of her breathing. He suffered a tinge of regret. In his haste to depart Highpoint, he did not bother to give her a name. She deserved one, a noble name. *Renegade, like him.* He pondered the name for a second. *Yes, that works.*

"Good night, Renegade," Tralderonn murmured.

His eyelids felt heavy and closed. Tralderonn yielded and let his need for sleep win.

Chapter Sixty-Two

Winter 532, Age of the Arch Mage

They shivered in the morning dawn. The air, wet and chilled, clung to their clothes and skin. A thin layer of frost blanketed the ground. The rising sun had crested the eastern horizon as they rested. Rays of gold and orange streaked a cloudless sky, offering them a glint of hope for some warmth. During the early morning hours, they exited the canyon. To their north, the mountains endured while those to the south morphed into hills and bluffs. A sparse forest lay ahead, a welcome relief from the rocks, stones, and dust comprising the barren landscape.

Roan told them they neared Udontawny. At least he hoped so. Wulf stowed his water and rations and rose to his feet. He saw Roan leaning against a tree, writing in a book. Wulf grinned at the sight. He recalled the many times he observed his brother, Seth, chronicling what they encountered on their rides. Wulf stood across from the ranger and waited. Roan finished his thought, closed his book, and lifted his gaze. Roan's cobalt eyes reflected his serious nature, his smile cordial.

"My Uncle Kiah taught my brother to document his findings in a book like yours," Wulf confided. "Seth spent hours describing what he saw, heard, smelled, and tasted."

"Your uncle was wise," Roan commended. "Your brother is wiser for complying."

"How did you make us invisible in the ruins?" Wulf blurted out. "Kiah could heal and mask his own movements, but he could not turn others invisible."

"I can heal as well," Roan chuckled. "And I did not turn us invisible. I veiled our presence."

"What's the difference?"

"Experienced rangers can blend into any environment. Seemingly vanish right in front of you, but we are still there if you know where and how to look," Roan explained. "We learn to manipulate our surroundings, bend the light and the shadows, if you will. Over time and practice, I have mastered the ability to extend this to others of my choosing."

"Will Seth be able to gain this ability?"

"In time, if he continues to study and learn," Roan confirmed. He stowed the book in his pack and came to his feet. He slapped Wulf on the back. "We need to go."

The others rose and pulled themselves into the saddle. Roan led the way, and the others fell in behind. He concentrated on the tracks they hoped would lead them to Francis and Kheel. Maybe even the relics. The earth warmed as the sun crept into the eastern sky.

Two miles farther on, he freed his senses, let them sweep over the landscape. The man and horse remained in place, stationary since he'd last checked. He kept his concern to himself. Mora had warned that Tralderonn might be unstable and unpredictable. Rage consumed Tralderonn, and he may lash out if provoked. Fighting orcs, worgs, and goblins was easy, tangling with a sorcerer could prove deadly. Roan decided he and Danny would go alone. It seemed risky for only two to go, but he wanted the man alive. Roan turned to his friends. "I found Tralderonn. Danny and I will go alone. We can move undetected."

"A ranger and a rogue, two hunters tracking their prey," Danny stated, wearing a broad grin. "The sorcerer will never see us coming."

Roan rolled his eyes and pulled up his cowl and battle mask while he slipped from his saddle. "The rest of you come fast if the fighting starts."

Ranger and rogue trotted into the wood line and looped south. Without sound, they stalked their prey. Nothing stirred, birds and animals were absent. Stale and unmoving, the air smelled of death and rot. Roan touched a towering tree. It was sick. Winter had not triggered its ashen hue. It was something else, something stronger than the seasons changing. The forest was dying. There was a magic here, raw and savage, sucking away life. An ancient magic far more powerful than the arcana contained inside the man they sought.

Roan located the man and the horse fifty yards ahead and paused. "Clip him, and no poison."

Danny scowled—apparently Roan knew about his drow arrows. The rogue watched the ranger until he vanished into the underbrush. Danny shifted to the right and settled in his hiding spot. He spied the man rolled into his cloak asleep, at least he hoped. Fighting a wizard or sorcerer was not anywhere on his list of lifetime accomplishments to achieve. Danny the assassin began progressing through his mental preparations, readying for the shot. He selected an arrow from his quiver—balanced to perfection, handcrafted, and drow. He ran his hand over the sharp arrowhead, free of poison, affixed to the tip. Danny gazed at the fletching feathers, fashioned from a mix of rooster and hen, attached near the notch. He licked his fingers, smoothed the feathers. He set the arrow onto the bowstring, drew the string tight to his cheek, and sighted in.

Unseen and unheard, Roan found cover behind an aged oak. He closed his eyes. An arcana, similar to Mora's, flowed freely within the man. Roan swore facing a sorcerer was beyond foolish. He checked his senses one more time. Hidden from sight, Danny had settled in place. The ranger peered around the tree. The man slumbered, his bald head resting on his saddle, his breathing steady. Roan scanned the campsite for any sign of the man's identity. His eyes returned to the man. A black staff leaning against a tree provided the answer. *Tralderonn.*

Roan held his breath and slipped past the sleeping horse to where the man dozed. The ranger felt out of place standing out in the open. A necessary risk or stupidity? he wondered to himself. He sat on a nearby log and studied the man for a moment. A black cloak wrapped about his tall and thin frame looked heavy and crafted by skilled tailors. Yet ragged tears and a fraying hem marred the cloak. Its tattered condition suggested his journey had been long and arduous to this point. His boots looked worn, the uneven wear on the left heel suggested he favored that leg. Large hands, ebony hued and scarred from recent wounds, clutched the cloak to his body. *This could go badly.*

Roan cleared his throat.

Tralderonn jerked awake and sat up, staring at Roan. His brown eyes were uncertain and feral as he reached for his staff.

"Don't," Roan warned. He gestured in Danny's direction. "My companion hidden out there is a master assassin. One shot is all he needs."

Tralderonn froze, not willing to chance further movement. His glare, fueled by rage and fear, met Roan's. The ranger gulped, understanding the danger facing him and Danny. He gathered himself. "I only want to talk. Are you Tralderonn?"

The sorcerer nodded.

"I am Captain Roan Ambrose." He pointed to his ears. "As you can see, I am not from around here."

"I don't care who you are or where you are from," Tralderonn jeered. "What do you want?"

A scowl appeared on Roan's face. His attempt at humor failed. "My companions and I seek Francis and Kheel."

"So," Tralderonn scoffed.

"Mora sent us to find them," Roan admitted.

"And?" He did not flinch, his countenance did not change. Tralderonn's mind swirled, his thoughts scattered like an autumn wind blowing fallen leaves. How did this elf know about Mora, Francis, and Kheel? *Curious.*

"I figured you would assist us," Roan confessed.

"Why would I help you?"

"He is your brother."

Tralderonn exhaled. The air created a hissing sound as it passed through gritted teeth. In a moment, his expression softened. A sadness replaced the rage reflected in his eyes. "True."

Roan relaxed a bit and signaled for Danny to join them. "This is Danny Caldwell."

Tralderonn acknowledged Danny with a slight wave.

Roan recapped the events that set him and his companions on a course to find Francis, Kheel, and the missing relics. Tralderonn did not interrupt. He sat in stoic silence, absorbing the information. When Roan finished, Tralderonn pulled on his boots and stood. He hobbled, favoring his left leg, to his horse, his body feeling the effects of what it had endured the last month. He turned as he ran a hand over his bald head. A smile, thin and weary, tugged at the corners of his lips. "You have spun quite a tale."

"Somehow I think you believe me."

"I do. The pieces fit together." Tralderonn motioned toward a satchel lying near his saddle. "I gained that satchel from the bounty hunters sent to capture me in Tejt. You will find the contents interesting."

Roan complied. He opened the flap and removed the articles. Roan read the letter. The writing was clear and precise. An educated person had penned the document. He scanned the map. It was far more accurate than the one provided to him. He glowered, then passed letter and map to Danny. "Do you suspect the princes' involvement?"

"I do," Tralderonn confessed, clenching his fists. "Treachery within the Citadelle runs deep."

"Agreed," Roan conceded. He was all too familiar with the princes' duplicity. "Why you?"

"I suspect I am a threat," Tralderonn admitted, his tone growing rough and angry. A scowl washed over his face, his body trembled. "I refuse to accept or conform to their stupidity and inaction."

Danny sensed Tralderonn's sudden change. The sorcerer's composure was fraying at the edges.

"What led you to Tejt?" Roan inquired, his words measured and calm.

"I headed for Beth Amen to join the fighting." Tralderonn snatched his saddle from the ground and set it on his horse. "Laid over in Tejt for a night."

"I see." Roan came to his feet. "What takes you to Udontawny?"

An answer did not come as Tralderonn finished tacking his horse and climbed into the saddle. "I am done talking."

"Where are you going?" Roan asked.

"To get my brother."

"Wait." Roan peeked over at Danny, then back to Tralderonn. The ranger realized he was losing control of the situation. "I have an idea."

Tralderonn reined his mare to a stop. "I am listening. But understand, with or without you, I am going to find my brother."

Chapter Sixty-Three

Winter 532, Age of the Arch Mage

After awkward introductions, the little company and Tralderonn gathered inside the wood line. Roan stepped away from his colleagues. He needed some space and quiet. He shut his eyes once more and projected his senses. A large garrison loomed at the limit of his range and a fierce evil lived within. So did orcs and men, too many to count. He sucked in a deep breath. He exhaled to clear his mind and block out the clutter. Roan put his head in his hands, trying to parse what his senses had detected. Francis, Kheel, and the relics remained beyond his grasp. Could there be magic in place, masking their presence? Were they even in the right place? Was the garrison he sensed Udontawny?

Ignoring his frustration, Roan walked to his companions who stood near their horses. They watched him as he approached. Tralderonn paced and grew more agitated as the minutes ticked by.

Roan hated this situation, and he worked hard to always avoid them. Doing so set him apart, made him the ranger he was today. He bristled at entering Udontawny blind and unprepared. He operated on facts and deliberate planning, not rash action. But he was stuck. Tralderonn sought revenge to satisfy his rage. The sorcerer's obstinance was forcing Roan's hand. If Roan delayed action for even a short time, Tralderonn would venture into Udontawny alone, ruining any chance to rescue Francis and Kheel or spoiling any possibility of recovering the relics. He cobbled together a hasty plan and presented it to his companions.

"We capitalize on the unknown. Which is us," Roan explained. "This Milton does not know who we are. We assume the role of the bounty hunter crew."

"So we just walk into an enemy camp pretending to be bounty hunters," Wrayer inquired.

Roan cracked a thin smile. Reticent, Tralderonn anchored his glower on Roan.

"Yeah, reckless," Wulf agreed. "I'm in."

Matthew eyed Wulf. "What is wrong with you?"

"What?" Wulf beamed. "Come on, Matthew, we did this all the time alongside the Highlanders. This is no different."

"I'm in," Naphtali added.

Sympathetic to Roan's dilemma, Danny remained quiet. His mind flailed. Assassins did not work in this manner. Each mission required detailed planning, strengths and weaknesses assessed, and ingress and egress routes identified.

"Okay, Captain. This may work," Tralderonn snapped, breaking his silence. "Who plays the prisoner?"

All eyes zeroed in on Tralderonn. "No! No way."

"Actually," Roan stated, his gaze drifting to Wrayer, "I think Wrayer is a wiser choice. Milton will not know the difference."

A clumsy hush ensued as the companions and Tralderonn eyed the elven prince.

"You think?" Wrayer questioned, wondering if Roan had misplaced his mind. "What about my ears? Sort of hard to hide."

"Yes," Roan responded. "Plus, you look more like a wizard than Tralderonn. Keep your cowl drawn atop your head, no one will know. We only need to fool Milton for a moment or two."

Wulf moved to Wrayer and looked him up and down. "I agree. You are kind of wizardly looking."

"Okay," Wrayer agreed, with a measure of uncertainty in mind.

"Good," Roan exclaimed. He looked at each member of his band and Tralderonn. "We are now bounty hunters. We ride to within a mile of the garrison, hide the horses, then proceed in on foot. The Troll's Head cannot be hard to find."

"If your plan doesn't work?" Tralderonn sneered.

"We adjust," Roan shrugged.

◊ ◊ ◊

A mile out, they dismounted and led their horses a hundred yards into the forest. They removed and hid saddles and bridles in the brush. Wulf pulled Maggie's head to meet his. "Stay here. This won't take long."

Maggie snorted and pawed the ground. Danny and Matthew shook their heads. Maggie never ceased to amaze.

Naphtali turned to Matthew. "Does she—"

"Yes," Danny and Matthew replied in unison.

With the horses hidden deep inside the woods, the troop and Tralderonn finished the last mile on foot. Across a swath of grasslands, they marched. Udontawny emerged as an unsightly blight rising from the plains. Set against the backdrop of a rugged mountain range, the town was an ugly stain, a dour blend of browns and grays. It was an unholy world of men and orcs drawn together for a singular purpose, Gaiand's destruction. Roan closed his eyes and projected his senses. Among the depraved, he perceived a small pocket of decency. *Francis and Kheel?* And there was more. He felt an intense evil. Only the abyss could produce an evil this vile and foul. *The relics.* They were close. Roan peeked at Matthew. The cleric mouthed an unheard prayer— he sensed the evil as well.

As they neared the garrison, the elves and half-elf pulled up their cowls. Roan tugged his battle mask over his face and loosely bound the elven wizard's hands, using a short length of rope. "Too tight?"

"No," Wrayer replied.

Clouds, heavy with rain, shrouded the setting sun. A gloom hung over the entire area, gray and foreboding. Old wooden structures, an unhappy collection of dilapidated shacks, intermingled among the recent construction. Dust rose to greet them as they trudged along dirt streets. A stench, foul and offensive, wafted in the air. Streets were empty, the threat of worsening weather kept most inside. Patrolling orcs growled and snarled but let them pass untouched as the companions and Tralderonn trooped deeper into the enemy's lair.

Roan led the way, followed by Danny. Next came Wulf, gripping Wrayer's left arm. Tralderonn, Matthew, and Naphtali brought up the rear. Near the north end of town, they arrived at the Troll's Head, a two-story building painted white. A single open door allowed access to the tavern. Laughter and coarse talk spewed from the tavern. Torch and candlelight streamed through large picture windows, casting elongated shadows onto the street. Roan peered inside, noting the occupants. Six Belhaaz soldiers reclined at the tables closest to the door, their crossbows close at hand. Four merchants drank at the bar. Behind a counter spanning the width of the room, a lone man tended bar, his movements wooden and deliberate as he poured ale into fresh mugs. He wiped a wisp of gray hair from his eyes and smiled as a pair of barmaids returned with empty trays. His smile gave his lined face a worn appearance. A set of stairs leading to the second deck sat against the east wall and a closed door on the west side of the tavern. Roan stepped from the door.

"I doubt Milton would be in the main room," Roan guessed. "Danny, see if you can find another entrance."

Danny slipped into the gloom and skulked through an alley. Garbage from overfilled trashcans lay spilled in the alley. A pungent odor from rotting refuse and urine and vomit invaded Danny's nostrils as he worked toward the back of the building. *Smells same as home.* Danny gazed around the corner, noting another entrance, a series of stairs leading to the second floor, and the glow of light coming from a window on the ground floor. He eased past the stairs to the door. He checked the door. *Locked.* Danny peered into the window. Torches hung along the walls illuminated the room. Danny noted three curtain-covered windows in the west wall and another two in the north wall. Eight Belhaaz soldiers and an overweight middle-aged man wearing gray robes sat at a large table filled with food and drink in the middle of the room. *Could the obese robed one be Milton?*

◊ ◊ ◊

Naphtali peeked to his left and noticed a four-man patrol drawing near. "Company."

Roan eased his back into the wall and let his eyes meet Tralderonn's. "Let me talk our way out of this. If not, we improvise."

Tralderonn scowled and clamped down on his lip. Wulf smirked—improvising is what he did best. Wulf tightened his grip on Wrayer, Matthew, Tralderonn, and Naphtali flanked on either side. Roan watched the soldiers as they closed. The torchlight reflected off their chain mail, their armor bearing five blood red stripes. Their long swords clanked against their legs on each step. Three soldiers maintained their distance and fanned out, cradling heavy crossbows. One approached, his hand resting on the hilt of his sheathed long sword. "What are we doing?"

The ranger studied the soldier. Roan combed the armor for a weak point, seeking a vulnerable location where a long knife could inflict some damage. The soldier's swagger marked him as a veteran, confident in his skills and experience. His jaw square and his face leathered from years in the field, his hair and beard, peppered with gray, portrayed a sense of wisdom. Roan stepped forward, forcing a smile. "My companions and I have business with Milton here at the Troll's Head."

"Milton Yeager?" the soldier inquired.

"Of course," Roan professed. "Delivering the wizard here."

"Bounty hunters? Wizard?" the soldier stated, his face twisted in disgust. "Carry on."

He pivoted and marched off, mumbling to himself about his disdain for bounty hunters and wizards.

◊ ◊ ◊

Danny hustled down the darkened alley, leading him back to his companions. The rogue slipped into the shadows and placed an arrow on the bowstring. He drew the string to his check and aimed at the soldier talking to Roan. *What are you doing?* Danny muttered under his breath while shifting his sights to another soldier. He lingered in his hiding spot until the patrol moved. Danny retired the arrow to his quiver and exited the dimness next to Roan.

◊ ◊ ◊

"I located a locked back door off the alley and stairs leading to the second floor," Danny reported. "Eight soldiers and a man in gray robes occupy the room."

"Milton Yeager?"

Danny shrugged. "Perhaps?"

"Maybe today is our lucky day?" Roan grinned. "Lead the way."

Chapter Sixty-Four

Winter 532, Age of the Arch Mage

Danny led his companions and Tralderonn down the alley, then around to the back of the Troll's Head. Danny pointed at the door. "In there."

"Door locked?"

Danny nodded his head.

Roan looked at the door, then back at Danny. He shrugged. "Do we knock?"

"I guess."

"Well, go ahead."

"Why me?"

"You found the door," Roan smirked. He gestured to the door. "You should have the honor."

Danny lifted an eyebrow, rapped on the door, and stepped back. Thirty seconds later, a soldier opened the door. He scrunched his face. "Leave."

Roan shoved past the soldier, his companions and Tralderonn following. Danny loitered in the shadows, seeking an opportunity to sneak in undetected. Roan's eyes flitted across the room, absorbing the details. He counted seven soldiers and a robed man seated at a round table. Three windows sat in the west wall, a door in the east, a bar near the north. The ranger grinned. "Milton Yeager."

The soldiers came to their feet, swords drawn. The gray-robed man peered around the soldiers.

"This is a private meeting," the man announced. "I suggest you leave now."

Roan grabbed Wrayer and shoved him towards the soldiers. "Your prize."

Milton squinted in the torchlight. "In one piece, I presume."

"Of course," Roan confirmed.

Milton waddled from behind the soldiers and adjusted ill-fitting robes. A tuft of hair, gray and unkempt, sat atop his balding head. Squat and wide, his belly spilled over the belt cinched around his waist. Seedy eyes sat beneath a furrowed brow. Fat rolled from bloated cheeks, jiggling with each movement. His thin smile did little to improve his appearance. "Remove the hood. Let me see him."

"Call off your soldiers first," Roan demanded, steeled eyes shuttered. In his mind, he knew his companions could kill everyone here in a matter of seconds.

Milton chuckled, his grin exposed stained and crooked teeth. "Stay your blades."

Roan eyed the soldiers as they lowered their swords. Rapid breathing, wide eyes, and the sweat forming on their brows betrayed their intentions. Roan snatched the cowl from Wrayer's head.

A gasp escaped Milton's mouth. He clapped his hands in approval. "An elf! Oh, this is even better than I imagined. This will please Zim Patok."

"You would agree we have fulfilled our end of the bargain?" Roan asked. He caught sight of Danny out of the corner of his eye slinking undetected in the shadows. A few more seconds and the rogue would be in position.

"Indeed," Milton agreed, his tone arrogant. An awkward hush washed over the room and nervous tension filled the air. He spun about and shuffled to the bar. Milton filled a mug and faced Roan.

"Let's settle the terms of our agreement," Roan pressed. "I expect payment in full."

"Patience ..." he paused mid-sentence. "I did not catch your name, bounty hunter."

"Names are not important, Mister Yeager," Roan countered, his grin wry and deceptive. His hand eased to the long knife tucked into his belt. Milton had no intention of paying. "Now, our money."

Danny slipped behind Milton, long knife drawn. Wulf suspected a fight. The soldiers fidgeted and their long swords remained unsheathed. Wulf slowed his breathing, his frame tensed as he clasped his bow tight. Words and sounds were subdued into nothing more than low drones. His eyes narrowed. He marked each soldier's location. Naphtali glanced over at the soldier standing near the open door. The soldier paid no attention to him. Matthew prayed and Tralderonn seethed, his face twisted in rage. The inaction, the needless banter, fueled the sorcerer's simmering temper.

Milton surveyed the chamber, a greedy grin spread over his chubby face. He hoisted his mug. "A toast—"

In an instant, the room erupted into a churning mass of chaos and death. The soldiers attacked. Roan reacted ahead of his companions. He drew and plunged his long knife into the soldier's neck. A gloved fist exploded another's nose, propelling the nasal bone into his brain. In a single fluid motion, the ranger nocked an arrow and readied a shot.

Before the soldiers could employ their swords, Wulf killed the two closest to him in swift succession. He rearmed his bow, and he set his sights on Milton.

Amidst the turmoil, Danny grabbed Milton by the scruff of his neck. He jabbed the tip of his long knife into Milton's back. Danny pressed the blade deeper through the folds of the robes to where the skin broke. As Milton squirmed to free himself, Danny tightened his grip on the man's collar. The rogue increased the pressure on the knife and leaned in close. "Not a sound."

Naphtali drove his shield up into the chin, shattering the jaw as a soldier raised his long sword. Crouching like a panther, Naphtali sprang straight up, bringing his legs to his chest. Naphtali angled his body and thrust his feet into another soldier's chest. The soldier reeled backwards, slammed his head into the wall, and crumpled to the ground. Naphtali rolled to his feet, sword in hand, seeking another target.

Tralderonn summoned his magic. Fiery darts leapt from his fingers. His missiles shredded armor and tore flesh. Two soldiers crumpled to the floor in a heap. Enraged, Tralderonn pivoted, his ire fastened on Milton.

Wrayer made for the door in the east wall. He motioned his fingers in precise movements, calling forth his cantrip. He touched his staff on the door and locked it using his magic. Only another wizard or sorcerer more powerful than he could undo his spell.

Matthew rushed to the open alley door and shut it. He rotated and gazed over the room. Violence and death were not new to him. He had suffered its consequences too often to count, to where he was almost numb to its effects. Yet it still bothered him. His soul silently cried out, mourning the dead. He considered that a blessing—it meant his humanity remained intact. As a priest in the duty of the Maiden, he considered all life precious. He prayed a muted appeal for forgiveness.

Roan surveyed the carnage. Eight soldiers lay dead. He swore and closed his eyes. His senses stretched out, probing for additional threats. *Nothing new.* Concerned their scheme had unraveled, Roan knew they must work fast.

Tralderonn seethed as he strode to Milton. Flames consumed his left hand. Milton screamed as the sorcerer neared. Danny clapped his hand over Milton's mouth, applied additional pressure on the knife. The rogue was certain he would die as well.

"Tralderonn!" Roan barked.

Consumed by fury, Tralderonn fixed his gaze on Roan.

Roan stowed his bow and returned the arrow to his quiver. He wanted to appear defenseless. He extended his arms, his palms facing upward. "Please."

Roan advanced, his steps measured and cautious. Tralderonn looked unhinged. His control hung by the thinnest of threads. His breathing was rapid, his teeth bared. The sorcerer's eyes reflected the roiling anger running rampant inside his soul.

"If we have any hope of finding your brother and nephew," Roan pleaded, "we need him alive."

Tralderonn took an additional step. Everything inside him screamed for vengeance. He wanted to obliterate Milton and desired to destroy the entire town. *Francis.* The ranger's words deflated his rage. He halted short of Milton, allowing the fire to dissipate. Tralderonn stood motionless, glaring at Milton.

Chapter Sixty-Five

Winter 532, Age of the Arch Mage

Zim Patok pulled on his black waistcoat and buttoned it up. He clasped the collar in place and buckled his long sword to his belt. He smoothed out any wrinkles and moved to the window. He caught his reflection in the glass and smiled—he liked what he saw. The time of Valaaham's return was imminent, just a few hours away. He was drunk with anticipation. The storm was growing along the horizon. Dark clouds, weighed down with rain, blocked out the moon and stars, leaving the sky blacker than raven feathers. He watched the lightning streak in the west, followed by the concussive claps of thunder that shuddered the windows. "Perfect weather for a perfect night."

Zim gazed over the torchlit courtyard. He saw the elongated shadows of the guards walking post on the ramparts and the inner ground. The three wagons that would deliver Francis, his son, and the Helm and Hammer to the Temple of Belhaaz were parked outside the front door.

He shifted his gaze to Udontawny and wondered if the bounty hunters from Highpoint would deliver the other prince in time for the ritual. It did not matter in the end. Francis and his son should be enough to appease Valaaham's fury. Zim Patok thought of Milton, and he frowned. For a second, he was unsure Milton Yeager could handle something so simple. "Maybe ... Nah, even that moron couldn't screw this up."

Zim Patok adjusted his waistcoat one more time, then strode out of his room. He still had a few tasks left to complete.

◊ ◊ ◊

Darkness persisted in his cell, all light banished from this hellish hole. Francis had just dozed off when they came for him and Kheel. He knew the moment neared for whatever they had planned for them. Despite his weakened state, he decided tonight he would fight back. For the past two days, he had abstained from their toxic food and drink. Free of their poisons, his mind was clear and ready to do battle. He heard their heavy footsteps, the rattle of the keys, and the audible clunk as the lock to his cell opened.

"On your feet," a guard ordered.

Feigning sleep, Francis mouthed the words, calling forth his cantrip. He allowed the first two guards to reach his cot. He waited, delayed the spell until they touched him. When he felt their grip on his shoulders, Francis grabbed their arms. They screamed in unison, their agony unmistakable. They reeled away and watched in horror as their hands and arms transformed white inside a thick coat of ice.

In less than a second, Francis gained his feet as two more guards entered his cell. He crouched like a cornered animal and hammered them with hail and sleet. Blinded, the guards careened off each other and crashed to the floor. Francis summoned another incantation. As he readied the spell, he felt sharp pangs from the darts piercing his neck. Francis fell back hard into the iron bars. His vision blurred, his thinking clouded. He fought the pain and battled their poison. And when they approached to take him, he fought them, too. Francis was unable to stand on his own, but it still required four guards to restrain him. It took two additional guards to apply the shackles and gag before he succumbed and passed out.

When Francis regained consciousness he lay in a puddle of his own blood, bound and gagged. His head and body throbbed from the thrashing he'd endured, yet Francis managed a meager smile, a slim satisfaction from the pain he had inflicted on the guards. He heard their screams, smelled their burning flesh.

Kheel was not surrendering without a fight. He mimicked his father and had refused their toxic food and drink as well. Dour and determined, Kheel lingered at the back of his stone chamber as the guards neared the cell gate. He growled and gnashed his teeth, ignoring their threats. Kheel paid no heed to the errant darts careening off the stone walls as they tried to subdue him before entering the cell. Consumed with revenge, Kheel raged. He trembled as raw arcane energy churned inside his body. It coursed through him like the air filling his lungs. He leered at them as they approached. Kheel sensed their fear, felt their trepidation. He understood their terror. Kheel sneered—they would suffer his wrath. He gathered his magic about him, and he waited for the guard to insert the key into the lock. As the key freed the lock, Kheel extended his hands. Fiery darts tore into armor and flesh. He called forth the magic once more and shot out his arms. His fireballs detonated, killing three guards and warping the steel bars.

Consumed by flames, their bodies dropped to the floor, blackened and burned.

Kheel advanced, wide eyed and feral. He mocked their fate and amassed the fire, permitted it to build in his hands once more. Prior to thrusting his arms forward, Kheel staggered. Frantic fingers groped for the dart embedded in his shoulder. Seconds later, another hit near the first. The pain and poison drove Kheel to his knees. His head slumped to his chest, his breathing became ragged and forced. He fought to remain conscious as his eyes closed. He shoved away the pain and poison and readied another spell.

Four guards hid behind their shields, drew their swords, and entered the cell, taking cautious steps. Their wide eyes focused on the wounded sorcerer while their companions aimed crossbows at the boy. Kheel listened to their deliberate footsteps and waited until they neared. *One more step.* His head snapped up, lightning streaked from his hands. His visceral energy ripped into the four guards, slashing their armor and scorching their skin. Their screams echoed off the stone walls. On his feet again, Kheel primed his next cantrip. Kheel tried to duck, attempted to avoid the butt of the crossbow slamming into the side of his head. Kheel gasped for air, then crumpled to the stone floor.

"Get someone in here to clean them up," the guard leader ordered. "Zim Patok will not be happy seeing them bloodied."

Shackled at the wrists and muzzled with cloth gags, Francis and Kheel sat on the stone floor, slumping against the iron bars. They were alone and locked in their cells, waiting for the guards to return. The stench from charred flesh and the rusty odor of spilled blood clung to the stale air. Sure of their fate, they plotted their next opportunity to fight their way free.

Chapter Sixty-Six

Winter 532, Age of the Arch Mage

Roan looked about the room and spat on the floor. In a matter of seconds, his hastily concocted plan had crumbled. This is why you did not rush headlong into unfamiliar situations, he reminded himself. His mind spun, trying to salvage what he could. Tralderonn stood nearby unmoving, his fists clenched, his breath sucked sharply through clenched teeth.

Roan concentrated on Milton.

"Milton Yeager, my patience has evaporated," Roan conceded, his voice low and barely audible. "What are the plans for Tralderonn, Francis, and the boy?"

A cumbersome quiet ensued. No one moved or spoke. All eyes focused on Milton.

"I can't answer your question. He will kill me," Milton whined. "Please take the gold, the silver. Take it all."

A loud rap on the door interrupted the interrogation.

"Mister Yeager," a voice from the tavern called out. "Is everything all right?"

Danny applied more pressure with the long knife and hissed close to Milton's ear, "You tell them yes and to go away."

"Yes. Leave me be," Milton yelled.

Danny patted Milton on the shoulder. "That's my boy."

Roan took another menacing step closer. He saw the beads of sweat rolling off Milton's forehead. He smelled the fear, beheld the terror in Milton's wide eyes. Danny tightened his grip on Milton. The rogue shoved the knife deeper, just enough to slit skin and cause warm blood to trickle down Milton's back. First his eyes rolled back into his head, next the knees buckled, then Milton crumpled onto the floor. Danny stepped clear, letting him fall. Milton hit the wooden floor with an audible thud.

"You need to lose some weight, Mister Yeager," Danny chuckled.

Roan stared at Danny in disbelief, then back at Milton. Roan grabbed for Milton until he a foul odor assaulted his nose. "Whoa. Did you wet yourself, Milty?"

Danny suppressed a laugh, but watching Milton faint and fall to the floor was hilarious. As the Jirocha crime family enforcer, he had interrogated many men in his former life, although none compared to this. Danny and Roan hauled Milton into his chair. Danny scowled and jabbed Milton in the chest with the hilt of a long knife. "Milty, you nasty."

Roan swooped in. He never let his guard down, not once breaking character. He peered at Milton like a hawk seeking its prey, his piercing eyes unsympathetic and wintry. Roan leaned in and suffered Milton's offensive odor. "Milty, I won't ask again."

Milton trembled and perspiration streamed from his forehead and into pockmarks dappling his pudgy cheeks. He gazed around the room sobbing. Eight soldiers lay dead. They had duped him. These so-called bounty hunters had played him. He lamented his situation. His plan, his treachery, was easy. Take possession of the prince, kill the bounty hunters, keep the money, and claim all the credit. Easy. Yet these bounty hunters had flipped the script. They rewrote it in their favor. Now they frightened him more than Zim Patok. He pondered his fate—death rapped on the door. Either way, he had lost, and he could not save himself. Milton's head sagged to his chest. He did not want to face the elf's glacier stare any longer. "They intend to sacrifice Francis and the boy in a ritual to free Valaaham from his prison on the Outer Planes."

"Go on," Roan said, sitting down directly in front of Milton, lending no reprieve. "What about the Helm and Hammer?"

"The Helm and Hammer are the gifts for Valaaham upon his return," Milton explained.

"And Tralderonn?" Roan insisted.

"An additional sacrifice," Milton whimpered.

Danny twisted Milton's collar, shoved the long knife hard enough to break skin.

"He lies," Danny alleged, his eyes meeting Roan's. The rogue winked. "Let's kill him now and get going."

"No!" Milton squealed. "Zim Patok dispatched me to meet the bounty hunters here. It's the truth."

"Where can we find Francis, the boy, and the artifacts?" Roan demanded.

"N-no ..." Milton's chest heaved. "I will have told—"

Roan slammed his fists onto the table, then flung it aside. Milton's eyes flew wide open. The elf now stood inches from him.

"Where can I find what I seek?" Roan hissed through clenched teeth.

"In Demonstaug under heavy guard," Milton moaned. "An hour before midnight, guards will move them to the Temple of Belhaaz."

"What is Demonstaug?" Roan asked.

"The temple stronghold," Milton wailed.

Danny twisted the blade, causing Milton to grimace.

"What direction?" Danny urged. "How far?"

"North," Milton cried out. "About a mile from the edge of town."

Wulf watched Roan and Danny interrogate Milton from the other side of the room—their performance awed him. The ranger and rogue worked as one. Together they convinced Milton his life meant nothing to them. Like the Highlanders, Wulf would have beaten Milton into submission.

Wrayer loitered near the side door. Danny's methods did not surprise him. This is how he believed assassins acted and he was half-elven after all. But Roan's behavior concerned him. Although of Graywild stock, Roan was still an elf. *Maybe this is a ranger's way as well?* Wrayer glanced about at his other companions, his gaze and thoughts accusatory and judgmental.

Neither Naphtali nor Wulf showed any concern regarding Danny's and Roan's actions. They were soldiers, no quarter expected, none given. And then Matthew, a Maiden of the Dawn cleric. He appeared to condone Roan's and Danny's actions. Wrayer felt a slight tug of regret. He paused his accusations and reconsidered his silent assessment of his companions. They were at war and the fate of Gaiand could hinge on their success or failure.

Roan shrugged. "I guess Mister Patok will have some late-night guests."

Danny smiled. "I bet Uncle Milty can show us the way."

"No, no," Milton cried. "I cannot lead you to Zim Patok. He will kill me."

"Gents, we need to get this done now," Roan exclaimed, gazing at his companions. "Danny, please bring our guide."

Milton pleaded for his freedom. Danny grabbed Milton by the collar and jerked him to his feet. "Uncle Milty, you have no choice."

Milton crumpled to the floor, whimpering. The rogue paused and grimaced, his smile icy and unforgiving. At the moment, he found Milton pathetic. He chuckled at the notion. It was strange that an assassin, a cold-blooded killer, would find someone like

Milton deplorable. *Ironic? Maybe.* Danny looked at Roan. "I am useless moving in a pack."

Roan nodded. *So am I.*

"I will meet you at the edge of town."

"Meet you there." Roan considered the half-elf assassin for a second. In hindsight, his initial assessment of the rouge seemed hasty and maybe his concerns about the drow arrows unjustified. Danny had proven his value to this little company many times over. Roan smiled beneath his mask. *The doubts were dwindling.*

Chapter Sixty-Seven

Winter 532, Age of the Arch Mage

A misty fog, cold and sodden, thickened the nighttime air, obscuring moon and stars as the companions exited the Troll's Head. In minutes a watery sheen adhered to clothes, weapons, hair, and skin. A stiff breeze blew in from the north, adding to their discomfort. Udontawny slumbered—an uncanny quiet pervaded the town. Torchlights, harsh and yellow, flickered in the lamps lining the streets. Under Roan's watchful eye and blade, Milton led them down a sequence of alleys and empty side roads. The dirt streets had transformed into a sea of orange mud. On several occasions, Milton tripped over his robes and ended up face down in a puddle, and each time Wulf hauled him to his feet. Milton halted when they cleared another back street. He stood motionless and stared across the open field in front of him.

◊ ◊ ◊

Danny lingered in the alley until his companions disappeared around the corner. The rogue slipped into the shadows and he headed east. An eerie hush blanketed Udontawny, the drizzle and wind muting the town. Even the taverns, gambling parlors, and pleasure houses were silent. Danny avoided the main avenues as he crept undetected through the alleyways and side streets for several blocks. He froze long enough to allow a four-man patrol to pass. A minute later, he attained the edge of town. He scanned the sweeping field to the north of him. Demonstaug loomed above the plains. *Great.*

◊ ◊ ◊

Shrouded in layers of fog, Demonstaug rose thirty feet above the earth. Stone walls, grim and dull, protected a two-story building. Torches lit the ramparts, outlining the guards patrolling the battlements. Roan pulled Milton close. "Zim Patok?"

"Yes," Milton whined.

Roan closed his eyes, cleared his mind, permitting his senses to stretch out. Danny was en route. Roan pushed his senses farther, detecting humans. Twelve soldiers patrolled the battlements and an additional forty-two loitered inside the stronghold. He felt evil, a menacing presence lurking beyond the walls farther north. Roan identified the Helm and Hammer, foreboding and demonic. But he uncovered more. An old human, depraved and dishonest, prowled the stronghold. Roan shifted west. Orcs and humans, too many to count, occupied another compound a mile beyond Demonstaug. Roan smiled, his eyes opened. Shining like a beacon of hope among the wicked, he perceived Francis and Kheel.

Danny eased next to Roan and tapped him on the shoulder. "Udontawny is quiet, no patrols in sight. What did you find?"

"Francis, Kheel, and the artifacts are in the stronghold," Roan whispered to Danny. Too many soldiers and too many orcs—they could not fight them all. He gathered his companions around him. "This won't work. They outnumber us. We must find another way inside."

"Castle Longpine has dozens of secret entrance and escape routes," Wrayer stated. "I am sure this stronghold has at least one we can exploit."

"Sure," Danny agreed. He grabbed Milton, spun him about, and set a long knife to his neck. "An escape route. You will show us."

Milton did not hesitate to answer and pointed east. "Forty yards past the east wall."

"Wulf, lead the others on," Roan ordered. "Danny and I will scout inside the stronghold. Wait for us at the entrance."

Wulf grunted, then shoved Milton forward.

◊ ◊ ◊

Roan and Danny sprinted north. Hidden by the drizzle and murk, they stalked toward the stronghold undetected. In minutes, they emerged from the gloom at the base of the east wall. Ranger and rogue allowed themselves a moment to detect guard patterns and tendencies. Roan motioned for Danny to scale the wall. Up they went, hands and boots gripping the wet stone. They squeezed through a crenel and onto the ramparts.

Roan counted a dozen guards carrying crossbows—six on the west wall and another six on the east. An additional four more patrolled the grounds. Danny studied the two-story building. Torches bathed the front entrance in a yellow light. Two guards stood near the door. Danny patted Roan's arm and pointed at three wagons carrying cages positioned near the building. Danny and

Roan spent a few moments more surveying the grounds, absorbing as much information as they could. Roan acknowledged Danny, then signaled for them to return to their companions.

◊ ◊ ◊

Cocooned in the dimness and rain, Wulf, Naphtali, Matthew, Wrayer, and Tralderonn trailed behind Milton across the open ground east of the stronghold. Several minutes passed until Milton brought them to a halt near a clump of bushes. "Here."

Wulf pushed Milton aside and knelt in the mud. He pulled the bushes away and discovered two iron doors. Gripping the handle, he yanked. The doors did not budge. His second effort yielded the same result. He stood and stared. "Naphtali, Matthew, help—"

Wrayer elbowed Wulf. "Move."

The elven prince spoke the words to summon his magic and tapped on each door using his staff. The heavy doors creaked and moaned as they opened, revealing a staircase leading down into the earth. "You work too hard."

Wulf furrowed his brow and grunted as Matthew and Naphtali chuckled.

Danny and Roan emerged from the dimness a moment later. Roan glared at Milton. "Where does this lead?"

"A guardroom near the dungeon," he moaned. "Now you will release me?"

"Nope," Roan replied, as his foot landed on the first stair. Roan knew the lack of light placed Wulf and Matthew at a disadvantage. Humans did not possess the elves' natural ability to see in the dark. Wrayer could alleviate the problem with his magic. Roan waved off the notion. He must maintain the element of surprise if they had any chance to succeed.

Into the unlit staircase they progressed. Roan led, followed by Danny. Next came Wulf, Milton, Matthew, and Tralderonn. Wrayer closed the door behind them as he and Naphtali secured the rear. They descended into the dark for ten feet, then twenty. At thirty feet below ground, they located a cramped tunnel opening ahead of them. The surrounding air smelled damp, stale, and stagnant.

For a hundred yards, they traveled through the darkened tunnel single file. The odor of must and mold adhered to their nostrils. Roan halted at a door. His senses told him the room beyond was empty. He closed his eyes, pushing his senses beyond the door. Francis and Kheel lingered close by. He found the artifacts—they sat two floors above. He counted thirty humans inside the building. Yet he could no longer detect the old human's presence.

"What did you uncover?" Tralderonn insisted.

"Your brother and nephew are close," Roan whispered. "So are the artifacts."

Tralderonn started for the door. Roan's iron grip brought him to a stop and spun him around.

"I call the shots, not you," Roan stated. He locked his cold cobalt eyes onto Tralderonn. "Your outburst at the Troll's Head could have cost us our chance to succeed."

Tralderonn did not speak. The rage in his eyes spoke for him.

Roan maintained his grip on Tralderonn and reached for the door. Danny grabbed Roan by the arm. "Step aside, ranger. You are in my world now."

The rogue hummed as he swept the door for traps and alarms. Finding none, he jiggled the handle. *Locked.* From a pouch on his belt, Danny produced a set of picks and a file. In a sequence of skillful progressions, the rogue sprung the lock.

"That seemed pretty easy," Roan admired.

"Yeah, it's one of my many talents."

Roan smirked. The odor of rank bodies and must escaped as Danny eased the door open and entered. Roan released his grip on Tralderonn and followed the rogue, his bow armed.

A single torch lit the room, a modest chamber constructed of interlocking granite blocks. Half-eaten rations and half-filled mugs sat on a table surrounded by chairs. An empty weapons rack hung near the exit. Danny stepped to the exit and listened. "All clear."

Roan nodded and grabbed a chair. "Come here, Milty."

When Milton was bound to the chair and gagged, Danny signaled for Roan to open the door, then slipped into a corridor built from the same granite blocks as the guard room. Small torches, interspersed at twenty-foot intervals, lent only small amber puddles of light. Concealed in the gloom, Danny eased down the corridor, trailed by Roan. Next came Wulf, Tralderonn, and Matthew. Wrayer and Naphtali brought up the rear.

A sharp squeal from a steel door dragging against stiff hinges reverberated down the corridor. Danny motioned his companions to halt. The rogue hesitated. He tilted his head, straining to listen for additional sounds. He signaled for his companions to stay and silently slipped away.

◊ ◊ ◊

Danny rounded a corner and slowed his pace. There appeared to be a second hall that branched right, and just past the intersection, the straight corridor ended in a heavy door. As he neared the end of the corridor, he saw the door was still ajar. Voices, grating and gruff, grew louder with each step. Onward he crept, keeping himself hidden inside the shadows. He recoiled and swore. The stench of charred flesh and death nauseated him. He retched, the bile burning his throat. He spat on the floor and wiped his mouth with the back of his hand. *Blech.* Inching through the door, Danny inventoried the dungeon. Five guards stood near one of three prison cells. Bound, gagged, and wearing black robes, the prisoners sat on the stone floor. *Hello.*

One guard produced a set of keys, unlocked the cell, and opened the door. "Get them."

The other four balked and eyed the prisoners. They did not want to die an ugly death like their compatriots had.

"Go on," the key holder growled.

The shield bearers, cautious and on edge, entered first, followed by the crossbowmen. Danny shook his head—it dropped to his chest. *Argh. How do I keep getting myself into these situations?*

The guards had the prisoners on their feet. The rogue was running out of time and his companions were too far to assist. Resigned to action, Danny nocked an arrow. His bow hummed as he killed the unsuspecting key holder and three guards with an assassin's deliberate speed and precision. The remaining guard leveled his crossbow and fired. Danny reacted fast enough to avoid a fatal wound. Instead of piercing his heart, the bolt grazed his side, tearing leather and drawing blood. Danny ignored the pain and rearmed his bow.

The guard discarded his crossbow and shoved Francis to the floor. He grabbed Kheel as he drew his dagger and set the blade to the boy's throat. "I will kill him."

"Nah." Danny discharged his bow. The guard released Kheel and clutched at the arrow buried in his forehead. The rogue set another arrow on the bowstring. "Do I need to use this?"

Kheel stared at Danny, unmoving, his eyes wide, his breathing shallow and uneven.

"I will take your silence as no." Danny returned the arrow to his quiver, navigated the mess of bodies he'd just contributed to, and entered the cell. He removed Kheel's gag. "You're Kheel and he is Francis?"

Kheel nodded.

Danny lifted the key from the keeper's corpse and freed Francis and Kheel from their shackles.

"Wait here! Some friends are coming for you," the rogue whispered as he slipped from the cell and back past the dungeon door.

Chapter Sixty-Eight

Winter 532, Age of the Arch Mage

Roan fidgeted and his companions chafed at the delay. The ranger knew lingering in an open passageway inside the enemy's stronghold was ill-advised. At any moment the guards could discover them. He grimaced at the notion. This entire journey was foolish. He glanced down the corridor, his elven eyes piercing the darkness. What kept Danny?

Tralderonn grumbled to himself not very quietly, earning himself a dark look from Wulf. Every second they wasted multiplied his rage, and time was not a luxury afforded to Francis and Kheel. He stepped from the wall. "Enough. I am going—"

"Nope," Wulf snarled, snatching Tralderonn by the collar. He jerked the sorcerer back in line.

Another minute passed, then two, then four more, before Roan spotted Danny waving them ahead.

"The dungeon is at the end of this corridor. Francis and Kheel are alive," Danny whispered. He produced a set of keys, handed them to Roan, and shrugged. "Call it a reluctant donation."

"What happened to your side?"

Danny smirked. "The guards and I had a minor disagreement."

Roan cocked his head and raised an eyebrow. "Locate the stairs to the first floor."

As Danny hustled off, Roan faced Wulf. "Lead the others to get Francis and Kheel. Wait for us outside the escape route entrance."

Roan spun about and trotted after Danny.

◊ ◊ ◊

Wulf and Naphtali kept watch from the passageway as Matthew and the others jogged for the dungeon. Fifty feet from the dungeon entrance, the stench of burnt and decaying flesh assaulted their senses. Tralderonn faltered on his next step. A hand placed against the wall kept him from falling. Nausea swept over him, his gut somersaulted. He gasped for air, then emptied his stomach.

Wrayer stood by Tralderonn's side, hoping his own last meal would remain inside. "I don't think I will ever get used to the smell."

Tralderonn groaned and used his sleeve to wipe off his chin.

Matthew spotted them. Free of their bonds, Francis and Kheel sat on a cot. Together, they struggled to stand. Eyes, guarded and hollow, met his. "Francis and Kheel, I mean you no harm."

Stepping over the dead guards, Matthew stopped short of the cell. "May I come in?"

"Yes," Francis croaked. He stared at Matthew, trying to figure out why he suddenly felt an overwhelming calm and peace.

"I am a cleric in the service of the Maiden. Sit down." Matthew knelt near Francis and Kheel. He removed his pack from his back and extracted two small flasks. "Drink this."

They choked down the thick elixir, coughing and gagging. In an instant, they felt a soothing warmth dispersing through their bodies as the potion took effect.

Wrayer, with Tralderonn in tow, came around the dungeon door. Tralderonn, desperate to get to his brother and nephew, tripped over the first corpse. Wrayer grabbed him by the arm. "Wait."

Matthew placed one hand on Francis and the other on Kheel, shut his eyes, and mouthed a silent prayer. A soft white glow emanated from the cleric's hands, causing Francis and Kheel slight discomfort. Directing his healing energy, Matthew repaired their internal wounds first. He reattached tendons, repaired torn muscles, and fused broken bones back together. Matthew's hand lingered on Kheel for a few extra moments. *He's endured severe beatings.* Next, he focused on the deep cuts and bruises on their wrists and ankles and faces. As the glow faded, Matthew withdrew his hands and stood.

"This is the best I can do for now," Matthew admitted, his voice low and steady. "Will you be able to walk?"

Francis and Kheel nodded.

"Okay. On your feet," Matthew encouraged.

"Amazing," Tralderonn whispered, his mouth agape.

Francis glanced up and smiled, thin and tired. "Tralderonn?"

Tralderonn brushed by Wrayer, leapt over the sprawled bodies and embraced his brother and nephew. Matthew tapped Tralderonn on the shoulder and pointed towards the exit. Francis stared at his brother. "How?"

"No time," Tralderonn stated.

Matthew shepherded them out of the dungeon to where Wulf and Naphtali stood watch at the intersection of the corridors. Matthew paused near Wulf. "Buy us time."

Wulf grunted.

"But don't be reckless. Remember Maria, your mother, and Seth," Matthew urged. "And Maggie."

"Me?" Wulf chuckled.

"Yes, you."

"You worry too much."

"Yes, I do," Matthew agreed. "Especially since I started hanging around with you."

Matthew rolled his eyes. The cleric turned to Wrayer and Tralderonn. "Let's get Francis and Kheel out of here."

Wrayer waffled. "They need you more than they need me. I can assist Wulf and Naphtali."

Matthew did not argue.

◊ ◊ ◊

At the end of the passageway, Danny lingered at the bottom of a staircase. Roan stopped near the rogue and closed his eyes. A dozen soldiers moved about on the first floor. He pushed his senses farther. He found the relics above them on the second floor.

"If you stay close, we can pass unnoticed," Roan whispered, his words confident.

"I was already doing that!" Danny said, a little too loudly. "I've been doing that this whole time!"

"Well, I'm casting a spell to mask our presence," Roan stated.

"Your whating a what?" Danny muttered.

"I did the same thing at … Never mind, there is no time to explain. Just stay close," Roan ordered. He waved his hand and shut Danny up. In an instant, an invisible shroud cloaked and silenced their movements. Roan started up the stairs. Danny grabbed Roan's cloak, bringing the ranger to a stop. "So no one can hear or see us?"

"Correct." Roan resumed climbing.

"So we are invisible?" Danny queried, pulling Roan's cloak one more time.

"No, undetected," Roan clarified, taking another step and yanking his cloak out of Danny's hand.

"Are you sure?" Danny yelled as he jumped up and down and smacked his dagger on the wall.

Roan stopped at the bottom of the landing and faced Danny. The ranger stared at the rogue as a parent would stare at an impetuous five-year-old. Danny grinned a broad, toothy smile and waved. They ascended the remaining stairs in several easy bounds, reaching an archway that opened into a foyer.

"Oh, I'm a ranger. I'll just cast an invisibility spell," Danny mocked, trailing Roan into the foyer. "We humble rogues only have our intellect, light touch, and stunning amounts of natural talent to rely on when we do our jobs. And that does not include our good looks. Had I known rangers just used spells, I would not have been so impressed with you all before."

"Are you done?" Roan asked as he swatted at Danny without looking back.

"Oh, sure," Danny said, then continued. "Hey, did you ever hear about Frederick Copperfield?"

Roan failed to respond and kept moving. Two guards loitered near an open door leading outside. Two more stood post near a second door in the west wall. They hugged the wall and slipped unseen to another staircase ascending to the second floor. Danny snuck a peek out the door. Rain fell in sheets and lightning, chased a few seconds later by thunder, creased the sky, leaving a bright trail behind.

"Anyway, he was this political boss back in South Hampton. Heaps of money, always traveled with at least two guards," Danny babbled on. "Know him? Well, I was fourteen and I got assigned to assassinate old Copperfield in broad daylight. At like noon, we're talking sun way up in the sky, no clouds, no rain or a bit of shade from a nearby tree."

Without making a sound to those around them, they climbed the stairs until they attained the second floor. The stairs emptied into a lantern-lit corridor. Roan turned to Danny. "The room where the relics are being kept is just up ahead. Would you like to finish your story here or in the room?"

Roan did not wait for an answer. He turned left and kept going.

"Nevertheless, I had to sneak up on Copperfield in broad daylight, right?"

The ranger paused at a closed door halfway down the corridor. Roan shuddered at the evil he sensed beyond the door. He grabbed the handle and tried to open the door. *Locked.*

"And as you know, I can't cast any spells. But I am not yanking on your leg, I snuck up on that guy—"

Roan stopped Danny's rambling by smacking him on the shoulder. "Uh huh, uh huh. Pick this lock."

Danny removed his picks and file. "Right, it's done. Long story short, they still don't know who killed ol' Copperfield."

Danny pushed the door open, entered, and looked over at Roan. "You coming in here, too?"

In seconds, they were inside. Danny scanned the room. Other than a window, the door was the only way in or out. The empty room was large and unfurnished except for a single table. Danny stared at the table. He could see a Helm and Hammer setting on the table and they looked exactly like Sheldon described them. *Valaaham!*

Roan followed Danny in and locked the door. "Well?"

"Well, what?" the rogue asked, his eyes fixed on the Helm and Hammer.

"Did you kill ol' Copperfield?"

Danny pivoted about. He smiled, threw his arms out to his side, and bowed.

"I'll guard the door." Roan grinned. "Use your immense amount of natural talent and good looks to steal the relics. I figure you are better at stealing things than I am."

Danny scoffed at the notion. He approached the table and circled the artifacts. A fortune sat right in front of his eyes, each one handcrafted from pure gold and platinum.

Undetected for the moment, Roan dissipated his masking spell and cast out his senses one more time.

"Hurry, they will not hurt you," Roan prodded, his voice hushed but his tone urgent. "More guards approach."

Danny gave Roan an uncivil hand gesture—the rogue would not rush. He removed his cloak and wrapped the artifacts. As he placed them in his pack, he heard a clunk coming from the lock. Danny shouldered his pack, then faced the door as it opened. He watched as four guards passed into the room. Danny eyed Roan.

"Can they see me?" Danny mouthed.

From behind the door, Roan nodded and shrugged.

"What did you say?" a guard inquired, raising his crossbow.

"Oh, I said the artifacts are ready," Danny lied. "So lead the way. I know Zim Patok is anxious."

"Who are you?"

"The one who packed up the artifacts," Danny acknowledged, his eyes fixed on the guard. "Are we going to Zim Patok or stand here debating who I am?"

"I don't recognize you," the guard declared, taking a tentative step forward.

"I don't know you either," Danny confessed, holding his ground. "Kind of makes us even."

"Where are the relics?"

"Are you dull?" Danny asked. "I told you I have them in my pack. I am done bantering with you. What is your name, soldier? I am going to have to report you to Zim Patok."

Not sure what to do next, the guard looked at his companions. As if conjured, a long knife appeared in Danny's gloved hand. The rogue whipped the blade at the guard. The guard clutched at the knife buried in his neck and fell to the floor dead. Roan closed and locked the door and drew his rapiers. Swift thrusts into the gaps in chain mail armor killed two guards. The last guard fired his crossbow in the rogue's direction. Danny rolled to his left, avoiding the bolt. Back on his feet, Danny hurled another long knife. The blade impaled the guard in the forehead. He reeled backwards and crashed hard into the wall.

Danny glared at Roan. "I thought you said we were invisible."

"No, you said we were invisible. I said we were undetected," Roan corrected. "There is a difference."

"Okay, undetected." Danny tossed up his hands in frustration. "They could have shot me. What happened?"

"I can't use my senses and stay undetected at the same time," Roan confessed, unable to prevent a wry smile from spreading beneath his battle mask.

"That might have been—"

Fists pounding on the door and yelling interrupted their argument. Roan ignored the commotion and fixed his eyes on the rogue. "What are you fussing for? You didn't get hurt."

"Well ... yeah. But—"

"We're out of time."

The door cracked and moaned—it would not hold much longer. Roan and Danny looked at each other. They did not need to speak. They pushed the table against the wall and flung the window open. Rain splashed into the room, puddling on the floor.

"You first," Danny urged.

"Why me?"

"Rangers lead the way."

Roan grinned beneath his mask and jumped. Danny shook his head at the stupidity of the entire situation. Out the window he went, falling two stories to the ground.

Chapter Sixty-Nine

Winter 532, Age of the Arch Mage

Wulf, Naphtali, and Wrayer tarried at the intersection of the two corridors.

"You sure you want to stay?" Naphtali inquired. The responsibility of protecting the elven prince weighed heavily on him.

Wrayer did not respond. He set his hand on the Watchman's shoulder, grinned, and pointed towards the stairwell. "Pay attention."

Naphtali became serious. "Your father would be proud."

Wrayer nodded and summoned a spell, his eyes focused straight ahead.

Matthew, Tralderonn, Francis, and Kheel shuffled by them and headed for the guardroom. Wulf snuck a peek around the corner. He saw the guards emerge from the staircase. Wulf nocked an arrow and strode into the corridor. The guards faltered near the bottom step. Wulf bridled his breathing. His body relaxed as he tightened his grip on the bow. Words and sounds muffled to an indistinguishable hum. Wulf's arrows killed two, forcing the guards to retreat for a moment. Wulf took a quick gander behind him. Francis's and Kheel's painful gait hindered Matthew's and Tralderonn's progress. A hundred feet stood between them and the safety of the guardroom. Wulf, Naphtali, and Wrayer must hold a few moments longer.

Naphtali and Wrayer joined Wulf. Naphtali snapped his head, clicking his helmet visor into place. He spun his sword and crouched to meet the guards. The guards started moving once more, this time in tight formation—four abreast and two deep. The shield men, their swords drawn, came first, followed by guards wielding crossbows.

Weaving his hands back and forth, Wrayer called forth his spell. Fiery shards leapt from his fingers. Glowing white hot, the darts roared down the corridor. Four guards lurched, their chain mail breached, their flesh torn, their lives ended.

Crossbows fired errantly. Bolts clanged harmlessly off the stone walls and floor. Wulf fired his bow twice, killing two more. Wrayer threw up a wall of fire, choking off the corridor. Arcane flames, torrid and angry, stifled the guards' attack and provided additional precious seconds for Matthew and the others to reach the guardroom. Enraged shouts arose from beyond the flames. Officers implored their men to resume the attack. Naphtali looked behind him. "They are in the guardroom."

"Wrayer, go," Wulf shouted.

Wrayer nodded and trotted for the guardroom. Wulf and Naphtali withdrew a few feet at a time, their eyes focused on the wall of fire. A flurry of crossbow bolts careened down the corridor. Wrayer felt a bolt crease his shoulder. He shrugged off the pain and kept going. Another bolt nicked his side. Wrayer stumbled and reached for the stone wall to keep himself upright. He took a step and staggered as two more bolts struck—one punctured his lung and the other pierced his heart.

◊ ◊ ◊

"No!" Mora screamed, like she was waking from a nightmare. In the tunnels deep beneath the Keep, she trembled in fear. Mora clutched her chest as an overpowering sense of dread poured over her, the same feelings she had suffered when she perceived first Elaire's and, many years later, Kysellah's deaths. She swore out loud. Mora hated this ability and loathed its presence within her. Across the length and breadth of Gaiand, it did not matter when or where. When natural magic perished, she felt the sting. She detested sensing the death of a sorcerer. It was a burden she endured. Not a blessing, but a tremendous curse. She could not limit this affliction just to sorcerers. Somehow it allowed her to perceive the demise of elven wizards as well. Wizards dying from other races remained undetectable and went unnoticed. It made some sort of sense in her mind. Elves were capricious creatures of magic and light.

Tears filled her eyes and flowed over her cheeks. She tasted their saltiness on her lips. Thin fingers ran through her unkempt hair as she set her feet on the cold stone floor. *Wrayer is dead.* She waded through a flood of memories. Evergreen, a realm of arcana and elves. A land of ancient forests and green vales. A place she loved more than any other place in Gaiand. When her father feared for her life, he placed her in the care of the elves. For many years, she had called it her home and refuge. She recalled two of her dearest and longest friends, King Joshua Longpine and Prince Isaiah Tytonidae. As a trio and before they knew what challenges life would bring, they roamed the woods and glens surrounding Oakrun without care. Their childhood adventures were forever stamped in her memory. Mora tried to stand. Her knees failed, and she fell back onto her cot. "Oh, Isaiah, your boy is dead."

◊ ◊ ◊

Matthew smirked, entering the guardroom. He found sick humor in seeing Milton bound and gagged. Matthew removed the gag and patted Milton on a chubby cheek. "Miss me?"

"Rot in …" Milton averted his eyes from the cleric and decided it was not worth finishing the sentence.

Francis and Kheel labored for each step, their faces lined with pain, and they gasped for every breath. A few minutes off their feet would be best.

"Let's get them into chairs," Matthew ordered.

They eased Francis and Kheel into the chairs. Tralderonn stood and stared at his brother and nephew. He clenched and unclenched his fists. Their marred faces, blackened eyes, and sunken cheeks became too much for him to endure. Wrath roiled inside him. Revenge begged and pleaded to be released.

"Do something useful," Matthew barked. He sensed the sorcerer was unbalanced. "Watch the door."

Matthew returned to Francis and Kheel. He handed each a waterskin, then turned for the door. Tralderonn was gone.

◊ ◊ ◊

Tralderonn stormed from the guardroom, his brow furrowed, his eyes shuttered. Vengeance would be his today. His widespread desire for revenge blinded him. In his rage, he did not see Wrayer's pierced body lying on the floor. He snapped his fingers. Flames grew in his palms, engulfed his hands. Onward he strode, his arcane fire enveloping his arms.

◊ ◊ ◊

Dread swept over Naphtali and Wulf as they watched the wall of flames dissipate. The guards ran at them, releasing a barrage of bolts. Three bounced off Naphtali's armor and shield. One bolt sliced Wulf's thigh, another grazed his shoulder. He scowled at the pain. Wulf stowed his bow and drew Ill Wind from its sheath. The ancient sword felt good in his hands. Naphtali glanced over at Wulf. "Yeah, that's what I'm talking about."

Wulf grunted and advanced, Ill Wind held out in front of him.

"Oh, this is even better," Naphtali shouted, matching Wulf stride for stride.

The guards hesitated, then stopped as Wulf and Naphtali closed the distance. The crossbowmen fired once more. Their shots sailed wide. Wulf increased his speed—he ran and Naphtali followed his lead as the crossbowmen hurried to reload. Wulf and Naphtali smashed into the shield men, knocking them into the crossbowmen behind.

Wulf gained his feet, drove Ill Wind into a faltering guard. He raised his sword and parried a strike aimed for his head. Wulf stepped to his right and thrust Ill Wind into the guard's stomach.

With the grace found only in elves, Naphtali coiled himself and exploded upwards. His shield caught his opponent under the chin, snapping the head back and breaking the guard's neck. Three quick slashes from Naphtali's long sword killed another.

The crossbowmen dropped their crossbows and drew their swords. One attacked Wulf, his swing wide and looping. Wulf shifted right to avoid the strike. Naphtali never saw the sword as it struck flat-side against his helmet. The Watchman staggered, his head bounced off the wall. His helmet absorbed the blow but tumbled from his head. In a violent slash, Wulf killed the guard. The remaining guards fell back and disappeared into the stairwell.

Wulf did not pursue. He held his ground, knowing this was their opportunity to retreat. He grabbed Naphtali by the arm and guided him towards the guardroom as the first notes from the alarms pealed inside the stronghold. Naphtali's ears rang, his vision blurred, and blood seeped from his nose, ears, and mouth. He shook his head to clear his mind. Naphtali stopped. "My helmet."

Wulf pivoted back to the stairs. Additional guards spilled into the corridor, converging on the two warriors.

"No time," Wulf growled.

◊ ◊ ◊

Matthew led Francis and Kheel into the tunnel. Several long minutes later, they reached the ladder and climbed to the surface. Rain continued to fall as Matthew scanned about. He could see the torches burning atop the stronghold's battlements and above the patrolling guards. Matthew motioned for Francis and Kheel. When father and son cleared the entrance, the three men hid themselves in the shadows to wait for their companions.

◊ ◊ ◊

Mora lay awake on her cot staring at the ceiling, any further desire for sleep gone. She gasped as a sense of relief spread through her body. *Kheel. My son lives. Francis?* Mora did not know. She could only hope they were together.

◊ ◊ ◊

Wulf almost crashed into Tralderonn. The sorcerer shoved Wulf aside and continued marching toward the guards.
"Tralderonn, don't—"
Tralderonn glared at them. Fury burned in his eyes. At that moment, he became unhinged and unyielding—beyond reason.
Bathed in arcane energy, Tralderonn raged. Like a demon bent on revenge, Tralderonn advanced, unleashing fireballs in rapid succession into the passageway. The fire trapped the guards, their armor and shields unable to save them. The front ranks evaporated, the second and third rows enveloped in flames. Wulf and Naphtali stood in awe of Tralderonn's destruction. A thick smoke, acrid and choking, filled the corridor, the walls and floors striated and scorched. Next, blinding streaks of bright blue and white light exploded from Tralderonn's fingertips. The lightning arced towards reinforcements emerging from the stairwell. The guards screamed in agony as raw power ripped into their bodies, charring flesh and tearing organs. Tralderonn's bolts slashed armor and ignited exposed skin. For what seemed like hours, Tralderonn hurled his magic until he exhausted himself and collapsed to his knees.
Feeling the heat Tralderonn emitted from his body, Naphtali and Wulf stepped back. Naphtali stared at Tralderonn, then at Wulf. "What happened?"
"I don't know." Wulf shook his head. He scanned the area—an ominous hush fell over the corridor. The enemy was absent, but the smoke and smell of death hung heavy in the air.

"We should go," Wulf suggested. He shrugged and grinned a silly smile. He knew what he'd just said was stupid. "Uh, monitor the stairwell."

"Watch the stairwell?" Naphtali declared, trying to stifle a laugh. "I can't see ten feet in front of me."

Wulf knelt next to Tralderonn. A swarm of heat swept over him. He touched the sorcerer and recoiled. "Blast."

"Is he dead?" Naphtali queried.

"I don't know." Wulf thrust his arms under Tralderonn and pulled him to his chest. A scream passed over Wulf's lips. The odor of his burning flesh and leather nauseated him. He gasped at the stench, fought the urge to vomit. This was a new sense of affliction and did not compare to any pain he had ever endured. He gazed at his hands and arms. They burned and had begun to blister. The heat ruined his gloves and leather gauntlets. Wulf cursed and grabbed Tralderonn again. He shoved the pain aside and brought Tralderonn to his feet.

"Naphtali, remove him from here," Wulf yelled. "I will cover you."

Naphtali hoisted the unconscious sorcerer over his shoulder. Inside his armor and on his face, Naphtali sweltered from the heat emanating off Tralderonn. Burdened by Tralderonn's mass, he lumbered through the corridor. Naphtali caught sight of Wrayer's lifeless body slumped on the floor and stuttered.

"Go!" Wulf hollered.

Naphtali resumed his pace. Wulf did not slow. He scooped up the elf's body and slung it over his shoulder. The thin silver band fell from Wrayer's head, a solemn reminder of a life sacrificed. They raced into the guardroom. Ignoring Milton, still tied to the chair, Naphtali and Wulf sped into the tunnel.

◊ ◊ ◊

Two stories they fell, crash landing into rain puddles and mud. Danny and Roan gathered themselves and hustled into the shadows. Alarms rang out marshaling the garrison. Angry shouts came from the broken window, and crossbows fired blindly into the night. Racing along the north wall, Roan freed his senses. Soldiers assembled inside and outside the stronghold. Orcs, too many to count, were less than a half mile away. His companions ... *Wrayer!* Roan faltered and grabbed Danny's arm. He swept the tunnel again with his senses. He accounted for everyone except Wrayer.

Squatted next to the wall, Danny looked at Roan. Even in the gloom and rain, he could see the concern reflected in the ranger's eyes. The rogue peered through the murk, scanning the compound. "What?"

"I can't find Wrayer," Roan admitted in frustration.

"Is he masking his presence?" Danny inquired.

"I don't know."

Chapter Seventy

Winter 532, Age of the Arch Mage

Black robes concealed his scarecrow frame. He leaned on his staff, limping to the Altar of Belhaaz. Sweat formed on his brow, streaked his cheeks, and rolled down his back. Natural light—moon, stars, and sun—was unwelcome here. Anything decent and good banished. This hell, hot and oppressive, was reserved for demons and devils. Here they celebrated their evil intent. In this place they employed their dark arts.

He knelt in the shadows cast by a hundred burning torches. He bowed before the altar alone in silent supplication. His mind focused on the pending ceremony. Only the crackle from the torches and his own breathing interrupted the ominous hush permeating the cavern. Midnight neared, and he trembled in anticipation. He enjoyed a deep sense of satisfaction. The relics were in his possession. He had Francis and his son locked in the stronghold's dungeon—the perfect sacrifices. Months of scheming and preparations were barreling to a conclusion in a few hours. Would Belhaaz appear? He hoped for it. He lifted his aged eyes to the empty altar in front of him. Soon the sacrifices and the Helm and Hammer of Valaaham would occupy the marble slab. Shortly, the Cleric of Belhaaz would resume his rightful place at the master's side. And Gaiand would be forever altered. This time, no one wielded the power to stand against Belhaaz. Felix Gallantry was no more than a fading footnote in history. His heir, if one lived, was nowhere to be found. Humans, elves, gnomes, and dwarves would bow before the master's throne. Then …

"No!" Exploding magic and the ringing alarms interrupted Gambier's musings. Gripped by a sudden fear, he struggled to his feet.

He slammed his staff into the ground. In seconds, Gambier appeared outside the dungeon cells.

◊ ◊ ◊

A steady rain fell as Naphtali and Wulf exited the escape tunnel. They found their companions clustered near the opening. Alarms continued, their mournful plea echoing across Udontawny and Demonstaug. The stronghold was now on full alert and soon soldiers would scour the area for them. Matthew shot to his feet as Wulf and Naphtali burst from the tunnel. He saw Wulf carrying Wrayer and Naphtali burdened by Tralderonn. More casualties further taxing his abilities to heal.

Wulf eased Wrayer's limp body to the ground. His imploring eyes met the cleric's. Matthew knelt and set his hands on Wrayer. A soft glow emanated from Matthew's hands. Wulf told himself over and over Wrayer was not dead. If Wrayer were, Matthew would not be trying to revive him. Matthew prayed, his mouth moving in silent appeal. He could find nothing, no heartbeat, no pulse, no breathing. Matthew realized he could not save Wrayer. He hesitated for a moment and stared at the lifeless elf. He felt Wulf's hulking presence hovering over him. Matthew knew Captain Blackhawk, understood that his friend struggled to accept death. He had seen his friend's blank stare many times before. Matthew grimaced. "There is nothing I can do. He is beyond my power."

Wulf blinked and ran a ruined glove through his hair, soaked with rain, sweat, and blood. He bent down to Wrayer and touched the dead elf's forehead with his hand and realized his crown was gone.

Naphtali laid Tralderonn onto the sodden ground and sank next to the sorcerer. His gaze found Wulf and Matthew huddled near Wrayer. He could see Wrayer, his body broken and unmoving. He gained his feet and hobbled to where they stood. Naphtali shot Matthew a pleading look. Matthew frowned and shook his head before walking away. Naphtali dropped to his knees and removed his gauntlets. The Watchman's head slumped to his chest and his body trembled, a combination of sorrow and rage and failure.

Matthew stooped to check on Tralderonn. He felt the heat, saw the steam rising from Tralderonn as he lay in the wet grass. "By the Maiden, what happened?"

Francis touched his brother's arm, then pulled it back. "He is burning up."

Tralderonn's eyes snapped open as if awakened from a fitful sleep. He groaned and sat up.

"What did you do?" Francis whispered.

Tralderonn did not answer as he held his head in his hands.

"Naphtali, we are still in danger," Wulf insisted, his tone compelling but gentle. He rose to his feet. "We need to leave."

The Watchman nodded, his gesture barely noticeable. He stood staring at his friend. "I can't leave him here."

"We don't have to," Wulf assured. "Warriors don't leave anyone behind."

Wulf studied his companions. They looked broken and defeated and exhausted. He empathized. He felt like they did but swore they would not fail. Despite Wrayer's death, they had won. Francis and Kheel were free, and perhaps Danny and Roan had possession of the relics. "On your feet."

"What about Roan and Danny?" Matthew questioned.

"I think the ranger can find us," Wulf assured him.

Wulf looked at Tralderonn, Francis, and Kheel.

"Can you walk, or do I need to carry you?" Wulf growled, reaching for Tralderonn and pulling him to his feet.

"I can walk," Tralderonn grumbled weakly.

"About time," Wulf snarled. "We head east until Roan and Danny catch us."

◊ ◊ ◊

The stench of death and burnt flesh hung in the air as Gambier stepped over the dead clogging the passageway. Each cell was empty, Francis and Kheel gone. A half dozen soldiers froze. None dared to speak. They feared the ancient wizard. Gambier swore, moving into the corridors. More deceased soldiers, the stone walls scorched and blackened. He knelt among the corpses. He noted that bow and blade had killed them. But it was those who were burned and disfigured that concerned him most. He closed his eyes. Gambier sensed the magic spent here. He considered the dead lying all about him. At first he thought he detected two types of magic. Gambier struggled to parse the difference. A wizard? Maybe. Yet very few wizards wielded the power to cause this much death and destruction. A sorcerer? Perhaps. But who? Sorcerers remained rare in Gaiand and he could only recall one at the moment but he was in Auroryies.

His mind spun as his aged eyes searched for a clue. A glimmer in the torchlight caught Gambier's attention. He stopped and stared. A thin silver band lay on the stone floor. He stooped and picked it up. He studied the band, flipping it over in his hands. A thin sneer spread over his face. "Elves. Why would an elven royal enter Demonstaug? What are you doing, Joshua Longpine?"

Gambier spun and walked toward the stairs. As he approached, he saw the damaged helmet. He bent down and grabbed it. "Scarlet Watch? What is—"

A fresh wave of panic swept over Gambier. *The Helm and Hammer!*

He tapped his staff on the stone floor.

In an instant he arrived inside the relic room. Gambier saw the smashed door and table, the broken window, and the dead guards. The old wizard handed the silver band and helmet to a guard. "Hold these."

He scanned the room—he could not see the relics. Gambier exhaled, attempting to calm himself. He scoured the room a second time on the chance he'd missed something. They were gone, the Helm and Hammer. His anger flared. Gambier seized another guard by his collar and pinned him against the wall. "Where are the relics?"

"W-we d-don't know," the guard stammered.

"Bring Zim Patok to me," Gambier hissed. He released the guard and limped to the window. He felt the wind, felt the mist on his skin as he peered into the dark. Another rush of lightning. One more roll of thunder. Another storm battering the Border Lands. He shook his head as despair replaced his fury. What did it matter? The relics and the prisoners were gone. The opportunity, their chance to return Valaaham had passed. Belhaaz and Deemos would not endure this failure. Someone must take the fall, pay the price. *Not me!* He paused and wheeled back to the window. Gambier sensed the Helm and Hammer close by. Maybe he still had time to recover them?

Zim Patok entered the room accompanied by a sobbing Milton and the Guard Captain.

Gambier spun, his eyes reflecting his rage. At the moment, all thoughts concerning the Helm and Hammer vanished.

Patok smirked. He considered Gambier an old fool. A former Prince of Auroryies who had betrayed his order. Patok found it hard to take the wizard seriously and even harder to trust him. Patok shoved Milton toward Gambier. "Milton needs to confess his sins."

Milton fell to his knees, groveling for his life. Gambier grinned, for he had found his sacrifice. He hoisted the staff over his head and brought it crashing down on Milton's skull. Milton fell to the side in a lifeless heap. Gambier looked at the Guard Captain. "Deploy the garrison to the east. I want every soldier and orc searching for the relics and the sacrifices. Don't stop searching until you recover them."

The Guard Captain froze, trying to wrap his mind around the old wizard's brutality. He gazed at Milton's unmoving body, then back to Gambier.

"Now!" Gambier screeched.

The Guard Captain saluted and bolted out the door. Gambier stepped over Milton's dead body, his hardened eyes fixed on Patok. "What do you know about sorcerers?"

Patok recoiled and cleared his throat. "Nothing?"

Gambier scowled and took another step towards Patok. "Nothing? I detected sorcerer's magic in the tunnels."

Patok backed into the wall and brought up his arms to protect himself. His mind failed, he had no answers. Patok could not avoid the wizard's frozen gaze. "He, um, well, I, uh, spoke with the master—"

"You spoke with Belhaaz?" Gambier spat, pinning Patok against the wall with his staff. "And did not bother to inform me?"

"Valaaham's return consumed your time," Patok stated. "I did not want to interrupt your planning."

"Go on," Gambier raged.

"The master told me to expect a Prince Tralderonn, a gift from the messenger and an additional sacrifice to further appease Valaaham," Patok explained.

"Prince Tralderonn?" Gambier recognized the name and knew Tralderonn possessed a sorcerer's magic.

"Yes," Patok answered. "Bounty hunters were to bring him here."

Gambier slapped Patok across the face. "Did you task Milton to receive them?"

"Y-yes," Patok admitted, wiping blood from his mouth and nose.

"What about elves, Patok?" Gambier demanded, pointing at the frightened guard holding the silver band and the helmet. "How do you explain those?"

"Milton told me elves were among the group who brought Tralderonn to him. They must—"

Gambier slapped Patok again. "You idiot! Elves don't earn their keep as bounty hunters."

Gambier stormed to the window. *The messenger? Why? Why risk hiring bounty hunters when the messenger could have had Tralderonn killed instead?* His head fell. He could no longer sense the relics. He slowly turned back around. The silver band and helmet lay on the floor and Patok and the guard had fled.

◊ ◊ ◊

Danny scoured the compound and frowned. Hundreds of torches flickered against the dark and rain. Their pale light shed an eerie pall on the soldiers bearing the torches. "Roan, you and I have bigger problems."

Roan agreed.

"How about doing that invisible thing again?"

"Stay close." Up the wall they climbed undetected to the battlements, then down the other side. Free of the stronghold, they settled into an easy jog. Tiny pinpricks of light danced in the distance. Ranger and rogue slowed. Roan dismissed his spell and released his senses. Four guards loitered near the entrance to the tunnel. Roan widened his search. His companions progressed east and out of danger for the moment. With bows armed, Roan and Danny crept forward, melting into their surroundings. They were shadows inside the murk. Illuminated by the torches they carried, the guards pointed in all directions, their words harsh and loud.

Roan contemplated killing them for a second, then decided otherwise. He motioned his decision to Danny and the rogue nodded in agreement. Roan shrouded them once again in his magic.

A wide arc led Danny and Roan north, leaving the guards far behind. They increased their pace, vanishing into the rain and gloom.

Chapter Seventy-One

Winter 532, Age of the Arch Mage

Headlong through sheets of rain, they trudged, each step harder than the last. At times, the rain fell so hard they could not see the man in front of them. The dropping temperature added to their misery. No one spoke. It required too much energy. Each one imprisoned themselves inside a self-imposed shell. Their gait was sluggish, the downpour and mud impeding their progress. They stopped often, allowing Francis and Kheel to rest. Several times Wulf offered to carry Wrayer and, with each attempt, Naphtali fervently refused.

Francis stared ahead, his vision blurred. His thoughts were fragmented and scattered all about. He knew his mind was shutting down. Francis glanced over at his son slogging beside him. Kheel remained silent, not a word spoken since their rescue. He thought of Mora. Would he see her again? Francis peeked at Tralderonn. What was he doing here? And who were these men, an odd assortment of elves, a half-elf, and humans?

An hour passed before they reached the forest. As they neared where they hid their horses, Wulf hastened his pace. His heart ached. Wulf hated—no, he loathed losing a fellow soldier. It sickened him. Wrayer's death hit too close. It stung him like Sergeant Kurhaden's had. Knees buckled, he almost fell. *Blast! Pull yourself together.* A trot became a run. A run became a sprint. Exhaustion and wounds did not matter. Tree limbs and brush swiped at him, drawing blood. He missed his father and Kiah. Loved his mother and brother. In love with Maria. But he needed Maggie. She was his rock, his anchor in life's storms. He yelled her name.

Maggie answered, her whinnies cutting through the rain. He yelled again. She moved to the sound of his voice. He stopped—he could hear her crashing through the woods to get to him. Out of the gloom, Maggie emerged. Wulf exhaled and opened his arms. She nickered, extended her head over his shoulder, and drew him close with her chin. Wulf closed his eyes and clung to her neck. He was certain he would lose himself if he let go.

Naphtali laid Wrayer beneath a tree and covered him with his cloak. Matthew situated Francis and Kheel out of the wind and rain the best he could and checked them over one more time. It took Wulf, Naphtali, and Tralderonn twenty minutes to round up the horses and get them tacked. They had finished settling Francis and Kheel on Wrayer's horse when Danny and Roan entered the clearing.

Roan's eyes shot to Wrayer. A somber hush rolled over the clearing, the sole noise coming from the rain splattering the earth. No one stirred, their focus on Roan. He knelt next to the elven prince, his worst fear now confirmed. Wrayer's lifeless body unearthed long-forgotten memories from earlier wars. Faces from the past, dead elves, drow, and the innocent, blurred his vision—the ache of loss threatened to submerge him and he fought for breath. After a moment, Roan rose to his feet. "How?"

"Bolts," Naphtali whispered. "I should have—"

Roan clasped Naphtali's shoulder. "There is no blame here. Wrayer knew the risks."

Naphtali heard the ranger's words but they rang hollow in his ears. A Watchman's sworn duty was to protect elven royalty. He had failed and it cost the realm a prince. His failure had cost him a friend.

"There are soldiers and orcs searching for us," Roan reminded them. "We must ride."

Without a word, the men pulled themselves into their saddles, knowing their travels this night were far from over. Naphtali draped Wrayer's body behind his saddle. He refused to bury his friend here.

The rain lessened, then quit, and the clouds drifted west. Throughout the night and early morning, they traveled east. The morning sun climbed above the eastern horizon and began to dry the earth. Bright tendrils of yellow, orange, and crimson marked the coming of a new day, exposing the bleak and broken landscape. Soaked and frayed, the companions and their horses plodded on. With each difficult step, they put more distance between themselves and Udontawny. Roan scanned west with his eyes while his senses searched in all directions. They were alone and now was their opportunity to rest. He brought them to a halt, slid from his saddle, and set off to find shelter. A mile off the trail, Roan found an empty cave in a rock outcropping large enough to provide them and their horses could provide them temporary refuge.

◊ ◊ ◊

Sunlight washed over the Border Lands by the time Roan returned and pointed his troop toward the cavern. He gave the reins of his horse to Wulf to lead. Once his companions and their horses had passed, Roan followed on foot, carefully sweeping away their tracks with some scrub brush branches. The rising breeze would soon help to further obliterate any evidence of their passing as it stirred the dust.

A small freshwater spring leaked from the rock face near the cave's entrance and trickled along the base of the outcropping, forming little pools around some large stones. Tufts of tall, coarse grass remained around the pools to provide some nourishment for hungry mounts. Roan directed that the horses rest in the cavern for the morning. Once the longer shadows of afternoon came, they would be able to venture out and still be nearly undetectable.

Tralderonn entered the cave, trailed by Matthew. He flung his pack against the wall and sat. His eyes met Matthew's. "What?"

"I need to ensure you're okay," Matthew requested. "What happened back there?"

"Leave me be," Tralderonn hissed. He ignored Matthew, unfolded his lanky frame, laid his head on his pack, and was asleep in an instant.

Matthew shrugged and left the sullen sorcerer alone. He wandered over to Francis and Kheel. Wrapped in dry cloaks pulled from Wrayer's saddlebags, they also slept.

Matthew wandered to the mouth of the cave. From there he observed Roan, Naphtali, Danny, and Wulf standing over a pile of rocks. Here, deep in the Border Lands, was where Wrayer's body would remain. Elves were children of magic and the wild, fey folk as old as Gaiand itself. Ancient forests and glades were where the elves roamed, not the ugliness of the Border Lands. It did not seem right to abandon him in this forsaken terrain. From childhood until he departed seminary, Matthew had appreciated the elves. He grew up with them, knew and understood their ways.

The decision to leave Wrayer's corpse behind proved painful for Naphtali and Roan as well. Through mournful eyes, Naphtali found Matthew standing near the mouth of the cave. The cleric surveyed the Watchman as he approached. Once pristine armor was now sullied and tarnished from battle. His helmet was gone, his scarlet cloak shredded. Rain and dried blood matted his blond locks to his head. His desire to test himself in combat was now fulfilled. His sword and shield had drawn blood, although it came at the high price of losing a friend. Naphtali stopped a few feet short. Dirt and soot streaked Naphtali's boyish face, his right cheek red and blistered. He managed a meager smile. "As a cleric of the Maiden, I think it appropriate you say a few words. Please."

"I would consider it an honor," Matthew avowed.

The cleric and the Watchman joined the others at Wrayer's grave.

"Our Maiden," Matthew prayed. "We commit our fellow warrior into your loving arms. His sacrifice will not go unnoticed or neglected. Be with us as we struggle to reconcile his passing. His loss stings beyond any words we can speak. Reassure us in our grief. Let us take comfort in knowing Wrayer now walks in your presence."

They stood together for several silent minutes, offering their last goodbyes. Then one by one, Wulf, Danny, and Roan slipped away until only Matthew and Naphtali remained.

"Thanks," Naphtali muttered, his eyes fixed on Wrayer's grave.

Matthew patted the Watchman on the back and walked to the cave.

◊ ◊ ◊

Roan knelt near one of the spring pools and splashed water onto his face. The icy water felt good. He stared at his reflection and suddenly felt old. And tired. Cobalt eyes, once bright, appeared dull. His face bore scars from a thousand battles. Lines and creases around his mouth and upon his brow revealed he did not smile enough and worried too much. For two hundred years he had walked Gaiand. He spent most of those two hundred years fighting orcs, drow, goblins, and dwarves. Death was nothing new. He had seen hundreds of soldiers die. Hundreds of the enemy had died on his blades and from his bow. So why was the elven prince's death so appalling? His youth? Perhaps. His inexperience? Maybe. That Wrayer was a royal? Conceivably. Possibly it was a merger of the three. Or it showed he still cared. Life remained precious even after all the death and destruction he'd endured and all the death and destruction he had dealt. He let his musings hang unfinished. Reflection was best left alone in the moment. His mission now shifted to safeguarding his companions and the relics back to Highpoint.

Roan rose and scanned his surroundings. He leapt the stream and trotted south. One more look around was required and then he could sleep. He relished the thought.

Chapter Seventy-Two

Winter 532, Age of the Arch Mage

Wulf stripped off his sodden armor and draped it over the rocks. Muscles ached, his wounded leg throbbed, and his hands and arms stung as if they were on fire. He experienced a new level of pain, and he winced each time he moved.

The cleric tended to Naphtali. He assessed his injuries and cleaned the blood from Naphtali's head and face. "You'll have some swelling and bruising for a couple of days."

Naphtali frowned. "Anything permanent?"

"What?"

"You know, a scar," Naphtali replied, his voice hopeful. "Something, anything to show off."

"Well, maybe a bit of a mark here." Matthew touched Naphtali's scalp an inch or so above his ear. "But your hair will hide it."

Matthew chuckled, listening to Naphtali mutter under his breath. Matthew ambled to the cave entrance where Wulf stood, wringing out his waterlogged shirt. The cleric noticed Wulf's hands and arms, red and blistered, and then saw the wound in his thigh. "By the Maiden. What happened?"

"Tralderonn," Wulf admitted, his voice hushed. "The heat from his body burned my arms and hands. The leg took a bolt in the tunnels."

"Blast, Wulf Blackhawk, you are as stubborn as a Highlander's donkey," Matthew uttered. "Why didn't you say something earlier?"

"Stop fussing like an old mare," Wulf exclaimed. "You know the Highlanders don't use donkeys and you were busy tending to Tralderonn, Francis, and Kheel."

"Give me your hands," Matthew demanded.

Matthew whispered a quiet prayer. In seconds, a faint white light radiated from the cleric's hands, causing Wulf to jerk. Matthew smiled, as if enjoying Wulf's distress. Wulf felt the healing energy wash over his burned hands and arms and spread through his leg. As the light faded, the swelling and blisters were gone and the wound closed.

"Don't wait next time," Matthew ordered. "Infection could have set in."

Wulf grunted and sat. He stared at Matthew, then at his hands, arms, a fresh pale scar on his thigh. *Amazing.*

◊ ◊ ◊

When Roan returned, he chuckled. Cloaks, shirts, and trousers hung over several ropes stretched between the rocks and scrub to dry in the sun. Matthew, Tralderonn, Kheel, and Francis slept. Wulf, Danny, and Naphtali soaked up the sun, cleaning their swords outside the cave. Naphtali raised his eyes. "Anything to worry about?"

"Not right now," Roan assured, his smile forced and weary. He removed his cloak and armor and hung them among the other garments. He sat down near Wulf, Danny, and Naphtali and pulled off his boots and socks. "Any of you get some sleep?"

"Not yet," Wulf admitted, as he resumed wiping down his sword.

"I'm not ready right now," Danny chimed in.

"I figure I will take the next watch," Naphtali offered, his gaze returning to Roan. "You must be tired."

"Once I eat," Roan yawned, "and clean my blades, I will sleep."

"Why does Matthew call you the Orc Slayer?" Naphtali asked Wulf without looking up from his sword.

"It's a name given to me when I was fifteen following a skirmish with some orcs in the North River." Wulf shrugged. "I guess it stuck."

Naphtali glanced over at Wulf. "So, your sword. Where did you get it?"

"It is a family heirloom," Wulf beamed. "My grandfather carried it during the Goblin Wars."

"Can I see?" Naphtali requested. "Not a lot of great swords used in Evergreen."

"My pops said the blade is elven," Wulf added, giving Naphtali the sword. "He told me the inscription says Ill Wind."

Roan stopped what he was doing. He glanced at Wulf and then at the sword. Wulf fidgeted under the elves' inquisitive glare.

"Ill Wind?" Naphtali questioned, tracing the inscription with his fingers. His eyes met Wulf's. "Uh, Wulf, this is a drow blade."

Danny laughed, then caught himself. His expression became serious. He knew of the hatred between elves and drow.

"Drow?" Wulf inquired. "You mean dark elves."

"Yeah," Naphtali answered, offering Roan a look. "Ill Wind is a drowan war cry."

"Huh. Well, my grandfather often told my brother and me stories about Caleb Blackhawk, the Nomad Warrior," Wulf explained. "Grandpops said the Nomad Warrior spent time in Evergreen amongst the elves, learning their customs and traditions. They banished him when he took a drow bride. I guess elves don't much care for the drow."

"A drow bride!" Naphtali shouted.

Roan chuckled, then raised his hand to Naphtali. "There are no concerns. This blade is centuries old."

Naphtali laughed. "It could be orcish for all I care. I will fight by your side any day."

"That's quite a story, Wulf," Roan grinned, handing Ill Wind back. "I have heard tell of the Nomad Warrior and his exploits. Never once thought them true. I may need to reconsider."

Wulf shrugged. He was not sure what else to say. He slid Ill Wind into its sheath, then stepped inside the cave. Wulf could see his grandpops tugging at his ears.

Roan grinned at Danny and Naphtali then shook his head, wondering if his companions possessed anymore surprises. "I need to sleep for a few hours."

"Go ahead," Naphtali said. "I got the watch."

Afternoon passed without incident, then yielded to the evening. As dusk descended over the Border Lands, Roan rose. He gathered up his weapons and donned his armor. His companions still slept. He ventured from the cave and found Naphtali at the creek filling his waterskin. "Quiet?"

"Very," Naphtali provided. "A little eerie after the last couple of days."

"Agreed," Roan concurred. His eyes scanned west, south, and east. Nothing moved. His gaze drifted to Naphtali. "Better?"

"Yeah." Naphtali stared over at the rock pile. "I guess."

"Get some sleep, Watchman," Roan ordered. "We have a long journey ahead."

"Yes, sir."

Roan closed his eyes and released his senses. For five miles, they stretched into the waning day. His eyes came open. Nothing.

They remained alone. He glanced over his shoulder at the cave. His companions would sleep under his watch tonight.

◊ ◊ ◊

Midnight neared, the time when demons and devils danced around the flames of the abyss. Roan reclined against the rocks outside the cave. Clouds drifted in from the west, shrouding the moon and stars. The ranger scanned the sky and sucked in a deep breath. Another storm, one of many they had endured in the last few days, was preparing to buffet the Border Lands. He sensed movement to his right.

"May I join you?" Francis requested.

"Yes."

Francis groaned, lowering himself onto a rock ledge. "Who are you and your companions?"

"Well ..." Roan started, then stopped. "Not sure how to answer your question. How about three elves from Evergreen, two humans from Beth Amen, and a half-elf from South Hampton?"

"Who sent you?" Francis inquired. "And why?"

"The princes," Roan stated. "To retrieve you and your family and the relics."

"For what reason?"

"The princes admitted to falsely convicting you and said if we recover you and the relics, it will shorten the war." Roan replied.

"Who are they?"

"Prince Singjeye and Prince Sheldon."

Francis fell silent and rubbed his chin as he processed the information. A thousand questions scrambled his brain, yet his words failed him. He finally fixed his gaze on Roan. "How did you find Kheel and me?"

"I tracked you from Ripley's—"

"You were at the Keep?" Francis pressed. "Mora, did you see Mora?"

"Yes."

Francis set his head into trembling hands. Roan sensed Francis's relief, heard the muttered words of thanks. The ranger reached into his tunic and extracted the Location Stone. "Here. Mora said you would know how to use this."

Chapter Seventy-Three

Winter 532, Age of the Arch Mage

Roan stood alone beyond the cave's entrance, his eyes and senses scanning the barren terrain. He shut his eyes and pushed his senses farther. He found them. They were coming. A horse-mounted patrol, forty-one strong, loitered at the outer fringe of his range. Roan lifted his eyes skyward. Sunrise approached and at their current pace, the enemy would be upon them in two hours. Elven curse words passed over his lips. They had lingered too long. Flee or fight were his sole options. To fight meant eight against forty-one. Not a promising outcome, he concluded. Fleeing east with eight riders on seven horses? Also not favorable. Either choice would prove difficult. He decided to keep the nearing patrol to himself, and he determined that escape was their only alternative.

Dawn broke gray and overcast, cloaking the rising run. During the early morning, rain clouds rolled in from the west. A steady drizzle fell over the Border Lands as the companions stirred inside the cave. Francis, Kheel, and Tralderonn woke with aches and pains but rested. The others ate their breakfast, iron rations and water, cold and in silence. Roan entered the cave and surveyed his companions.

"Pack up. We leave in ten minutes," Roan declared.

Naphtali stowed his gear, gathered his sword and shield, and exited the cave without speaking. He knelt near Wrayer's grave. Grief and regret etched his boyish face once more. He struggled to come to terms with the finality of Wrayer's death. Naphtali fumbled for a few last words to say to his friend. He searched for something elegant and profound. But that was not his way. Two simple words were all he could muster. "Forgive me."

The Watchman rose, shouldered his pack, and walked to his horse.

Francis edged from the cave. He stared at the Location Stone sitting in the palm of his hand. He studied the blue amulet and silver chain for a minute.

"Mora," he whispered as he clutched the amulet to his chest.

◊ ◊ ◊

Mora rested against Ripley's shattered gate. Her world and mood wore a gray shroud, dull and dour. Her hope for seeing her husband and son waned as the minutes passed. Mora's eyes scoured the lonely landscape. Clouds, dark and burdened by rain, veiled the morning sun. Mora lingered as a north breeze ushered in the mist. She wiped the droplets from her face and sighed. Not today or even tomorrow, but soon she would have to decide. Remain in Ripley's, hoping for Francis's and Kheel's reappearance, or venture someplace else? Her strength was returning as her body filtered out the remaining poison. But where? Auroryies? Certainly not. Evergreen? Maybe. Mora felt at home among the elves and knew she would find refuge there.

Mora leaned on her staff as she limped to the house. She gazed across the compound, broken and deserted. The Location Stone flared. Mora stopped. *It can't—*. The stone flared once more. Her hands trembled as she pulled the amulet from beneath her blouse. It flared again. She heard his voice calling her name. *Francis!*

◊ ◊ ◊

"Kheel and I will see you soon." Francis grinned, ignoring the tears streaking his cheeks. "I must go. I love you."

"I love you, too." Mora lingered as the amulet faded. She lifted her eyes into the gray skies and smiled. "The boys succeeded."

◊ ◊ ◊

Out of their secluded location, they rode east. The sheeting of mist concealed them. It adhered to weapons, armor, skin, and horses. In fifteen minutes, they were soaked and chilled once more. The mist wandered east as morning conceded to midday. Roan set a steady pace through the terrain they had journeyed several days ago. Fragmented bits of sunshine broke through layers of clouds late in the afternoon, bringing relief to the weary riders.

Another day passed without incident and on each step the haggard band drew closer to Ripley's. As mid-afternoon on the following day came to a close, Roan sent forth his senses for what seemed like the hundredth time in the last several hours. They were alone, a welcome relief. The patrol he located that morning was a distant memory. He had not detected them since before noon. He was satisfied with his decision to flee. At the edge of his range, the ranger detected the Keep. Three hours separated them from the ancient bastion.

◊ ◊ ◊

Mora emitted an audible gasp as they emerged from the gloom. She stared at them for several moments as if she did not trust her eyes. Mora pressed her lips tight to prevent the tears from falling. She failed—tears tumbled down. She had thought them dead and gone. Yet they, husband and son, were alive and standing in front of her. She limped to Francis and Kheel as fast as her legs would go, her arms wide. Mora sobbed, clutching her husband and son. She clung to them as her worst fears vanished in an instant.

-- Now Mora? --

Soon, very soon.

Mora released her grip on her family and turned to face Wulf, Roan, Matthew, Danny, and Naphtali. She seemed fragile and old to them. She swiped at the tears and brushed back a strand of hair from her face. Mora studied the five remaining companions for several moments before speaking. "I have no words or possessions worthy enough to express my gratitude."

Mora took an uneasy step towards them. "I am sorry for Wrayer's death."

The company shot each other odd glances. Her declaration astounded them. How did Mora know of Wrayer's death? Was she a seer or some kind of conjurer? Roan bowed his head and exhaled. This woman seemed an enigma, a force of nature he could not explain. Fear was a foreign concept to the ranger, yet this petite woman terrified him.

Mora discounted their confusion as she pulled each one to her level, kissed them on the cheek, and stepped back. "You are now and forevermore my heroes."

She whirled about, took Francis and Kheel by the arms, and ambled into the house. At the door, Mora stopped and shot Tralderonn a knowing look and winked.

◊ ◊ ◊

Matthew, Naphtali, Danny, and Tralderonn shuffled into the house. Wulf loitered for a moment, watching Roan ascend the stairs to the ramparts.

The ranger removed the cowl from his head, closed his eyes, then inhaled to clear his mind, to focus his thoughts. He loosened the grip on his longbow, trying to relax. He released his senses, sent them reaching out to detect the threat he knew searched for them. *Nothing.*

Wulf studied Roan from the courtyard. Roan paced across the parapet like a caged mountain cat. *What does he see? What does he sense?*

Scanning across the vast darkness enfolding the Border Lands, Roan paused. He sensed Wulf nearing. When he reached the stairs, Wulf climbed to the battlements and joined Roan. "You think they pursue us, don't you?"

"Yes," Roan answered, keeping his gaze fixed on the landscape in front of him. "We damaged them, set them back, and disrupted their plans. We stole valuable property. Somebody will pay a steep price."

"When?" Wulf inquired.

"What do you think?" Roan asked.

"They will look here later today or early tomorrow morning," Wulf responded.

"Agreed," Roan confirmed. "You possess great instincts and insights, Wulf Blackhawk. I underestimated you and I won't do it again. Sleep, Captain Blackhawk. We need you sharp and ready to fight when the time comes."

"What about you?" Wulf queried. "You must be tired as well?"

Roan grinned. "Elves need very little sleep, my friend—maybe four hours a day, and I need even less."

Maggie greeted Wulf when he reached the courtyard. Mud streaked her flanks and clung to her legs. She was a mess. "You're still beautiful to me, Princess Marguerite."

Her nicker said she agreed. Side by side, they headed for the stables. He removed her saddle, tack, and cleaned her the best he could. Wulf found a spot near the tack room, sat down, and pulled a tin of rations from his pack. Wulf ate his dinner cold as his thoughts drifted off to Maria.

Chapter Seventy-Four

Winter 532, Age of the Arch Mage

Francis rose early and absorbed the gray dawn. He sighed contently, seeing Mora and Kheel sleeping nearby. He felt relief wash over him. Mora was secure and her health improving. Kheel was talking again and hopefully forgetting their terrible ordeal. Francis yawned and walked to the kitchen. He stoked the fire in the stove box and scrounged up the last of the coffee. In minutes, the aroma of brewing coffee woke Matthew and Danny from their slumber. Kheel and Mora arrived carrying empty cups. Mora pouted as she sipped the coffee. "Where is the dwarven mead?"

"Glad to see you are back to your old self," Francis chuckled. He kissed her on the cheek and filled another cup. "I need to check on Tralderonn."

◊ ◊ ◊

A bright rising sun welcomed in a new day. Tendrils of yellow, orange, and pink snuck over the eastern horizon, bringing warmth to the chilled air. Roan rolled out of his cloak and buckled on his weapons. He slung his quiver across his back and grabbed his bow. He ascended the stairs to the ramparts and saw Naphtali patrolling the north wall. Roan grinned to himself. The Watchman's once pristine armor remained soiled and marred, his helmet gone, any doubt as to Naphtali's combat prowess forever banished.

The ranger scanned over the broken terrain. He closed his eyes, allowing his senses to advance. For several minutes, he searched the Border Lands for threats. *Nothing.* He opened his eyes as Naphtali neared.

"Anything?" Naphtali asked.

"Nothing," Roan sighed. "Whatever I sensed yesterday has moved on."

"That's good, right?" Naphtali questioned.

"Yes, for now," Roan responded. "We need a plan for leaving here Naphtali. We can't stay much longer."

◊ ◊ ◊

Francis carried the coffee and walked to the room where Tralderonn slept. He found his brother reclining against the wall and pulling on his boots. Francis sat next to his brother and handed him a cup. "You look bad. How do you feel?"

Tralderonn shook his head as he sipped on the coffee. "Mom is dead. I sensed her passing."

"I know."

"How?" Tralderonn queried. "Did you sense it as well?"

"No, Mora," Francis admitted, avoiding eye contact. "She told me last night."

"Curious," Tralderonn smirked. "Dad is safe, though?"

Francis glanced over at his brother and recognized the look on his face. Tralderonn stared at the wall, wearing a flimsy smile. Francis knew Tralderonn would pursue the matter until he got a suitable answer.

"Yes, Mora discovered him in Evergreen," Francis confessed, his voice reluctant.

"How?" Tralderonn pressed, already knowing the answer, but wanted to hear it from Francis. "He does not possess magic."

"He carries a ward created from Elaire's magic," Francis answered.

"Well, at least he is safe among the elves." Tralderonn gave his brother a half smile. Tralderonn's eyes narrowed as he contemplated his next words. "Francis, is Mora the—"

Francis held up his hand, cutting off Tralderonn mid-sentence. He stared straight ahead, refusing to answer his brother's question using words. Francis lifted his gaze to meet Tralderonn's. His eyes betrayed him and Tralderonn received the answer he sought. *Curious.* "When will she—"

Francis held up his hand again. "I don't know."

"Curious."

"Traldy, how did you end up in Udontawny?" Francis inquired, trying to change the subject.

"Looking for you," Tralderonn provided, letting his brother off the hook. He described his outburst in the chambers and his confrontations with Xavian, Marcelinus, and Cornell. He explained his intent to join the fighting in Beth Amen and his capture in Tejt.

"Who would send them …" Francis realized the stupidity of his question as soon as the words left his mouth.

Tralderonn cocked his head and smirked. "Who do you think?"

"Sorry."

"Auroryies is in disarray," Tralderonn stated. "Francis, we cannot trust the princes, to include Cornell. For some reason, they want us out of the way. Their duplicity runs deep."

Francis did not speak for a long moment. He knew Tralderonn spoke the truth. It was just so hard to accept the idea. Not all of them could be corrupt, he wanted to believe. Especially Cornell. His older brother may be misguided, but he was not treacherous. Surely some remained loyal to their calling. Francis blew out his cheeks. "Traldy, someone framed me."

"I am aware," Tralderonn acknowledged. "Uriah told me."

Tralderonn stood, offering Francis his hand, and pulled his brother to his feet.

"I am sorry for the meltdown the other day," Tralderonn confessed. For a second, his thoughts wandered to Carjlin and the Matron Sister. He smiled at their memory. "Controlling my temper remains a daily battle."

"I heard it was impressive, though," Francis admitted, as a half-smile tugged at the corner of his mouth.

"Perhaps," Tralderonn suggested. "But I placed everyone in jeopardy and hurt the young trooper."

◊ ◊ ◊

Matthew filled a mug for himself and one for Wulf. He stepped from the house and searched the courtyard. Matthew located Wulf sleeping in front of the stables and Maggie standing nearby. He smiled. *Where else would he be?* Matthew nudged him with his boot and placed the mug near Wulf's nose. "Wake up, princess."

"Ah, thanks." Wulf came to his feet and stretched. He took the mug and drew in a few sips.

"Sure." Matthew headed back to the house. He stopped midway as Tralderonn approached.

"I ask your forgiveness," Tralderonn requested.

"Forgiven and forgotten," Matthew declared. "Feel better?"

"Yes," Tralderonn answered.

"Good to hear," Matthew acknowledged. "Excuse me. I must check on Mora, Francis, and Kheel."

Tralderonn resumed walking to the stables. Wulf was strapping Ill Wind across his back when he saw Tralderonn approach. Wary eyes watched the sorcerer. Wulf knew of the stories concerning magic users, especially the ones who fought in the Goblin Wars.

Despite their history, the Horse Tribes possessed an inherent distrust for wizards, particularly the Princes of Auroryies. Right or wrong, Wulf held similar opinions as his adopted homeland. His dealings with Princes Singjeye and Sheldon further solidified Wulf's beliefs. Even Wrayer had made him a little uneasy.

Tralderonn perceived Wulf's apprehension and stopped short. "Thank you for pulling me from the fight."

Wulf nodded, his eyes locked on Tralderonn.

"Forgive me," Tralderonn appealed. "I did not mean for you to get hurt."

"Of course," Wulf offered. He relaxed a bit and softened his glare. "That was one hell of a display."

"I suppose," Tralderonn muttered. He cast a sheepish glance around the courtyard. "You could say I have anger issues."

"You don't say," Wulf chuckled. "How do you do that? All that fire and lightning."

"I come by it naturally," Tralderonn explained. "It's as easy for me as breathing."

"Tralderonn and Wulf, we need you in here," Roan shouted as he and Naphtali descended the rampart stairs.

◊ ◊ ◊

Once everyone had assembled inside the main house, the ranger surveyed the room.

"The forces in Udontawny will seek us," he said, "and I believe they will start their search here. We must leave as quickly as possible."

"I agree," Francis confirmed. He rose from the hearth. "Did you sense anything?"

"A threat lingered near the limit of my range last night," Roan explained. "I don't sense them now, but I am confident they will return."

Francis faced Mora, Kheel, and Tralderonn. "We must return to Auroryies."

"Well, we cannot stay here." Mora stated. "Our location stands compromised. I disagree with returning to Auroryies. My concern is the relics. They lost the Helm and Hammer once, so how can they protect them in the future?"

"We can take them to Evergreen," Tralderonn suggested.

"No!" Mora and Roan responded in unison. Roan cast an odd glance in Mora's direction.

"King Longpine will not allow such evil in Evergreen," Mora shrugged. Her expression said she knew more about the elves than she let on.

"We have no other choice," Francis argued. "The relic vault is the only secure location."

An uneasy hush fell over the room. Francis drifted to the broken windows. The torn curtains fluttered in a cool morning breeze. He paused and rubbed his chin, his eyes focused on something far afield. Kheel stood among the group, absorbing the conversation. Relics and elves he did not comprehend. What he understood was someone in Auroryies intentionally hurt his mother and father. That someone would pay.

"Too many questions," Francis mused. "How did the relics get to Udontawny? How did the enemy know we were here? And why was Traldy attacked by bounty hunters?"

He fixed his gaze on Mora and Tralderonn. "None of this makes sense."

Mora and Tralderonn exchanged reluctant glances.

"If the answers we seek are in Auroryies," Mora stated, allowing her gaze to meet Tralderonn's, "then I guess we should return."

"As distasteful as it may be." Tralderonn winced. The idea of returning to Auroryies was revolting. He had sworn he would never step foot inside the Citadelle again.

Francis peeked over at Roan, Wulf, Matthew, Naphtali, and Danny.

"It would be worth watching them squirm," Danny blurted out.

"And I have to kill Singjeye," Wulf reminded.

Matthew slapped himself on the forehead, and Roan dropped his head to his chest. Naphtali and Danny clamped down on their lips, trying not to laugh. Mora, Francis, Tralderonn, and Kheel stared in disbelief.

"What?" Wulf said, self-conscious at their attention. "I told you I was going to kill him. I am honor-bound."

"We can discuss you killing Singjeye later," Matthew proposed, the frustration in his voice apparent.

"There is nothing to discuss," Wulf assured.

"Francis, I think we agree," Roan confirmed, wanting to put an end to the conversation. "I recommend we leave soon."

"Settled," Francis announced.

◊ ◊ ◊

Mora left her pack in the center of the courtyard and strolled to the shattered gate. She stood at the gate and stared into the gray. In the distance, thunder rumbled, and lightning arced across the clouded sky. Rain rolled east across the Border Lands. Soon it would arrive at Ripley's Keep.

-- My child --

Yes.

-- The staff awaits your return --

My time has come, and I am ready.

Mora paused when she realized her confession.

-- You are not alone --

Mora turned back toward the house. Francis, Kheel, Tralderonn, and her heroes were gathering in the courtyard. She smiled, one filled with hope. *I know.*

"Mora," Francis shouted. "You ready?"

-- You are ready --

"Yes, Francis. I am ready."

Chapter Seventy-Five

Winter 532, Age of the Arch Mage

Deemos dawdled in his candlelit quarters. Ill news from across Gaiand soured his mood. He leaned back in his chair and placed his boots on the desk, his eyes fixed on the Scrawlstone sitting in the corner. The Scrawlstone had gone silent, and its light slowly faded. Gambier reported awful news from Udontawney. The Helm and Hammer thieved away, preventing Valaaham's return. The sacrifices, a Prince of Auroryies and his son, missing as well. Gambier mentioned he'd discovered in the tunnels below Demonstaug an elven silver headband worn by elven royalty. What was an elf doing in Udontawny? He cursed Gambier, the old fool.

And what of this second prince? The one named Tralderonn. Why would the messenger hire bounty hunters to capture and deliver him to Udontawny? How did he figure into this? Deemos swore to himself. The messenger no longer held his trust. Like Gambier, the messenger was a liability. Deemos knew he must make an adjustment in Highpoint, and Essa was the perfect choice to enact the change. He was the puppet master. Deemos must stay above the fray and hidden in the shrouds of deceit. He could not afford to dirty his hands in the matter.

Deemos grabbed a map from his desk. The outlander nations endured. A remnant in Crawsteri fought on despite the loss of its army. Beth Amen remained defiant and held the Mulford River. The Highlanders continued to defeat every assault thrown at them. Evergreen's counterattack drove the orcs from the elven nation and back across the North River. The elf army now advanced into the Border Lands. His eyes moved to the Sea of Marhgot. Only Teach Drummond and his marauders experienced any success these days.

Jaisia stood in the corner judging his inaction, arms folded across her chest and her face concealed in the pleats of her cowl. She exhaled, a loud hiss escaping clenched teeth. She did not try to conceal her impatience. "Are you going to just sit here and stew?"

Deemos disregarded Jaisia's exasperation and her question. He would not waste his time or breath bantering with the drow maiden. He stared at the bag containing the kobold's head. It smelled. He shifted his gaze to the talisman in his hand. He sensed the ancient magic emanating from the charm. A powerful magic formed centuries past, and it was now his to claim. Deemos's sneer did nothing to improve his looks as a plan, foul and bold, rumbled around his brain. The talisman, a black dragon carved from obsidian, was the centerpiece of his sinister scheme. If properly employed, it could alter the course of the war. The talisman, along with patience and cunning, traits his master did not possess, would bring the Southern Realms to their knees. Then he would lord over them, not Belhaaz. Deemos clenched the talisman tight in his fist, snatched the sack, and rushed from his quarters.

Unannounced, Deemos stormed into the master's chambers. Passing the Odjarhary guards posted at the door, he strode over the bridge without hesitation or fear. The heat was oppressive, the humid air visible. Beads of sweat formed on Deemos's forehead, streamed down his back and chest.

Belhaaz lifted his gaze. He watched as his emissary strode toward him. Deemos carried a sack. The demon considered this intriguing. Deemos came on, did not wait for Belhaaz to summon him to approach.

Deemos halted short of the dais and let the demon suffer his indignation.

"Seems we have overstepped our bounds," Belhaaz snorted. His yellow eyes flashed in anger. "I do not tolerate insubordination, even from you."

Defiant, Deemos held his tongue and his ground, kept his eyes fixed on the demon. Belhaaz shifted his massive girth. A long silence ensued. Neither was willing to retreat from the pending confrontation.

"Careful, my precious emissary," Belhaaz cautioned, rising to his feet. "Gagging on misplaced ambitions could prove fatal."

The Odjarhary standing near the demon took a wary stride towards Deemos. An icy gaze and a wave of his hand froze the Odjarhary in their tracks.

"Impressive. Your power grows," Belhaaz admitted, his words mocking, his grotesque face twisted in a rage. "I suggest caution."

"It is you, master," Deemos pressed, "who should exercise caution."

"Hm, how so?" Belhaaz growled.

Deemos studied the demon before answering. Clawed hands clenched, nostrils flared, eyes narrowed. There was no hiding Belhaaz's rage. Deemos scoffed at the demon's posturing. Deemos would not falter now.

"The Helm and Hammer are missing, along with the sacrifices. Gambier managed to lose them all," Deemos reported. He sucked in a quick breath. "Beth Amen, the Highlanders, and the elves hold. They refuse to bend to your will. Everywhere you look, your forces fail. Your war, master, is slipping from your claws."

"Have you come to grovel?" the demon inquired, a thin smile emerging on his beastly face. "To beg my forgiveness for your abundant failures?"

"Certainly not," Deemos answered. "You refused to heed my warnings."

"Then why do you stand here?" Belhaaz demanded.

"The kobold failed," Deemos announced. He tossed Aeros's head, and it rolled to within a few feet of the dais. "Your heir is dead. Your bounty hunter killed her."

Deemos did not wait for a reaction—he did not care. He spun on his heels and marched off. With his patience gone, Deemos vowed to prosecute the war against the Southern Realms on his own. When he cleared the chambers Deemos stopped and leaned against the wall. He snorted and a thin smile creased his face. *I can deceive Belhaaz anytime I want.*

Belhaaz lowered his frame onto his throne. His yellow eyes, filled with hate and disgust, watched Deemos depart from his presence. When the door shut and Deemos was gone from his sight, Belhaaz stood, clenched his fists, and leaned his head back.

The demon roared.

Chapter Seventy-Six

Present Day 568, Age of the Arch Mage

Fitzhugh lifted his gaze from the leather-bound book and removed his glasses. Diminishing light through the windows signified dusk had ushered the day's unseen sun west. The snow had fallen throughout the day and once the sun set, the temperatures would plummet. Mora refilled her mug as he removed a handkerchief from the pocket of his jerkin. He wiped his tired eyes and the perspiration from his brow, then neatly folded it and put it back in its place. He flipped through the remaining pages. Seven blank pages remained unfilled. He sighed. Maybe his labors were ending for the day.

"How many empty pages do we have?" Mora quizzed, sitting again at the table. She brushed a lock of hair from her face and pulled a drink from her mug.

"A half dozen, my lady," he answered.

Mora leaned back in her chair and smiled. "Well, this day went fast."

"Yes," Fitzhugh grinned. It appeared thin and forced. He recharged his pen from the ink well and put on his glasses.

"Now where were we?" she wondered aloud.

Fitzhugh turned the page. "You were preparing to depart the Keep."

"Ah, yes," she agreed, pulling another drink. "I can remember feeling anxious, almost nauseated, as we rode from the shattered Keep. The source of my consternation was not the long trek through the Border Lands to Highpoint. It was our pending return to Auroryies."

As he finished writing, Mora pulled a long draw from her mug and sat motionless for a minute. Then another. Mora's gaze rested on the floor. He hesitated to speak—he did not want to disturb her. She lifted her eyes to meet his. Fitzhugh peered at her over his glasses. "I am ready, my lady."

"Mister Walsh," she said, her voice harsh and irritated. Her ashen eyes flared, her lips tightened. She felt a tinge of regret tugging at her soul for not sensing Belhaaz's return all these decades agao. "On the ride south ... There were so many unanswered ..."

Her voice trailed off. Fitzhugh witnessed Mora struggling to translate her memories into words.

"Strange," she mumbled to herself. In an instant, her mood changed. She smiled, her eyes brightened. Mora rose from her chair, sauntered to the keg, and replenished her mug. She faced about. "Can I offer a mug or a glass of wine?"

"Wine? Please," Fitzhugh requested. He studied her while she pulled the cork and poured the wine. His opinions about her were gradually changing. Yes, he still feared Mora's power, but she was revealing another side to her. A softer side she allowed only a select few to witness. There was more, he concluded, to Mora Gallantry than bearing the mantle as the Second Arch Mage of Gaiand.

Mora placed the wine next to his arm, then sat. "I think our day has concluded."

A sense of relief washed over Fitzhugh. His eyes were tired and his hand ached. He swirled the wine in his glass and breathed in its bouquet. Fitzhugh sipped from the goblet and smiled. "Ah, a vintage Solice cabernet. One of my favorites. How did you come to gain such a bottle?"

Mora chuckled. "Being the Arch Mage garners certain perks, Mister Walsh."

"As it should, my lady," he concurred. He drank again, slow and easy, letting the wine refresh his palate. "What year?"

"529, I believe," she answered.

"Yes." Fitzhugh grinned and studied the glass for a moment. His opinions were definitely changing.

She watched as he carefully stowed his writing instruments and the book into his satchel. When he was done, he finished his glass. "Tomorrow, my lady?"

"Yes, of course," she confirmed. "Should we meet at the Arnault in the morning? I think a change of scenery would be nice."

"It would be an honor to host you, my lady," Fitzhugh admitted.

"Another glass of wine."

"No, thank you," he answered. "It is late and the temperatures are falling."

"Understood." Mora stood and set her mug on the counter. She followed him into the living room and did not speak as he donned his coordinated coat, scarf, hat, and gloves.

"Pleasant night, my lady." He bowed and tipped his hat.

"Good evening, Mister Walsh." She lingered in the doorframe until he vanished into the falling snow. Clouds concealed the moon and stars, denying Deep Well the enjoyment of their heavenly light. The brittle night air was refreshing. It felt good gently brushing her face and arms. She heard Francis singing in the kitchen as she shut and locked the front door.

Mora smiled—she knew this song. It was a tune Francis sang often, a song from his youth. She leaned against the door and joined in. Halfway through, she paused and listened. Outside, carried by the wind, she heard a faint voice, angelic and lonely.

The song of Elaire.

About the author. After retiring from the Marine Corps, Chris Grooms settled in Virginia with his family.

Contact the author at: TalesFromGaiand@gmail.com

Made in the USA
Middletown, DE
01 March 2023